Praise for the novels of #1 *New York Times* bestselling author Debbie Macomber

"Debbie Macomber is one of the most reliable, versatile romance writers around."

—*Milwaukee Journal Sentinel*

"Prolific Macomber is known for her portrayals of ordinary women in small-town America. [She is] an icon of the genre."

—*Publishers Weekly*

"Macomber is a master storyteller."

—*Times Record News*

"Debbie Macomber [has a] gift for understanding the souls of women—their relationships, their values, their lives."

—*BookPage*

DEBBIE MACOMBER

Meet Me on Sunday

Any Sunday and *The Playboy and the Widow*

MIRA

/II MIRA

ISBN-13: 978-0-7783-0641-2

Recycling programs
for this product may
not exist in your area.

Contents

Any Sunday

In memory of Darlene Layman.
My treasured friend through the years.

One

Marjorie Majors's deep brown eyes widened as a flash of burning pain shot through her side. Feeling hot and flushed again, she guessed she was running a fever. Her smile was decidedly forced as she walked across the showroom floor, weaving her way around the shiny new Mercedes while lightly pressing her hand against her hipbone. She'd thought that if she ignored the throbbing ache, this unexplained malady would vanish on its own. So far her reasoning hadn't worked, though, and the mysterious discomfort had persisted for days.

"Is your side hurting you again?" Lydia Mason, the title and license clerk for Dixon Motors, called from behind the front counter.

"A little." Now that had to be the understatement of the week, Marjorie mused. The shooting pain had been coming and going all day with no real rhyme or reason. She should have known she wasn't going to be able to fool Lydia. Her friend had a nose for news. Little transpired at Dixon Motors without Lydia knowing about it.

"Honestly, Marjorie, why don't you just see a doctor?"

"I'm fine," she protested. "Besides, I don't have a doctor."

Lydia, who stood barely five feet tall and wore heels that increased her height an additional two inches, moved around the counter. Her mouth was pinched into a tight line of determination. "But you haven't been feeling good all week."

"Has it been that long?"

"Longer, I suspect," Lydia murmured, shaking her head. "Listen, no one is going to think less of you for needing a doctor, for heaven's sake. Just because you're one of only three female salespeople here, that doesn't mean you have to behave like Joan of Arc."

"But it's just a little stomachache."

"What did you have for lunch?"

Marjorie shrugged noncommittally, preferring not to lie. A wry smile lifted the corners of her full mouth as she pretended to survey the parking lot, hoping a prospective buyer would magically appear so she would have an excuse to drop the conversation. She didn't want to admit that with her stomach acting up, she hadn't bothered to eat lunch. And now that she thought about it, breakfast hadn't appealed to her, either.

"You didn't have any lunch, did you?" Lydia challenged.

"I didn't have time since . . ."

"That's it, Marjorie—that's the final straw. I'm making you an appointment with my gynecologist."

"You're what?"

"You heard me." Lydia didn't wait for an argument. With her manicured fingernails, she flipped the hair that had fallen across her cheek to the back of her shoulder and marched around the counter with the authority of a marine drill sergeant.

"Don't call a gynecologist! That's crazy. I don't need a woman's doctor—an internist maybe . . ."

Ignoring Marjorie's protest, Lydia pressed the telephone receiver to her ear and turned her back to her friend. "What's crazy," she said, twisting her head around, her eyes sparking with impatience, "is suffering for days because you're afraid to see a doctor."

"I am not afraid! And a gynecologist is the last person I want to see." Marjorie couldn't seem to get it through her friend's thick skull that a queasy stomach was unworthy of all this fuss. From the way Lydia was behaving, Marjorie fully expected her friend to dial 911 to report a minor pain that came and went without warning. She'd lived with it for the last few days—a little longer wasn't going to matter. More than likely it would disappear as quickly and unexpectedly as it had come. Or so she continued to hope.

"Today, if possible." Lydia spoke firmly into the telephone. She placed her hand over the receiver and turned to Marjorie. "Listen, I had a friend once with similar symptoms, and it ended up being female problems and—" She broke off abruptly. "Five o'clock would be fine. Thanks, Mary."

Although Marjorie knew it wouldn't do any good, she tried again. "Lydia . . ."

The telephone was replaced in its cradle before Lydia turned around. "And something else. Dr. Sam isn't your run-of-the-mill doctor. He's wonderful! If you need to see someone else, he'll refer you, so stop looking so worried."

"But I'm sure this pain is nothing."

"Then checking it out won't be any big deal. Right?"

Marjorie shrugged.

"He has an opening this afternoon at five."

"His name is Dr. Sam?" Now Marjorie had heard everything. "Will Nurse Jane be there, too?"

"He's really terrific," Lydia announced with a loud sigh, obviously choosing to ignore Marjorie's sarcasm. "I think I fell in love with him in the delivery room just before Jimmy was born. He was so gentle and understanding when I was in labor. He made me feel like I was the most noble, heroic woman in the world for enduring the pain of childbirth."

"Hey, I've got a stomachache. I'm not looking to find Prince Charming."

"But he's handsome, too."

"Does Dr. Sam have a last name?" She wasn't bothered by the thought of seeing a physician, exactly, but the simple truth was that Marjorie hated relying on anyone else. She could take care of herself very well, and relying on another person went against her fiercely independent nature.

"His name is really Sam Bretton, but everyone calls him Dr. Sam."

Marjorie rolled her eyes toward the ceiling. "I don't know if I can trust a man who sounds like he keeps an office on Sesame Street."

"Wait and see," Lydia claimed, writing out directions to the medical center on a piece of paper and ripping it free of the tablet before handing it over to Marjorie. "He's marvelous—trust me."

Marjorie folded the paper in half and stuck it inside her purse. If nothing else, it would be interesting to meet the guy. Lydia wasn't generally free with her praise, yet she hadn't been able to say enough good things about this guy.

"You'll like him, I promise," Lydia added.

Marjorie made a barely perceptible movement of her head, as if to say it made no difference to her how she felt about him. She didn't care what he looked like as long as he could give her something for this blasted pain.

At precisely ten minutes to five, Marjorie pulled into the parking lot of the large medical complex north of Tacoma General Hospital. The ache that had troubled her most of the day had vanished, just as she'd known it would, and she felt better generally. If she'd had a fever earlier, she was convinced it was gone now. Briefly she toyed with the idea of heading back to her apartment and forgetting the whole thing, but that would be irresponsible, and if Marjorie knew anything, it was the meaning of responsibility. Besides, her friend would be furious with her for canceling at the last moment.

Two other women were seated in the waiting room. Both were in the advanced stages of pregnancy. One sat with her hands resting on her protruding belly, looking content, while the other was knitting. The thick needles, encased in a pastel shade of yarn, moved furiously. Their smiles were friendly as Marjorie stepped up to the reception desk to announce her arrival. An older, gray-haired woman asked Marjorie to fill out several forms and handed her a clipboard.

Marjorie took it and located a seat in the corner beside a dying houseplant. The yellowish leaves did little to boost her confidence in this unknown physician.

"Is this the first time you've seen Dr. Sam?" one of the soon-to-be-mothers asked.

Marjorie nodded. "My friend recommended him."

"He's absolutely wonderful."

"And good-looking to boot," the knitter added.

"Real good-looking!"

The two pregnant women eyed each other and shared a smile.

"I suppose all women fall in love with their doctors," the woman with the knitting needles commented, "but I've never known a man who's as caring as Dr. Sam is."

"I'm not pregnant." Marjorie didn't know why she felt it was necessary to tell them that. This physician might do wonders with mothers-to-be, but all Marjorie cared about was his expertise with sharp, persistent pains.

"You don't have to be pregnant," the two were quick to assure her.

"Good." Marjorie completed the information sheets and returned them to the receptionist, then subtly glanced at her watch. She hadn't experienced any real discomfort in hours and was beginning to feel like a phony. Again, the thought of skipping out of the appointment sprang to mind. Sheer stupidity, of course. If nothing else, it would be interesting to stick around and meet this doctor who seemed to be a paragon of virtue. From what Lydia and the two patients in the waiting room had said, Dr. Sam Bretton was a cross between Brad Pitt and Mother Teresa.

"It'll only be a few minutes," the receptionist told her.

"No problem," Marjorie answered softly, wondering if the woman had read her mind.

A few minutes turned out to be fifteen. Marjorie was escorted into a small cubicle by a nurse who was dressed as though she were shooting a scene from a daytime soap opera. Her gray hair was perfectly styled in a bouffant, and even after a full day in the office, not a single strand was out of place.

Marjorie stopped just inside the room, her mind whirling. She'd been in her teens when she'd last seen a physician. Over the years there'd been minor bouts with the flu and a bad cold now and again, but overall she'd been incredibly healthy. There might have been times when she should have seen a physician and hadn't, mainly because she wasn't particularly fond of anyone poking around her body, but usually she could take care of herself just fine.

"Go ahead and have a seat," the nurse instructed, gesturing toward the upholstered examination table.

Reluctantly Marjorie walked into the room and pressed her backside against the oblong examining table, her elbows resting on top of the padded cover. She crossed her ankles as though she posed this way regularly, hoping to give the picture of utter nonchalance. Chagrined, she realized she'd failed miserably.

Thankfully the nurse didn't seem to notice. "What seems to be the problem?"

Marjorie shrugged. "A little pain in my side. I'm sure it's nothing."

"We'll let Dr. Sam decide that." The woman pulled out a digital thermometer and, before Marjorie could protest, stuck it under her tongue. Motioning with her hand, the nurse told Marjorie to sit on the end of the table and skillfully took her blood pressure.

"Go ahead and get undressed," the nurse said afterward. She leaned over and pulled a paper gown from a cupboard. "When you've finished, put this on. The doctor will be with you in a couple of minutes." She left, quietly closing the door.

Marjorie mumbled grumpily to herself as she pulled the paper gown over her head and sighed with disgust when the opening for her arm hung far wider than necessary. Keeping her arms tucked close to her side for fear the gown would reveal the sides of her breasts, she wrapped the tissue sheet around her waist and sat on the end of the paper-lined examination table. The whole idea of introducing herself to a man when she was nude felt ridiculous. All right, so he was a physician, but all that stood between her body and this stranger was a piece of tissue that felt as though a big sneeze would destroy it.

Her bare feet dangled, and she kicked at the air aimlessly. Her brilliant red toenails looked funny, and she absently decided to change the color. Next time she would use a more subdued shade.

Just when she had convinced herself she was wasting her time, a polite knock sounded at the door. The knob twisted, and Marjorie painted a welcoming smile on her lips, doing her best to swallow the panic that unexpectedly gripped her.

Dr. Sam Bretton entered the examination room, reading

Marjorie's chart, his wide brow furrowed as he took in the information.

The first thing Marjorie noticed was his stature. Five foot seven in her stocking feet, she'd never considered herself short, but this man dwarfed her. His shoulders were broad and fit his height. His chest was deep. He wore his hair short, and his sideburns were clipped neatly around his ears. A few strands of gray at his temple provided a distinguished, sophisticated touch. He was good-looking—not strikingly handsome, but attractive enough to give credence to Lydia and the other women's claims. His eyes were a deep, dark shade of brown and the gentlest Marjorie had ever seen in a man. For an instant they mesmerized her into speechlessness. A stethoscope hung from his neck and rested against his broad, muscled chest.

"Ms. Majors." Sam smiled at his newest patient. Mary, his receptionist, had come to him earlier and asked about fitting this young woman into his already-tight schedule. A friend of Lydia Mason's, Mary had said, and Sam had agreed because he was fond of Lydia. Later he'd regretted the impulse. His day had started early, and he was tired, but with one look at the wide, frightened eyes of the woman sitting on the examination table he realized he'd made the right decision. Rarely had he seen a more expressive pair of brown eyes. Marjorie Majors was as nervous as a young mother and struggling valiantly to disguise it. Her chin trembled slightly, yet she met his gaze with pride and more mettle than he'd seen in years. She resembled a lost kitten he'd once found in a rainstorm; her wide eyes were round and appealing, and she looked as though she might turn and bolt at any moment.

"Doctor." The return of her voice brought with it the reappearance of her poise and aplomb. Her chin came up with the forced determination not to let him know how nervous she was. She handed him her business card.

"I realized I forgot to put my work number on the form," she said by way of explanation.

He removed the card from her stiff fingers, read it casually and nodded before sticking it inside the folder. "Your chart states that the last time you saw a physician was at age fourteen." He grimaced; whatever was bothering her now must be traumatic for her to seek medical help. In the last ten years he'd seen everything, and now a list of possibilities ran through his mind, most of them unpleasant.

"I had an ear infection." Marjorie pointed to her right ear while her heart beat at double time. She was literally shaking. She couldn't understand why she was reacting this way. Certainly this doctor didn't frighten her. His demeanor inspired confidence, not fear.

"You're experiencing pain in your right side?"

"That's correct," Marjorie said, and her voice wobbled as she jabbered on witlessly. "I don't think it's anything to be concerned about . . . probably one of those common female problems. No doubt it will go away in a couple of days."

"How long has it been bothering you?"

"A few days . . . maybe longer," she admitted reluctantly.

His thick brows contracted into a single, dark line. "Fever?"

Marjorie nodded. "But not high. It seems to be worse at night."

"Nausea? Dizziness?"

Again Marjorie answered with a nod.

"How has your back felt?"

"Sore." She wondered how he knew that. "Is that bad?" she asked hurriedly. "I mean, I can suffer with the best of them . . . In fact, I have a high tolerance for pain, and if you tell me it'll simply go away, I'm sure I can get through it."

"There's no need for you to do any suffering. Go ahead and lie back." He gave her his hand to guide her into a reclining position.

His hand curved around her fingers, and Marjorie's grip was surprisingly tight. What the others had said was true: Dr. Sam did inspire faith. She only wished he would stop looking at her as though she were a pathetic, scared doe caught in a hunter's sights.

"There's no need to be nervous," he said softly. "I promise not to bite."

"It's not your teeth that bother me."

He smiled again and stepped closer to the table to stand at her side. "Are you always such a wit?"

"Only when I'm forced to introduce myself to a strange man when I'm in the nude."

"Does this happen often?" Sam couldn't believe he'd asked her that. He clamped his jaw tightly. As a physician, he had taken an oath to treat all patients equally, but this one struck a chord, and the danger of looking upon her as a warm, desirable woman was strong.

"Meet men when I'm nude? No!"

He laughed outright at that, relieved. "I guessed as much." Carefully he lifted up the tissue sheet at her waist and placed his fingers on her abdomen, suspecting he would find rigidity and tenderness at McBurney's point, halfway between the navel and the crest of the hipbone.

"Actually, I've been feeling better the last couple of hours," Marjorie said hurriedly, hoping to suggest that whatever was wrong was curing itself. His hand felt cool and soothing against her heated flesh, and she closed her eyes. However, the instant he glided his fingers to her side and pressed down, her eyes shot open at the excruciating pain searing through her like red-hot needles.

She swore loudly and jumped from the examination table. "What do you think you're doing?" she shouted, her hands crossed protectively over her stomach. The agony lingered, and she nearly doubled over with the force of it.

"Miss Majors . . ."

"And what were all those platitudes about not needing to suffer?"

"Miss Majors, if you'd kindly return to the table . . ."

"Are you crazy? So you can do that again? Forget it, buddy."

"I may be able to forget it," he said solemnly, with a hint of chastisement, "but you won't. The pain isn't going to go away. In fact, it will get worse. Much worse. You should have seen a doctor days ago."

"It's already worse, thanks to you."

"Miss Majors . . ."

"For heaven's sake, call me Marjorie."

"Marjorie, then. Running out of here like a terrified rabbit isn't going to make everything all right."

So he'd noticed the way she was eyeing the neat pile of her folded clothes. She wouldn't run, because that would be silly and stupid, but she couldn't keep from looking at the door longingly.

"You have an inflamed appendix."

She swallowed past the tightness in her throat. The shooting pain hadn't ebbed; if anything, it had gotten steadily worse from the moment he had touched her tender abdomen. Oh, dear heaven, her appendix. She didn't need a fortune-teller to explain what would happen next. Surgery. The sound of the word was as ominous as that of a trumpet in a funeral march.

"Your temperature is rising, and my guess is that your white cell count is sky-high," he continued. "A blood test will confirm that easily enough."

A weak smile wobbled at the corners of her mouth. "My appendix," she repeated.

Sam nodded. "Go ahead and get dressed. When you've finished, I'll have my nurse draw some blood and escort you into my office. That'll give me a few minutes to make the necessary arrangements. We'll talk, and I'll explain where we go from here."

"Okay." Her voice sounded scratchy and thin, like an ailing frog's.

He eyed her again, his gaze tender and concerned. He regretted having hurt her. The look of suppressed pain in her eyes bothered him more than he'd expected, and he tried to lend her some of his own confidence. "Don't look so worried—everything's going to be fine."

"Everything's going to be fine?" Marjorie echoed, unable to disguise her sarcasm. "Sure it is." The minute he left the room, she snapped her teeth over her bottom lip and bit down unmercifully. Her hand trembled as she brushed a thick strand of hair away from her face, and the room appeared to sway slightly. The last time she'd felt this shaky had been at her parents' funeral.

As if on cue, the nurse reappeared the minute Marjorie had completed dressing and led her into another room, where she drew blood from her arm.

While he waited for Marjorie, Sam contacted Cal Johnson, a surgeon and good friend. His instincts told him the sooner they had her in the hospital, the better. When he explained her symptoms to Cal, his friend concurred and agreed to take the case. His second telephone conversation was with a member of the staff at Tacoma General.

When Marjorie appeared in the doorway of his office, Sam saw her from the corner of his eye. She hesitated, and he motioned for her to come inside and take a seat.

"I don't think we should wait any longer," he said into the receiver. "Good. Good. Yes, I can have her over there in a half hour. I'll assist."

In an effort to keep from looking as though she were listening in on his conversation, Marjorie scanned the walls. Certificates, diplomas and service awards decorated every available spot. His desk was neat and orderly. The sure sign of a twisted mind, she mused darkly. She glanced his way again and sighed. Heavens, she hoped he wasn't discussing her! He must have been. If he felt surgery was necessary, then she would at least like a couple of days to mentally prepare herself. A week would be even better.

Marjorie's soft, expressive eyes pleaded with him, but Sam's gaze just missed meeting hers, and she realized that, although he hadn't mentioned her name, he wasn't likely to be talking about another patient.

"Sorry to keep you waiting," he said, when he'd hung up.

"No problem." She smiled, and her fingers curved around her purse in her lap.

"I was just talking to Tacoma General."

Marjorie pointed her finger over her shoulder. "Did you know that you have a dying houseplant in your waiting room?" she asked in an effort to delay the bad news she knew was coming.

"I wasn't aware of that."

"You want to operate on me, don't you?"

"We don't have a lot of options here, Marjorie. I've contacted a friend of mine. He'll be doing the actual surgery, but I'll be there, as well. Your appendix is at a dangerous stage and could burst at any time."

He said her name in a soft, caressing way that she knew would have made another woman's knees turn to tapioca pudding. Not Marjorie's. Not now. Panic was overwhelming her, dominating her thoughts and actions.

"Where's your family?" he asked in a low, reassuring voice.

"I don't have one."

The memory of the orphaned kitten returned to Sam's mind. Cold. Lost. Frightened. And vulnerable.

At his look of surprise, Marjorie hurried to explain. "No parents, that is . . . One sister, but she doesn't live in Washington State. Jody's attending the University of Portland."

"What about a boyfriend?"

With effort she held her head high, her chin jutting out proudly. "I've only been in Washington a few months." She was about to add that she didn't have time to date much, not when she had to earn enough money to support herself and keep her sister in school. She managed to stop in the nick of time. This man was almost a complete stranger, yet she had been about to spill her guts to him. He had a strange effect on her, and Marjorie found that oddly intimidating.

"Is there anyone you can call?"

"No." No one she felt she could trouble. She'd made it on her own this far; she could get through the operation and a lot more if necessary. "When do you want to do the surgery?"

"Soon. Cal Johnson will make that decision."

A lump worked its way up her throat. The battle to hold back the fear was nearly overwhelming. Even breathing normally had become a difficult task as she labored to appear unaffected and calm.

"So *you* won't be doing the surgery?" This was a man she could trust. Like the others, she had known that instinctively. Now he was pawning her off on another physician, and the thought was almost as terrifying as the actual operation.

"Do you think you should trust a doctor with a dying houseplant?"

"I . . . don't know." Marjorie realized he was attempting to help her relax, and she appreciated the effort. He really was a nice man. Lydia and the others were right about that. She envisioned him with other women, offering security and assurance. He'd chosen his profession well.

"The truth is, I may not have a green thumb, but when it comes to surgery you don't have any worries."

"Then why won't you operate on me?"

"The appendix isn't my area of expertise. Dr. Johnson has

done countless appendectomies, whereas I've only done a few. I'll assist."

"But I know you." As soon as the words ran over her tongue, Marjorie realized how ridiculous they sounded. They'd met less than a half hour earlier.

"You'll do fine with Dr. Johnson."

"I suppose I will," she said without much confidence.

"I can honestly say that you're the first woman who's jumped off the examination table, ready to swing at me." His smiling eyes studied her.

"Hey, that poke hurt."

"I know, and I apologize," he answered sincerely. "I don't want you to worry about this surgery. I'll be there with you. Cal Johnson's an excellent surgeon, and there shouldn't be any problems, since we've caught this in time."

Marjorie nodded.

"I'm not going to let you down."

"You say that to all your patients, don't you?"

His eyes widened briefly. "No." He opened the top drawer and took out a single sheet of paper. "Here. Let me show you what we're going to do."

Marjorie wasn't sure she wanted to know. He must have read the doubt in her eyes, because he added, "I learned long ago that my patients aren't nearly as nervous if they have an idea of what's going to happen."

She nodded and cocked her head so that she could see the picture he had started drawing.

"As you're probably aware, the appendix is a small pocket, from one to six inches in size." He illustrated it, dexterously moving his pencil across the sheet of paper.

Marjorie understood only a little about what he was telling her, but she nodded as though she had recently graduated from medical school and knew it all.

He talked for several minutes more, explaining where Dr. Johnson would be making the incision and what he would be doing. "Once you're admitted to the hospital, you'll undergo a series of tests, including several X rays."

"X rays? Why?"

"We want to be sure that your lungs aren't congested. No need to borrow trouble."

"I see," Marjorie commented, although she didn't really. Whatever he and the other doctors thought was fine with her.

"You'll only be in the hospital a couple of days, depending on how you feel, and you'll be back to work within three weeks."

"Three weeks," Marjorie echoed. "I can't take off that much time!"

"You don't have any choice."

"Wanna bet?" Defiantly, she slapped the challenge at him. "In case you don't realize it, a car salesperson works solely on commission. If I don't sell cars, I don't eat."

His mouth tightened momentarily. "Let's play that part by ear. No doubt you'll surprise me."

"No doubt," she echoed.

Sam rubbed the pencil between his palms. "How'd you get into car sales?"

Marjorie shrugged. "The usual way, I suppose. I started out working in a computer store four or five years back. We worked on commission, and I did well."

"That figures. So where did you go from there?"

"Boats."

"Do you know a lot about them?"

She crossed her knees, winced in an effort to hide the pain, then grinned sheepishly. Naturally he noticed, but he was kind enough not to comment. "At the time I didn't know a thing, but before long I learned everything there was to know."

"And from there it was a natural progression to cars?"

"More or less. I like selling a top-of-the-line product, so selling Mercedes sedans and sports cars was a natural next step."

He continued working the pencil back and forth across his palms. He didn't normally spend this much time with a patient, but he wanted her to feel comfortable with him. She was alone and scared to death, and it was his job to do what he could to reassure her. Success in health care had a lot to do with attitude, and he wanted Marjorie Majors to feel confident and secure about whatever lay ahead.

"I've always wanted a Mercedes," he said.

Marjorie realized he was doing everything he could to ease her fears and help her relax. It was working; the tense terror that had gripped her only moments before was slipping away.

He placed his hands against the edge of the desk and rolled back his chair. "I'll see you at Tacoma General," he said, his gaze holding hers.

"I wasn't planning to run away."

"I didn't honestly think you were."

The smile that curved his mouth did funny things to her heart rate, but Marjorie quickly dismissed the effect as having anything to do with attraction. She was grateful, that was all. Grateful—nothing less, nothing more.

Two

Marjorie felt strange. She lay on her back, staring above her as the dotted white tile loomed closer and closer, then gradually faded back into place. Her eyes narrowed, and she tried to tell herself that the ceiling wasn't actually closing in on her. This phenomenon was the result of the shot the nurse had given her a few minutes earlier to help her relax before they came to roll her into the operating room.

"How are you feeling?" Sam Bretton moved beside her gurney and placed his hand over hers.

Again Marjorie was struck by how gentle his dark eyes were. A man shouldn't possess sensitive eyes like that. In her drugged condition her imagination was running away with her, suggesting thoughts she had no right to think. She stared back at him, then blinked twice, because it seemed as though she could see straight into his heart. It was large and full, and his capacity to care and love seemed boundless.

"Marjorie?"

She pulled her gaze past the I.V. drip to Sam and lightly shook her head in a futile effort to clear her befuddled mind.

"You wouldn't believe the treatment I got," she said, trying to disregard the strange effect of the medication.

"You met Cal Johnson?"

She nodded. He wasn't another Sam Bretton, but he would do, especially if Sam felt he was the right man for the job.

"So they put you through the mill?"

His smile dazzled Marjorie, and she reminded herself anew that at the moment her senses couldn't be trusted. "Your call must have done the trick, because there was a whole crew just waiting to get their hands on me the minute I walked in the door."

"You can thank Cal for that."

"Oh sure! If you think I believe that, then there's some swampland in Nevada that might interest me, right?"

"Are you saying you don't trust me?" Sam's eyes widened with feigned outrage. He liked Marjorie. Even now, when she was dopey from the effects of medication, he found her sense of humor stimulating. Her ready smile had wrapped itself around him the moment he'd walked into the room. She was fresh and alive; her mind was active, her wit lively, and her courage in difficult circumstances was admirable.

"I'll have you know that in the last hour I've been poked, pinched, prodded and a bunch of other disgusting things I don't even want to discuss."

His lips trembled with suppressed mirth, and he squeezed her fingers reassuringly. "Is there anything I can get you?"

Marjorie tried to smile, but her mouth refused to cooperate. "That sounds suspiciously like a last request."

The dark eyes that studied her crinkled at the corners as he revealed his amusement. "It wasn't."

"You mean I don't need to ask for a priest?"

"Not this time around. Anything else?"

The inside of her mouth felt thick and dry. "Something to drink. Please."

He reached behind him and took a chip of ice from a water jug. Again the urge to reassure her, to stay with her, was strong. Her hair spilled out across the pillow, and the red highlights suggested that her temper would be as quick as her smile. "This will have to do for now. Suck on it and make it last."

Obediently she opened her mouth, and he slipped the ice chip inside, then paused to wipe a drop of moisture from her chin. It wasn't until then that Marjorie noticed he was dressed entirely in green. A cap covered his head, and a surgical mask hung free around his neck.

"Green surgical gowns?" she asked, holding the ice chip against the back side of her mouth so she could speak clearly. "Is that because red stains are so difficult to remove from white fabric?" She sucked in her breath and closed her eyes. "Don't answer that—I don't want to know."

"Don't let your courage fail you now, Marjorie, you're doing fine."

Her eyes shot open. "It's not you who's going under the knife. I'll be scared if I want, and I don't mind telling you, I'd rather be anyplace else in the world but right here." Shot or no shot, sedative or no sedative, she'd never been more unsure about anything. More than that, she was astonished that she had admitted how afraid she was to Sam. It wasn't like her. That shot must have contained a truth serum.

"Everything's going to work out," he said in that calm, confident voice of his.

Without much effort Marjorie could envision him talking someone out of jumping off the Tacoma Narrows Bridge. He had the kind of voice a salesman would kill for—low-pitched, confident, effortless, sincere.

"Don't worry," she said with feigned composure, seeing herself standing on the edge of the steel precipice, looking into the swirling waters far below. "I'm not going to jump."

He gave her a funny look but made no comment.

"That didn't make any sense, did it?" She tossed her head from side to side in an effort to clear her thoughts. It didn't work. Everything scrambled together until she wasn't sure of anything.

He patted her hand. "Don't worry about it. The medication has that effect."

Marjorie wondered if it actually was the shot. No, she was convinced his silk-edged voice and kind eyes were the cause of all this, mesmerizing her. Her eyes drifted closed, and she moistened her lips as she imagined Sam Bretton leaning over her and whispering words of love in her ear, then taking her in his arms and kissing her with such tenderness, such passion, that her thoughts forcefully collided inside her head. A fireworks display that rivaled a Fourth-of-July celebration exploded, and she forced her eyes open and felt the blood rush through her veins.

"Go ahead and sleep," he said softly. "I'll be here when you wake up."

"Please don't leave me." Her eyes rounded, and her mouth filled with the bitter taste of panic. She needed this man she barely knew more than she'd ever needed anyone. The terror that gripped her as she stared ahead at the wide double doors that led to the operating room was intense and nearly overwhelming.

"I'm not going anywhere," Sam assured her, continuing to hold her hand, his fingers firmly entwined with hers.

Somehow it seemed vitally important that he be there every minute. Still, she hated needing anyone. People had always let her down. She was a stronger person than this, and Dr. Sam Bretton was little more than a stranger. Yet she trusted him enough to place her life in his capable hands.

"Don't worry, I'll be fine," she said, and realized her voice was barely audible. "You . . . you don't need to stay with me. I'm a big girl. I'll get through this . . . really . . . Don't tell Jody, she'll only worry . . . Must call Lydia."

"That's all taken care of," he said, and his voice seemed to come from a great distance.

"Thank you, Sam," Marjorie mumbled, and started slipping into a light sleep.

A female voice made its way through to her fading consciousness. "Dr. Johnson is ready, doctor."

An invisible force pushed the gurney forward, and Marjorie struggled to open her eyes. Someone lifted her head and placed her hair inside a confining cap.

She managed to open one eye and was greeted by blinding lights. Sam was at her side, and Cal Johnson, who she'd briefly met earlier, stood on the opposite side of the room, examining her X rays. Sam leaned over her and explained that the anesthesiologist would be there any minute. Marjorie nodded, even managed a weak smile, then decided that it was better not to look around. She settled back down and tightly shut her eyes.

Soon other voices met over her head, some deep, others crisp, and a few soft. In her drug-induced drowsiness Marjorie sorted through them and tried to assimilate only Sam's words. The nurses joked and flirted with him like a longtime friend. She sighed with the realization that if his patients fell in love with him, then the women on the hospital staff must be equally vulnerable to his charms. Maybe he was already married. Of course, that was it! Sam Bretton had a wife. Her disappointment was keen. He was married. He had to be. Rats! All the good ones were already taken.

Finally it got too difficult to concentrate, and she gave up trying. When she woke, this troublesome episode would all be over, and she could get on with her life and forget that any of this had ever happened.

Impatiently, Marjorie waded through huge billows of thick, black fog. She shivered with cold and sighed when Sam's familiar voice asked for a heated blanket. She felt the weight of a quilt on top of her, and she sighed contentedly. The fog parted as warmth seeped into her bones, and for the first time she could decipher a path that led through the haze. She tried to speak, but her lips seemed glued together, and no amount of trying could pry them apart.

"Marjorie?"

Getting her eyes to open required an equal amount of effort, but when she managed that task, she was blinded by a flash of high-intensity light. She groaned and lowered her lashes.

"Am I in the morgue?" she mumbled, having difficulty getting the words over her uncooperative tongue.

"Not yet," Sam answered.

"That's reassuring."

"You're in the recovery room. Everything went without a hitch. We're lucky we got the appendix when we did. From the look of things, it was ready to burst, and then there could have been some unpleasant complications."

"Close, but no cigar, huh?"

"In this case you don't want a cigar."

"So I'll live and love again?"

Sam brushed the hair from her temple. "You're good for at least another fifty years."

For some inexplicable reason it seemed easier to concentrate with her eyes closed. Her lids fluttered shut even though she strained to keep them open.

"Go ahead and sleep," Sam told her softly. "I'm here, like I promised."

Marjorie wanted to thank him; she searched for some way to let him know how grateful she was that she hadn't woken up alone. The hospital might seem a warm, congenial place to him, but he was there every day. To her, it was a disinfected torture chamber, and she was scared witless. It seemed so important to tell him that his presence comforted her that she wrestled to keep awake even as she felt herself slipping back into the thick, dark fog.

Pain woke Marjorie up the second time—a dull, throbbing ache in her side, quite different from what she'd experienced before meeting Sam. She raised her hand, rubbed her eyes and yawned. The room wasn't as brilliant as before. The light appeared muted, and she was grateful. She rolled her head and realized she was in a small room. The drapes were closed, but a ribbon of light entered between them. A noise distracted her, and she turned her head in the opposite direction and discovered Sam Bretton sitting at her bedside, reading the latest Scandinavian thriller.

"Sam?"

He closed the book, turned to face her and smiled. "Hello again."

"What time is it?"

He rotated his wrist. "Almost six."

"In the morning?"

He nodded and stood, setting his novel aside. He took her wrist and pressed his fingers over her pulse while he stared at the face of his watch.

"Have you been here all night?" It seemed incredible that he would have stayed with her ever since her surgery. She noticed then that the blood-pressure cuff was wrapped around her upper arm, and fear renewed itself within her. There had been problems! Big problems! She swallowed around the tightness in her throat. All night she'd teetered on the brink of death, and Sam had stayed with her and fought for her very life. For hours her fate had hung by a delicate thread, and this man had valiantly battled to save her.

"What happened?" Her question was hoarse, revealing a hundred doubts.

"Nothing," he answered crisply. "All surgeries should be such a breeze."

"Nothing went wrong?"

He frowned, puzzled. "Nothing."

"But . . . the blood-pressure cuff . . . And you stayed with me all night. Why?"

His frown deepened, marring his smooth brow with three nearly straight lines. "Because I said I would. You needed someone."

Guilt fell heavily upon her shoulders. She certainly hadn't meant for him to do this. He must have gone without sleep the entire night, and all because of a few silly words she'd uttered in the throes of panic. "But, I didn't—"

"Hey, don't worry about me," he interrupted quickly. "I've got the day off."

"I suppose you golf on Wednesdays?" she asked.

"I don't play golf."

Marjorie feigned shock. "You don't golf? Just what kind of doctor are you? No one told me that before I made my first appointment with you."

"Count your blessings, Majors."

"Oh?"

"I could charge by the hour."

The effort to smile was painful, but holding back her amusement would have been impossible. "Hey, don't make me laugh—it hurts." She groaned and placed her hand over her abdomen. "How soon will the pain go away."

"In a few days."

"A whole lot of good that's doing me now."

"Stop being so impatient."

He spoke with just enough of a challenge for her to quit arguing. She would grin and bear it.

"I'll get the nurse," Sam informed her, smiling. "Cal left instructions for you to sit upright once you woke."

Marjorie snapped her mouth closed and pressed her lips together to smother a protest. Dr. Johnson didn't actually expect her to move, did he? She couldn't—not yet. If breathing hurt this much, she could only imagine the agony that sitting up would cause. Great! Sam and his friend had grabbed her from the jaws of death, only to let her die a slow, torturous death from pain.

From the moment she'd met Dr. Sam, Marjorie had been looking for some imperfection. Anything. He was much too wonderful to be real. Now the flaw stood out like a fake diamond under a jeweler's eyepiece. Clearly, she decided in her still-drugged state, Sam Bretton enjoyed watching people suffer.

Again Sam proved her wrong. The nurse who came to her room came alone. Her name tag was pinned to her uniform: Bertha Powell, R.N.

"Dr. Sam sent me," Bertha announced.

Marjorie studied the older woman, who looked as though her previous profession had been mud wrestling. She was built as solid as a rock, and from the glinting light in her eyes, she was just waiting for Marjorie to start something.

"Where's Sam?"

"*Doctor* Sam asked me to tell you that he'll be back later this afternoon."

"Wonderful," Marjorie muttered, and wiggled her big toe as an experiment. The pain wasn't debilitating, but she wasn't exactly up to swinging from jungle vines, either.

Bertha pulled back the sheet. "Are you ready?"

Marjorie wondered what the other woman would do if she announced that she refused to move. Briefly she toyed with the idea, then decided against it. Her teeth gritted, she cautiously did what had been requested of her.

Exhausted afterward, Marjorie slept for six hours. Someone moving inside her room woke her. When she stirred and opened her eyes, she found Lydia standing at the foot of her bed with a small bouquet of flowers in her hand.

"Hi, Marjorie," Lydia said in a soft voice.

"I had my appendix out," Marjorie grumbled. "I stopped your friend in the nick of time from doing a lobotomy."

Lydia looked relieved and set the flowers on the bedside table. "Same ol' Marjorie."

"I didn't mean to snap at you."

"Hey, no problem. I'm used to it, remember?"

Marjorie tried to wipe the tiredness from her eyes. "I bet you're waiting for me to tell you how right you were."

"It'd feel good, but I can wait." Obviously she couldn't, because she added, "Didn't I tell you it had to be more than a queasy stomach? I figured it out long before you, didn't I?"

"Yup, you did," Marjorie returned, with more than a hint of amused sarcasm. "Where would I be without you?" That much wasn't in jest. She was sincerely grateful her friend had made the appointment when she did, especially after what Sam had told her.

Lydia pulled a chair close to the hospital bed and plunked herself down. Without so much as pausing to inhale, she started off with a long series of questions. "How do you like Dr. Sam? Isn't he wonderful? Didn't I tell you he was a marvel? Now that you've met him, you'll probably be like everyone else and fall madly in love with him."

"No doubt."

Lydia's face blossomed into a wide grin. "I knew you'd like him."

Just managing to avoid her friend's gaze, Marjorie asked, "What's his wife like?"

"His wife?" That stopped Lydia cold. She opened and closed her mouth twice. "I didn't know he was married."

"You mean he isn't?" Hope flared. Naw, he had to be married—

and probably had a passel of kids to boot. All in diapers, no doubt. Knowing the type of doctor he was convinced Marjorie that Sam Bretton would be a devoted husband and father. She, on the other hand, was definitely not the mother type.

"I don't know anything about a wife," Lydia answered thoughtfully, chewing on the corner of her bottom lip. "I really don't think he's married. I can't remember seeing a wedding band, can you?"

"It doesn't matter," Marjorie muttered. He'd been wonderful . . . more than wonderful, but she had far more important matters to deal with that didn't involve risking her heart over a physician whose second job entailed throwing women's equilibriums off balance.

In order to change the subject Marjorie scooted her gaze past Lydia to the bouquet of carnations and roses on the bedside table. "Thanks for the flowers."

"Hey, no problem. They're from all the salespeople at Dixon's."

"All?" Marjorie cocked one delicately shaped brow suspiciously. "Even Al Swanson?"

Lydia grinned sheepishly. "He tossed in a buck and suggested I buy a cactus."

That Marjorie could believe. Al had made it clear that he didn't approve of women in the car business. That was tough, she mused, since she was at Dixon Motors for the long haul, no matter what Al or anyone else thought. It wasn't that Al had taken a dislike to her and her alone. He had a problem with everyone. He had yet to learn that sales work was often a team effort. Marjorie's gut feeling was that Al Swanson wouldn't be around Dixon much longer.

"Oh!" Lydia exclaimed. "I nearly forgot. Dr. Sam phoned and told me to get the key to your apartment so I could pick up some personal items you're going to need."

Once again the man had amazed Marjorie with his thought-fulness. "I hate to put you to all the trouble."

"It's no trouble. Honest. You'd do the same thing for me."

Marjorie smiled her thanks. Accepting anyone's assistance was difficult for her—more than it should have been, she realized. She'd practically raised Jody with little or no help from any state agencies. With a limited college education she'd forged her own way in the world, designed her career, and earned enough to support herself and pay for her sister's college tuition. Sam Bretton had the wrong impression of her, and to Marjorie's utter embarrassment, she had to admit she'd been the one to give it to him.

"The key," Lydia reminded her.

"Oh, it's in my purse." Guessing where it would be stored, she nodded toward the closet door.

Lydia stood and moved in that direction. "Dr. Sam gave me a list, but you might want to read it over."

"I'm sure he thought of everything," Marjorie responded distractedly. She had to set Sam straight. She wasn't a helpless clinging vine, although he had good reason to believe she was. The memory of how she'd pleaded with him not to leave her was a keen source of her present chagrin.

Triumphantly Lydia held up Marjorie's key chain. "I'll run over to your place and get your things now."

Marjorie could do little more than nod. Her thoughts were light-years away, spinning out of control. She would talk to Sam the next time he stopped in to see her. She would explain everything. Yawning, she placed her hand over her mouth and determinedly tried to suppress the exhaustion that gripped her. How strange it felt to become so weary so easily. Of their own accord, her eyes drifted closed.

Sam was there when she woke. He smiled down on her before noting something on her chart. "How's the patient feeling?"

"I don't know yet. Give me a minute to sort through the various pains." To her surprise she noticed that her purple velvet housecoat was neatly folded across the bottom of her bed. Lydia must have returned with her things, and Marjorie realized she had somehow managed to sleep through her friend's second visit.

"Dr. Johnson wants you up and walking before dinner."

The protest that sprang automatically to her lips died a quick death. Sitting up in bed earlier had been difficult enough! Sam had to be out of his mind if he believed she was going to traipse around this room or down these halls, dragging an I.V. pole with her, and all because some man she barely knew had ordered her to. She, of all people, should know when she was ready to risk life and limb by walking again.

Sam glanced up from his notations, his eyes studying her. "What, no argument?"

"When can I get out of here?"

"Soon, but that's up to Cal," he answered noncommittally. "Listen, before you think about leaving the hospital, focus your energy on getting out of bed and moving."

He sounded so reasonable, so calm and confident, that the brick walls of her rebellion crumbled before she had them completely raised. Marjorie cautiously moved the sheet aside and struggled a little higher against her pillows.

"Careful, Marjorie. Don't try to move on your own." Sam closed her chart and hung it at the end of the bed.

"No," she said through gritted teeth. "I'll do it myself." One foot freed itself from the tangled sheet, and she raised herself up onto one elbow.

Disregarding her words, Sam placed his arm around her shoulders and helped her into an upright position. Flushed and embarrassed by how incredibly weak she was, Marjorie reached for her housecoat, astonished that the simple task of sitting could tire her so much that she was practically panting.

Sam draped her robe over her shoulders, then located her slippers and slipped them onto her feet. "Okay, let's take this nice and easy."

"Trust me, I'm not exactly ready to jump off this bed and race down the corridor." The spinning room gradually circled into place and came to a stop. "I think I'd feel better about this in the morning."

"Now, Marjorie."

She wanted to argue with him but hadn't the strength. "I'm not normally like this," she said, with as much force as she could muster. "I'm sorry I asked you to stay with me . . . I realize now I shouldn't have. . . ."

"Marjorie, I stayed because I wanted to, not out of any obligation." He stepped around the bed and stood directly in front of her, leaning down only slightly. Because the hospital bed was so high, their eyes met. His were warm and sincere, while hers flashed with frustration and regret.

Although his words had filled her with an absurd amount of pleasure, Marjorie still felt compelled to explain herself. "But I'm not like that . . . really."

"Like what?"

"Weak and sniveling."

"I never once thought that."

"Oh, you're impossible!"

Sam's thick brows shot upward. "I'm what?"

Marjorie lightly tossed her head. "Nothing."

"Do you doubt my word?"

"Not exactly. It's just that I feel I've given you the wrong impression of me. I'm a capable, responsible adult. I even figured out my own taxes last year."

"I'm impressed." He pushed a small stool across the floor so she could use that as a step to climb off the bed.

"You're actually going to make me do this?" Marjorie couldn't seem to get her body to cooperate. One foot eased itself down-ward as she cautiously scooted to the edge of the mattress.

Sam placed a supporting arm under her elbow to help her down. She felt small and incredibly fragile in his embrace. Once again she reminded him of the rain-drenched kitten he'd discovered all those years ago. And like the half-drowned feline, Marjorie Majors required love and attention, too. Only Sam wasn't in any position to give those things to her. She was his patient, not a potential girlfriend. The two didn't mix. Couldn't mix.

With both feet firmly planted on the floor, Marjorie paused, half expecting to keel over. When she didn't, she felt a glowing sense of triumph. She'd made it, actually made it.

"Good job," Sam said, and reluctantly dropped his arm. "Now take a few steps."

"You don't really mean for me to walk, do you?" She was only hours from having been under the knife. Hours from the most frightening experience of her life.

"I certainly do want you to walk. You know, one foot in front of the other in a forward direction."

She flashed him a look of irritation.

"And soon, if you're good, I'll take you upstairs."

"Upstairs? Is there something up there that would interest me? Like food?"

"You're hungry?"

"Famished! I haven't eaten in two days." That was entirely true. Marjorie liked her food and seldom skipped a meal. Luckily, gaining weight had never been a problem. She guessed she was fortunate in that department, but it seemed she would quickly melt away if this hospital had anything to say about it. She hadn't been offered a single meal so far.

Sam knew her digestive system couldn't handle anything solid for a few days, but he decided against telling her so. He would leave as many unpleasant tasks as possible for Cal Johnson. After all, Cal was the physician of record.

While guiding the I.V. pole beside her, Sam manipulated them through the doorway and into the broad hallway.

"This afternoon, while you were sleeping, I delivered a set of twins," Sam boasted proudly. Birth, even after countless deliveries, had never ceased to humble him, and twins were always special. "They're upstairs," he continued. "I'll take you to see them later, if you want."

Marjorie looked at him and blinked. She didn't know how to explain that babies frightened her. All right, they terrified her. Some women took to motherhood and dirty diapers like hogs to mud. But, unfortunately, that would never be the case with her. The only times she'd ever been around babies, they'd cried. Within ten minutes she'd been ready to wail herself. After several embarrassing episodes in her youth, she had decided that anyone under two was allergic to her.

"I . . . I think I'd better wait until I've got more strength," she said.

"Of course," Sam agreed. "I wouldn't dream of dragging you upstairs your first time out. Tomorrow, maybe, or the next day."

"Sure. Anytime," Marjorie answered, but the words nearly stuck in her throat.

Three

Marjorie stared at the orange tray and grimaced in pure disgust. If she so much as looked at another bowl of plain gelatin, she was going to start screaming and say something unladylike that would shock the entire hospital staff. Everything they'd brought to her so far only vaguely resembled food.

"Good morning," the nurse's aide greeted her, as she strolled into the room. "And how was your breakfast?"

"You don't want to know."

The young girl glanced at the untouched tray. "You didn't eat a thing."

"I couldn't," Marjorie muttered. It wasn't this poor woman's fault that the hospital had chosen to starve her.

"Aren't you feeling better? Usually my patients are more than ready to eat by this time. Are you in a lot of pain? Perhaps I should notify Dr. Johnson."

"Contacting the doctor isn't going to convince me to eat . . . this. I'd rather die," Marjorie said dramatically. "I refuse to swallow anything that slithers down my throat."

The aide chuckled. "Let me see what I can do." She left,

and Marjorie stared after her with visions of cheesy pizza, crisp fried chicken and a thick, juicy steak playing havoc with her imagination. Marjorie was convinced she smelled bacon frying in the distance, the odor wafting toward her and tormenting her with delicious dreams.

"Problems?" Sam sauntered into the room, looking sympathetic.

"Sam," Marjorie said, and brightened instantly. She hadn't seen him in nearly twenty hours and had rarely been more pleased to lay eyes on anyone. Sam Bretton could be trusted. She wasn't so sure about anyone else in this antiseptic place, but Sam would help straighten out this mealtime mess.

"You didn't eat your breakfast." His voice was only lightly accusing.

"I couldn't," she said, her eyes softly pleading with his. "The oatmeal had more lumps than a camel, and heaven only knows what flavor of gelatin they wanted me to eat . . . Liver, I think, and even with whipped topping, it looked disgusting. As for the tea and toast, could they be any more boring? Why can't I have a mushroom omelet, with home fries on the side? Something . . . anything, but gelatin and oatmeal."

"Soon."

Marjorie's face mirrored her reaction. Obviously *soon* wasn't going to be this morning, and she needed nourishment *now*, if not earlier. Disappointment consumed her. She'd thought of Sam as her ally, her friend. The amazing part was that he seemed to look better to her every time he walked in the room. When he was with her, even the pain lessened. He filled her room with an assurance of well-being and safekeeping. He lent her confidence, stamina and the conviction that this, too, would pass, and when it did, he would be there for her.

Sam reached for her hand, and his eyes gentled. "Marjorie, listen." He did understand her position, but she had to realize that stronger foods had to be reintroduced gradually into her digestive system. "You're not being a very good patient."

"Oh, spare me," she snapped, quickly losing a grip on her fragile patience. Her temper was always quick to fire when she was hungry. "No one told me I had to pretend I was on the good ship Lollipop."

"All we're asking is that you do as we say."

"And die of starvation in the process."

"You're a long way from that. Most women look forward to dropping a few pounds during their hospital stay." The moment the words slipped from Sam's mouth, he recognized his terrible mistake. It was too late to retract his statement; his only hope was that she would let it slide. He tried smiling, praying the action would take any sting from his words. It didn't.

Marjorie's face grew as red as a California pepper, and her anger was just as hot. "Are you insinuating Tacoma General is a fat farm and that I'm overweight?"

"No, you misunderstood—"

"Your meaning was more than clear," she said coldly, and reached for the buzzer to call the nurse. Immediately the red light above her bed flashed on.

"Marjorie . . . I didn't mean to be so tactless. You're not the least bit plump . . . I'm doing a poor job of this." Sam wiped a hand around the back of his neck and sighed. He regretted getting trapped in this no-win conversation. When it came to dealing with his patients, he usually had more finesse than this.

She ignored him and tossed aside the sheet, sticking her bare leg out in an ungraceful effort to climb down from the high hospital bed. "Nurse," she cried, but her voice was weak and wobbly.

"Marjorie, you have to stay where you are and eat your breakfast," Sam said.

Their eyes met and clashed. Marjorie was hurting and hungry, a lethal combination that resulted in the most embarrassing reaction. Tears. Embarrassed, she turned her face away from him and motioned toward the door, wordlessly asking him to leave.

Sam hesitated. Once again his heart went out to her, and he had to force himself to walk out of the room. In the few days since he'd met Marjorie, she'd touched him in ways few women ever had. He had been a silent witness to her courage and realized that she possessed a rare personal strength. Her laughter was a sweet melody, her movements innately graceful. Several times over the past twenty-four hours he'd found his thoughts drifting to her, and he smiled at the memory of her waking from the operation to ask if she was in the morgue. At each meeting he realized all the more how proud she was. Proud. Fiery. Straightforward. He found it utterly astonishing that she wasn't married. And he was grateful. He wanted to get to know her better—a whole lot better.

Sam knew he'd made a mess of this and was angry with himself. He patted her shoulder and turned to leave the room.

The nurse's aide met him outside her door and raised questioning eyes to him. "Doctor?"

"I believe she'll eat her breakfast now," Sam answered, his thoughts distracted.

"Very good." The younger woman beamed him a warm smile—impressed, he imagined, with his ability to deal with a difficult situation.

Sam did his best to return the friendly gesture. He had a reputation for working well with unreasonable patients, but Marjorie wasn't that, only confused and miserable.

And he'd made a mess of things.

Marjorie heard Sam tell the nurse's aide that she would be eating her meal and glared after him, half tempted to toss the liver gelatin at his arrogant backside. She didn't, though, because he was right. Once again she'd made an idiot of herself in front of him and the hospital staff. She didn't like herself when she behaved this way, yet she seemed powerless to change.

The moisture on her cheeks felt like burning acid, and she brushed the tears aside, thoroughly embarrassed by their appearance. She wasn't a crybaby—at least she hadn't been until Sam Bretton walked into her life. Then everything had quickly fallen to pieces. Whatever it was about that insufferable, wonderful man that reduced her to this state should be outlawed.

The tea was only lukewarm, but at least it was strong enough to satisfy Marjorie's need for caffeine. The dry wheat toast was surprisingly filling, and the oatmeal passable as long as she dumped three sugar packets over the top. The gelatin she ignored.

In order to avoid the triumphant look on the nurse's aide's face, Marjorie pretended to be asleep when the woman returned for the tray. To her surprise, she actually did fall into a restful sleep and woke midmorning with a game show blaring from the TV positioned against the wall.

"I see you're awake." The mud-wrestling star was back. Bertha Powell, R.N., looked stiff in her starched white uniform. "Dr. Johnson wants you up and walking today. Ten laps."

"Laps?" Marjorie repeated, still caught in the last dregs of sleep. Did the hospital provide a running track for surgery patients?

"The corridor," the muscular woman informed her primly. "Ten times up and back. That's your goal for today. But don't do too much at once. Two or three round trips at a time. No more."

Marjorie resisted the urge to salute. Bertha Powell seemed to be looking for a few good men—or women—to gleefully whip into shape. Marjorie didn't doubt that the nurse would count every single lap.

To her credit, the nurse aided Marjorie into an upright position and helped her on with her robe. There was some confusion with the I.V., but Bertha figured it out, and after only a few minutes, Marjorie was on her way.

Steadier on her feet than she'd been before, she was pleased with her slow but sure progress. Although it was hours until noon, the hospital was a hive of activity. If she'd been in a grumbling mood, she would have pointed out that Dr. Johnson had suggested she get plenty of rest, but the hospital staff had awakened her before the sun was anywhere close to the horizon. The only people up at that time of the morning were mass murderers, teenagers and nurses' aides.

The woman who had brought in her breakfast tray grinned as Marjorie passed the nurses' station.

"Hey, you're doing great."

Marjorie smiled back. "Yes, I think I'll donate my body to science."

"Science fiction might appreciate it more," said a deep male voice from behind her.

"Sam?" Marjorie laughed and turned her head, pleased to see him again.

"To your room," he instructed.

Marjorie was more than happy to comply and glanced with wide-eyed curiosity toward the brown paper sack in his hand. "What's that?"

"You'll see."

"I thought you had appointments all day," she said once they were back in her room, not that she was disappointed to see him. Nothing could have been further from the truth; she was overjoyed.

"I just finished my rounds."

"Oh." Once again Marjorie couldn't take her eyes from his dazzling smile. "How are the twins?"

"As cute as a bug's ear. I'll take you to see them this evening, if you want."

It was all Marjorie could do to nod. She'd brought up the subject of the babies because she knew they were close to Sam's heart. She was interested, but not to the point of overcoming her instinctive apprehension. When the time came that she couldn't avoid it any longer, she would look through the glass and ooh and aah with appropriate enthusiasm, and Sam would never guess she was frightened to death.

"I brought you something to tide you over until lunch," he said, holding out the sack to her.

Marjorie took it and eagerly peeked inside. The chocolate-coated ice-cream bar produced a small squeal of delight. If they'd been anyplace but the middle of a hospital, she would have thrown her arms around his neck and smudged his face with kisses to thank him properly.

"Thank you, Sam. Really."

"It's my pleasure."

Those gorgeous eyes of his seemed to look straight into her heart. "I felt terrible about the scene I made earlier," Marjorie admitted, centering her greedy gaze on the melting Dove Bar. Her mouth started to water. This man was special. Really special.

"There's no need to apologize," he said. "I wasn't exactly helpful."

"But you tried." She didn't understand why he was so good to her, but she wasn't willing to question it. From the moment she'd walked into his office, he'd befriended her, then seen her through the most difficult days of her life, all the while hardly leaving her side. No wonder his patients were so willing to admit they fell in love with him.

Sam's heart throbbed painfully with desire. Marjorie's wide eyes regarded him with such sweet gratitude that it seemed the most natural thing in the world to lean forward and press his mouth to hers. He didn't, of course, but that didn't stop his imagination from running rampant. He could all but taste her honey-sweet lips. He could all but feel her mouth shaping and fitting to his own, and her ripe body pressing against him.

Inhaling deeply to discipline his thoughts, Sam took a step back. Marjorie Majors had caught him completely off guard. Over the years he'd been subjected to every female ploy imaginable, but the majority of women who were interested in him were mostly concerned with the money he was making and the social position that would go with becoming his wife. They hadn't soured him on marriage, but they *had* made him extra cautious. He didn't succumb easily to a woman's charms, and he wasn't about to start now. He was looking for a special woman to become his wife. A partner and a friend.

And now there was Marjorie. Her candor had caught him unaware. She was a natural beauty. Even without makeup and with her dark hair tied lifelessly away from her face, he couldn't help being attracted to her. From the moment she'd angrily jumped off his examining table, Sam had been enraptured with her. Everything about her acted as a powerful aphrodisiac, but nothing could come of this attraction until after she was released from the hospital.

Sam left abruptly, but Marjorie was too busy eating her ice-cream bar to pay much attention. She sucked on the wooden stick until the last bit of chocolate had long since melted on her tongue, then carefully set the stick aside.

Dragging the I.V. stand with her, she walked slowly and carefully down the corridor until she reached the nurses' station. There wasn't any way to be tactful about what she needed to know, but she was in dangerous territory here, feeling the way she did about Sam Bretton.

"Ms. Powell?" she said as sweetly as she could.

"Yes?" Bertha Powell glanced up from the chart she was updating, and her eyes narrowed with displeasure.

"I've done five laps."

"That leaves five more for this afternoon."

"Right."

The woman returned her attention to her work.

"Ms. Powell?"

"Yes." Once again the older woman's voice revealed her lack of patience. She gripped the pen tightly and glanced up at Marjorie before slowly exhaling one long breath.

"Dr. Bretton was in earlier. I was wondering if I could ask about . . ."

"His wife?" the older woman finished for her.

The room swayed, and the floor felt as if had buckled under Marjorie's unsteady feet. She gripped the edge of the counter until she regained her balance and the hospital had righted itself once more. But she had to ask, and surely the hospital staff would know for sure, while Lydia had only been guessing.

"That *is* what you wanted to know, isn't it?" the woman pressed.

It was all Marjorie could do to nod and say, "He's married, then?"

"Not as far as I know," Bertha answered almost kindly. "But I swear that man breaks more hearts than George Clooney. There isn't a woman on this floor who wouldn't give her eyeteeth to be married to him. He's the type we're all looking for."

"But . . ."

"Be smart, Ms. Majors. Listen to the voice of experience and learn from it. All Dr. Sam's patients fall in love with him. It's gratitude, I suppose. Heaven knows he's hunk enough to melt anyone's heart—even mine."

Marjorie clenched her jaw to hide her reaction.

"Now I don't want you to feel bad about this. It's common enough, believe me."

The heat that exploded into Marjorie's cheeks was hot enough to fry eggs. She hadn't realized her feelings were so obvious. Under normal conditions she didn't fluster easily, but when it came to Sam, she lost all her poise.

"He's a wonderful person," Marjorie managed to say with some semblance of calm.

"Honey, you don't know the half of it. I saw that man sit for hours with a young couple after their baby died. More than once I've been a witness to his tenderness—that's why I'm telling you what I am. Believe me, if I were twenty years younger, I'd be in love with the man myself. Truthfully, I *am* in love with him. We all are."

"Thank you." Already Marjorie was walking away, trying to disguise her embarrassment. She'd tried to be subtle, tried to find out what she could without making a total idiot of herself. And she'd failed.

After a few moments to think the nurse's words over, Marjorie relaxed. An odd reassurance replaced her chagrin. It was good to know she was merely one of the masses. Bertha Powell was right. Women tended to fall in love with their doctors. It was a common enough malady, and one she should have anticipated.

The sooner she was released from the hospital, the better, Marjorie decided. With a determination that drove her to the brink of exhaustion, she did five more laps up and down the long corridor, then fell into a deep sleep the minute the dinner tray was removed from her room.

"Morning, doctor," Marjorie said casually when Cal Johnson paid his morning visit. He was a bald, grandfatherly type who certainly hadn't affected her the way Sam had.

"I see you've made considerable progress," he said, reading over her chart.

"I hope so."

"You're walking?"

"Every minute I can."

"Good." He nodded approvingly.

"When can I be discharged?" The question had been on her mind from the moment she talked to Bertha Powell. "I feel great—I want to go home."

"I'm pleased to hear that. However . . ."

"Doctor, please, I need to get home."

The grandfatherly brows molded into a tight frown. "I want to keep you until I'm sure you're a little stronger. A couple of days—maybe."

"Two days!" Marjorie would never last that long. For the sake of her sanity, she had to get out of this place. Heaven only knew what would happen when she saw Sam next. The way matters were progressing, she would profess her love for him the moment he walked in the door. That was just the kind of crazy, foolish thing she might do.

"We'll see how things progress today," Dr. Johnson said on his way out the door.

A half hour after Dr. Johnson had left her room, Sam appeared.

"How are you feeling?"

"Fine," Marjorie responded in a flat, emotionless tone. She did her utmost to pretend she was looking straight at him when in reality her gaze rested on the wall behind him. Even looking in Sam Bretton's direction was dangerous to her equilibrium. She should be reassured that she was like every one of his other patients, but she wasn't. Such strong emotions were strangers to her and best avoided.

"Marjorie, what's wrong?"

"I want out of here!"

"You aren't alone in that, you know. Everyone who ever stays in the hospital is eager to get home."

"But I feel terrific." That wasn't entirely true. "I'm as strong as an ox."

"Why don't you leave it in Dr. Johnson's hands?" he offered gently. "He knows what he's doing."

"But two days is an eternity," Marjorie insisted.

Sam's cajoling smile vanished. "Cal suggested you could leave then?"

"Yes."

"I'm sure he's mistaken."

"What do you mean?" Marjorie grumbled.

"Dr. Johnson's obviously forgotten that there isn't anyone at your apartment to watch over you when you're released."

"In case you hadn't noticed, I'm a big girl. I've been taking care of myself for a long time now. I'm not going to keel over because someone isn't there to hold my hand and place wet washcloths over my forehead every ten minutes."

"That's not the issue, Marjorie."

"Then what exactly is?"

"You've gone through a life-threatening episode. Take advantage of this time to be waited on and pampered."

"Take advantage of it?" She laughed sharply. "You've got to be kidding. What's with you doctors? Do you get a kickback for every additional day a patient stays in the hospital?"

Marjorie's ability to attract him paled beside her capacity to anger him. He knotted his hands into tight fists, and clenched his jaw to keep from saying something he would regret. Her suggestion was so outrageous and so unfair that it offended him beyond anything he'd felt in years.

"I think it would be best if I left."

"By all means go, Doctor."

Sam retreated, shoving the door with such rage that it nearly slammed against the wall. A kickback? She couldn't actually believe that, could she?

Marjorie watched him go and swallowed down a mouthful of remorse, nearly choking on the aftertaste. She hadn't meant to suggest such a ridiculous thing, hadn't planned to say the words. But she was desperate to escape. How ironic it was that a man—a doctor who had dedicated his life to saving lives—could be responsible for breaking so many hearts.

All Marjorie wanted to do was to put this unfortunate episode behind her and get on with her life. Every day she spent in the hospital was another day without income. She hadn't been joking when she told Sam that if she didn't sell cars, she didn't eat. Most of her customers tended to glamorize her job, but it wasn't anything like they imagined. She was in a cutthroat business.

In her frustration, she walked the halls until she was convinced her feet had made imprints in the polished linoleum squares. When Lydia arrived at five-thirty, she was so pleased to see her friend that she nearly threw her arms around the other woman and wept for joy.

"You look great. I don't believe it! Your color's almost back." Lydia slid the lone chair closer to Marjorie's bed and took a seat. "Dixon's doesn't seem the same without you."

Despite her bad mood, Marjorie laughed, then sucked in a pain-filled breath and pressed her hand against her side. She hadn't healed as much as she thought.

"Are you resting enough?"

Just the mention of sleep produced a yawn that Marjorie hid with the back of her hand. "You wouldn't believe it. I haven't slept this much since I was a newborn."

"What about Dr. Sam? Have you seen much of him?"

"He's been in a few times," Marjorie said in a flat tone. The scene from that morning played back in her mind, along with the awful accusation she'd thrown at him. Once again, Marjorie was struck by her own foolishness.

Lydia paused and closely studied her friend. "What's the matter? You said that as though you don't want anything to do with the man."

"Oh, Sam Bretton is everything you said he was . . . and more. But to be frank, he simply doesn't interest me."

The perfectly shaped eyebrows above Lydia's dark eyes drew together sharply. "He doesn't interest you?"

"Not really." Marjorie studied her fingernails with feigned interest.

"Do you have a raging fever, girl? Are you stupid? He's wonderful . . . He's handsome enough to tempt any red-blooded American woman."

"Not me," Marjorie claimed, her voice gaining conviction. "Nice guy, but not my type."

"He's every woman's type!"

"Maybe." That was as much as Marjorie was willing to concede.

The way Lydia was regarding her, Marjorie had the feeling her friend was considering having her arrested for treason. If she didn't watch it, she would be dragged before a firing squad at dawn.

"I don't understand you," Lydia said in a low, curious tone. "The last time I came to visit, the scent of a good old-fashioned romance was so thick in this room that I walked away intoxicated. I was convinced you were hooked and would be head over heels in love with him within a week."

"I'm sorry to disappoint you."

"What went wrong?" Lydia crossed her arms and glared at Marjorie as though she'd let a million dollars' worth of gold slip through her fingers. "When Dr. Sam phoned before the surgery, he sounded . . . I don't know . . . interested, I guess. We must have talked for a half hour. He asked a hundred questions about you."

"He did?" Marjorie wasn't sure she wanted to hear that.

"I don't know what happened between then and now, but obviously something did."

"I'm his patient," Marjorie insisted, because to do anything else would be ludicrous. That relationship was not to be tampered with. All afternoon she'd forced herself to view it as something like the relationship between a woman and her priest. It was much safer that way.

"That's too bad," Lydia said with an exaggerated sigh. "I was really hoping things would work out between you two."

"Why?"

"Why?" Lydia repeated, astonished. "Because I think Dr. Sam is the most amazing man I know, and because you're my best friend. That's why. The two of you are perfect together."

"You've got to be kidding!" Marjorie cried. Her words resounded throughout the room; the echo taunted her for long hours afterward.

Four

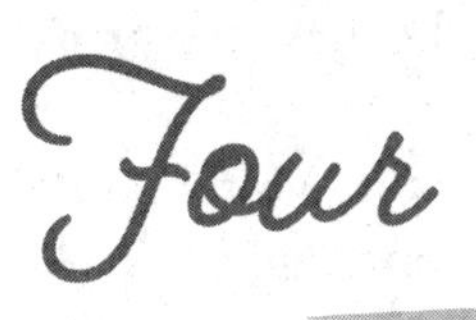

Marjorie paused just inside the Mercedes showroom and drew a deep breath. It felt wonderful to be back. Wonderful and right. Three weeks recovery time was what Sam had told her she would need, and she had used every minute of those twenty-one days to recuperate. Even now she felt weak and a little shaky, but the thought of another day holed up in her tiny apartment was enough to make even the most sane person go stir-crazy.

With a sense of appreciation that never waned, Marjorie ran her hand over the trunk of an SLK roadster. Rarely had she been more eager to get to work. Bit by bit she had regained her strength, and now she would quietly resume her life.

"Welcome back," Lydia called eagerly from behind the customer-service counter. "How are you feeling?"

"Terrific, thanks." Marjorie realized her clothes were a little loose and her complexion a bit chalky, but all in all, she felt great.

"Has your sister gone back to Oregon?"

Marjorie nodded. Her sister had left a few days before, and it had not been a minute too soon. When Jody had learned about the surgery, there had been no stopping the twenty-year-old from coming to her sister's aid. Despite Marjorie's protests, Jody had dropped her studies and immediately driven to Tacoma to play the role of the indulgent nurse. Marjorie loved her sister, but after one entire week of Jody giving an Academy Award-level imitation of Clara Barton, Marjorie had been on the brink of madness.

Within the first hour of her return to Dixon Motors, two of the salesmen stopped by her desk to welcome her back. At ten Lydia delivered a cup of coffee, closed the door and pulled out a chair. "Well?" she asked, as she plunked herself down and leaned forward intently, propping her elbows on the corner of Marjorie's desk. Her eyes were both wide and curious.

Marjorie blinked back her surprise. "Well, what?"

"Did you hear from Dr. Sam?"

"Of course not." With jerky movements she tore off three weeks, a day at a time, from her desktop calendar.

"Dr. Sam didn't contact you?" Lydia's voice rose dramatically in disbelief.

"I just told you he didn't." Marjorie had seen Sam exactly twice since that heated episode when she'd accused him of getting a kickback from the hospital. Both times had been strained, as she battled her very strong and very real attraction toward him. Again and again she was forced to remind herself that women patients tend to fall in love with their doctors and that she wasn't any more immune to his charms than the rest. Keeping her perspective had been difficult, especially when Sam returned the following day and behaved as though nothing had happened. He had chatted easily with her, but she noted regretfully that he stayed only a few minutes. His second visit had been even shorter.

"That depresses me," Lydia lamented, as she gracefully rose from her chair. "I was convinced he really liked you."

It depressed Marjorie, too, but it didn't surprise her. Overall, she was grateful to have met Sam Bretton. He'd taught her several surprising lessons about herself—mainly that she wasn't as invincible as she would like to think. And secondly, as much as she strove to avoid relationships that were more than casual, her heart was vulnerable. He'd proved beyond a doubt that plenty of red-hot blood flowed through her veins.

Painful experience had taught her that most men liked their women soft and clinging. A woman who could change her own oil, balance a checkbook and build a bookshelf seemed to intimidate them. That left the strong, independent types, like herself, out in the cold.

Sam Bretton sat in his office and chewed on the end of a pen. His thoughts were dark and heavy. He hadn't seen Marjorie in more than two weeks, but still she kept popping into his mind when he least expected it. He had seen her smile on a new patient's face as he entered the room to introduce himself. His coffee cup had made it halfway to his lips when he thought he heard Marjorie's laugh. Last week he'd been convinced he'd seen her in the parking lot. Even his dreams had been affected. A couple of times he'd caught himself staring into space, remembering something witty she'd said or the way her eyes narrowed when she was angry. Friends had begun to comment that he seemed preoccupied.

Preoccupied? That wasn't the half of it. Forcefully he opened his desk drawer and tossed the pen inside. He'd been thinking about her for days—all right, weeks—and still he wasn't convinced anything between them would work. She was so proud, so headstrong, and he wasn't entirely persuaded she was interested in him. Without being egotistical about it, Sam realized that there were plenty of women who found him attractive. Unfortunately, Marjorie didn't appear to be one of them.

Well, he was a big boy; he could deal with that. What was difficult to handle was the fact that he wasn't convinced that a future for them was out of the question. Her streak of independence was a mile wide; she didn't want or need anyone. At least that was what she wanted to think. He wasn't so sure, but so long as she stuck to her guns, he was stymied. He just wished he could put her out of his mind.

Marjorie looked at Lydia sitting across the table from her in the deli opposite Dixon Motors. She watched as her friend checked suspiciously between the thick slices of rye bread for the mustard she'd ordered with her pastrami sandwich. "I've been thinking," Lydia muttered under her breath.

"Careful," Marjorie warned, hiding a smile. "That could be dangerous."

"No, I'm serious." Her look gave credibility to her words.

"About what?" Marjorie continued to study her friend while she wrapped the second half of her own turkey sandwich in a paper napkin to take back to the office for a snack later.

"Didn't you tell me Dr. Sam was interested in buying a Mercedes?"

"I . . . Yes, now that you mention it, he did say something along those lines."

The edges of Lydia's mouth lifted with unsuppressed delight. "Then get moving, girl! I've never known you to look a gift horse in the mouth."

"I . . ." Marjorie's tongue felt glued to the roof of her mouth.

"If you don't move on this, then you know Al Swanson will."

The arrow hit its mark. Al Swanson was her nemesis, and he wouldn't think twice about robbing his own mother of a sale. "I'll think about it," Marjorie said, and gave her friend a bright smile.

Lydia pushed her plate aside and stood, looking pleased with herself. Marjorie thought she looked determined to get her together with Sam even if she had to lock them in a room herself.

Marjorie checked her watch and was grateful to note that she was free to leave in fifteen minutes. After her second day back at work she was eager to get home and relax. Her afternoon hadn't gone well. She'd crossed swords with Al Swanson when he'd attempted to steal a sale. One of her clients had taken out a sedan for a test drive, and when he'd returned, Al had explained that Marjorie was out to lunch and had asked him to wrap up the deal. Luckily, she had overheard him, and quickly inserted that she was back and would take over for him.

Incidents like this had happened in the past, and she refused to stand for it. She didn't like tattling to the manager, but she wasn't about to let Al cheat her out of her commission.

The bell chimed as the large double doors opened, indicating that a customer had entered the showroom. The salespeople took turns dealing with the influx of prospective buyers. She'd only recently finished helping a young executive, so she left the field open to Jim Preston, the senior salesman.

"Marjorie," Jim called, and stuck his head in the door. "Someone's here to see you."

Once again, she glanced at her watch. Staying late hadn't been a problem before, but she tired easily now and was eager to head back to her apartment. "Thanks, Jim," she muttered, and pushed herself away from her desk with both hands.

Out in the showroom, she paused in midstep and nearly faltered in an effort to disguise her surprise.

"Sam." His name came out in a rush of confusion and delight.

Sam turned away from the light blue convertible he'd been examining. He liked the sleek lines and the classic style of the

SLK, but fifty-five thousand dollars for a car, any car, was more than he cared to spend.

"Hi." Some of Marjorie's composure had returned, and she greeted him with a careful smile. She didn't want to appear overjoyed to see him, although her heart felt as if it were doing somersaults inside her chest.

Sam couldn't take his eyes off her. She looked wonderful. If he'd found her attractive before, it was nothing compared to the way she appeared to him now. To think he'd once pictured this woman as a lost kitten trapped in a storm. This kitten wasn't an ordinary, run-of-the-mill stray. She was of the highest pedigree.

Without even realizing what he was doing, Sam gave a low wolf whistle. He couldn't stop looking at her and finally managed to say, "I see you've recovered."

"You promised I'd live and love again."

Sam grinned and, still a little bemused, rubbed the side of his jaw, unable to carry on the conversation.

Marjorie knew that men found her attractive, but what amused her was the shocked look on Sam's face. "I didn't think the brochure had time to reach you," she said, her gaze holding his.

"Brochure? What brochure?" He suspected he was beginning to sound like an echo.

"I mailed one off to you yesterday afternoon," she said, and casually crossed her arms over her double-breasted tweed jacket. "You'd mentioned something about wanting a Mercedes, and I extended an invitation for you to come in and take a test drive."

"I'd enjoy that," Sam murmured, glancing toward the sticker on the side window of the car he'd been inspecting.

"Perhaps it would be best if I explained the different models," Marjorie continued, her gaze following his. "Our cars start in the range of fifty thousand dollars," she said in an even, smooth voice, "depending, of course, on the options you decide on."

"Naturally."

Leading the way into her office, she turned back and asked, "Would you care for a cup of coffee?"

"Please."

Marjorie's thoughts were racing as she directed him toward a chair. From the corner of her eye she happened to catch a glimpse of Lydia, who flashed her a triumphant grin and the universal signal for okay.

Once Sam was comfortably seated, she poured him a mug of coffee. Although she remained outwardly poised, her heart was pumping so fast that she felt dizzy and a little shaky. She knew her face was flushed.

When Marjorie was dealing with a prospective buyer, she usually approached them with an angle. This involved asking a few subtle but pertinent questions and discovering their individual concerns. Some potential buyers were looking at a Mercedes for performance—the German-made automobile was built to cruise at twice the speed of U.S. freeways. Marjorie realized, though, that Sam wasn't interested in traveling over a hundred miles an hour. From what she knew about him, he wasn't the type who cared a great deal about prestige, either. The safety issue would evoke a response in him.

"The Mercedes-Benz is one of the safest cars in the world." She handed him a brochure from her desk drawer and took her seat.

As a saleswoman, she was as slick as frost on mossy rocks, Sam thought. Yes, she was a beautiful woman, but once she had a customer's attention, it was cars she was there to sell.

"I like to tell prospective buyers that purchasing a Mercedes-Benz is another form of life insurance," she continued. "As a physician, I'm sure you can appreciate our cars' many safety features."

Sam flipped through the pages of the glossy pamphlet and nodded. She knew her stuff, he had to give her credit for that. "You're very good."

Marjorie paused. "How do you mean?"

"As a salesman."

"Salesperson," she corrected with a smile.

"I don't think many men would be able to turn you down."

A couple of the salesmen had protested that very point when Marjorie was first hired, claiming she had an unfair advantage over the rest of them. They claimed that, sitting across the table from a good-looking female, a man would have a difficult time negotiating a price. The men might have convinced a few of the others they had a point, but Bud, the manager, was behind Marjorie. Her sales record spoke for itself. She sold cars, and that was the purpose of the dealership. If she possessed an unfair advantage, the manager didn't care as long as cars moved off the lot. But Marjorie knew that she didn't need to use her feminine wiles; the cars sold because she was a good salesperson.

"I get turned down plenty of times," she responded, her smile fading.

Sam turned the page of the brochure and read over the information on the E350. "I'll take this one."

"Pardon." Marjorie wasn't completely sure she had heard him right.

"This sedan—in a light blue, if you have it."

"You mean you want to buy one now?"

"Is that a problem?" He withdrew his checkbook from inside his coat pocket.

Marjorie had sold plenty of cars, but never any quite this way. "Don't you want to drive one? Negotiate the price?"

"Not particularly. I know you aren't going to cheat me."

"But . . ." Experience told her to shut up. She didn't need to kill a sale by arguing with him. She clamped her mouth closed and swallowed her questions. Sam was an adult; he knew what he wanted. Far be it from her to stand in his way.

"I trust you to be fair," he continued, adding the pertinent details to the blank check. "How much should I fill in for the amount?"

Hours later Marjorie was still completely bemused. She wandered around her apartment, moving from room to room, listless and bored and, at the same time, excited. She'd seen Sam again, and even if he had come into the showroom to buy a car and not just to see her, she was thrilled. At the same time, she regretted the encounter. Knowing that other patients fell in love with him had been reassuring, but to her dismay she'd learned that the attraction she'd experienced toward Sam hadn't lessened with time. It had been weeks since she'd last seen him, and he looked better to her than ever. All the emotions she'd struggled so valiantly to bury had surfaced the minute she'd walked into the showroom to discover him standing there. All the pleasure of seeing him again had returned to remind her how strongly Sam Bretton appealed to her.

When Sam walked back into Dixon Motors late the following morning, every word that Marjorie had rehearsed so carefully, every scenario she'd spent hours plotting, fell by the wayside. All she could see was the gentle man who had sat at her bedside and held her hand.

"Hello, Sam." It was amazing that she'd been able to utter those few words. She was trembling inside. No longer was she an inept hospital patient but a woman who knew what she liked—and Sam Bretton was it. The thought terrified her.

"Hello again."

"Everything's ready." She straightened the French cuffs of her sleeves, bemoaning the fact that virtually everything she owned was either blue, black or gray. It wasn't any wonder dates were few and far between. Marjorie swallowed her self-doubts and gestured toward the customer-service counter. "Lydia will need you to fill out a few forms."

Sam looked mildly surprised, but he followed Marjorie into the other office. Lydia greeted him with a wide smile, and Sam was left with the impression that he'd done something very right to have gained her undying gratitude.

Surely buying the Mercedes couldn't have been any more obvious, even to Marjorie. Against his better judgment, he'd decided he wanted to see her again. He'd planned on getting a luxury car someday, and now seemed as good a time as any. Besides, he wanted her to have this sale. He remembered her telling him once how she lived on commissions alone. This was his way of helping her through what was sure to be a difficult month, since the first three weeks had been spent recuperating from surgery. Because of that, he had even decided against negotiating the price.

While Sam was with Lydia, Marjorie stood on the showroom floor, pacing back and forth while she waited for him to finish. Her hands felt damp, her throat dry, and yet to all outward appearances she was as cool as a pumpkin on a frosty October morning.

When Sam was finished, she approached him with a grin and handed him the keys to his shiny new E350 sedan, which she'd arranged to have waiting for him in front of the dealership.

"That didn't take long," she said as if surprised, but it was just a means of starting a conversation. From experience, she knew the paperwork didn't take more than ten or fifteen minutes.

"Have you got time to take a spin with me?" Sam invited.

She nodded, hoping she didn't appear as eager as she felt. "Of course."

Like the true gentleman he was, Sam held open the passenger door for her, and she gracefully slipped inside. He joined her a moment later, inserted the key into the ignition, and paused to inhale the fresh scent of new leather and study the dials in front of him.

It was on the tip of Marjorie's tongue to give him another sales pitch and quote what *Car and Driver* had to say about the E350. She knew her stuff, but the sale had already been made, and he only had to drive the vehicle to be impressed.

Wordlessly Sam eased the sedan into the busy Tacoma traffic, quickly acquainting himself with the mechanics of the car. They rode past the digital signboard above the Puget Sound Bank.

"Actually, you being able to pick up the car this morning works rather well," Marjorie said.

"How's that?" Sam looked away from traffic long enough to glance in her direction.

"I can treat you to lunch." As soon as the words slipped from her lips, she was flabbergasted. She didn't know where the invitation had come from.

"Marjorie . . ."

"That is unless you can't . . . I mean, if you're due back at the office . . . The reason I asked is that I always treat new customers to lunch. It's my way of showing my appreciation for your business." She was convinced her lies would someday return to haunt her.

"But *I* was thinking of taking *you* out."

"I owe you this one," she insisted. "For the car, yes, and everything else."

"You're a difficult woman to refuse."

How Marjorie wished that were true. "How do you like Mexican food?"

"Love it. But I really would prefer it if you allowed *me* to buy lunch."

"You'd break tradition." She was convinced her nose would start growing at any minute.

Sam grinned. The more he came to know this woman, the more he learned about pride. "Are you always so stubborn?"

"Always," she answered evenly, and pointed to the left-hand side of the street. "The restaurant is about a block farther on. There's parking on the street and a small lot around back."

Sam parked easily. Once inside, they were forced to put their name on a list, but Marjorie assured him the food was well worth the wait. They were seated within ten minutes; the waitress seemed to know Marjorie.

"Do you come here often?"

She nodded and finished munching on a warm tortilla chip before answering. "At least once a week. I'm worthless in the kitchen, and it's easier for me to eat out."

Sam's insides tightened. He should have guessed that she would be a terrible cook, and he felt almost guilty because it bothered him. He'd always thought the woman he was looking to build his life with should possess at least the rudimentary culinary skills.

"The last time I experimented with a recipe," Marjorie continued, "I set off the fire alarm and cleared the entire apartment complex. Under direct orders of the building manager and the Tacoma Fire Department, I've been asked to refrain from any kitchen activities," she joked.

The sound of Sam's strained chuckle mingled with the chatter in the small restaurant.

"My sister swears that I'll make someone a wonderful husband." In many ways what Jody claimed was true; Marjorie could fix just about anything. But cooking and sewing were lost arts to her.

Sam found the food to be as good as Marjorie had claimed. He watched her eat with undisguised gusto and then pause, obviously embarrassed, to explain that she was only now regaining her appetite.

As she dabbed a drop of hot sauce from the corner of her mouth with a paper napkin, Marjorie's gaze fell to her empty plate. No doubt most women Sam dated were dainty things who ate like sparrows and wore a size two. She downed the remainder of her Mexican beer, equally sure she'd done the wrong thing by ordering it. Sam's women probably drank tea diluted with milk. For once in her life she wished she could be different. She wanted Sam to like her even with her healthy appetite and appreciation of good beer.

The waitress returned for their plates and served two cups of coffee. Sam noted the sudden lag in the conversation that followed and picked it up easily, entertaining Marjorie with anecdotes from his youth.

She was so engrossed in his stories that when she finally checked her watch, she saw that it was one-forty-five.

"Oh, Sam, I've got an appointment at two." A stock-broker was coming in to test-drive a S600 sedan, and she couldn't be late.

They hurried out of the restaurant, and Sam had her back at the dealership with minutes to spare. Even though her customer was due to arrive at any time, Marjorie was reluctant to get out of the car. She turned to face him, her hand on the door handle, wanting to tell him so many things and not knowing where to start.

"Thank you, Sam," she said softly. That seemed so inadequate. "It seems I'm always having to thank you for one reason or another. Have you noticed that?"

"No," he answered evenly. "Besides, I should be the one thanking you."

"It was only lunch." And she owed him so much more than a simple meal. He'd given her another argument when the tab arrived, but she'd won. She realized now that it probably would have been better if she'd let him pay, male pride being what it is.

"Next time it's my turn."

Marjorie was outside the car before his words registered. "Right," she answered, and her smile broadened.

He waved. "Bye, Marjorie."

"Bye, Sam." She waited until he'd driven away and was out of sight before she entered the dealership.

No sooner had she stepped onto the showroom floor than Lydia appeared. "Where in heaven's name did the two of you take off to? You've been gone for hours! Where'd you go? Did he ask you out again? I told you he was interested. Remember what I said?"

"We went to lunch."

Lydia nodded approvingly. "I bet he took you to a fancy place on the waterfront for lobster."

Marjorie had a difficult time containing her amusement. "Actually, I treated him at The Lindo."

"That Mexican place you're always bragging about?"

"The food's wonderful."

"And you paid?"

"I . . . I told him I do that with all first-time car buyers."

Lydia's frown relaxed into a soft, encouraging smile. "Hey, not a bad idea."

"He said he'd treat next time." Marjorie cast her gaze longingly toward the street. "Do you think he'll phone?" She hated feeling so insecure, but more than anything else, she wanted to see Sam again.

"I bet you ten dollars he calls by tomorrow."

Lydia lost the bet.

Two days later Marjorie had chewed off two fingernails and was quickly becoming a nervous wreck. She'd never been a patient person, and waiting for Sam to contact her was slowly but surely driving her crazy.

"You aren't going to sit still for this, are you?" Lydia said over lunch.

"What other choice do I have?"

"Oh, come on, Marjorie!" Lydia declared, crumpling her napkin and tossing it atop her empty plate. "I've watched you chase after a sale when anyone else would have given it up. You have a reputation for putting deals together when others would have thrown their hands in the air."

"Yes, but selling cars and dealing with a man are two entirely different matters."

"No they're not," Lydia disagreed sharply.

"You think I should phone him?" The idea didn't appeal to her. Sam had left her with the impression that he'd contact her.

"No . . ." Lydia gazed thoughtfully at the ceiling fixture. "You need a more subtle approach."

"I suppose I could do what *he* did," Marjorie murmured thoughtfully.

Lydia's stare was blank. "What do you mean?"

"Meet him on his own ground. I could call for an appointment, claim I was having problems with the insurance company or something."

Lydia nearly tipped back the chair in her enthusiasm. "That's perfect, and there wouldn't be anything out of the ordinary in you showing up with the forms."

Even though it sounded easy, it took Marjorie nearly all afternoon to work up the courage to contact Sam's office. Since she feared the receptionist would probably handle any insurance work, she asked for an actual appointment and was given one later the following week. Now that she'd taken some positive action, she felt a hundred times better—until she saw Lydia's shocked face later that afternoon.

"What's the matter?"

"Dr. Sam's office just called."

"And?"

"And, well . . . apparently Dr. Sam looked over his schedule and saw your name."

"So?"

"Marjorie, I'm sure there's a logical explanation."

"Lydia, for heaven's sake, will you stop beating around the bush and tell me what's going on?"

"You know Mary and I are good friends, don't you?"

From what she remembered, Mary was Sam's receptionist. "Yes, what did she say?"

"Mary told me that when Dr. Sam saw your name, he got upset, swore under his breath, and asked Mary to call you and suggest you make an appointment with another doctor."

Five

Marjorie turned on the television, and plunked herself down on the overstuffed sofa, crossing her arms in a defiant gesture. Five minutes later she dug through the sofa cushions to find the remote and switched channels, not that it helped any. She was too furious for coherent thought, and the possibility of a mere television movie salving her injured ego was nil.

Men! Sam Bretton in particular! None of them were worth all this aggravation. She had behaved like a fool over Sam, and knowing it made her lack of savoir faire all the more difficult to swallow.

Hindsight nearly always proved to be twenty-twenty, but she should have known not to trust a man who preferred mild salsa on his enchiladas. If he couldn't eat a jalapeño straight from the jar, he wasn't her type. She liked her food *and* her men spicy and pungent. Sam was too . . . too wonderful. That was it, much too wonderful.

Depression settled over her shoulders like a dark mantle, and she rubbed her forearms to ward off a late-evening chill that had little to do with the mild Puget Sound weather. Sam and she were simply too different. Sam no doubt liked moonlight walks and a glass of wine in front of the fireplace, and she liked . . . moonlight walks and a glass of wine in front of the fireplace. Well, going over every detail a hundred times wasn't going to settle anything. He didn't want to see her again, and that was that.

She was an adult; she should be able to handle disappointments. Obviously Sam was interested in meek, mild women who knew their place. She was neither, and it was far easier to face that truth now than later, when her heart was completely infected and the prognosis for recovery would be against her.

Once Marjorie had sorted through her myriad thoughts, she felt better, even good enough to put this unpleasantness behind her and think about fixing herself something to eat. She left the television on and wandered into the kitchen. The freezer contained a wide assortment of prepackaged meals, but none of them appealed to her. Popcorn suited her mood—something crunchy and salty would help to vent her frustration. Microwave popcorn, naturally. What she'd told Sam about her lack of expertise in the kitchen had been true. She could manage spreadsheets and calculators in her sleep, but recipes baffled her. Having her anywhere in the vicinity of hot grease was like putting a submachine gun in the hands of a raw recruit. In fact, she didn't even own a complete set of cookware. The less she involved herself with a stove top, the better.

Marjorie inserted the popcorn bag, set the timer and waited. Soon the sounds and smells of the butter-flavored kernels filled the small apartment.

She had just opened the bag and munched down the first handful when the doorbell chimed. A glance at the wall clock told her it was after nine. She certainly wasn't expecting anyone. The hope that it might be Sam caused her to hurry. It wouldn't be him, of course—she knew that—but she so wanted to see him again that her mind tormented her with the possibility.

With an eagerness that was difficult to explain, she opened her front door. Sam was standing on the other side. It was as though her wishful thinking had conjured him up.

"Hello, Sam." She greeted him as though she'd been expecting him all along, revealing no surprise.

He looked terrible. Exhausted, overworked and not himself. She would have thought he would never allow a strand of hair to fall out of place, but his hair wasn't the only thing rumpled; everything about him looked unkempt. His clothes hung on him, and the top two buttons of his shirt were unfastened. He hadn't shaved in a couple of days, or so it appeared.

"I have had the most exhausting day of my life," he announced, walking past her and into the apartment.

Bemused, Marjorie remained at the entrance, her hand on the doorknob. She'd expected contrition, guilt, grief, but not this out-and-out appeal for sympathy.

"It's been one thing after another," he continued undaunted. Without invitation, he picked up her remote and cued up the guide at the bottom of the screen.

"Would you like something to drink?" she offered, choosing to ignore his opening statement.

"Please." He sank onto her sofa and leaned forward to wipe the tiredness from his eyes. He'd planned on calling her hours earlier and inviting her to dinner. Before he could get to a phone, Nancy Brightfield had gone into labor, and he'd spent the next five hours at the hospital with her. The delivery had been difficult, and he hadn't been able to get away until now. The unexpected trip to the delivery room and the arrival of Baby Brightfield had been a climax to a long, tedious day.

Sam realized that arriving unannounced on Marjorie's doorstep probably hadn't been one of his most brilliant ideas, but he wanted to straighten out a few things between them, and delaying the discussion was potentially unwise. He was beginning to know Marjorie Majors, and the message she was bound to read into the canceled appointment would be all wrong.

Marjorie went into her kitchen to survey her meager supply of refreshments. All she could find was a two-liter bottle of flat cola in the back of her refrigerator, a can of tomato juice with a rusty crust over the aluminum top, and a carton of milk she'd been meaning to toss for the past week.

"Is instant coffee all right?"

"Fine, fine." He really didn't care. All he really wanted was the chance for a long talk with her. He leaned back and inhaled deeply, paused, then asked, "Do I smell popcorn?"

Grinning, Marjorie stuck her head around the corner of her kitchen. Nothing smelled better than freshly popped popcorn. "Want some?"

Sam shook his head. "No, thanks. I haven't had any dinner."

"This is my dinner."

His face twisted into a mock scowl that revealed his amusement. She had to be joking with him. "You're kidding, right?"

"No."

Sam jumped up from the couch with a reserve of energy he hadn't realized he possessed. "You can't eat that for dinner . . . it's unhealthy."

"I disagree." Everything she'd read contradicted Sam. The kernels were reported to be a good source of fiber, and since she ate her main meal at noon, it made sense to have something light in the evenings.

"Don't you know you're not supposed to argue with a doctor?" Actually, Sam wasn't as concerned about the nutritional value of popcorn as he was that her choice for her evening meal gave him an excellent excuse to invite her out.

"Sam, it isn't any big deal. . . ."

"Come on, I'll take you to dinner."

Marjorie hedged. "But you just said today's been the most exhausting day of your life. What you need is to put up your feet and enjoy a good home-cooked meal." Oh, heavens, why had she suggested that? Sam would assume she planned to do the cooking, and then there would be real trouble. She might be able to bluff her way through some things, but a complete meal was out of the question.

The idea of Marjorie preparing a meal for him appealed to Sam, but he studied her carefully. Maybe he'd misunderstood her earlier. "You told me you don't cook."

At that moment she would gladly have surrendered three commissions to Al Swanson in exchange for the ability to whip together a three-egg cheese-and-mushroom omelet, but she knew better than to offer. Still, the temptation was so strong. She opened her mouth and closed it again. "I make excellent microwave popcorn," she offered weakly, and gestured toward the open bag sitting on the counter behind her.

"Then popcorn it is," Sam said, lowering himself back onto the couch. While he waited, he glanced back at the television and recognized an old-fashioned romance from the late fifties. He wouldn't have thought Marjorie would appreciate anything so sentimental. But then, she'd surprised him before.

"Here's your coffee and dinner. It's the specialty of the house." She brought in a steaming cup and handed it to him, along with a breadbasket filled with hot popcorn. "I'll be back in a minute."

"I owe you a dinner, you know."

"As I recall, it's a lunch, and if you're counting that, you might as well add a movie and popcorn to the list." He didn't owe her anything. Not really. She was the one in debt to him. Sam had given her so much more than she could ever hope to repay.

He relaxed against the thick cushions and felt his body release a silent sigh of relief. He'd missed Marjorie over the past couple of days. Missed her wit. Missed her warmth. Missed her smile. He'd wanted to see her again despite his reservations. For two days he'd been trying to find the time to call her, but there were never more than those odd five minutes here or ten minutes there. Besides, what he had to say would be better said in person. There was too much room for misunderstanding over the phone. But letting another day pass without seeing her would only add to his mounting frustration, so he'd headed over here tonight despite the late hour.

She joined him a minute later, stretched her legs on top of the coffee table and crossed them at the ankles. Judging exactly where she should sit had been a problem. If she sat too close, he might read something into that. On the other hand, if she positioned herself as far away as possible, he might think she didn't want him around, and nothing could be further from the truth.

They sat quietly and watched the movie for a moment, then she ventured into conversation. "So. Tell me about your day."

"It was nonstop busy, and then, just as I was getting ready to leave, a woman came in, ready to have her first baby. And then, as sometimes happens, I had a difficult delivery."

Even as she tried not to, Marjorie started laughing. "*You* had a difficult delivery? How's the poor mother doing?"

"Better than me, I think. She got her girl."

"And what did you get?"

The same reward that came with every new life he brought into the world: pride and a deep sense of satisfaction.

"Plenty," he answered, in a gentle way that assured her that no matter what problems he faced, he was content with his life.

The unexpected vision of Marjorie with a baby, their baby, in her arms produced such an intense longing that his breath jammed in his lungs. He shook his head to dispel the image, but it remained, clearer than before. For years Sam had brought children into the world. He'd spent countless hours encouraging new mothers and an almost equal amount of time soothing soon-to-be fathers, but only rarely had he thought about the woman who would give *him* children one day.

Their eyes met, and Sam's smile embraced her. She didn't know what he was thinking, but if she'd been holding her coffee cup, it would have slipped from her fingers. Sam had the most sensuous smile of any man she'd ever known.

"So how have *you* been?"

"Good." She nodded once, then swallowed and headed for the deep end. "About that appointment . . ."

"Yes, I wanted to talk to you about that."

"I got the insurance papers straightened out—no problem."

"Insurance papers? You made the appointment to go over some papers?" Sam felt like a heel now. He'd thought she'd wanted a physical or something else equally impossible.

Her excuse to see him sounded so flimsy now that a deep flush crept up her neck and over her ears.

"It would be best if you got another physician," Sam said, and cleared his throat. "I'd be more than happy to recommend one if you want."

Marjorie couldn't believe what she was hearing. He said it so calmly, without so much as a hint of regret, as though they were discussing the weather or something equally trivial. With those few words he was telling her that he wanted her out of his life.

Unable to trust her voice, she nodded.

"It's important for everyone to have a regular physician," Sam insisted. "Cal Johnson will be doing the follow-up after your appendectomy, but he's a surgeon, and you need a general practitioner."

Marjorie's throat closed up on her, the tightness making it difficult to breathe evenly.

The wounded look in her eyes tore at Sam's heart. It was apparent that she still didn't understand. He would have to spell it out for her.

"I think you're wonderful, Marjorie."

Sure he did. Enough to dump her right when she needed him.

"I'd like to see a lot more of you," Sam continued, "and I can't do that if you continue to be my patient."

Marjorie jerked her head around. What had he said? He wanted to see her? As in date her? Spend time with her? Be with her? She blinked and pointed her index finger at her chest. "You want to see more of me?"

"Don't look so surprised."

"I'm not . . . It's just that . . ."

"It shouldn't seem all that sudden. You must have known in the hospital I was interested. Believe me, I don't spend that much time with all my patients."

"I know, but . . . I don't know . . ." She was unsure, confused. Her gaze narrowed as she studied him. It would be best to clear away any misconceptions up front. "It's not gratitude, you know."

"It's not?" He didn't quite follow her meaning.

"Of course I'm grateful for everything you've done, but if we'd met on the street, I'd have felt the same things I do now."

"Which are?" he prompted, scooting closer to her. His dark eyes surveyed her with renewed interest.

"Never mind," she said with a small laugh. She could see no reason to inflate his ego any higher than it was already.

With his eyes steadily holding hers, Sam tucked a finger beneath her chin and slowly raised her mouth to his. Marjorie's eyelids fluttered closed as she awaited the warm sensation of his lips settling over hers. He didn't keep her waiting long. His arms encircled her, drawing her gently against his hard chest.

Their lips met in an unrushed exploration, as though they

had all the time in the world and there wasn't any reason to hurry anything. His mouth was moist and pliant against her own, moving with such gentleness, such care that a tiny shudder worked its way through Marjorie, and with it came a helpless moan.

After torturous seconds Sam's lips reluctantly left hers. He buried his face in the curve of her shoulder and inhaled a calming breath. He'd felt physically drained when he'd arrived. Now he was alive, more alive than he could ever remember being. Holding Marjorie, touching her, energized him, filled him with purpose, exhilarated him, eased the ache of loneliness that followed whenever he returned to an empty house after a delivery.

The wealth of sensation took Marjorie by surprise. A simple kiss—their first—had left her with a hunger as deep as the sea. Emotion clogged her throat, and she held him to her, her fingers weaving through the thick strands of his dark hair.

"Marjorie?"

"Hmm?"

"Do you always smell this good?"

Her eyes remained closed, and she grinned. "I think it's the popcorn."

"Not this. It's roses, I think."

"My perfume."

"And sunshine."

"I showered when I got home."

He shook his head, declining her explanation. "And something more, something I can't define."

"*That's* probably the popcorn."

Sam shook his head. "Not this," he countered softly. "Not this."

The reluctance with which he loosened his hold thrilled her. They straightened and went back to watching the movie. He tucked his arm around her, and she rested her head against his shoulder. The warmth of his nearness convinced her that the man beside her was indeed real and not the product of a fanciful imagination or some delayed anesthesia–induced illusion.

A multitude of unanswered questions ran through her mind. It was on the tip of her tongue to blurt out everything she felt for him, but she feared ruining this special evening.

"So you enjoy old movies," he said, the thought pleasing him.

"Especially the classics. They did romances so well in those days."

"You like romance?"

Marjorie nodded and hid a smile. "I'm liking it more all the time."

"I am, too," Sam agreed, and turned her toward him. He wanted to kiss her again, taste her sweetness and experience once again that special power she possessed that filled him with such energy.

It was a long time before Marjorie saw any more of the movie. Or cared.

Six

"You aren't going to let Al get away with it, are you?" Lydia cried in outrage, indignation flushing her cheeks.

Marjorie didn't need to be angry about Al Swanson's latest attempt to steal a customer from her; Lydia was furious enough for the both of them. "Bud will be the one to decide."

"But you know Al is lying."

"It's my word against his, and unfortunately Bud's only the manager, not Solomon."

"But it's so unfair."

"Tell me about it," Marjorie grumbled.

Once again Al had tried to horn in on her deal. Only this time he'd succeeded. Marjorie had spoken to a couple about a E63 AMG sedan, worked with them, called twice to keep them interested, and even rode with them as they went on four different test drives in order to answer their numerous questions. The last time, the couple had gone home to sleep on the decision and returned the following day with a deposit. Al had met them at the door, claimed Marjorie had stepped out of the office, and they had accepted his offer to write up the deal on her behalf. This was the same trick he'd used once before, only this time it worked. Once the paperwork was firmly clenched in his hand, Marjorie didn't have a leg to stand on. She had complained to the manager, insisted she had been at the dealership and not out, as Al had alleged. Since Bud had been gone and there wasn't anyone to verify her story, things didn't look good for her. But she knew the manager wasn't completely naive when it came to Al. She was certain he'd heard complaints from several of the other salespeople. Bud's fair assessment of the situation was Marjorie's only real hope. Unfortunately, Al's name was on the paperwork.

The commission scale was based on how much profit the dealership made on the sale of each new car. Marjorie collected thirty percent of the capital gain. In this case she'd worked hard to give the couple the best deal possible. Her share was meager enough. If forced to split her commission with Al, she would have worked long, hard hours for practically nothing. Everything rested on Bud's decision.

"But Bud doesn't know Al the way we do," Lydia continued insistently.

Marjorie studied her friend and was hard-pressed to hold back her own indignation. Al might think he was getting away with something, but if she had anything to do with it, the cheating salesman would spend the next fifty years regretting his underhandedness. Given enough rope, Al Swanson was bound to hang himself sooner or later, and she intended to be around to see it happen.

"If he's tried those things with me, you know he's done it with the others," she said thoughtfully after a while. Yes, she was furious, but losing her cool wouldn't solve anything.

"It's the meantime that I'm worried about," Lydia mumbled, crossing her arms and righteously over her chest. "When's Bud going to let you know?"

Marjorie glanced at her watch. "As soon as he gets in."

The low hum of the intercom caught their attention. "Marjorie, call on line three. Marjorie—line three."

"I better get that," Marjorie mumbled, and sighed. "It could mean another sale."

"Not if Al can get his greedy hands on it," Lydia responded sourly, and returned to her place behind the customer-service counter.

With her friend's words ringing in her ears, Marjorie walked over to her office and reached for the phone. "Marjorie Majors," she said in a cordial, businesslike tone.

"Dr. Sam Bretton here," Sam returned.

She sat down and propped her elbows on the desktop. A rush of pleasure washed over her, taking with it some of the bitter aftertaste of Al's trickery. "Hello."

"I was just thinking about you."

"Oh?" She knew that she sounded about as intelligent as mold, but he'd taken her by surprise.

"I just returned from the hospital, and my first appointment isn't scheduled for another five minutes, so I thought I'd give you a call. You don't mind, do you?"

"No . . . it's a pleasant surprise."

"How's your day going?"

"Fair." It would have been much better if things were settled between her and Al, but none of this mess was Sam's problem. "How about your morning?"

"Hectic, as always." Actually, he'd been preoccupied, thinking about Marjorie and angry with himself for not setting a date for their next . . . well, date. He'd left her apartment feeling exhilarated and excited. They'd sat and talked long after the movie had finished, easily drifting from one subject to another. She was well-read and knowledgeable about current affairs. He'd found her opinions insightful and intelligent, and marveled that he'd found a woman who stirred his heart as well as his mind. So she didn't cook; he could deal with that. He enjoyed her company, relished their time together and longed to see her again soon. Unfortunately, his head had been in the clouds, and he hadn't thought to make plans. He'd tried calling her apartment, but she'd already left for work. He knew she worked long hours and decided his best chance of catching her was at Dixon's. He didn't want to wait another two days to see her again.

"I suppose I should apologize for last night," she said softly.

"Why?" Something was wrong. Sam could detect the subtle difference in her voice. Whatever it was, he hoped she would share it with him.

"I feel bad about not being able to offer you anything more appetizing than microwave popcorn."

"I can't remember when I've enjoyed a meal more."

Marjorie was sure that couldn't be true. No doubt there were a thousand nurses out there who longed to lure him into their arms with hot chocolate-chip cookies straight from the oven. Her microwave couldn't hope to compete with all the talented, domestically inclined women who wanted him.

"Are you free tonight?" he asked, thinking about taking her to the waterfront for a lobster dinner. He wanted to wine and dine her, and give her an evening she would remember the rest of her life. He thought about bringing her to his home and showing her his view of Commencement Bay. He wanted to sit by the fireplace with her and watch the flickering light dance over her face.

"Tonight?" she asked, confused by the unexpected invitation.

Sooner, if possible, Sam thought, but he knew his schedule wouldn't allow it.

"Actually, I'm working late, so maybe . . ."

"What time do you get off?"

She wished he wasn't so insistent. With Bud's decision hanging over her head, she needed some time alone to clear her thoughts. When she was with Sam, she wanted to look and feel her best. "Would it be all right if I called you next week sometime?"

Sam's breath caught at the implication. There wasn't a woman alive who threw him off course with as much ease as Marjorie. Just when he was prepared to overlook her flaws and lay his heart at her feet, she made it sound as though going to dinner with him was an inconvenience.

"Sure," he returned flippantly. "You call me. That won't be any problem."

But it was, and Marjorie recognized it from his stiff tone. She had just opened her mouth to explain when he spoke again.

"Listen, I've got to get back to my patients. We'll talk soon." He was eager to get off the phone. The entire conversation had left a bad taste in his mouth. He'd read Marjorie wrong, read everything wrong. It wasn't the first time she'd led him astray. The stock market was more predictable than Marjorie Majors.

"Right." But her voice was barely audible. "Goodbye, Sam. Thanks for calling."

He didn't answer, and she bit her bottom lip to keep from shouting that she would love to see him any night, any time, if only she didn't have this mess with Al to settle first. The phone went dead, and Marjorie felt physically ill. She'd ruined everything.

The polite knock outside her office lifted her from the pit of despair.

"It's only me," Lydia said, opening the door and peeking inside. "Hey, you look like you just lost your best friend. What happened? Another deal fall through?"

The words congealed in Marjorie's throat, and it took a few moments for her to unscramble her thoughts. "That was Sam."

"Dr. Sam?"

It was all Marjorie could do to nod. "I blew it."

"Oh, good grief," Lydia said. "Not again."

Marjorie dropped her gaze to the floor. "I'm afraid so."

"What did you do?"

"He suggested we get together tonight, and I said I was busy and that it would be better if I contacted him next week."

A moment of stunned silence followed.

"You didn't! Tell me you didn't say that!" Lydia marched into the room and pressed both hands on top of Marjorie's desk, leaning forward so that their faces were scant inches apart. "If the two of you ever get together, I swear it will be a miracle. Good grief, what made you put him off that way?"

"I don't know. This thing with Al's really got me down, and I wanted Sam to see me at my best, not my worst."

Lydia closed her eyes and slowly shook her head. "I've got more bad news for you."

"What's that?"

"Bud's here," Lydia announced starkly. "And he's in one hell of a bad mood. He wants to see you right away."

Even before Marjorie left the dealership at a quarter after nine, she knew she wasn't heading home. Sam's Brown's Point address was tucked safely away in her purse, and she had every intention of talking to him before she did anything else. Maybe she could undo some of the damage.

She located the house without a problem, pulled into the wide driveway and turned off her engine. Sam's home was a magnificent sprawling ranch house made of used brick. Huge picture windows faced the street.

Her heart was pounding like a locomotive chugging uphill. Now she understood what courage it had taken for him to arrive unannounced at her apartment. She didn't often do this sort of thing, and the need to swallow her pride made it all the more difficult.

While her conviction held, she climbed out of the car and marched up to his front door like a soldier making his way to the front of a firing squad. Her hand faltered as she rang the bell.

She heard Sam's footsteps long before the door was opened.

"Marjorie." He blinked, certain she was a figment of his imagination.

"I know I should have called, but . . ."

"No," he said, and smiled that slow, sexy smile of his as he stepped aside. "Come in, please."

Relieved by his warm welcome, she entered his home. The first thing that she noticed when he led her into the huge, tiled entryway was the large, unobstructed view of Commencement Bay from the floor-to-ceiling living-room windows. The twinkling lights of barges and ferryboats lit up the inky black night and reflected off the water.

"Oh, Sam," she said, her voice low in wonder. "This is so beautiful . . . it's marvelous." Words failed her, and she simply stared into the night.

"I love it, too." He didn't know what had brought her here, and he didn't care. She'd been on his mind all day. He regretted the abrupt way in which he'd ended their telephone conversation, and all because his fragile ego had been pricked. Most of the evening had been spent trying to come up with a way to see her again and preserve both his pride as well as hers.

"Sam," she said, tearing her gaze from the water and turning to face him. Her features were strained with an expression of practiced poise. "I've come to apologize for this morning."

"No," he countered quickly, sensing her apprehension. "I should be the one to do that." The appeal in her gaze cut a path straight to his heart, but he kept his own features tightly controlled.

"You?" she said, and laughed shortly. "I was the one who was rude."

"Something was troubling you. I knew it the minute you spoke." He longed to ease whatever was bothering her and kicked himself more than once for having been such a fool.

Her eyes narrowed as she studied him. If Sam found her so readable, it would be difficult to hide anything from him.

"Come in and relax," he offered, leading her into the living room. The white leather couch was

L-shaped, and decorated with several huge pillows in brilliant shades of blue to complement the plush carpet.

Marjorie sat, and her gaze drifted once more to the panoramic view of Commencement Bay. Just being here with Sam soothed her. All day she'd been battling her resentment toward Al and what the loss of this commission would mean to her already strained budget.

"Do you want to tell me about it?" Sam asked, taking a seat beside her.

Marjorie nodded. "I owe you that much, at least." For the next half hour she explained what had happened with Al—though she was careful not to name names—and how his devious methods had cheated her out of half the commission. By the time she'd finished, Sam was pacing in front of the coffee table with barely restrained anger. The corners of his mouth were pinched and white, his hands knotted in tight fists.

"What's being done about this?" he demanded.

"Nothing."

"Nothing?" Sam repeated incredulously.

"The decision's already been made."

"But he lied."

"I know that, and so does nearly everyone else, but it's his name on the contract, so he's entitled to a commission no matter how much time I spent with those people. At least my protest to the manager earned me half of it. That's the way things are done in sales."

It had been a long time since Sam had felt this angry. He wanted to find Marjorie's coworker in a dark alley some night and teach him a lesson. The intensity of his fury shocked him; he hated unnecessary violence.

"I'll take care of this for you," Sam said without any real plan in mind. He knew how hard Marjorie worked—the long hours with few free weekends. She'd climbed her way up the sales ladder and deserved to be a success. The last thing she needed was someone sabotaging her efforts. The burning desire to protect her seared through him like a surgical laser beam.

"Sam, please. I'm a big girl, I'll find a solution my own way."

"No." He shook his head once, hard. "I want to handle this."

"Sam." His reaction wasn't a joke, she realized. If she'd known this was the way he was going to be, then she wouldn't have told him about Al. As it was, she was glad she'd been careful not to mention Al's name. "Listen to me. I appreciate your concern, but I don't involve myself in your business, so I'm asking you not to interfere in mine. Things have a way of working themselves out."

"But this heel deserves—"

"Everything he's going to get." She stood and placed her hand on his forearm. "I don't need anyone to rescue me. I've been on my own for a long time now. This guy hasn't made many friends at Dixon's. He won't last long."

"You're sure?" At her nod, Sam relaxed a bit. "Have you eaten yet?"

"No," she answered with a smile, surprised to realize how hungry she was. "Are you offering to feed me?"

"Better than that," he answered with a slow, sensuous grin that edged his strong, well-shaped mouth upward. "I'm willing to cook for you."

Just looking at Sam made Marjorie feel light-headed. She could drown in those appealing eyes of his, dark, deep, penetrating.

"Follow me," he instructed, taking her hand and leading her into his kitchen. He was a good cook and thought he might be able to teach her a thing or two.

Sam's kitchen was huge and equipped with every modern convenience. An island with restaurant quality gas burners was set up in the middle of the expansive floor. A wide assortment of copper pots, pans and skillets was suspended from the ceiling above the island.

"Wow," Marjorie said, and released a slow, wondering breath. "You must be some chef."

"I try." He pulled out a stool for her to sit on. "First things first." With that he opened the wine refrigerator and, with little hesitation, drew out a bottle, then chose two tall wineglasses from a cabinet.

Expertly he removed the cork and poured them each a glass, pausing to taste his first. He gave his approval before handing the second glass to Marjorie.

While she sipped her Chablis, Sam set to work with a huge wok, a large supply of fresh vegetables and a sharp cleaver.

It had been hours since she'd last eaten, and the first glass of wine went straight to her head. "Here, let me help," she offered, slipping off the stool.

"No, you don't. You're my guest," Sam insisted, noting the way her cheeks were reddening. She was already a little tipsy.

He refilled her glass, and she sat down again and took another sip. "So you don't want my help. Have you been talking to the fire department?"

"No." Sam chuckled and set about slicing the vegetables in neat, even sections. "This is a recipe a friend of mine from Hong Kong taught me several years back. It's authentic and delicious."

"Is there anything you can't do?" she asked, only a little intimidated.

"A few things."

She sighed, crossed her legs and sipped some more wine. "My grandmother used to do all the cooking."

"Your grandmother?" he prompted. She rarely talked about her childhood, he'd noticed.

"Jody and I went to live with her after Mom and Dad were killed in an automobile accident."

"How old were you?"

"Twelve going on twenty. Grandma loved us, don't get me wrong. She tried to make a decent home for the two of us, but she was old, and her health wasn't good. The main problem was money. Grandma took care of Jody and the house, and I found work to bring in extra income."

Sam reached for the wine bottle and replenished her glass. The Chablis was loosening her tongue.

"So your grandmother raised the two of you?"

She nodded, holding the stem of the glass with both hands. "Right. This room feels awfully warm?" she said, and fanned her face.

Suppressing a smile, he gazed at her, trying not to laugh outright. "I think I'd better feed you, and the sooner the better."

"I'd rather you kissed me," she told him, then blinked and covered her mouth with her hand. "Oops, I didn't mean to say that."

Sam pushed the vegetables aside. "Did you mean it?"

Sheepishly, she nodded. "I think the wine's gone to my head."

"I think so, too." He walked around to stand directly in front of her. His smile was filled with confident amusement.

Her dark eyes followed his movements and innocently pleaded with him for a kiss. Unable to resist her, he leaned forward and gently covered her mouth with his own. His intention had been to appease her until he'd finished stir-frying their dinner, but the instant his lips met hers, he was lost. He deepened the kiss, his lips playing over hers as though she were a rare musical instrument.

His kiss burned through Marjorie like fire raging through dry brush. When he reluctantly lifted his head from hers, she swayed, and his hands on her shoulders were all that kept her from tumbling to the floor.

"I think you're right," she admitted. "I need something to eat . . . quick."

Sam's eyes burned into hers, and his strong, steady voice shook slightly. "I was just thinking that we should forget about dinner and continue with the kissing."

She tilted her head up to look into his eyes, resisting the urge to reach out and cling to him. "You were?"

"But you're right."

"I am?" At the moment she didn't think so as she watched him turn back to the stove. After a while she stood on shaky feet, unfastened her jacket and removed it. By the time she'd finished loosening the top buttons of her shirt, Sam had their meal ready.

He handed her a plate and pulled another stool up beside hers. The tantalizing scent of hot oil and ginger wafted toward her, and her stomach reacted with a loud growl. She placed her hand over her abdomen and smiled sheepishly. "Sorry."

"When was the last time you had anything to eat?"

"Noon." Soup. She'd been too upset to down anything else, so now she was famished.

Sam used chopsticks, holding the plate with one hand while dexterously using the wooden sticks with the other. She tried the same thing and nearly dumped her dinner on her lap.

"You'd better use a fork," he advised, humor lurking in his eyes.

She nodded meekly. Once she had a fork in her hand, she discovered the food was both hot and spicy. Closing her eyes, she savored each mouthful as though she hadn't eaten in weeks instead of hours.

"Oh, Sam, this is really good."

"I do my best," he answered, but his interest wasn't in the dinner. Marjorie, the woman who had tormented his dreams for weeks, was sitting across from him. Part angel, part temptress. Complicated, vital and ripe, an opulent beauty. He'd dreamed of having her with him in his home, envisioned carrying her into his room and laying her across his king-size bed. He wanted to love her, ease the ache of loneliness he read in her eyes and make up to her for the childhood she'd lost.

Following the meal, Sam made a fresh pot of coffee. Marjorie, feeling sober and steady on her feet after the delicious dinner, poured them each a cup and carried them into the living room. They sat close to each other, and she tucked her feet up under her and placed her head on his sturdy shoulder.

"You're not going to drift off on me, are you?" he asked gently. His hand curved around her nape, and his fingers stroked the slope of her neck and shoulder.

"If you keep doing that, I will." She felt him smile against her hair. "I'm sorry to be such poor company," she said, uttering the words through a loud yawn.

"You're not."

She half lifted her head. "I don't know what it is, but every time I'm around you all I do is sleep."

"I often have that effect on women," Sam said, and chuckled. The rich sound of his amusement echoed around the room. He was thinking of going to bed, too, but not in the same sense she was. Holding her close was a tough temptation to handle.

She tried unsuccessfully to stifle another yawn. "Believe me, I know how women react to you."

"I'd better get you home, Kitten."

"Kitten?" No one had ever called her anything but her name, at least not to her face.

"You remind me of one," he explained softly. "You're all soft and cuddly."

"I have claws."

Again he smiled. "Now that's something I can personally attest to."

Marjorie was smiling when she unfolded her legs from beneath her and stood. She collected her jacket and purse, and paused in the entryway. "It seems I'm always in your debt."

Sam's brow furrowed as he rose. "How's that?"

"First you rescue me from the jaws of death . . ."

"That's a slight exaggeration."

"Then you buy a car from me . . ."

"One I intended to purchase anyway."

"Next you feed me."

There was a lot more Sam was interested in doing for her, and if she didn't hurry up and leave, he was going to have more problems refusing her.

"Thank you, Sam, once again."

"Thank *you*."

They paused in front of the door, and Sam turned her in his arms. His hands locked at the small of her back, pulling her closer against the solid wall of his chest. His hips and thighs pressed against hers, and still they weren't close enough.

Marjorie had no intention of refusing his kiss, not when she craved it herself. His mouth closed possessively over hers, searing his name onto her heart. Again and again he kissed her with a fierce tenderness, shaping and fitting her lips with his own.

Sam's arms circled her protectively while his tongue explored the soft recesses of her mouth until she shook with a sensation she had never known.

"Sam . . ."

"Kitten," he murmured.

Wildly consuming kisses followed, and Marjorie felt as though she were on fire. Never had she felt so willing, so sensuous. There'd been little time for puppy love when she was young. Later, the men she'd dated had resented her streak of independence. When it came to lovemaking and men, she was shockingly innocent. The sensations Sam had awakened in her had been dormant far too long. Now that she'd discovered love, she wasn't going to let go lightly.

An insistent beeping surrounded them, and Sam's impatient groan told her the noise wasn't the bells on the hill tolling their love.

"What is it?" she whispered, hardly able to find her voice.

"Not what, but who."

She blinked, not understanding.

"That's my pager. I'm needed at the hospital."

Seven

The phone pealed loudly in the darkened bedroom. At first Marjorie incorporated the irritating sound into her dream. By the third ear-shattering ring she realized it was her telephone.

Without lifting her head from the pillow, she stretched out her arm and groped for the receiver, locating it in time to cut off the fourth ring.

"Yes," she mumbled, and brushed the wild confusion of hair from her face.

"Kitten?"

Her eyes flew open, and she struggled into a sitting position and reached for the small clock on her nightstand. "Sam?"

"I'm sorry to wake you, but I wanted to be sure you got home safely."

She blinked and focused her gaze on the illuminated clock dial. It was a few minutes after four. "I didn't have any problems. How did things go at the hospital?"

"Great. Wonderful, in fact."

She relaxed and leaned against the thick goose-down pillow,

savoring the warmth that never failed to infuse her whenever Sam called. "Did you deliver another baby?"

"Two, actually, or I would have been back hours ago."

"Girls? Boys?"

"One of each." He felt like a fool, calling her at this ungodly hour, but he'd walked into his empty house, and everywhere he looked, he thought of Marjorie. The memory of her presence swirled around him like the soft scent of summer. Often the stark loneliness of his lifestyle had hit him after a nighttime delivery, but never more than it had this time. He would have given anything in the world to have found her curled up and sleeping in his bed, waiting for him. Hearing her voice was a poor substitute, but one he couldn't deny himself.

"I realized when I got back to the house," he continued, "that I hadn't asked to see you again." Even to his own ears, the explanation sounded lame.

"No, we both had other things on our minds."

"Dinner tonight, then?" he asked.

Marjorie wasn't thinking clearly; her mind was clouded with the last dregs of sleep. "What day is this?"

"Friday."

Her disappointment was potent enough to produce a bout of aching frustration. "I can't," she moaned. "My sister is driving up from Portland, and I'm working late both days this weekend."

"I'll take both you and your sister to dinner, then." That was an easy enough solution.

"But, Sam . . ."

"No arguing. Your sister, and anyone else you want, is welcome to join us." He didn't care if he had to buy dinner for every employee at Dixon Motors as long as he could spend time with Marjorie.

"You're sure?"

"Absolutely. And while we're on the subject of dinners and dates, I know it's next week and you might be busy, but do you have plans for July Fourth?"

"No."

"You don't have to work?"

"No," she murmured, and smiled. "That would be un-American. What makes you ask . . . about the Fourth, I mean?"

"Another doctor and his wife, Bernie and Betty Miller, have a cabin on Hood Canal, and they invited me up. Would you spend the day with me?"

Marjorie closed her eyes to hold back the tears of joy. "I'd be thrilled."

"I'll let the Millers know, then."

They must have talked for another half hour before Marjorie realized that Sam's slow responses revealed his exhaustion.

"Oh, Sam, I'm sorry. You must be dead on your feet, and I'm talking your head off."

His grin was both lazy and content. "No. Listening to you relaxes me. Normally when I get back from the hospital, especially this late, I'm too tense to sleep—too keyed up. Now I feel like I could easily drift off."

"Good night, then," she murmured softly, regretfully. She was falling head over heels for Sam Bretton. She knew the pitfalls and still wanted to love him.

"A doctor?" Jody squealed with unrestrained delight. At twenty she was a younger version of Marjorie, the only difference being her hair, which was cut fashionably short, and her sportier and more colorful clothes.

"You behave yourself," Marjorie warned. Now that her health was back and she didn't have to submit to Jody's orders, she could more fully appreciate her sibling.

Jody looked her sister full in the eye. "You mean I can't tell

Sam about the time you snuck out of the house to kiss Freddy Fletcher behind the toolshed?"

"You do, and I'll smack you upside the head."

The light, musical sound of Jody's laughter filled the cozy apartment. "I have to admit, though, you look a hundred times better than the last time I was here. I wonder if your doctor friend has anything to do with that?"

"I look better because I haven't been forced to eat your cooking, which is even worse than my own."

Jody pretended the remark had greatly offended her, but neither of them had been blessed with talent in the kitchen, and they enjoyed teasing each other about that fact.

"So Sam was your doctor," Jody said, as she slumped on the couch and crossed her legs Indian style beneath her. "How come you didn't mention him before now?"

"I . . . He . . . Well, what really happened is . . ."

"Oh honestly, Marjie, look at your face. You're actually blushing. I can't believe it. My big sister is in love. Well, good grief, it took you long enough."

Marjorie's hands flew to her cheeks in embarrassment. They did feel hot and were no doubt as flushed as her sister claimed.

"You're in love with him, aren't you?" Jody asked, pretending to study her nails, but actually aiming her gaze toward her older sister.

"Yes," Marjorie answered honestly.

"Have you gone to bed with him yet?"

"Jody!"

"Well, have you?"

The heat in Marjorie's face intensified a hundred-fold. "Of course not! What kind of question is that?"

Jody's eyebrows rose suggestively. "But you'd like to, wouldn't you."

"I can't believe we're having this conversation." With as much composure as she could muster, which wasn't much, Marjorie reached for her glass of iced tea and took a large swallow.

Amused, Jody pinched her lips together in mock disapproval. "Come on, Marjie, would you stop being my mother long enough to talk to me like a big sister? Tell me everything. I want to know the most intimate desires of your heart."

Despite the subject matter, Marjorie relaxed. "My desires? That's easy."

"Sam?" Jody coaxed.

"Sam," Marjorie repeated. "I can't believe this is happening to me after all these years of being so sensible about men. With Sam, everything's different." She paused and then continued, telling her sister how Sam Bretton had stayed with her in the hours following her surgery. "I didn't know any man so wonderful existed. I feel giddy every time I'm with him."

Jody nodded knowingly and smiled through a haze of tears.

"Honey, what's wrong?" Marjorie asked quickly.

Jody wiped the moisture off the high arch of her cheekbones. "This is the first time I can remember when you've talked to me like a . . . sister. You never shared anything with me before—at least not like this. I'm happy for you, really happy."

Marjorie blinked back her surprise, ready to argue the point. Then she thought about how right her sister was. She had never felt she could share with Jody; her sister was so much younger that it hadn't seemed right to burden Jody with her problems. Jody had to be protected, and because of that their relationship had to be part parent, part sibling. She'd had to be Jody's mother and sister both.

"You know something," Jody said, her voice unsteady. "I love Sam already."

"Wait until you meet him," Marjorie answered, her own voice wavering. "He's been so good to me."

"You deserve him, and he deserves you."

They wrapped their arms around each other and squeezed tightly, neither willing to let the other go. They had reached a deeper understanding of what it meant to be sisters, and for that Marjorie would always be grateful.

Sam arrived about fifteen minutes later, amazed at Jody's warm welcome. He liked her immediately but wished he could have had time alone with Marjorie. It seemed a hundred years since he'd last talked to her, and a thousand since he'd held her sweet warmth against him and relished the special feel of her in his arms.

The evening proved to be a fun one. He treated the two women to a delicious seafood dinner in a four-star restaurant that overlooked Commencement Bay. Following the meal, the three of them walked along the dock outside the Lobster Shop and gazed at the bright lights that sparkled like shiny stars from the opposite shore.

"I can't remember the last time I ate this well," Jody said, holding her stomach and exhaling a deep, contented sigh. "I'm stuffed."

Marjorie's worried gaze instantly flew to her younger sister. "I knew it! You're not eating right."

"I'm in perfect health."

Sam's arm around Marjorie's waist tightened, and she managed to hold back any further argument.

Jody looked at the two of them, and with a smile lifting the corners of her full mouth, she feigned a loud yawn. "I can't believe how tired I am all of a sudden. That drive from Portland can really wear a person out."

Sam and Marjorie shared a secret look and struggled to hide their amusement. Jody couldn't have been any less subtle had she tried.

"I think she's offering us some time alone," Sam whispered

close to Marjorie's ear. He was hard-pressed not to flick his tongue over her lobe, knowing her instant response. "Are we going to accept?"

Marjorie's nod was eager.

"Just drop me off at the apartment, and you two can escape," Jody announced, looking pleased with herself. "Far be it from me to block the path of true love."

"Far be it from me to let you," Sam joked, as they headed toward the restaurant parking lot.

Sam drove directly back to Marjorie's apartment, and Jody hurriedly scooted out of the car, winked and reached for Marjorie's keys. "Don't hurry back on my account."

"We won't," Sam assured her. He appreciated what Jody was doing, but he wouldn't keep Marjorie out long. It was obvious the two sisters were close. He'd seen for himself the various roles Marjorie played in Jody's life, slipping from one to the other with hardly a breath in between.

Marjorie remained in Sam's car while Jody let herself into the apartment. Then he reached for her hand, squeezing gently. "I like your sister."

"She's impressed with you, too." That was a gross understatement, Marjorie thought to herself. Jody had been giving her signals all night that showed her wholehearted approval of Sam. In the ladies' room she had gone so far as to suggest that if Marjorie didn't want Sam, she'd take him.

But Marjorie wanted Sam Bretton even more than before. She couldn't look in his direction without her eyes revealing everything that was stored in her heart. She couldn't hide her love for him any longer.

"I have to stop off at the hospital for a minute," he said, as he pulled out of the parking lot of the apartment complex. "Is that a problem?"

"No, of course not. If you want, I'll stay in the car."

"There's no need for you to do that," Sam came back quickly. "I want to introduce you to a couple of my friends. And this will give you a chance to see the two babies I delivered the other night."

Marjorie's heart shot to her throat. Babies. Sam was as comfortable with them as she was with interest rates and electromechanically fuel-injected engines. Anyone under the age of two terrorized her; babies made her nervous and served to remind her of how inadequate she was in the traditional female role. Her biggest fear was that Sam would bring her into the hospital and expect her to go inside the nursery. He might even expect her to hold an infant, and then he would learn that not only were babies allergic to her, she was allergic to them.

"How does that sound?" Sam asked, cutting into her troubled thoughts.

"About the babies?" she hedged.

"Yes, they're—"

"Sam, listen," she said, rushing her words. "Maybe it would be better if I went back to the apartment with Jody."

He shot her a puzzled frown. The disappointment that welled up in him was strong. He couldn't understand her sudden objection. Sure, she hadn't especially enjoyed her hospital stay, and he could understand why. But her hesitation now puzzled him. "Go back to the apartment? Whatever for?"

Marjorie made the pretense of glancing at her watch. "It's late and . . ."

"It's barely after nine," he countered, studying her. She was growing paler by the minute.

Marjorie couldn't look into Sam's eyes and refuse him anything. "You're right," she said, determination squaring her shoulders. "I'm being silly. Of course I'll go with you and meet your friends and see the babies. Everything will be wonderful."

She knew her tone was falsely cheerful, but she decided it

was far better for her to confront her fears than leave them un-conquered. He would be with her—nothing would go wrong.

He helped her out of the car, and led her through a side entrance and to the elevator beyond. When the door shut, he punched the floor number and pulled her into his arms for a brief, ardent kiss.

She tried to respond, but her heart was beating as hard and loud as a drum, and her insides were quivering with apprehension. She wanted to do everything right with Sam, and her fear of babies was sure to ruin her chances.

He pulled her close to his side and stared at the closed doors. Marjorie was perfect, with her soft skin, her wide, soulful eyes, and a heart he longed to fill with his love.

The elevator doors smoothly glided open, and Marjorie braced herself for the inevitable. Sam meant so much to her, and it was vital that she be the kind of woman he needed. Without meaning to, she pressed her flattened palms together and rubbed them back and forth several times. When he looked her way, he frowned, so she smiled tightly and freed her hands, letting her arms drop lifelessly to her sides.

With his hand at the base of her spine, Sam directed Marjorie over to the nurses' station and introduced her to three of the staff members he worked with regularly. The purpose of this visit was more social than anything else. He'd partially fabricated the need to stop in, in an effort to casually introduce her to his peers. It seemed as though she'd been a natural part of his life forever.

"Is Bernie around?" Sam asked the oldest of the nurses, who reminded Marjorie of Bertha Powell. The two could have been sisters.

"Dr. Miller's in the lounge."

Sam reached for Marjorie's hand, lacing his fingers through his as he led her down the wide hallway.

"Nice to have met you," Marjorie said brightly over her shoulder.

"A pleasure," the oldest nurse returned. The other two said nothing. Their wide-eyed stares told her that both of them were convinced she wasn't good enough for their beloved Dr. Sam. The feeling of being watched persisted long after the staff members were out of sight.

Bernie Miller was sitting at the round table in the middle of the doctors' lounge, holding a cup of coffee. He was leaning over the table and holding his head up with one hand. When Sam and Marjorie entered the room, he raised his head, his gaze brightening. His fatigued features relaxed into a slow grin.

"Bernie, I'd like you to meet Marjorie Majors."

Slowly Dr. Miller rose to his feet, but his gaze didn't waver from Marjorie's. "Hello there."

"Hi." She stepped forward and offered him her hand.

"So this is her?" Bernie's gaze shot from Marjorie back to Sam as they ended the brief handshake.

"In the flesh." Sam draped his arm across Marjorie's shoulder as he smiled down on her, his gaze filled with warmth. He hadn't told many of his friends about Marjorie, but hiding the news of how he felt from his best buddy had been impossible. Bernie had known he'd met someone important the minute Sam casually mentioned her a few days earlier. Bernie had wanted to know all about her, but Sam had hesitated. He hadn't been sure of his own feelings then. Marjorie appealed to him more than anyone in a long time, but she wasn't exactly the happy home-maker, and that realization had pulled him up short. Until he'd met Marjorie, the woman he'd pictured in his life had been able to both seduce him in the bedroom and whip up a five-course dinner.

"I understand that you're joining us for our picnic on Wednesday."

"Yes," Marjorie said, and nodded for emphasis. "Thank you for including me."

Sam poured two more cups of coffee while she sat down and talked to Bernie, then joined them at the table. Marjorie mused to herself that things were going well. If only they could stop here. She had no trouble relating to adults; it was infants and children who caused her to break out in hives.

"I'm going to take Marjorie to the nursery," Sam was saying.

Doing her utmost not to choke on her coffee, she pushed her cup aside and stood. If she thought her heart had been pounding in the elevator, now it was crashing like a Chinese gong as she followed Sam out of the doctors' lounge. No doubt the three nurses she'd met earlier never had this problem. Most likely any one of them would gladly surrender her eyeteeth to have Dr. Sam Bretton.

He led her down the wide corridor and into the nursery. Rows of bassinets were lined up in uniform fashion. Some of the infants were blanketed in pink, others in blue. Their surnames were written in bold letters in front of their mock cribs. Two of the nurses that Marjorie had just met now sat in rocking chairs, soothing crying infants.

Sam donned a surgical robe and handed Marjorie one.

"Sam," she whispered, barely able to speak. "There's something you should know."

"Just a minute," he murmured, grinning boyishly. With a gentleness she'd witnessed several times in the last month, Sam lifted a small pink bundle from a crib and looked up at Marjorie, beaming proudly.

"What do you think?" he asked, scooting sideways so she could more easily view the squirming infant in his wide embrace.

Her eyes dropped to the scrunched-up face and minute fists as the baby struggled to get free of her bindings. She forced a smile, unable to think of anything to say.

"Would you care to hold her?"

Her dark eyes widened with alarm, and she forcefully shook her head. "No . . . thanks." By the time she'd finished speaking, she'd backed herself out the door.

"Marjorie, are you feeling all right?"

"I'm a little . . . I'm fine," she managed somehow. "Really."

As carefully as he'd lifted the infant, Sam replaced her in her bassinet. By the time he'd finished, Marjorie was leaning against the wall in the corridor outside the nursery.

"What's wrong?" he asked softly, coming to stand beside her.

"I . . . it's no big thing."

"You look like you're about to faint."

"Don't worry, I'm not the type," she said. "I'm not the kind of woman who goes all mushy at the sight of a baby, either. In case you hadn't noticed, not all of us are alike. There are some of us who cook and crochet and get pregnant at the drop of a hat. And then there are others, like me, who are allergic to baby powder and dirty diapers, and content to eat TV dinners the rest of our miserable lives."

Sam's eyes were incredulous. "Are you trying to tell me you don't like babies?"

"Sure, I do," she said. "In somebody else's arms."

Sam blinked, hardly able to believe his ears. He felt as if the world were crashing in around him. He'd decided not to worry about Marjorie's lack of culinary skills, deciding that her strength and independence were more important than any domestic qualities. But when it came to having children, he wouldn't—couldn't—compromise.

"Babies are fine for the right kind of woman," she said. Her voice had gained in volume with the strength of her convictions. "Unfortunately, I'm not one of them."

"You don't mean that." His words were sharp.

By now their heated exchange had attracted the attention

of the hospital staff. If Sam's nursing friends had disapproved of her earlier, it was nothing to the censure she felt being aimed at her now. They thought Sam deserved someone far better than she would ever be, and every accusing glare said as much.

Without thought for the wisdom of her actions, she turned and half ran, half walked, down the polished corridor to the elevator, fighting back tears all the way.

"Marjorie, wait!" Sam cried.

Since the elevator wasn't there yet anyway, she didn't have much choice if she wanted to maintain her dignity. They descended in tense silence. Even when they left the hospital building and headed toward Sam's car, neither of them spoke. By that time her throat was so clogged that it felt as though someone had a stranglehold on her. With everything that was in her, she yearned to be all Sam wanted in a woman, yet she'd failed miserably.

Sam opened her door for her. His feet felt heavy as he walked around the car and let himself in. He didn't know what to say or how to say it. He wanted a family, longed for children, and he yearned for Marjorie to give them to him.

She watched him with despair. The tears that had been so close to the surface ran down her cheeks like water over a dam after an early spring thaw, and she turned her head away so he couldn't see. At that moment she would have sold her soul to be different. She took a deep, shuddering breath. "You want children, don't you?"

Her heart cracked when he was silent, and she realized he couldn't deny it. Sam Bretton would make a wonderful father; he was a natural.

"Yes," he answered finally. He couldn't deny his desire for a family. Almost from the beginning, he'd pictured Marjorie with a child in her arms—their child. For years he'd been seeking a woman who was strong enough to stand on her own, and tender enough to need and love him. These last weeks with Marjorie had led him to believe he'd found that special woman . . . until tonight.

"I'm no good with babies, and I'm even worse with children," she whispered in a choked voice. "That's not going to change."

Eight

For the second time that morning, Marjorie checked the picnic basket. Her nerves were shot. She hadn't heard from Sam, nor had she contacted him. For three days she'd done nothing but think about him and how wrong they were for each other. The realization didn't do any good, though; she still loved him, still wanted him, still yearned for them to build a life together. She would give anything to be the right person for him, but she couldn't change what she was, couldn't become someone different.

Now it was the Fourth of July, and she wasn't even sure he would show up to take her to the picnic and wouldn't blame him if he didn't.

She paused to take a calming breath and rubbed her hands down the thighs of her new jeans. They had been Jody's idea. Marjorie hadn't told her sister what happened between her and Sam, but Jody had guessed something was drastically wrong. The following morning she had insisted they go shopping, claiming there wasn't any ailment a department store couldn't cure. The jeans, Jody claimed, did great things for Marjorie's legs. For all Marjorie cared, they could have been made from sackcloth.

The weather outside wasn't promising; thick gray clouds had formed overhead. As an afterthought, she tucked a thick sweater inside the basket.

The doorbell chimed, and her heart lurched. She swallowed and opened the door. Sam, dressed in jeans and a T-shirt, stood on the other side. He didn't look any better than she felt. Although he was outwardly composed, turmoil and regret were evident in his eyes and the hard set of his mouth.

He stepped inside her living room and hesitated, then smiled. The movement transformed his face.

"What's wrong?" she asked, convinced she should have worn anything but jeans. Denim might help her legs, but it didn't do a thing for her hips.

"The jeans," Sam managed.

"They're all wrong, aren't they?" Silently she blamed her sister. Marjorie knew better than to listen to the advice of a college student who was toying with the idea of tinting her hair blue.

"No," he murmured.

"I can change, don't worry," she went on brightly. "It'll only take a minute."

"Don't," he said, and smiled briefly. "You look fantastic." His gaze was warm and sincere.

Marjorie thought she would cry. She'd been as taut as a violin bow, as well as nervous and worried. Until the minute he spoke, she'd had no idea what he was thinking. Apparently he'd decided to put the incident in the hospital behind them—at least for today. She knew that they should talk and try to settle this problem, but in three days she hadn't been able to come up with a solution, and from his haggard look, she suspected that Sam hadn't, either. Today they would put their troubles aside and enjoy the holiday. She was grateful.

"Every woman should look so good in Levi's," he said.

A smile curved her mouth. "You honestly like them?"

"Yes, Kitten, I do."

Sam longed to take her in his arms and hold her, but he didn't dare. These last days without her had been a self-imposed nightmare. After years of searching for a woman he could love, respect and admire, he'd been convinced he'd found her in Marjorie. No, she wasn't exactly the woman he'd pictured, but he'd discovered he could accept her quirks, loved her all the more because of them. They were part and parcel of who she was. But children . . . He'd dedicated his life to reproduction and childbirth. To him, children were as essential as food and water. He needed a woman who wanted to give him a family. He could find no way to compromise on an issue so basic to his happiness.

After that night at the hospital, Sam had decided to make a clean break from her. There didn't seem to be any purpose in prolonging the agony. But he'd learned it wasn't that simple. He thought about her constantly, longed to talk to her. After two torturous days he'd known that forgetting about her would be impossible. He would have to think of something to help him solve this problem.

"I've missed you," he murmured, as his eyes held hers.

"I've missed you, too," she answered, and her voice was filled with regret. "Sam," she whispered, "I'm so sorry."

"I am, too, Kitten." He drew a deep breath, then exhaled slowly. She couldn't change what she was, and he couldn't help loving her. He prayed they could find a solution to this, because now that he had found Marjorie, he couldn't let her go.

"Betty," Sam said, his arm loosely draped over Marjorie's shoulder. "This is Marjorie Majors. Marjorie, Betty."

"Hi," Betty Miller said cordially, her blue eyes twinkling. She was bouncing a toddler on her hip, and the shy little boy hid his face against his mother's shoulder. "I'm so pleased you could make it. Can you believe this weather? Only on Puget Sound would we have a fireplace going on the Fourth of July."

"Thank you for inviting me."

Betty was slender and pretty, exactly the type Marjorie had always pictured as a doctor's wife. Her deep blue eyes were warm and gentle, and Marjorie doubted that Betty Miller had an enemy in this world.

"The ruffian on my hip is Kevin. He's three," Betty added, and encouraged her son to look up long enough to greet their company. Kevin, however, held his fists over his eyes and refused to acknowledge Marjorie *or* Sam.

"Hi, Kevin," Marjorie offered stiffly but to no avail.

The little boy buried his face deeper into his mother's shoulder. "He's a little bit shy," Betty explained, her face flushed with embarrassment.

"That's all right," Marjorie said, in an effort to reassure her. She understood far better than Betty could realize. Kids instinctively knew she was rotten mother material. She didn't know how they knew, but they did.

"Kevin, do you want to show Uncle Sam where your daddy is?" Betty asked, and there was a hopeful note in her voice.

To everyone's surprise, Kevin nodded eagerly and climbed off his mother's hip. Without looking in Marjorie's direction, the three-year-old held out his hand in order to lead Sam away.

Sam must have noted the distress in Marjorie's eyes, because he murmured something about being right back.

"Take your time," Betty returned. Once Sam and Kevin were out of sight, she let out a soft sight and changed the topic as she led the way toward the cabin, which was located on the fertile bank of Hood Canal and was surprisingly modern. She gestured expansively. "You'd think Bernie had constructed the Empire State Building for the amount of time and effort that's gone into this infamous deck."

"Bernie built the deck himself?" Marjorie had to admit she was impressed with the wraparound structure, as she followed her hostess into the kitchen. A series of stairs led down onto the sandy, smooth beach below.

"Don't encourage him," Betty warned with a short laugh. "In his former life Bernie claims to have been a carpenter. He thinks he missed his calling." Still grinning, she poured them each a tall glass of iced tea and led Marjorie into the living room. A small fire gave the room a cozy feeling.

Marjorie sat in the overstuffed chair opposite her hostess.

Betty's chest rose with a deep breath, and she smiled at Marjorie. "You don't know how relieved I am to finally meet you."

"Me?"

"Sam's hardly talked about anything else from the day you went in for surgery."

"He told you about me?" Amazed, Marjorie flattened her hand over her heart.

"In elaborate detail. Does that surprise you?"

"It shocks me." And pleased her. And excited her. Then she remembered there could be no future for them.

"Bernie and I have been waiting years for Sam to finally meet the right woman. We'd almost given up hope. He's so dedicated to his patients. The one thing that's suffered most over the last few years has been his personal life."

"He *is* a wonderful doctor."

"You won't get any arguments out of me. I should know—Sam delivered both Kevin and Shelley."

"Shelley?" She was going to have to deal with more than one child?

"Shelley's sleeping, like all good four-month-olds. You'll see her later."

Marjorie only nodded. She liked Betty and didn't want to disillusion her with her own lack of anything approaching the maternal instinct.

"You know, I knew Sam before I even met Bernie," Betty explained, gazing into her iced tea. Her face took on a solemn look.

"Are you a nurse?"

Betty nodded. "I know that sounds old hat, but the path of romance was anything but smooth for Bernie and me. It isn't like we saw each other from across a crowded room and instantly heard fate calling."

"No?"

Betty crossed her legs and grinned sheepishly. "Well, to be honest, I was dating Sam when I met Bernie. Later Bernie was assigned to the ward where I was working."

"So it was being in close proximity that ignited the fires between you?"

Laughing, Betty shook her head. "Hardly. If there were any fires ignited, they were from the arguments we had. Bernie and I couldn't agree on anything, and I found him impossible to work with. Once he even went so far as to warn Sam that I was a meddling busybody and he'd do well not to see me again."

Marjorie found all this a little difficult to believe. She'd met Bernie and seen for herself the way his gaze softened when he mentioned his wife's name.

"I know it sounds unbelievable now, but we had serious problems." Betty paused and ran the tips of her fingers over the chair's armrest, caught up in her memories. "It seemed that no matter what I did or how careful I was, I couldn't please the demanding Dr. Miller. Every time he and I were together, we ended up in a shouting match. There wasn't a staff member on the entire floor who would come within twenty feet of us when we got going."

"What happened to change all that?"

Betty shrugged, then a lazy smile began to grow until it practically lit up her round face. "Bernie came to my apartment one night after work. I'll admit he looked terrible, but we'd had another one of our confrontations that day, and I wasn't in any mood to be friendly."

"What did he say?" Marjorie couldn't help being curious.

"He wanted to talk." Betty paused and grinned. "I told him to take a flying leap into the nearest cow pasture."

Marjorie laughed outright. The idea of tiny Betty standing up to a stern-faced Bernie made for a comical picture. "I don't imagine he was any too pleased with that suggestion."

"No. I could tell he was struggling not to tell me where I should fly. But he didn't. Instead he asked me how serious I was about Sam."

Marjorie suspected that Bernie had been attracted to Betty from the first, but he was decent enough not to get involved with his best friend's girlfriend.

"Sam was a friend," Betty continued. "A good one. We'd dated off and on for years, but there was never anything serious between us. Fun stuff. You know—a baseball game, hikes now and again, that sort of thing. Neither one of us ever thought it was a romance for the ages."

"But you let Bernie think otherwise."

"Why not? He'd been a pill from the first. Besides, what was happening between Sam and me wasn't any of his business. I told him that, too."

"I suppose he left then."

"Yeah, how'd you know?"

"Lucky guess," Marjorie said, holding in a knowing smile.

"We didn't argue after that. Not once. Bernie treated me like every other nurse on the ward, and within a week I was so bored I wanted to cry. Until that moment I didn't realize how much I looked forward to sparring with him." She smiled as she remembered. "That was when Sam invited me to have coffee with him in the cafeteria after work one day. When I sat down, the first thing he did was ask about Bernie. I said I didn't have any idea what he was talking about. Sam looked surprised at that. He claimed Bernie had gotten drunk one night and stormed at him to hurry up and marry me before he—Bernie—did something stupid."

"I can imagine Sam's reaction to that."

Betty grinned and continued. "Sam told him he liked me fine, but he couldn't see the two of us ever getting married."

"What did Bernie say to that?"

Betty rolled her eyes toward the ceiling. "Apparently he tried to swing on Sam. You have to understand how out of character that is for Bernie to fully appreciate him doing something like that."

"I think I can understand," Marjorie said. Any person who would dedicate his life to the care and well-being of his fellow man would naturally deplore violence. "How did the two of you ever manage to get together?"

"It was easy once I sorted through my feelings. I figured that since he'd come to me once, I'd have to be the one to approach him. Not right away, mind you. It took some thinking on my part. The most difficult part was realizing I was in love with Bernie Miller and had been for weeks. The hardest thing I've ever done was invite him over for dinner. Funny thing, though, once we stopped arguing, we discovered how much we had in common. Within a month of our first dinner date we were engaged, and you can guess the rest of the story."

Marjorie took a sip of her tea. "The two of you are perfect together. It's obvious talking to either one of you that you and Bernie are in love."

"We work on it." Betty slapped the armrest. "Enough about me. I want to know about you."

"There really isn't much to tell." A bit uneasy, Marjorie spoke in general terms about her job and her sister. The whole time she was talking, she was aware that there was nothing that made her any different than the other women Sam had dated in the past ten years.

"He's crazy about you," Betty commented. "You know that, don't you?"

Marjorie could feel the other woman studying her. Sam might have been crazy for her at one time, but she had ruined that.

"To be honest, I wondered what made you different. But ten minutes with you and I can understand it. You're exactly the type of woman Sam needs."

Marjorie's look must have revealed her disbelief.

"A doctor needs a woman in his life who has a strong and independent nature. So many other people are constantly making demands on his time and his energy that sometimes there's not much left for anyone else. Above anything else, Sam needs a respite from the demands of work. For men like Sam and Bernie, death is the enemy, and they'll fight for a life with little or no thought to the physical or emotional cost to themselves."

Marjorie nibbled on her lower lip. "I hadn't thought about it like that." Betty had far more insight into Sam and Bernie's needs than she'd considered. All she herself knew was that she loved Sam Bretton and that she would consider herself the most fortunate woman in the world to be his wife.

"I know Bernie so well that I recognize the signs now. He doesn't need to say a word," Betty went on. "There's a look about him, a tiredness in his eyes and in the way he walks. All of those things tell me the kind of day he's had. He'll snap at me every now and again, but I forgive him because I know that he's probably had to tell someone's son or daughter that their mother won't be coming home from the hospital, or he's had to tell someone that their test results show they have cancer."

The thought of having to give someone such bad news tightened a knot of compassion in Marjorie's stomach.

"The last thing Bernie needs when he gets home is a list of demands from me. I wouldn't do that to him, and you wouldn't do that to Sam. He knows that, just the way I did as soon as we met."

A cool sip of her drink helped alleviate the tightness in Marjorie's throat. "I'm not the right woman for him. I don't deserve him."

Betty settled back in her chair and grinned. "He said almost exactly those same words to Bernie about you."

Marjorie blinked back her surprise and lowered her gaze. Her heart was filled with such misery that it was impossible to hold it all inside. She felt as though she would burst into tears in another minute.

"In fact, Bernie got so sick of hearing about you that he threatened to cancel their poker night if Sam didn't bring you around and introduce you."

"He must have taken him seriously, because we made a trip to the hospital Friday night."

"Bernie mentioned that, too. He told me that one look at the two of you together and he knew Sam had finally found the right woman. By the way, what is it about Sundays with you?"

"Sundays?"

"Yes. Sam phoned the other day and said the only time he can play poker from now on is Sunday afternoons."

Marjorie set the tall glass aside. "I work weekends. Hopefully someday I'll have Sundays free, but unfortunately, that probably won't be for some time yet."

Slowly Betty shook her head. "Believe me, when a man puts a woman before a long-standing poker game, he's serious about her."

Marjorie dropped her gaze and felt obliged to add, "We aren't serious. There are . . . problems."

"Wait and see, you'll settle them," Betty returned with unshakable confidence. "Sam's never been more ready for a wife than he is now."

Betty looked as if there were more she wanted to say, but before she could speak the sliding-glass door opened, and the two men, plus Kevin, walked into the house.

"Have you shown Marjorie my deck yet?" Bernie asked, beaming proudly.

Betty tried not to smile and failed. "It was the first thing I mentioned."

"I've been thinking that since this project went so well, I might try my hand at something a little more complicated."

Betty eyed her husband speculatively. "Like what?"

"An addition to the house," he said enthusiastically. "I could add on to the master bedroom. You've told me more than once that we need more closet space."

"Men," Betty groaned under her breath to Marjorie.

Sam walked over to Marjorie and sat beside her on the cushioned arm of the chair. He slipped his arm around her and cupped her shoulder.

A warm sensation filled her, and when she glanced up, she discovered Sam studying her. The love that filled her eyes was as unexpected as it was embarrassing.

His fingers bit into her shoulder as his gaze held hers. "I love you," he whispered. "We'll work this out."

"But, Sam . . ."

He bent down and kissed the top of her head. "Listen, we'll adopt kids. Older kids. Okay?"

Biting her bottom lip, Marjorie nodded.

Sam reached for her hand, lacing their fingers together, as though bonding them. She loved this man more than she ever thought it was possible to care about another human being.

Whatever problems they faced in the future could be conquered with Sam at her side. She was sure of it.

"When are we going to eat?" Kevin demanded, placing his hands on his hips. "I'm hungry." The little boy still wouldn't look directly at Marjorie, but that was an improvement from hiding his face in his mother's shoulder.

"The barbecue's already hot," Bernie told his wife. "I'll put the steaks on now, if everything else is ready."

"I want a hamburger," Kevin insisted.

"And you will get one," his father promised. "Come along, big boy, and you can help your dear ol' dad and Uncle Sam with the cooking."

"I'll start setting the table out on the deck," Betty said.

"Is there anything I can do?" Marjorie volunteered, quickly rising to her feet. "I brought some chips and dip, and some potato salad and sliced pickles." Sam caught her eye and revealed his surprise. "Deli made," she whispered, and he grinned back.

"Why don't you unpack those while I set the picnic table?" Betty suggested.

The others left to take care of things, and Marjorie found herself alone in the kitchen. She went over to the wicker basket and lifted the top. The potato salad was nestled between the pickle jar and the dip. As she was drawing it out, she heard a faint cry coming from the back of the house. She paused, then remembered Betty mentioning that the baby was napping. Marjorie went to the cabinet and proceeded to take out a couple of bowls and fill them with the potato salad and dip. To her chagrin, the infant's crying grew louder.

A quick check outside told her that Kevin had managed to distract his mother from the job of setting the table. The two of them were down on the beach. Betty was bent over, examining something Kevin was pointing to in the sand. The men were across the yard, busy chatting while Bernie stuck T-bone steaks onto the hot grill.

Before Marjorie could call out to anyone, the baby's cry split the air.

Alarmed, she ran into the back bedroom. The infant's cries died to a soft gurgle once she arrived.

"Hi," she said stiffly, standing a good three feet from the crib. "Your mother's on the beach. Would you like me to do something before she gets here?"

The baby's fists flailed in the air.

"Don't cry, okay? I'm sure she'll be back any minute."

The infant whimpered softly, and that alone was enough to cause Marjorie to take two steps in retreat. Once four-month-old Shelley realized she was losing her audience, she let go with another loud, earnest cry. She paused then, and inserted her fist into her mouth, sucking on it greedily.

"Oh, I get it," Marjorie murmured, retracing her steps. "You're hungry." She dropped her gaze to her own full breasts. "Sorry, I can't help you in that department." She smiled at her own joke.

The baby gurgled again, seemingly amused by Marjorie's attempt at humor.

"I suppose you've got a wet diaper, as well."

Shelley made a chuckling sound that cut straight through Marjorie's heart. "I don't think I'm going to be much help in that area, either. You see, babies and I don't get along."

Shelley giggled at that. Two arms and legs punched the air as she smiled up at Marjorie, who found she had somehow ended up leaning over the crib.

Sam came into the house and took a Pepsi from the refrigerator. He looked around for Marjorie, and when he didn't find her, he opened the front door, thinking she might have forgotten something in the car. She wasn't there, either. Concerned now, he started for the deck to find Betty.

A faint noise stopped him. It was almost indiscernible at first, so faint that he didn't recognize it until he paused and listened intently. It was a baby cooing happily. He turned into the narrow hallway that led to Shelley Miller's bedroom and found Marjorie at last.

She was sitting in a rocking chair, cuddling Shelley in her arms as though she never intended to let the baby go. Tear tracks streaked her face, creating a bright sheen on her flushed cheeks. She sniffled loudly and wasn't able to keep her chin from trembling.

"Marjorie," he murmured, falling to his knees in front of her, hardly able to believe his eyes.

Nine

"**S**am," Marjorie whimpered softly. "I'm holding a baby."

"I see that, Kitten."

"She's so beautiful." A teardrop rolled down her face and landed ingloriously on Shelley's cotton jumpsuit. Cooing, the baby reached out to catch the next drop.

With the gentleness she had come to expect from him, Sam tenderly brushed his hand over her face, wiping away the tears. "I've never seen a woman as beautiful as you are right this minute."

"Sam, I didn't think I could get close to a baby. I didn't dare dream I'd feel this way—ever."

"I suspected as much," he countered, resisting the urge to wrap her and the baby in his arms and hold them both for eternity. "I prayed it would only be a matter of time until you recognized the mothering instincts were there. They have been all along."

"They're here, all right," she whispered, smiling and crying at once. "I feel so tender inside—I don't know how to describe it. Sam," she said, raising her eyes to meet his, "if I feel this strongly about a baby I barely know, I can't imagine how much love I'd have for one of my own."

"We'll discover that together, Kitten."

The tightness that jammed her throat made it impossible to speak. He was talking about them having children together, and although the thought frightened her, it thrilled her far more. She yearned to ask him if he meant it and to tell him she was willing, but every time she opened her mouth, all that came out were soft, strangled sounds. She managed to free one hand from beneath Shelley to caress the rugged line of Sam's jaw. Closing her eyes, she pressed her cheek against the side of his head.

He edged away from her, and their gazes met and held. The promise between them was more potent than anything she had ever known. She didn't need words to recognize what was in his heart; his feelings were all there for her to read in his eyes.

Sam bent toward her, and her dark eyes shimmered with an aching need for his love, a need that was echoed in his own heart. Her parted lips offered him an invitation he couldn't ignore.

This was the man she loved, the man who had filled her life with purpose and realized her dreams. He'd helped her to conquer her fears, laying the groundwork to destroy one after another with unlimited patience. He had gently proved to her that there wasn't anything they couldn't face together, nothing the force of their love couldn't overcome.

"Oh, Sam," she murmured, not wanting him to stop but knowing he had to. "The baby . . ."

He nodded and straightened, although his hands continued to grip her shoulders. The sight of Marjorie holding Shelley, knowing that someday she would be cradling their own baby, burned through him with the effectiveness of a hot knife. He felt weak with desire, weak and yet so powerful.

"Was that Shelley I heard?" Betty asked as she came into the small bedroom. If she noticed Marjorie's tears, or the fact that Sam was on the floor beside her and the baby, she didn't comment. "Thanks for getting her up for me," she said smoothly, and reached for her daughter.

With some reluctance, Marjorie surrendered the infant. "She's a wonderful baby."

"I'm convinced she gets that easygoing disposition from her mother," Betty said with a cheerful smile.

Bernie coughed in the background. "What about her old man?"

"*And* her father," Betty amended, and shared a secret smile, a wordless disclaimer, with Marjorie.

Marjorie managed to smother a laugh. When she stood, Sam slipped his arm around her waist and gently hugged her. "Do you think it'd be considered impolite to eat and run?" he whispered, so she alone could hear.

"Not if we're not too obvious," she said after a moment. As much as she liked Bernie and Betty, there were so many things she wanted to tell Sam, so much she yearned to share.

"It's selfish, I know, but I want to be alone with you," he added, after their hosts had taken the baby and headed into the other room.

Marjorie wanted it, too, and her gaze told him so.

"Soon," he promised.

"Soon," she agreed.

By the time they returned to the living room, Bernie had finished barbecuing the steaks. They all worked together, and within a few minutes the picnic table on the Millers' newly finished deck was set. The salads, potato chips and other dishes were brought out.

Sam sat beside Marjorie, and the four of them talked and joked throughout the meal. When they'd finished, Marjorie sat on the lounge chair and cradled Shelley as though she'd been handling babies all her life. Every now and again she felt Sam's loving gaze, and they shared a special look that said more than mere words.

"I can't get over the way Shelley's taken to you," Betty commented, joining her. The weather had cleared as the lazy afternoon sun burned off the clouds.

"Marjorie's a natural with children," Sam said proudly. "I don't suppose she told you, but she nearly raised her sister."

"Sam!" she cried, embarrassed. "I'm not a natural at all."

A sharp shake of his head discounted that notion. "She's been around children most of her life," he added. Studying her, his mouth curved into a faint smile. He had prayed that, given time, she would recognize most of her fears as unfounded. The mothering instinct was as strong in her as it was in any woman, only Marjorie had failed to recognize it.

She held out her hand to him, and he gripped it firmly. In many ways he understood her better than she did herself. Sometime, somewhere, she'd done something very good in her life to deserve this man.

Late Saturday afternoon Marjorie had changed her outfit twice, unable to decide what to wear. Sam wanted her to meet his parents. Although she had readily agreed to dinner with his family, she was a nervous wreck. She'd been in and out of clothes faster than a quick-change artist. Worse, she was convinced that his mother was bound to disapprove of her lack of domestic skills, though Sam himself had dismissed that fear.

Five minutes before he was due to arrive, she chose a soft knit dress Jody had suggested when she made a frantic call to Portland. It was more casual than anything she wore to work, and she was doubtful. This meeting was so important, and she longed to make a good impression so as not to embarrass Sam.

She needn't have worried. His parents stepped onto the

front porch when he pulled into the driveway, and they looked as anxious as she felt.

"Don't be so nervous," Sam said, reaching over to squeeze her clenched fist. "They're going to love you."

"Oh, Sam, I hope so." She forced herself to relax, uncoiling her fingers and flexing them a couple of times to restore the blood flow. Normally she was able to disguise any uneasiness, but the prospect of meeting his family had completely unnerved her.

"Mom and Dad have been waiting years to meet you."

"I only hope I'm not a disappointment."

"You won't be, Kitten, I promise."

Sam's mother came down the front steps and walked toward the car. Marjorie studied the streaks of silver in the older woman's dark hair, then shifted her gaze to the classic profile. None of the other woman's features resembled Sam's. Not the faint gleam in her dark eyes, not the warm, friendly glow in her complexion. Yet if Marjorie had met her in a crowded room, she would have known instantly that this woman was his mother.

Sam helped Marjorie out of the car and slipped his arm over her shoulders.

"Mom and Dad," he said proudly, "this is Marjorie Majors. Marjorie, my parents, Roy and Irene Bretton."

"I hope you don't mind us coming out to greet you like this, but Roy and I couldn't wait another minute." Irene took both of Marjorie's hands in her own and nodded approvingly. "I can't tell you how very pleased we are to meet you—at last."

"Thank you. The pleasure is all mine." Marjorie felt stiff and awkward. The inside of her mouth was dry, yet her hands were moist. Sam's warmth was the only thing that kept the chill of anxiety from seeping all the way through her bones. She had so little to impress this family with—no real background or prestigious relatives. She could offer them nothing but her love for their son.

"Please come inside. Dinner's almost ready," Irene invited, leading the way. "I fixed your favorite, Sam—friend chicken, potatoes and gravy, with my homemade biscuits."

"Mom's a wonderful cook," Sam explained, grinning down at her. He hoped Marjorie knew that he wasn't concerned about her ability to burn water.

Marjorie's return smile was feeble at best.

"I'll give you all his favorite recipes if you want them," Irene offered Marjorie.

She nodded her thanks, knowing it would be a complete waste of time, but she hated to disillusion Sam's mother so quickly. Later she would explain that her presence in the kitchen invariably resulted in a fiasco, that when she turned on the stove, the entire Tacoma Fire Department went on standby.

"I better go check on the chicken," Sam's mother said, as soon as they entered the house.

The luscious smells that greeted them could have rivaled a four-star restaurant. It was obvious that Sam had underplayed his mother's culinary abilities.

"Let me help," Marjorie offered hurriedly.

"Nonsense, you're our guest." Irene gestured toward the sofa. "Sit down and make yourself at home. I insist."

Marjorie smiled and tried to relax. Sam's parents were exactly as she'd expected: warm and sincere.

She lowered herself onto the wide sofa. An afghan, crocheted in fall colors of gold, orange and brown, was spread across the back.

Sam claimed the seat next to her and reached for her hand. His father saw the gesture and grinned proudly, as though he were personally responsible for bringing the two of them together.

A moment later Irene Bretton returned. "Dinner will be ready in another fifteen minutes," she announced, and took the chair beside Sam's father.

Roy Bretton looked all the more pleased. "Good. We have enough time for a glass of wine first." He eyed his son intently, as though he expected Sam to make some momentous proclamation.

"Dad patronizes several local vineyards," Sam explained, ignoring his father's look.

"There are a dozen or so excellent wines bottled right here in Washington state," Roy added, filling in the conversation. "I found another superior winery recently, near Bonney Lake."

Marjorie nodded and started to relax against the back of the sofa. There wasn't anything to be nervous about, especially since Sam's parents appeared to be even more anxious to make a good impression than she was.

"Give me a hand, son," Roy said, standing.

"Sure."

The two men left the room, leaving Marjorie and Irene alone.

"Sam has spoken fondly of you on several occasions," his mother said, clearly seeking a way to start the conversation. "His father and I are very proud of him."

"You have every right to be."

"It will take a special woman to share his life."

Marjorie dropped her lashes, fearing that Sam's mother was suggesting that she wasn't the right one for their only son. Her heart pounded wildly, filled with doubts.

"I knew from the moment he mentioned your name that you were special to him." Irene smiled and smoothed her hand across her skirt in a nervous gesture. "A mother knows these things about her children. For instance, I knew long before Sam—or even his father—did that he would be a physician. Roy was sure Sam's career would involve animals. He had pets from the time he was little and was forever collecting more."

"He's the kindest, most generous man I've ever known."

"He always was," Irene said. "I swear, that boy brought home more stray dogs than the city pound ever collected. His heart would melt over things that you and I would hardly notice." She warmed to her subject and scooted forward in the chair, her face bright with love for her son. "I remember one time—he must have been around ten or twelve—anyway, he found an orphaned kitten in a rainstorm, a sickly, weak, half-drowned little thing. By the time he got her home, she was more dead than alive."

Marjorie's smile went weak. Sam called her Kitten, had for weeks now, and like the stray cat he'd found in his youth, she, too, was an orphan. Little things played back in her mind. Minor incidents came into focus. Puzzle pieces fell into place, painting a clear picture. Sam was a rescuer, always had been and always would be. He'd seen it as his duty to take care of her the night she went into surgery.

When they'd first started dating, he had tried several times to rescue her. He'd wanted to step in when Al had cheated her out of her commission. He'd bought the Mercedes more for her benefit than his own. Now that she was seeing him regularly, she knew that he had a perfectly serviceable car and had no reason to purchase another.

"What happened with the kitten?" She was almost afraid to ask.

"He nursed her back to health. You should have seen that silly cat. She was the most prickly, bad-tempered thing— wouldn't let anyone near her. You'd think she would have been more appreciative of everything he had done for her."

The knot in Marjorie's stomach tightened to a punishing level of discomfort. After her surgery she'd lashed out at Sam at every turn. She'd even accused him of getting a kickback from the hospital for every patient he forced to stay. At least she'd felt guilty later and had apologized.

"He . . . Sam kept the cat, though, right?" she asked, sure she already knew the answer.

"Named her Kitten and ignored her bad moods."

"Didn't he get tired of her moods and lose interest after a while?" Once again, she was certain of the answer, and her stomach sank.

Irene nodded. "It was bound to happen. Summer came, and Sam had his friends. But he kept her, and she became a regular member of the family. I remember the funniest thing about that cat. The first time Kitten became a mother, she wouldn't let anyone close to her except Sam. He was with her when she gave birth. Years later, when she died, Sam was in his first year of high school, and he was real broken up for a long time afterward. But he got over her, and he's owned several cats since."

Marjorie struggled to disguise her distress. All his talk about accepting her as she was, loving her and needing her, was a lie. Sam hadn't accepted her. He never had. To him, she was a pitiful, lost soul, helpless and in need of being rescued. From what his mother had told her and from what she'd seen herself, she was forced to admit that Sam had yet to accept how truly independent she was. And like the kitten from his youth, Sam would eventually replace her, too. His interest would wander, and his feelings for her would change.

A numb, tingling sensation spread to her arms and legs. She felt physically ill along with being emotionally distraught.

How she made it through dinner was a mystery to her, but somehow she managed to say and do what was expected of her as though nothing were wrong. She answered his parents' questions and responded appropriately to what was going on around her. Yet all the while the world was crashing down around her feet.

At one point Sam's father commented that she didn't eat enough to keep a bird alive, and Sam responded that he planned on taking care of her from now on. It had taken every ounce of composure she possessed not to inform him that she was perfectly capable of taking care of herself. She didn't need him to see to her meals or ensure that she made enough money to pay the rent or anything else.

By the time they left, she had never been so grateful to get away from anywhere in her life. The sun had set, and dusk had settled over the landscape. Grateful for the cover of impending night, she hoped that Sam wouldn't notice how pale she was or how sick to her stomach she felt.

Neither spoke as they rode back to her apartment, and when they arrived, he climbed out of the car and walked her to her door.

"Invite me inside," he said.

She felt so unsure, so unsettled. Still, she couldn't resist him, so she nodded and unlocked the front door. "I'll make coffee," she murmured, heading toward the kitchen.

Sam followed her. She'd been unusually quiet on the ride back, but then again, so had he. All evening he'd been mentally rehearsing everything he wanted to say to her. It wasn't every day a man asked a woman to be his wife, and he wanted to make this moment special.

Briefly he toyed with the idea of pulling the diamond out of his pocket and just handing it to her. But that seemed so abrupt, especially when there was so much he longed to tell her. First he planned on saying how loving her had changed his life. Since he'd met her, he felt totally alive. He loved her—that much was obvious and had been for weeks—but simply telling her that he loved her was too inadequate, especially since there was so much more to the way he felt than mere words could express.

Marjorie's hands shook as she turned on the faucet to fill the teakettle. Her back was to him as she spoke. "I like your parents."

"They like you, too, Kitten. I knew they would."

She flinched. "Why do you call me that?"

"Kitten?"

Nodding, she set the kettle on the stove.

"I'm not exactly sure," Sam responded. "I had a cat named that once."

"The one you found in a rainstorm?"

He glanced up, surprised. "Yes. How'd you know?"

"Your mother mentioned it." She swallowed tightly, still unable to turn and face him. "She told me what a prickly, ungrateful cat she was."

Sam chuckled. "She came around in time."

"Like I did," Marjorie said in a wobbly but controlled voice.

"You?" Sam asked, surprised. "I thought we were talking about Kitten."

"We are!" She whirled around to face him, her hands braced against the counter behind her. "Me. *I'm* Kitten."

Sam looked stunned. "That's ridiculous!"

"Tell me, Sam, why did you buy the Mercedes? You didn't need another car."

He shifted uncomfortably. "No, but my other one's a couple of years old now and . . ."

"And you wanted me to collect the commission from the sale."

"All right," he said, struggling not to respond to the anger in her voice. "That's true, but I was looking for a way to see you again, and buying the car seemed a perfect solution."

"It was an expensive one, too, don't you think?"

"I didn't care."

"This may surprise you, Sam Bretton, but *I* care. In fact, I care a great deal. I don't want your charity. The next time you want to throw money away, give it to cancer research."

"It wasn't charity!" he shouted.

Marjorie ignored him, clenching her hands into tight fists at her sides. "What was it about me that attracted you in the first place?" She didn't give him a chance to respond as she hurried on. "There's nothing that makes me any different than a thousand other women who parade through your office."

Drawing a calming breath, Sam waited a moment before answering. "This conversation isn't getting us anywhere. I suggest—"

"You can't answer me, can you, Sam?"

"I think it would be best if I left and gave you a chance to calm down."

"I don't need any time!" she shouted, and to her horror, her voice cracked.

Unable to see her cry and not do something to ease the pain, Sam took a step toward her and held out his arms. "Kitten, listen . . ."

"Don't call me that!" she cried, pointing at him and retreating several steps. "Or I'll . . . I'll . . ." She couldn't think of anything to threaten him with. "Or I'll scream," she said finally.

"Or worse yet, you might cook for me."

Marjorie's eyes widened with the pain his words inflicted. "Just leave, Sam. The next time I need someone to rescue me, I'll give you a call. But don't wait around for me to phone. It might astonish you to learn that I'm a capable human being."

His frustration was nearly overwhelming, and Sam paused to rub his hand along the back of his neck. "I didn't mean that wisecrack about your cooking."

Her back stiffened with resolve. "No? Well, I meant every word *I* said," she responded coolly, struggling to maintain her crumbling composure.

"No, you don't. You love me. You need me."

He was so confident, so sure of himself, that Marjorie wanted to kick herself for being so gullible. The signs had been there from the beginning, and she'd refused to see them, refused to believe them. Her love for Sam had blinded her to the truth.

She was a charity case to him in the same way that kitten had been all those years ago. He might believe he felt something for her now, but time would prove him wrong. He honestly believed she couldn't get by without him.

"Marjorie, I'm not exactly sure what's going on in that wonderfully crazy mind of yours, but if you want me to tell you that I associated you with that lost kitten, then I'll admit as much—but only in the beginning."

The room swayed, and she reached out a hand in an effort to maintain her balance. Briefly she closed her eyes. "You admit it?"

"Yes. But only in the beginning," he repeated softly. "You were so fragile, so afraid, and there was no one there for you when you were ill."

"Do I hear violin music in the background?" she taunted. It dented her considerable pride to hear Sam refer to her in those terms, though, to be fair, she remembered how she'd clung to him, begging him to stay with her. That had been a low point in her life, and now he was using it against her. Worse, he hadn't an inkling of why she was so offended, and she'd thought he knew her so well.

"Later I was attracted to your courage," he added, ignoring her gibe. "And your pride and your candor. I discovered that I spent half my time thinking about you. When you were discharged, I racked my brain for days trying to think of a way to see you again. I wanted to help you—and I finally came up with the idea of buying the car. By then I knew you were special."

"As I explained before, I don't need your charity."

"It wasn't charity, not in the way you think!" Sam shouted, losing his patience. "The only thing I did was help you, and you make it sound as if I've committed some terrible crime."

As far as Marjorie was concerned, he had.

"I was in love with you then—only I didn't know it. And now I know I love you. More than I thought it was possible to love another human being. If you don't want me to call you *kitten* again, then fine, I won't."

A tense silence wrapped itself around them. She couldn't believe that she was having the most important discussion of her life while standing in her kitchen waiting for the kettle to boil.

Sam's level gaze trapped hers from across the room. His anger had vanished as quickly as it had come, leaving his face an impassive mask of pride. Abruptly, he spun away, his impatient strides carrying him to the door. He paused and turned toward her.

"There's a diamond ring in my pocket, Marjorie. I'd planned to ask you to be my wife."

Calmly she met his gaze. She wanted Sam. The temptation to swallow her doubts and dismiss her pride nearly overwhelmed her. She would have, too, if she hadn't remembered what his mother had said about him losing interest in the kitten after a while. He had his friends, his mother had said. There was nothing to guarantee that anything would be different when it came to *her*, that within a few months he wouldn't regret having married her.

"I think you already know my answer to that," she said, looking everywhere but at the huge diamond he now held in his hand.

"You're right—I do know." With that, he slipped the ring back inside his pocket. Then he turned and walked away from her in lightning-quick strides.

The door slammed. Feeling incredibly weak, Marjorie cupped her hands over her face and sagged against the counter.

Ten

Confounded, Marjorie stepped out of her manager's office and paused, her hand lingering on the doorknob. Her mind was racing with the details of her conversation with Bud.

"Well, what happened?" Lydia wanted to know. She walked around the customer-service counter and stood expectantly in front of her friend. When Marjorie didn't immediately respond, Lydia waved her hand in front of her bemused face.

The action captured Marjorie's attention. "I got a promotion," she said, shaking her head, still befuddled. Starting the first of the month, her Sundays would be free. For weeks her schedule had conflicted with Sam's. Now, when it didn't matter if she had the day off, her Sundays were open. Life was filled with such ironies.

"A promotion!" Lydia cried. "Cool!"

"I can't believe it myself," Marjorie returned, and shook her head in an attempt to dispel her pensive mood. She'd been numb for days; nothing seemed to penetrate the dull ache that had ruled her thoughts and actions since she'd last seen Sam. Not even this promotion, which would have given her plenty of reason to celebrate a week earlier, could penetrate the fog of her sadness.

"What did Bud say to Al Swanson?" Lydia asked next, her eyes wide with curiosity.

"I'm not sure . . . he's still in there." Marjorie had noted how disgruntled he'd looked when Bud announced her promotion. That alone had been worth the apprehension she'd suffered all morning before the meeting.

"And you thought you were going to get fired." Lydia flashed her a triumphant smile and shook her head knowingly. "What did I tell you?"

"Not to worry," Marjorie quoted back to her friend in a monotone, and rolled her eyes toward the ceiling.

Lydia was obviously pleased that her words had proven to be prophetic. "Now all I have to do is straighten out this mess between you and Dr. Sam."

Marjorie stiffened at the mention of his name. "Don't even try," she said forcefully. "As far as I'm concerned, the subject of Sam Bretton is off-limits."

"What did he do, for heaven's sake?"

"Lydia, I already told you, I refuse to discuss the matter!" Purposeful strides carried her across the showroom floor. Once again she was running away, doing anything she could to escape the emotional pain that blossomed when anyone asked her about Sam. Before she'd met him, she had prided herself on her ability to confront unpleasantness. Since her last evening with him, she found it easier to hide than deal with her feelings.

Undeterred, Lydia followed her friend. "Hey, we're talking about the man who had you waltzing around here with your head in the clouds not more than a week ago. Something happened, and I want to know what it was."

"Lydia, please, just drop it." The pain was so fresh that even hearing someone casually mention him produced an ache that came all the way from her soul.

She walked into her office and braced her hands against the side of her desk, inhaling deeply, praying the action would alleviate the surge of emotional pain. She'd done a great deal of thinking since the last time she'd seen Sam. As much as she hated to admit it, she needed him. The realization that she depended on him hadn't been easy to swallow. She loved him, but she hated to think she was nothing but the subject of his charity.

Following close on Marjorie's heels, Lydia came into the office and shut the door. "Listen, I've tried to be a good friend and—"

"I know," Marjorie said, cutting her off. "And I appreciate that, but there are some things that are better left alone." She couldn't deal with Lydia's questions *and* answer her own. She whirled around to confront her friend. "And this is one of them."

Lydia hesitated, then. "If you'd just tell me what he did that was so terrible, then I could hate him, too."

Marjorie could deal with any multitude of problems—irate customers, unreasonable loan officers, cheating salesmen—but her friend's persistent inquisitiveness had finally worn her down.

She crossed her arms over her chest and exhaled a slow, laborious breath. "He called me *kitten*."

Before she could go on, Lydia's mouth fell open in astonished disbelief. "That was it?"

"No. He asked me to marry him, too."

A pregnant pause followed as Lydia's eyes narrowed in speculative scorn. "You're right," she finally said in mock disgust. "The man should be sent before a firing squad. He wanted to marry you. Well, of all the nerve!"

All Marjorie could manage was a sharp nod.

Lydia ran her fingertips over the top of the desk, avoiding eye contact. "Marjorie . . . when was the last time you had a decent vacation?"

"About ten years ago. Listen, I can see what you're getting at. You think I've gone off the deep end, and maybe I have. I don't know anymore. I . . . turned Sam down, but my reasons are my own. Just accept that I know what I'm doing, and it's for the best, and kindly leave it at that."

"I can't believe you turned Dr. Sam down." Lydia glared at her as though Marjorie should be psychoanalyzed that very minute. "The most marvelous man I've ever known, and he wanted to marry you and . . ."

"And I refused him," Marjorie said flatly.

"You're not going to see him again?"

"No . . . I don't think so."

"And that's the way you want it?" The incredulousness was back in Lydia's voice, raising it half an octave.

Marjorie couldn't answer. Lying by saying "yes" to Lydia was one thing, but trying to fool herself was another. She was slowly shriveling up without Sam. Her days felt like empty, wasted years. The hours dragged, especially when she was home alone. The walls seemed to close in around her, suffocating her. Normally she enjoyed her own company, but since she'd been without Sam, even the everyday routines seemed useless. The happy expectancy was missing from her life, as was the excitement. Without him, her future looked astonishingly bleak.

It would have been far better, she decided, if she'd never met the man. Again and again she'd gone over the events of that last evening with his family, seeking a solution that would salvage both his pride and her own, some misunderstanding about the way he saw her. But he had made that impossible. He'd admitted openly that he pitied her, and she was scared to death of the fact that she needed him. What a mess this had turned out to be.

Lydia's steady gaze lacked any sign of sympathy. "It's your decision."

Marjorie's gaze held her friend's. "I know."

Lydia headed out of the office. "Be miserable, then. See if I care."

With Lydia gone, the emptiness inside the small office was oppressive. Dejected, Marjorie sat at her desk and read over some paperwork she'd been putting off. However, nothing held her attention for long, and within moments she was silently staring at the walls, her thoughts focused on Sam.

Suddenly Lydia burst into her office and excitedly clapped her hands. She marched around Marjorie's desk to confront her face to face.

"Lydia! What's going on?"

"You're going to love this. I certainly do."

Sam. Marjorie's heart rocketed into space. He'd come for her. He'd decided that his life would be an empty wasteland without her. He'd realized he honestly needed her.

"Sam?" Marjorie asked expectantly, half rising from her chair. "He's here?" Oh, please, God, she prayed, let him be here.

"Sam? Heavens no." Lydia gave her an odd look and shook her head. "It's Al Swanson. Bud just gave him the ax."

"Bud fired Al Swanson? You mean . . . he's leaving?"

"From the way he's packing up his things, I'd say he can't wait to get out of here. He'll be gone in five minutes."

"Oh." Marjorie was surprised by how little elation she felt at the news. A week ago, her behavior would have rivaled her friend's. Now all she felt was a cloying sense of disappointment that Sam hadn't come for her. Discouraged, she reclaimed her seat.

"Apparently," Lydia went on to explain, "one of Al's schemes backfired on him. Bud found out about it, and Al's out of here."

Marjorie had known from the first that Al was his own worst enemy, and that, given enough rope, he would do himself in without any help from anyone else.

Crossing her arms, a subdued Lydia paused to study her friend. "You thought Sam had come to talk to you?"

Marjorie's fingers tightened around the pencil she was holding; it was a miracle it didn't snap in two. "It wouldn't have done any good."

"Hey, he could have withdrawn his marriage proposal. That might have settled things, don't you think?"

Marjorie shook her head. "Lydia, please. I don't want to talk about him."

"Hurt too much?" her friend asked, lowering her voice into a soft, coaxing tone.

The answer was so obvious that the question didn't require a response. Marjorie was lost without Sam, but she would get over him in time. The only question that remained was how long it would take. A lifetime, her heart told her, but she refused to listen.

Two days later, a cocky smile curving her lips, Lydia sauntered into Marjorie's office, her hands clasped behind her back.

Pretending she'd been interrupted, Marjorie glanced up from the report she'd been trying to read. "You look like the cat that just swallowed the canary."

"Really?" Lydia swayed back and forth on the balls of her feet. "I have a tasty tidbit of information, if you're interested."

"About Al Swanson?" The details of what had happened between the salesman and the manager had been the favorite topic of conversation with the other staff members ever since his firing. The rumors had been flying around the dealership like combat planes, dropping bombs of speculation.

Lydia shook her head. "What I have to tell you involves a certain doctor, but according to you, I'm not supposed to mention his name."

"Sam?" Marjorie's heart stopped, then pounded frantically against her ribs.

"The one and only."

The temptation to strangle Lydia was powerful. Marjorie returned her gaze to the report. "I refuse to play your games."

"Okay," Lydia announced with typical nonchalance. "If you don't care, then far be it from me to announce that the very doctor in question happens to be in this building at this precise minute."

Marjorie's gaze froze. "Here?"

"Not more than twenty yards from this office door, if you must know."

The papers Marjorie had been holding slipped from her fingers and fell to the top of her desk. Uncaring, she left the scattered sheets there.

"But you are apparently over Dr. Sam," Lydia commented, studying the ends of her polished nails, "so it would be best if you stayed holed up in here and did your best to pretend he isn't anywhere around."

Without realizing what she was doing, Marjorie stood, her knees barely strong enough to keep her upright.

"I don't mind telling you," Lydia said, grinning, "I'm having a difficult time not giving Dr. Sam a piece of my mind. The man is obviously a degenerate."

Marjorie blinked, sure she'd misunderstood her friend. "Sam's nothing of the sort."

"Imagine Dr. Sam wanting to get married," Lydia continued with a sigh. "Doesn't he realize how old-fashioned that is? A woman should live with a man fifty, maybe sixty, years before making that kind of commitment. Dr. Sam expects too much."

As best she could, Marjorie ignored her friend's sarcasm. "Sam's here?"

Smiling unabashedly, Lydia nodded. "You'll see him the minute you walk out of this office."

Nothing could have kept Marjorie where she was.

As Lydia had claimed, Sam was in the dealership, standing at the service counter. For a solid minute Marjorie was unable to breathe. He looked tired, overworked, hassled. He wasn't taking care of himself, and he looked as though he'd lost weight. As if drawn by a magnet, she walked to his side.

"Sam." His name came from her lips without her even being aware she'd spoken out loud.

He tossed a look over his shoulder and froze when his eyes met hers.

"Hello," she said in an effort to avoid calling attention to herself. "How are you?"

"Fine," he answered stiffly. "And you?"

"Okay . . . wonderful, actually."

"Yeah, me too."

A tense silence followed while she struggled for something more to say. Her gaze fell to the service desk. "Is something wrong with the car?"

He shook his head. "It's time for an oil change."

The tense quiet returned.

". . . babies?"

". . . work?"

They spoke simultaneously.

Sam gestured with his hand. "You first."

"I got a promotion." She didn't mention that her Sundays would be free from now on; she couldn't see the point.

"Congratulations."

She attempted a smile. "Thank you." In the ensuing silence, she nodded at him, indicating it was his turn. "You look like you've been busy."

He nodded. "I delivered another set of twins last week."

"Girls?"

"No, both boys. Identical."

"Oh." For the life of her, Marjorie couldn't think of another thing to say. Small talk had always been her forte, and there were a thousand things she wanted to tell him but couldn't.

Seeing him like this made her feel so unsure, so uncertain. Her mind stumbled over her thoughts. "Kitten" wasn't such a terrible name, she realized. So she'd reminded him of a pathetic cat; no doubt that was the way she'd looked when she visited his office that first time. She loved the way his pet name for her sounded on his lips, almost as though the word were a gentle caress. So she needed him. That wasn't such a terrible thing. It was time—more than time—that she faced the fact that needing someone was normal and right. It was on the tip of her tongue to tell him so when Bud strolled past.

"There's a customer here to see you."

Feeling guilty, although she didn't know why, she nodded and glanced over her shoulder. "I guess I'd better get back to work," she said, getting back to Sam.

He didn't respond. "I suppose you should."

"Goodbye, Sam."

"Goodbye, Kitten." The instant the word slipped out of his mouth, he wanted to take it back. "I apologize. I didn't mean to say that."

"Don't worry. It's not such a bad name."

"Only it's not right for you," he said, his gaze unwavering.

Marjorie wasn't in any position to argue with him; holding back tears required all the energy she could muster. "Right," she answered weakly, giving up the fight.

Without looking back, she headed outside, where the insurance salesman she'd talked to earlier in the week was waiting for her. As she walked out the door, she heard Sam ask what time he could expect his car to be finished. By the time she returned, he was gone.

Lydia seemed to be waiting for her when she got back inside, though. Her friend came over to meet her. "Well, what did he have to say?"

"The insurance salesman?" Marjorie asked, playing stupid.

"Of course not. Sam!"

"Nothing."

"But he must have said something! You two talked for three minutes. I timed you. You must have gotten something settled in that amount of time."

"Unfortunately, we didn't."

"Marjorie, this craziness has got to stop. I talked to Mary, Dr. Sam's receptionist, and she told me he hasn't been the same from the moment you two split up. He's melancholy and moody, and everyone knows that's not the least bit like him."

"He'll get over it," Marjorie said flippantly.

"Maybe," Lydia returned with barely controlled skepticism. "But will you?"

Her friend's words echoed in her mind for the remainder of the afternoon. Lydia was right. Her world was crumbling at her feet, and she was too proud, too stubborn, to do anything about it. Just seeing Sam again had proven that. She was ruining her life over something incredibly silly. She'd overreacted and behaved stupidly, and the time had come to own up to that.

Filled with determination, she marched over to the service department.

"What time did you tell Dr. Bretton his car would be ready?"

Pete, the head mechanic, who had been with Dixon Motors for ten years, flipped the pages of the service book. "After three. As I recall, he told me he wouldn't be in to pick it up until six."

Marjorie nodded, pleased. "Have you finished with it?"

"Yeah. It seemed pointless to change the oil on a vehicle

that doesn't even have a thousand miles on it. But we did it—couldn't see the point in arguing with him."

That small bit of information sent Marjorie's spirits soaring. Sam must have used the Mercedes as an excuse to see her. Her relief felt like a thirst-quenching rain after a long August drought. "Could I have his keys, please?"

The mechanic gave her an odd look. "You want Dr. Bretton's car keys?"

"Right. When he comes in, send him to my office."

The barrel-chested mechanic scratched the side of his head. "If that's the way you want it, Ms. Majors."

"I do. Thanks, Pete."

The remainder of the afternoon crept by. At precisely six, Marjorie was waiting in her office. Sam didn't keep her in suspense long.

He knocked once and stepped inside. "What's this about you having my car keys?" he demanded, his temper showing. He'd been a fool to think that coming to the car dealership would solve anything between them. She wanted blood, and he wasn't about to give it to her. The more he reviewed their earlier conversation, the angrier he became. That wounded, hurt look in her eyes had accused him of greatly wronging her. All he'd ever wanted was to marry her and make her happy, and she'd reacted as though he'd insulted her.

Marjorie blinked. "Yes, I have your keys."

He held out his open palm. "I'd like them back."

"Of course." She remained outwardly calm, but adrenaline was racing through her system as though she were running the Boston Marathon. "I have a couple of questions first, if you don't mind answering them."

He made a show of glancing at his watch. "Make it quick—I have an appointment."

"Oh, Sam, you always were such a poor liar."

He snapped his jaw closed and pulled out a chair. "As it happens, I do have to be someplace in less than an hour. But obviously my word isn't to be trusted."

"This will only take a minute."

He crossed his legs, hoping to give the impression of indifference. Nothing could be further from the truth, but anger was his only defense against Marjorie. It was either yell at her or yank her into his arms and kiss some sense into her.

Her fingers closed around the cold metal keys. "It's about that ring you offered me."

Sam shot to his feet. "Listen, Marjorie, we're talking about our lives here, not a car deal. There are no counteroffers."

"Yes, I know."

"The offer stands as it was."

"All right," she said, her voice strong and sure.

"All right, what?"

"I'll marry you."

If Sam had been flustered before, it was nothing compared to the confusion he felt now. "You will?"

"That is . . . if you still want me for your wife."

He ran his fingers through his hair. "What happened? Did you check around and discover that you couldn't make a better deal than me?"

"No . . . that's not it at all." This was going so much worse than she'd hoped.

He eyed her speculatively. "I'll call you *kitten* any time I please!"

She nodded, because speaking would have been impossible.

"We won't have a long engagement, either. I want us married before the end of the summer."

She met his fiery gaze with feigned calm, then answered him with a quick nod of her head.

He mellowed somewhat and lowered his voice. "Do you have to check this out with your manager?"

"No."

His gaze moved to the shimmering moistness of her lips. He was dying to hold her, starved for a taste of her, and just looking at her disturbed his concentration. His control was slipping fast. Walking around to her side of the desk, he reached for her. Hungrily his mouth devoured hers as he pulled her hard against the solid length of his body so she would know how desperate he'd been without her. His hand roamed possessively over her, molding her to him, uncaring that anyone outside the office might be watching.

Only partially satisfied, Sam dragged his mouth from her, his hunger sated for the moment.

The iron band of his arms held her a willing prisoner. "Sam, I love you . . . I'm sorry to be so insecure. I don't know what made me say those things. It's just that I've been on my own so long that it hurt my pride to think you pitied me, and I . . ."

"It doesn't matter, Kitten," he said, his voice husky and thick against her hair.

Overcome by a searing happiness, she laughed breathlessly. The sound was short and sweet. "I can't imagine why I objected so strongly when I love the name *kitten*."

"Good, because I meant what I said about calling you that."

Her arms circled his waist, and her heart swelled. She was home, truly home, for the first time since she'd lost her parents.

"We're getting married as soon as I can arrange it."

She grinned, more than agreeable to any terms he wanted. "Any Sunday."

He paused and looked deep into her misty, diamond-bright eyes, letting her words sink in. "You got a promotion?"

She nodded and started to say more when Lydia burst into her office.

Her friend's mouth dropped open as she stopped abruptly. "Oh . . . hi."

"Hi," Marjorie answered for them.

"Have you two patched things up?" Lydia asked casually.

"It's either that or we have a peculiar way of arguing," Sam answered, and chuckled softly.

"So are you two getting married or what?"

"We're getting married," Marjorie said, beaming.

It looked for a moment as though Lydia doubted them. "When?" she asked speculatively.

Sam and Marjorie shared a lingering look. "Any Sunday," they answered in unison.

★ ★ ★ ★ ★

The Playboy and the Widow

To Jayne Krentz—
friend, fellow aerobic exerciser,
restaurant connoisseur

One

"Mom, I don't have any lunch money."

Diana Collins stuck her head out from the cupboard beneath the kitchen sink and wiped the perspiration from her brow. "Bring me my purse."

"Mother," eight-year-old Katie whined dramatically, "I'm going to miss my bus."

"All right, all right." Hurriedly Diana scooted out from her precarious position and reached for a rag to dry her hands.

"We're out of hair spray," Joan, Katie's elder sister, cried. "You can't honestly expect me to go to school without hair spray."

"Honey, you're in fifth grade, not high school. Your hair looks terrific."

Joan glared at her mother as though the thirty-year-old were completely dense. "I need hair spray if it's going to stay this way."

Diana shook her head. "Did you look in my bathroom?"

"Yes. There wasn't any."

"Check the towel drawer."

"The towel drawer?"

Diana shrugged. "I was hiding it."

Joan frowned and gave her mother a disapproving look. "Honestly!"

"Mom, my lunch money," Katie cried, waving her mother's purse under Diana's nose.

With quick fingers, Diana located five quarters and promptly handed them to her younger daughter.

Five minutes later the front screen door slammed, and Diana sighed her relief. No sound was ever more pleasant than that of her daughters darting off to meet the school bus. The silence was too inviting to resist, and Diana poured herself a cup of coffee and sat at the kitchen table, savoring the quiet. She grabbed her laptop and, automatically went in search of part-time positions. It was tempting, although Diana wanted to wait until the girls were a bit older. Before Stan had died, there'd been few problems with money. Now, however, they cropped up daily, and Diana was torn with the desire to remain at home with her children, or seek the means to provide extra income. For three years Diana had robbed Peter to pay Paul, juggling funds from one account to another. Between the social security check, the insurance check and the widow's fund from Stan's job, she and the girls were barely able to eke by. She cut back on expenses where she could, but recently her options had become more limited. There were plenty of macaroni-and-cheese dinners now, especially toward the end of the month. Diana could always ask for help from her family, but she was hesitant. Her parents lived in Wichita and were concerned enough about her living alone with the girls in far-off Seattle. She simply didn't want to add to their worries.

"Pride cometh before a fall," she muttered into the steam rising from her coffee cup.

A loud knock against the screen was followed by a friendly call. "Yoo-hoo, Diana. It's Shirley," her neighbor called, letting herself in. "I don't suppose you've got another cup of that."

"Sure," Diana said, pleased to see her friend. "Help yourself."

Shirley took a cup down from the cupboard and poured her own coffee before joining Diana. "What's all that?" She cocked her head toward the sink.

"It's leaking again."

Shirley rolled her eyes. "Diana, you're going to have to get someone to look at it."

"I can do it," she said without a whole lot of confidence. "I watched a YouTube video online that tells you how to build a shopping center in your spare time. If I can repair the outlet in Joan's room, then I can figure out why the sink keeps leaking."

Shirley looked doubtful. "Honey, listen, you'd be better off to contact a plumber . . ."

"No way! Do you have any idea how much those guys charge? An appointment with a brain surgeon would be cheaper."

Shirley chuckled and took a sip of her coffee. "George could check it for you tonight after dinner."

"Shirley, no. I appreciate the offer, but . . ."

"George was Stan's friend."

"But that doesn't commit him to a lifetime of repairing leaking pipes."

"Would you stop being so darn proud for once?"

Funny how that word "pride" kept cropping up, Diana mused. "I'll call him," she conceded, "but only in case of an emergency."

"Okay. Okay."

Diana closed her laptop. "Let me save you the trouble of small talk. I know why you're here."

"You do?"

"You're dying to hear all the details of my hot date with the doctor I met through Parents Without Partners."

"Not many women have the opportunity to have dinner with Dr. Benjamin Spock."

A smile touched the edges of Diana's soft mouth. "He's a regular pediatrician, not Dr. Spock."

"Whoever!" Shirley said excitedly, and leaned closer. "All right, if you know what I want, then give me details!"

Diana swallowed uncomfortably. "I didn't go out with him."

"What?"

"My motives were all wrong."

Shirley slumped forward and buried her forehead against the heel of her hand. "I can't believe I'm hearing this. The most ideal husband material you've met dances into your life and you break the date!"

"I know," Diana groaned. "For days beforehand I kept thinking about how much money I could save on doctor bills if I were to get involved with this guy. It bothered me that I could be so mercenary."

"Don't you think any other woman would be thinking the same thing?"

Diana's fingers tightened around the mug handle. "Not unless they have two preteens."

"Don't be cute," Shirley said frowning. "I have trouble being angry with you when you're so witty."

Standing, Diana walked across the kitchen to refill her cup. "I don't know, Shirl."

"Know what?"

"If I'm ready to get involved in a relationship. My life is different now. When Stan and I decided to get married, it wasn't any surprise. We'd been going together since my junior year in high school and it seemed the thing to do. We hardly paused to give the matter more than a second thought."

"Who said anything about getting married?"

"But it's wrong to lead a man into believing I'm interested in a long-term relationship, when I don't know if I'll ever be serious about anyone again."

"You loved Stan that much?" Shirley inquired softly.

"I loved him, yes, and if he hadn't been killed, we probably would have lived together contentedly until a ripe old age. But things are different now. I have the girls to consider."

"What about you?"

"What about me?"

"Don't you need someone?"

"I—I don't know," Diana answered thoughtfully. The idea of spending her life alone produced a sharp pang of apprehension. She wanted to be a wife again, but was afraid remarriage would drastically affect her children's lives.

Shirley left soon afterward, and Diana rinsed the breakfast dishes and placed them inside the dishwasher. Her thoughts drifted to David Fisher, the man whose dinner invitation she'd rejected at the last minute. He obviously liked children or he would have chosen a different specialty. That was in his favor. She'd met him a couple of weeks before and listened over coffee to the gory details of his divorce. It was obvious to Diana that he was still in love with his ex-wife. Although Shirley viewed him as a fine catch, Diana wasn't interested.

Not until she closed the dishwasher did Diana notice the puddle of water on her kitchen floor. The sink again! It would be a simple matter of tightening the pipes if the garbage disposal didn't complicate the job.

Unfortunately the malfunctioning sink didn't heal itself, and after Diana picked up Joan from baseball practice, disaster struck.

"Mom," Katie cried, nearly hysterical. "The water won't stop!"

When Diana arrived, she found that the pipe beneath the sink had broken and water was gushing out faster than it would from a fire hydrant.

"Turn off the water," Diana screamed.

Katie was dancing around, stomping her feet and screaming. By the time Diana reached the faucet, the water had reached flood level.

"Get some towels, stupid," Joan called.

"I'm not stupid, you are."

"Girls, please." Diana lifted the hair off her forehead and sighed unevenly. Either she had to call George or wipe out any semblance of a budget by hiring a plumbing contractor. Given that option, she reached for the phone and dialed her neighbor's number.

The male voice that answered sounded groggy. "George, I hope I didn't wake you from a nap."

"No . . ."

"Did Shirley mention my sink?"

"Who is this?"

"Diana—from next door. Listen, I'm in a bit of a jam here. The pipe burst under the sink, and, well, Shirley said something about your being able to help. But if it's inconvenient . . ."

"Mom," Katie screamed. "Joan used the S word."

"Just a minute." Diana placed her hand over the telephone mouthpiece. "Joan, what's the matter with you?" she asked angrily.

"I'm sorry, Mom, it just slipped out."

"Are you going to wash out her mouth with soap?" Katie demanded, hands on her hips.

"I haven't got time to deal with that now. Both of you clean up this mess." She inhaled a calming breath and went back to the phone, hoping she sounded serene and demure. "George?"

"I'll be right over."

Ten seconds later, a polite knock sounded on the front door. Diana was under the sink. "Joan, let Mr. Holiday in, would you?"

"Okay."

"Mom," Katie said, sticking her head under the sink so Diana could see her. "How are you going to punish Joan?"

"Katie, can't you see I've got an emergency here!" She raised her head and slammed her forehead against the underside of the sink. Pain shot through her head and bright stars popped like flashbulbs all around her. She blinked twice and abruptly shook her head.

"Mom," Joan announced. "It wasn't Mr. Holiday."

Pushing her hair away from her forehead, Diana opened one eye to find a pair of crisp, clean jeans directly in front of her. Slowly she raised her gaze to a silver belt buckle. Above that was a liberal quantity of dark hairs scattered over a wide expanse of muscular abdomen. A cutoff sweatshirt followed. Diana's heart began to thunder, but she doubted it had anything to do with the bump on her head. She never did make it to his face. He crouched in front of her first. His blue eyes were what she noticed immediately. They were a brilliant shade that reminded her of a Seattle sky in August.

"Who—who are you?" she managed faintly.

"Are you all right?"

Diana was ready to question that herself. Whoever this man was who had decided to miraculously appear at her front door, he was much too good to be true. He looked as though he'd stepped off the hunk poster hanging in Joan's bedroom.

Diana knocked the side of her head with her palm to clear her vision. "You're not George!" It wasn't her most brilliant declaration.

"No," he admitted with a lopsided grin. "I'm Cliff Howard, a friend of George's."

"You answered the phone?" This was another of her less-than-intelligent deductions.

Cliff nodded. "Shirley's at some meeting, and George had to run to the store for a minute. I'm watching Mikey. I hope you don't mind that I brought him along."

She shook her head.

Cliff was down on all fours by this time. "Now what seems to be the problem?"

For a full moment all Diana could do was stare. It wasn't that a man hadn't physically attracted her since Stan's death, but this one hit her like a sledgehammer, stunning her senses. Cliff Howard was strikingly handsome. His eyes were mesmerizing, as blue and warm as a Caribbean sea. She couldn't look away. He smiled then, and character lines crinkled about his eyes and mouth, creasing his bronze cheeks. She'd never stared at a man quite this unabashedly, and she felt the heat of a blush rise in her face.

"There's a problem?" he repeated.

"The sink," she murmured, and pointed over her shoulder. "It's leaking."

"Bad," Katie added dramatically.

"If you'd care to move, I'd be happy to look at it for you."

"Oh, right." Hurriedly Diana scooted aside, sliding her rear end into a puddle. As the cold water seeped through her underwear, she bounded to her feet, wiping off what moisture she could.

Something was drastically wrong with her, Diana concluded. The way her heart was pounding and the blood was rushing through her veins, she had to be afflicted with some serious physical ailment. Scarlet fever, maybe. Only she didn't seem to be running a temperature. Something else must be wrong—something more than encountering Cliff Howard. He was only a man, and she'd dated plenty of men since Stan, but none of them—not one—had affected her like this one.

"Does your husband have a pipe wrench?" he called out from under the sink. "These pliers won't work."

"Oh dear." Diana sighed. "Can you tell me what a pipe wrench looks like?"

Cliff reappeared. "Does he have a toolbox?"

"Yes . . . somewhere."

Women! Cliff doubted he would ever completely understand them. This one was curious, though; her round, puppy dog eyes had a quizzical look, as though life had tossed her an unexpected curveball. The bang on her head had to be smarting. She shouldn't be working under a sink, and he wondered what kind of husband would leave it to her to handle these types of repairs. This was a woman who was meant for lace and grand pianos, not greasy pipes.

"When do you expect him home?" he asked patiently. The flicker of pain that flashed into her eyes was so fleeting that Cliff wondered at her circumstances.

"I'm a widow."

Cliff was instantly chagrined. "I'm sorry."

She nodded, then forced a smile. In an effort to bridge the uncomfortable silence, she asked, "Does a pipe wrench look like a pair of pliers, only bigger, with a mouth that moves up and down when the knob is twisted?"

Cliff had to think that over. "Yes, I'd say that about describes it."

"Then I've got one," Diana said cheerfully. "Hold on a second." She hurried into the garage and returned a minute later with the requested tool.

"Exactly right."

He smiled at her as though she'd just completed the shopping center project. "Should I be doing something?" she asked, crouching.

"Pray," Cliff teased. "This could be expensive."

"Damn," Diana muttered under her breath, and looked up to find Katie giving her a disapproving glare. In her daughter's mind, *damn* was as bad as the *S* word. "Don't you have any homework?" she asked her younger daughter.

"Just spelling."

"Then hop to it, kiddo."

"Ah, Mom!"

"Do it," Diana said in her most stern voice.

A few minutes later, Cliff climbed out from under the sink. "I'm afraid I'm going to need some parts to get this fixed."

"If you'll write down what's necessary, I can pick them up tomorrow and—"

"You don't want to go without a sink that long. I'll run and get what you need now." He wiped his hands dry on a dish towel and headed toward the front door.

"Just a minute," Diana cried, running after him. "I'll give you some cash."

"No need," he said with a lazy grin. "I'll pay for it and you can reimburse me."

"Okay," she returned weakly. The last time she'd looked, her checkbook balance had hovered around ten dollars, give or take a dime or two.

Cliff took Mikey Holiday with him, but not because he was keen on having the youth's company. His reasons were purely selfish. He wanted to grill the lad on what he knew about his neighbor with the sad eyes and the pert nose.

"You buckled up?" he asked the eight-year-old.

Mikey's baseball cap bobbed up and down.

"Say, kid, what can you tell me about the lady with the leaky sink?"

"Mrs. Collins?"

"Yeah." Cliff had to admit he was being less than subtle, but he often preferred the direct approach.

"She's real nice."

That much Cliff had guessed. "What happened to her husband?"

"He died."

Cliff decided his chances of getting any real information from the kid were nil, and he experienced a twinge of regret. He'd met far more attractive women, but this one got to him. Her appeal, he suspected, was that wide streak of independence and that stiff upper lip. He admired that.

It had been a while since he'd been this curious about any woman, and whatever it was about her that attracted him was potent. A smile came and went as he thought about her dealing with the problem sink. It was all too obvious she didn't know a thing about plumbing. Then he recalled the pair of puzzled brown eyes looking up at him and how she'd sensibly announced that he wasn't George.

He laughed softly to himself.

The knock on the front door got an immediate response from Diana. "You're back," she said, rubbing her palms together. She seemed to have a flair for stating the obvious.

Cliff grinned. "I shouldn't have any problem fixing that sink now."

"Good."

The house was quiet as she led him back into the kitchen. Diana hadn't been this agitated by a man since . . . she couldn't remember. The whole thing was silly. A strange man was causing her heart to pound like a locomotive. And Diana didn't like it one bit. Her life was too complicated for her to be attracted to a man. Besides, he was probably married, even though he didn't wear a wedding band. If Cliff was George's friend, and if he was single, it was a sure bet that Shirley would have mentioned him. And if Cliff was available, which she sincerely doubted, then he was the type to have plenty of women interested in him. And Diana had no intention of becoming a groupie.

"I really appreciate your doing this," she said after a long moment.

"No problem. What happened to the kids?"

"They're upstairs playing video games," she explained, and hesitated. "I thought you might work better with a little peace and quiet."

"I could have worked around the racket."

Diana nervously wiped her hands on her thighs. Then, irritated with herself, she folded them as though she were about to pray. Not a bad idea under the circumstances. This man was so virile. He was the first one since Stan to cause her to remember that she was still a woman. Five minutes in the kitchen with Cliff Howard and she was thinking about satin sheets and lacy underwear. Whoa, girl! She reined in her thoughts.

"Could you hand me the wrench?" he asked.

"Sure." Diana was glad to do anything but stand there staring at the dusting of hairs above his belly button.

"I don't think I caught your first name," he said next.

"Diana."

He paused, his hands holding the wrench against the pipe. "It fits."

"The pipe?"

"No," he said, grinning. "Your name." He pictured a Diana as soft and feminine, and this one was definitely that. Her hair was the color of winter wheat. She smelled of flowers and sunshine; summer at its best. Her face was sensual and provocative. Mature. She'd walked through the shadow-filled valley and emerged strong and confident.

Self-consciously Diana placed her hand at her throat. "I was named after my grandmother."

Cliff continued to work, then altered positions from lying under the sink on his back to kneeling. "It looks like I'm going to have to take off the disposal to get at the problem."

"Should I be doing something to help?"

"A cup of coffee wouldn't hurt."

"Oh, sorry, I should have thought to offer you some earlier." Diana hurried to her antique automatic-drip coffeemaker and put on a fresh pot, getting the water from the bathroom. She stood by the cantankerous machine while it gurgled and drained. Soon the aroma of freshly brewed coffee filled the kitchen.

When the pot was full, Diana brought down a mug and knelt on the linoleum in front of Cliff. "Here."

"Thanks." He sat upright, using the cupboard door to support his back.

"Do you have children—I mean, you claimed you could work around the noise, so I naturally assumed that you . . ."

"I've never been married, Diana," he said, his eyes serious.

"Oh." He had the uncanny ability to make her feel like a fool. "I just wondered, you know." Her hands slipped down the front of her Levi's in a nervous reaction.

"I was wondering, too," he admitted.

"What?"

"How long has your husband been gone?"

"Stan died in a small plane crash three years ago. Both my husband and his best friend were killed."

Three years. He was surprised. He would have thought a woman as attractive as Diana would have been snatched up long before now. She was the marrying kind and . . . ultimately out of his league.

"I shouldn't have pried." He saw the weary pain in her eyes and regretted his inquisitiveness.

"I'm doing okay. The girls and I have adjusted as well as can be expected. I'll admit it hasn't been easy, but we're getting along."

The phone rang, and before Diana could even think to move, Joan came roaring down the stairs. "I'll get it."

Diana rolled her eyes and smiled. "That's one nice thing about her growing up. I never need to answer the phone again."

"It's Mr. Holiday." Joan's disappointment sounded from the hallway. "He wants to speak to his friend."

"That must be you." The moment the words were out, Diana wanted to cringe. She was making such an idiot of herself!

Cliff rolled to his feet and reached for the wall phone.

Because she didn't want to seem as though she were eavesdropping, Diana moved into the living room and straightened the decorator pillows on the end of the sofa, positioning them just so. They were needlepoint designs her mother had given her last Christmas.

Five minutes later, hoping she wasn't being too conspicuous, she returned to the kitchen. Cliff was under the sink, humming as he worked. The garbage disposal came off without a hitch, and he set it aside. Next he added a new piece of pipe.

"There wasn't anything in the video about replacing pipe—at least in the one I viewed, anyway," she explained self-consciously.

"I'm happy to do it for you, Diana," he said, tightening the new pipe with the wrench. "There." He stood and faced the sink. "Are you ready for the big test?"

"More than ready."

Cliff turned on the faucet while Diana squatted, watching the floor under the sink. "It looks worlds better than the last time I peeked."

"No leaks?"

"Not a one." She straightened and discovered they were separated by only a couple of inches. She blinked and eased back a couple of steps. Neither spoke. Sensual awareness was as thick as a London fog; Diana's blood pounded through her veins. Her gaze rested on the V of his shirt and the smattering of curly, crisp hairs. Gradually she raised her gaze and noticed that his lower lip was slightly fuller than the upper. It had been so long since she'd been kissed by a man. Really kissed. The memory had the power to stir her senses, and her hands gripped the sink to keep herself from swaying toward him. She was behaving like Joan over a new boy in class. Her hormones were barely under control. "I don't know how to thank you," she managed finally, her voice weak.

"It isn't necessary."

Feeling awkward, Diana said, "Let me write you a check for the supplies."

"They were only a few dollars."

That was a relief! He named a figure that was so ridiculously low that she could hardly believe it. She thought to question him, but recognized intuitively that it wouldn't do any good and quietly wrote out the check.

"I don't suppose I could have a refill on the coffee?" Cliff surprised himself by saying. Standing there by the sink, he'd nearly kissed her. She'd wanted it. He'd been partially amused by her obvious desire, until he'd realized that he wanted it, too.

"A refill? Of course. I don't mean to be such a poor hostess." She moved to the glass pot and brought it over to Cliff, who had claimed a chair at the table. Diana topped his cup and then her own, returned the pot and took a seat opposite him.

"Do you like Chinese food?" he asked unexpectedly, again surprising himself. It wasn't her beauty that attracted him so much as her spirit.

Diana nodded. Her stomach churned and she knew what was coming. She hoped he would ask her, and in the same heartbeat prayed he wouldn't.

"Would you have dinner with me tomorrow night?"

"I . . ."

"If you're looking for a way to repay me, then make it simple and share an evening with me."

"Joan's got baseball practice." Instead of looking for excuses, she should be thanking God he'd asked. "But Shirley could pick her up."

Cliff grinned, his blue eyes almost boyish. "Good, then I'll see you at six-thirty."

Diana responded to the pure potency of his smile. "I'll look forward to it."

The minute Cliff was out the door, Diana phoned her neighbor.

"Shirley, it's Diana," she said, doing her best to curtail her excitement. "Where have you been hiding him?"

"Who? I just walked in the door. What are you talking about?"

"Cliff Howard!"

"You met Cliff Howard?"

"That's just what I said. After all these months of indiscriminately tossing men at me, why didn't you introduce us earlier?"

A lengthy, strained silence followed. "I'm going to shoot George."

"Shoot George? What's that got to do with anything?"

Shirley raised her voice in anger. "I told that man to keep Cliff Howard away from you. He's trouble with a capital *T*, and if you have a brain in your head you won't have anything to do with him."

Two

"Mom, do you want to borrow my skirt?" Joan held up a skimpy piece of denim that was her all-time favorite.

"No thanks, sweetheart." Diana was standing in front of the mirror in her bathroom, wearing only her slip and bra.

"But, Mom, this skirt is the absolute!"

Diana sighed. "I appreciate the offer, sweetie, but it's about four sizes too small. Besides, I have no intention of looking like Katy Perry."

"But Cliff's so handsome."

Leave it to Joan to notice that. This year Diana had seen a major transformation take hold of her elder daughter. After one week of fifth grade, Joan had wanted her ears pierced and would have killed for fake nails. The youngster argued that Diana was being completely unreasonable to make her wait until junior high before wearing makeup. Everyone wore eye shadow and Diana must have been reared in the Middle Ages if she didn't know that. Boys were quickly becoming all-important, too. Fifth grade! How times had changed.

"Are you going to wear your pearl earrings?" Joan asked next.

The pair were Diana's best and saved for only the most festive occasions. "I—I'm not sure."

She wasn't sure about anything. Shirley seemed convinced Diana was making the mistake of her life by having anything to do with Cliff.

Her neighbor claimed he was a notorious playboy who would end up breaking her fragile heart. He was sophisticated, urbane and completely ruthless about using his polished good looks to get what he wanted from a woman, or so Shirley claimed. Next she had admitted that she was half in love with him herself, but as Diana's self-appointed guardian, Shirley couldn't bear thinking what could happen to her friend in the hands of Cliff Howard.

After Shirley's briefing, Diana was too curious to find out to consider canceling the date.

"Mom, the earrings," Joan repeated impatiently.

Her daughter's shrill voice broke into Diana's thoughts. "I don't think so."

"Do it, Mom."

"But if I wear them now, I won't have anything to razzle-dazzle Cliff with later."

Joan chewed on the corner of her lower lip, grudgingly accepting her mother's decision. "Right, but what about your hair?"

"What about it?" Diana's hair was styled the way she always wore it, parted on the side and feathered back away from her face.

Joan looked unsure. "You look so ordinary, like this is an everyday date or something."

"I don't think now would be the time to experiment with something different."

"I suppose you're right," Joan admitted reluctantly.

Diana checked her watch; she had plenty of time, but the

way Joan kept suggesting changes wasn't doing a whole lot for her self-confidence. Maybe her daughter was right, and it was time to do something different with her hair and makeup. But age thirty was upon her, and no matter how she parted her hair or applied her makeup, she wasn't going to look like Stacey Q., Joan's favorite female rock star. Well, almost favorite. Stacey Q. ran a close second to Katy Perry.

When Diana came out of the bathroom, she discovered her daughter sorting through her closet. "I have what I'm going to wear on the bed."

"But, Mom, black pants and a blouse are so boring."

"The blouse is silk," she told her coaxingly.

"Men like black silk, not white."

Diana preferred not to know where Joan had gotten that little tidbit of information. The child was amazing. While Diana slipped into the pants, Joan lay across the queen-size mattress and propped her chin up with her hands.

"You know who Cliff reminds me of?" Joan asked with a dreamy look clouding her blue eyes.

"Who?"

"Christian Bale."

"Who?" Diana stopped dressing long enough to turn around and face her daughter.

"You know, the actor."

Diana sighed. "I suppose he does faintly resemble him, but Cliff's hair is dark."

"Cliff's hot stuff, Mom. He's going to make your blood boil."

"Joan, for heaven's sake. The way things are going, I may never see him again after tonight."

Alarmed, Joan bolted upright. "Why not?"

"Well, for one thing my clothes are boring, and for another I don't look a thing like Katy Perry and my hair's all wrong."

"I didn't say that," Joan returned defensively.

The doorbell chimed and Joan tore out of the room. "It's him. I'll get it."

Diana let out an exasperated breath, squared her shoulders and did one last check in the mirror. She'd dressed sensibly, hoping to be tactful enough to remind Cliff that she was a widow and a mother. According to Shirley, Cliff had previously dated beauty queens, centerfolds and an occasional actress. Diana was "none of the above." Her reflection revealed round eyes and a falsely cheerful smile. Good enough, she decided as she reached for her sweater and placed it over her arm; nights still tended to be nippy in May.

Joan came rushing back to the bedroom. "He brought you flowers," she announced in a husky whisper. "Mom," she continued, placing her hand over her heart, "he's so-o-o handsome."

As Joan had claimed, Cliff stood inside the living room with a small bouquet of red roses and pink carnations. It had been so long since a man had given her flowers that Diana's throat constricted and she couldn't think of a single word to say.

He smiled, and the sun became brighter. Shirley was right. This man was too much for a mere widow.

"You look lovely."

Somehow Diana managed a feeble thank-you.

"Mom's got terrific legs," Joan inserted smoothly, standing between Diana and Cliff and glancing from one to the other. "I keep telling her that she ought to show them off more often." She slapped her hands against her sides. "But my mother never listens to me."

Diana glared at her daughter but said nothing. "I'll find a vase for these." As she left the room, Joan's chatter drifted after her. Her daughter found it important that Cliff know she was much too old to have a babysitter. Katie was over at the Holidays', but at eleven, Joan was far too mature to have anyone look after her.

"I thought you had baseball practice?" Diana heard Cliff ask.

"Normally I do," Joan explained with a patient sigh, "but I skipped today because my mother needed me."

Diana reappeared and Joan escorted the couple to the front door. It was on the tip of Diana's tongue to remind Joan of the house rules when she was alone, but one desperate glance begged her not to. Diana grudgingly complied and said everything that was needed with one stern look.

"Have a good time," Joan said cheerfully, holding the front door open. "And, Cliff, you can bring Mom home late. She doesn't have a curfew."

"I'll have her back before midnight," Cliff promised.

Joan nodded approvingly. "And don't worry, Mom, I'll take care of everything here."

That was what concerned Diana most. She kissed Joan's cheek and whispered, "Remember, bedtime is nine." Shirley would be over then to sit with the girls until Diana returned.

"Mom," Joan said under her breath, "you're treating me like a child."

Diana smiled apologetically. However, it would be just like her daughter to wait up half the night to hear the details of this date, and Diana couldn't face Joan and Shirley together.

Cliff's sports car was parked in front of the house. It was a two-seater that Diana couldn't identify. Cool. Very cool. He held open the door and helped her inside. She mumbled her thanks, feeling self-conscious and out of her element. Diana drove a ten-year-old SUV and wouldn't know the difference between a BMW and an MGB.

Cliff joined her a moment later, inserted the key in the ignition and turned to her, smiling. "Is she always like that?"

"Always. I hope she didn't embarrass you."

"Not at all." He looked more amused than anything.

"I sometimes wonder if I'm going to survive motherhood," Diana commented, her hands clenching her purse.

"You seem to be doing an admirable job."

"Thanks." But Cliff hadn't seen her at her worst. Katie called her the screaming meemie when she let loose. Diana didn't lose her cool often, but enough for the girls to know that the best thing for them to do was nod politely and agree to everything she shouted, no matter how unreasonable.

Cliff started the engine, doing his best to hold back his amusement. This daughter of Diana's was something else. He'd been looking forward to seeing this widow all day. He continued to be confounded by the attraction he felt for her. True, she was pretty enough, but years older than the women he normally dated. Diana had to be close to his age.

Several times during the day, he'd discovered his thoughts drifting to her, wondering what she was doing and what catastrophe she was fearlessly facing now. After he'd finished with her sink, he'd gone to the Holidays' and drilled George, wanting to ferret out every detail about Diana he could. Shirley arrived home then, and when she learned that he planned to take Diana to dinner, her disapproval had been tangible. She'd mumbled some dire warning about the wrath of God coming down upon his head if he ever hurt Diana.

However, it was never Cliff's intent to hurt any woman. He realized George and his other golfing friends credited him with the playboy image, but he wasn't Hugh Hefner. He wasn't even close. Oh, there'd been a few relationships over the years, but very few. It was true that most women found him attractive, and it was also fair to say he liked variety. The truth was his reputation far outdistanced reality.

When Cliff had drilled his friend about Diana, George hadn't been able to say enough good things about the young widow. To escape Shirley's threats, the two men had gone to the local pub and talked late into the night. Cliff went away satisfied that he'd learned everything George knew about his next-door neighbor.

In the car seat, Diana clasped and unclasped her purse. She was nervous. She hadn't felt this uptight since . . . never, she decided. A man had stepped out of the pages of *Gentlemen's Quarterly* and into her life. This shouldn't be happening to her. Events like that were reserved for fairy tales and gossip magazines. Not widows whose money couldn't stretch till the end of the month.

Diana wanted to stand Shirley up against a wall and shoot her for filling her with doubts. One date! What possible damage could one dinner date do? The one and only time she was interested in finding out details about a man, and all Shirley could do was point out that Diana was headed down the road to destruction. Shirley claimed lesser women crumbled under Cliff's charm. He broke their hearts, but he hated to see them cry. Diana, according to Shirley, was too gentle natured to be hurt by this playboy.

Consequently Diana didn't know anything more about Cliff than she had when he'd left her house the night before.

"How do you know George?" she asked, breaking the silence.

"George and I golf together," Cliff explained.

George was a real sports fanatic.

"Do you play?" Cliff asked.

"I'm afraid not." No time. She was the room mother for Katie's second grade class, did volunteer work at the elementary school the girls attended, taught Sunday school and was heavily involved in Girl Scouts. "I used to play tennis, though," she added quickly. "Used to" being the operative expression. Every Thursday had been her morning on the court, but that was before Joan was born and . . . oh, good grief, that was eleven years ago. Where had all the years gone?

They arrived at the Chinese restaurant and were seated in a secluded booth. "This place isn't high on atmosphere, but I promise you the food's terrific," Cliff said.

Diana studied the menu, and her stomach growled just reading over the varied list of entrées. If the food tasted half as good as it sounded, she would be satisfied. "You needn't worry," she said, "I'm easy to please. Anything that I don't have to cook is fine by me."

The waiter appeared, and they placed their order. Diana cradled a small teacup in both hands. "I know you fix leaky sinks in your spare time, but what do you normally do?"

"I'm an attorney." His gaze settled on her mouth. "Are you a working mother?"

Diana bit back a defensive reply. A man who had never been married wouldn't appreciate the fact that *every* mother was a working mother. "Not outside the house," she explained simply. "I keep thinking I should find a part-time job, but I'm delaying it as long as possible."

"What have you trained for?"

"Motherhood."

Cliff grinned.

"I suppose that sounds old-fashioned. But you have to remember that Stan and I married only a few months after I graduated from community college. The first couple of years, while Stan worked for Boeing, I attended classes at the University of Washington, but I got pregnant with Joan and didn't earn enough credits for a degree. At one time I'd hoped to enter the nursing profession, but that was years ago."

Their hot-and-sour soup arrived. "Why don't you do that now?" Cliff wanted to know.

"I could," she admitted, and shrugged, "but I feel it's too important to spend time with the girls. They still need me. I'm all they've got and I'd hate to be torn between attending

Joan's baseball games and doing homework, or squeezing in an additional night class." She paused and dipped her spoon in the thick soup. "Maybe that's an excuse, but my children are the most important investment I have in this life. I want to be there for them."

"What if your husband were alive?"

"Then I'd probably be in nursing school. The responsibilities of raising the girls would be shared." She hesitated. She doubted that Cliff would understand any of this—a bachelor wouldn't. "To be honest, I'm not toying with the idea of getting a part-time job because I want one. Money is tight and it gets tighter every year. I suppose by the time Joan's in junior high, the option will be taken away from me, but by then both girls will be better able to deal with my being away from home so much."

"Joan seemed eager enough to have you leave tonight."

Diana nodded, hiding a smile. "That's because she thinks you look like Christian Bale."

"I'm flattered."

Diana noted that she didn't need to explain to him that Christian Bale was an actor. "I hope you don't find this rude, but how old are you, Cliff?" Diana knew she was older. She had to be—if not in years, then experience.

"How old do you think?"

She shrugged. "Twenty-five, maybe twenty-six."

"How old are you?"

A hundred and ten some days. Fifteen on others. "Thirty last September."

His grin was almost boyish. "I'm thirty-one."

The conversation turned then, and they discussed local politics. Although they took opposing points of view, Diana noted that he respected her opinions and didn't try to sway her to his way of thinking. Cliff was far more liberal than Diana. Her views tended to be conservative.

From their conversation, she discovered other tidbits of information about him. He skied, and had a condo at Alpental on Snoqualmie Pass. His sailboat was docked at the Des Moines Marina and he enjoyed sailing, but didn't get out often enough. He was allergic to strawberries.

Diana hated to see the evening end. It had been years since she'd had such a fun date. Cliff was easy to talk to, and she was astonished when she happened to notice the time. They'd been sitting in the booth talking for nearly three hours.

"How about a movie?" he suggested on the way to the restaurant parking lot.

Regretfully Diana shook her head. "Sorry, Cliff, but it's after ten. I should think about heading back."

It looked for a moment as though he wanted to argue with her, but he changed his mind. Diana was sure that most of his dates didn't need to rush home. More than likely they lingered over wine in front of a romantic fireplace, shared a few kisses and probably more. It was the "probably more" that got her heart pumping. It would be a foolish mistake to let this relationship advance beyond friendship. All right, she admitted it. She was attracted to the man. Good grief, what red-blooded female wouldn't be? But they lived in different worlds. Cliff was part of the swinging singles scene and she was like a modern-day Betsy Ross, doing needlepoint in her rocking chair in front of the television.

"You're looking thoughtful," he said as they left the restaurant.

"I do?" she murmured.

Once again he opened the car door for her, and she scooted inside as gracefully as she could manage. Again her fingers moved to the clasp on her purse. For some reason she was nervous again. She liked Cliff more than any man she'd dated since Stan's death, but it went without saying that she wasn't the woman for him.

Cliff pulled out of the parking lot and was soon on the freeway heading south. They chatted easily, and Diana could see where Cliff would make a good attorney. He could be persuasive when he wanted to be. Darn persuasive.

"That was my exit," she told him when he drove past it. She jerked her head over her shoulder as though it were possible for them to reverse their direction.

"I know."

"Where are you taking me?" She was more amused than irritated.

"If you must know, I want to kiss you and I wasn't exactly thrilled to do it in front of an audience."

As Joan had predicted it would, Diana's blood reached the simmering point. A kiss would quickly accelerate it to the boiling stage.

"Joan and Katie will be in bed by now." He needn't worry about them peeking through the living room drapes.

"I was thinking more of George and Shirley," Cliff told her.

Diana laughed; he was probably right. She could picture Shirley waiting by her front window, drapes parted, staring at the street.

Cliff took the next exit to the small community in the south end of Seattle called Des Moines. "I want you to see something," he explained.

"Your sailboat?"

"No," he said softly. "The stars."

Romantic, too! She could resist anything but romance. It wasn't fair that in a few hours he could narrow in on her weaknesses and break down all her well-constructed defenses.

There were several dozen cars in the huge parking lot. A wonderful seafood restaurant was an attraction that brought many out on a lovely spring evening.

Cliff parked as far away from the restaurant as he could. He turned off the ignition and climbed out of the car. By the time he was around to her side, Diana's heart was pounding so hard it threatened to break her ribs.

With his arm draped around her shoulders, Cliff led her down onto the wharf. The night was lovely. A soft breeze drifted off the water and the scent of seaweed and salt mingled with the crisp air. The sky was blanketed in black velvet, and the sparkling stars dotted the heavens like diamonds.

"It's lovely, isn't it?" she said, experiencing the wonder of standing beneath a canopy of such splendor.

Cliff's answer was to turn her in his arms. She looked up at him, and her hair fell away from her face. He raised his hands to touch her cheeks and stared down at her. His fingertips slowly glided over each feature. Such smooth skin, warm and silky, and eyes that could rip apart a man's heart. Slowly he lowered his mouth to hers, denying himself the pleasure for as long as he could endure it.

Their mouths gently brushed against each other's like rose petals caught in a breeze. Velvety smooth. Soft and warm. Infinitely gentle, but electric. Again he kissed her, only this time his mouth lingered, longer this time, much longer.

Diana felt her knees go weak and she swayed toward him, slipping her arms around his neck. A debilitating sensation overcame her. She couldn't think, couldn't breathe, couldn't move.

Cliff groaned and his grip tightened and moved to the back of her head. He slanted his mouth across hers, sampling once more the pure pleasure of her kiss. He'd been right; she tasted incredibly of sweet butterscotch. Hungrily, his lips devoured hers, again and again, unable to get enough of her. Diana felt the tears well in her eyes, and was at a loss to know where they came from or why. One slipped from the corner of her eye and rolled down the side of her face, leaving a shiny trail.

At first her tears were lost to him, he was so involved with the taste of her. When he realized she was crying, he stopped and drew away from her.

"Diana?" he asked tenderly, concerned.

Embarrassed, she tucked her chin against her shoulder, not knowing what to say.

"Then why . . ."

"I don't know. I am such an idiot." She jerked her hand across her face and smudged her carefully applied mascara. "I don't know, Cliff. I honestly don't know."

He tried to hold her, but she wouldn't let him.

"Because it was good," she offered as an explanation.

"The kiss?"

"Everything. You. The dinner. The stars." She sobbed once and held her hands over her face. "Everything."

"I didn't have anything to do with making the stars shine," he teased softly. Although she didn't want him to hold her, Cliff kept his hands on her shoulders, seeking a way to comfort her.

Diana knew he was attempting to lighten the mood, but it didn't help.

"Come on, let me take you home." This wasn't what he wanted, but he didn't know what else to do.

Miserable, she nodded.

"I have to admit this is the first time my kisses have caused a woman to weep."

She attempted to laugh, but the sound that came out of her throat was like the creak of a rusty hinge. No doubt this was a switch for him. Women probably swooned at his feet. Tall, handsome, rich men were a rare species.

He draped his arm around her shoulders again as he led her back to his car. When he opened the door for her, he paused and pressed a finger under her chin, lifting her face so that she was forced to meet his gaze.

"It was just as good for me," he told her softly.

Diana longed to shout at him to stop. All this wasn't necessary. The last thing she wanted was for him to sweep her off her feet, and already she was so dangerously close to tumbling that it rocked her to the bottom of her soul. They weren't right together. Cliff was wonderful, too good to be true. His tastes leaned toward someone young and sleek, not a widow with two daughters whose lifetime goals were to grow up and succeed Katy Perry.

All the way back to the house, Diana mentally rehearsed what she planned to say at the door. He'd ask her out again, and she'd tell him in hushed, regretful tones that she had to decline. She had to! The option had been taken away from her the instant he'd pulled her into his arms. Shirley was right—this man was more dangerous than fire!

Only Cliff didn't give her the opportunity to refuse him. Like the perfect gentleman, he escorted her to the door, thanked her for a lovely evening, gently kissed her forehead and walked away.

Diana was grateful he hadn't made her say it, but her heart pounded with regret. Cliff had realized there could be no future for them, and although she would have liked to find a way, it was impossible.

A week passed, a long, tedious week when life seemed to be an uphill battle. Joan went through two packages of press-on nails, and they turned up in every conceivable corner of the house. Katie's allergies were acting up again, and Diana spent two dreary afternoons sitting in a doctor's office waiting for the nurse to give Katie her shot.

Shirley was over daily for coffee and to reassure Diana that she'd made the right decision about not seeing Cliff again. It seemed Cliff had recovered quickly and was said to be dating Dana Mattson, a local television talk show hostess. Diana thought of Cliff fondly and wished him well. In many ways she was grateful for their one evening together. She'd felt more alive than at any other time since Stan's death. She was grateful that he'd shown her the light, but now she didn't know if she could be content with living in the shadows again.

The Thursday afternoon following their dinner, Diana planted marigolds along the edges of the flower bed in the backyard. The huge old apple tree was in bloom and filled the air with the sweet scent of spring, but Diana was too caught up in her own thoughts to notice. All day she'd been in a blue funk, depressed and irritable. Every time she saw the wilted bouquet of roses and carnations in the center of the kitchen table, she felt faint stirrings of regret. Friday there wouldn't be any choice but to toss the flowers. It was silly to allow a lovely bouquet to mean so much.

After depositing her garden tools in the garage, she stepped into the bathroom to wash her hands. Joan was standing on top of the toilet, leaning across the sink and staring in the mirror. Her young mouth was twisted in a grimace.

"What are you doing?" Diana demanded.

"I'm practicing so I look cool. See." She turned to face her mother, her mouth twisted in a sarcastic sneer that would have wilted daffodils.

"You look terrible."

"Great. That's exactly the look I'm going for."

"Joan, sweetheart," she said with growing impatience, "I just put five hundred dollars down at the orthodontist's so that you could have lovely, straight teeth."

Joan stared at her blankly.

"Do you mean to tell me I'm spending thousands of dollars to straighten the teeth of a child who plans never to smile?"

"Boy, are you a grouch," Joan announced as she jumped down off the toilet. "What's the matter, Mom, is Aunt Flo visiting?"

It took Diana a moment to make the connection with her monthly cycle. When she did, her knees started to shake. In an even, controlled voice, she turned toward her daughter. "When did you learn about Aunt Flo?"

"A year ago."

"But . . ." So much for the neat packet she'd mailed away for that so carefully explained everything in the simple terms that a fifth grader would understand.

"I figured you'd get around to telling me one of these days," Joan said, undisturbed.

"Oh, dear." Diana sat on the edge of the tub.

"It's no big deal, Mom."

"Who told you . . . when?" Diana's voice shook as she realized that her little girl wasn't so little anymore. "Why didn't you come to me?"

"Honestly, Mom, I would have, but you think a fifth grader is too young for panty hose."

"You are!"

"See what I mean?" Joan declared, shaking her head.

"Who told you?"

"The library . . ."

"The Kent library?" Good grief, it wasn't safe to take her daughter into the local library anymore.

"You see," Joan explained, "we had this discussion in fourth grade that sort of left me hanging, so I checked out a few books."

"And the books told you everything?"

Joan nodded and started to speak, but was interrupted by her younger sister, who stuck her head in the bathroom door.

"I'm starved—what's for dinner?"

"I haven't decided yet."

Katie placed her hands on her hips. "Is it going to be another one of *those* dinners?"

"Can't you see we're having a serious mother-daughter discussion here?" Joan shouted. "Get lost, dog breath."

"Joan!" Diana cried, and quickly diverted an argument. "Don't call your sister that. Katie, I'm hungry, too. Why don't you check what's in the refrigerator? I'm open for suggestions."

"Okay," Katie cried eagerly, and hurried back into the kitchen.

"Are you mad?" Joan asked in a subdued voice. "I didn't tell you before, well, because . . . you know."

"Because I won't let you wear panty hose."

Joan nodded. "You've got to remember, I'm growing up!"

Diana swiped the hair off her face. At this moment she didn't need to be reminded of the fact her elder daughter was turning into a woman right before her eyes.

Katie had emptied half the contents of the refrigerator on top of the counter by the time Diana entered the kitchen. "Find anything interesting?"

"Nothing I'd seriously consider eating," Katie said. "Can we have Kentucky Fried Chicken tonight?"

"Not tonight, honey."

"How about going to McDonald's?"

"If we can't afford KFC, we can't afford McDonald's."

"TV dinners?" Katie asked hopefully.

"Let me see what we've got." She opened the freezer door and glared inside, hoping against hope she'd somehow find three glorious flat boxes.

The doorbell chimed in the distance. "I'll get it," Joan screamed, and nearly knocked over the kitchen chair in her rush to get to the front door first.

"Oh, hi." Joan's voice drifted into the kitchen. "Mom, it's for you."

The list of possibilities ran through Diana's mind. The paperboy, Shirley Holiday, the pastor. She rejected each one. Somehow she knew even before she came into the room who was at the door. She'd longed for and dreaded this moment.

"Hi," Cliff said, smiling broadly. "I was wondering if the three of you would like to go on a picnic with me."

"Sure," Joan answered first, excited.

"Great," Katie chimed in.

Cliff's gaze didn't leave Diana's. "It's up to your mother."

Three

"I thought we'd go to Salt Water Park," Cliff said, his gaze holding Diana's. He resisted the urge to lift his hand, touch her cheek and tell her she'd been on his mind from the minute he'd left her. After their dinner date he'd instinctively realized that if he were to ask her out again, she'd refuse. The only way he could get her to agree to see him again would be to involve her daughters.

"Can we have Kentucky Fried Chicken?" Katie asked, jumping up and down excitedly.

"Katie!" Diana cried. That girl worried far too much about her stomach.

"As a matter of fact," Cliff answered, "I've got a bucket in the car now."

"Mother," Katie pleaded, her eyes growing more round by the second. "KFC!"

"I'll get a blanket," Joan said, rushing through the living room and down the hall to the linen closet.

"I've got to change shoes," Katie added, and zoomed after her sister, leaving Diana and Cliff standing alone.

"I take it this means you're going?"

Diana decided his smile was far too sexy for his own good, or for hers. "I don't appear to have much of a choice. If I refuse now, I'm likely to have a mutiny on my hands."

Cliff grinned; his plan had worked well. A streak of dried dirt was smeared across her chin, and her blond hair was gathered at the base of her neck with a tie. Her washed-out jeans had holes in the knees. Funny, but he couldn't remember the last time a woman looked more appealing to him. She was everything he'd built up in his mind this past week, and more.

What he'd told her that night was true—he'd never had a woman respond to his kisses with tears. Unfortunately, what Diana didn't know was that he'd been equally shaken by those moments in the moonlight. He'd been attracted to her from the minute she'd stared up at him from beneath her kitchen sink and described a plumber's wrench. She'd amused him, challenged his intelligence, charmed him, but what had attracted him most was her complete lack of pretense. This wasn't a woman whose life centered around three-inch long fingernails. She was gutsy and authentic.

Over dinner, he'd discovered her wit and humor. On social issues she was opinionated but not dogmatic, concerned but not fanatical. She was unafraid of emotion and possessed a deep inner strength. All along he'd known how much he wanted to kiss her. What he hadn't anticipated was the effect it would have on them both. A single kiss had never touched his heart more. Diana had been trembling so badly, she hadn't noticed that he was shaking like a leaf himself. He experienced such a gentleness for her, a craving to protect and comfort her. He felt like a callow youth, unpracticed and green. Thrown off balance, he hadn't enjoyed the feeling.

On the way home from the marina, they'd barely talked. By then Cliff was confident he wouldn't be seeing her again. That decided, a calmness had come over him. A widow with children was no woman to get involved with, and Diana was the take-home-to-mother type he generally avoided.

Picturing himself as a husband was difficult enough, but as a father . . . well, that was stretching things. He'd always enjoyed children and looked forward to having his own someday; he just hadn't planned on starting with a houseful. He did like Joan and Katie—they were cute kids. But they were kids. He hardly knew how to act around them.

Then why had he gone back to Diana's? Cliff had asked himself that same question twenty times in as many minutes. He'd been out a couple of times that week, but neither woman had stimulated him the way those few hours with Diana had. He heard her laugh at the most ridiculous times. A newscast had left him wondering what her opinion was on an important local issue. He'd waited a couple of days for her to contact him. Women usually did. But not Diana.

Interrupting his thoughts, Joan returned to the living room, dragging a blanket with her. The eleven-year-old was quickly followed by a grinning, happy Katie.

"You ready?" Cliff asked.

"We won't all fit in your sports car," Diana said, fighting the natural desire to be with Cliff and angry with herself for wanting it so much. She'd changed clothes and washed her face, but she still felt like Cinderella two nights after the ball.

"We can take two cars," Joan suggested, obviously not wanting anything to ruin this outing.

Palm up, Cliff gestured toward her elder daughter. "Excellent idea."

Joan positively glowed. "Can I ride with Cliff?"

Diana's brows involuntarily furrowed in concern.

"I . . . ah."

"It's fine with me," Cliff told her, and noticed that Katie

looked disappointed. "Then Katie can ride with me on the way home."

"Okay," Diana agreed reluctantly.

Diana followed Cliff toSaltwater State Park, which was less than ten minutes from the house. She'd taken Joan and Katie there often and enjoyed the lush Puget Sound beachfront. On their last visit, the girls had watched several sea lions laze in the sun not more than twenty feet off the shore on a platform buoy.

When Cliff turned off the road and into the park entrance, Diana saw him throw back his head and laugh at something Joan had said. A chill went up Diana's back at the thought of what her daughter could be telling him. That girl had few scruples when it came to attractive men. But Diana was concerned for another reason. Both her girls liked Cliff, which was unusual, and although she'd dated a number of men during the past few years, rarely had she included the children in an outing. As much as possible, she tried to keep her social life separate from her family.

Cliff pulled into a space in the parking lot, and Diana eased the SUV into the spot beside him. Even though it was a school night, there seemed to be several families out enjoying the warm spring evening. Both Joan and Katie climbed out of the respective cars and rushed across the thick grass. Within seconds they returned to inform Cliff that there was an unused picnic table close to the beach.

Diana waited while Cliff took the bag of food from the trunk of his car. She felt awkward in her sweatshirt and wished she'd taken the time to change into a new pair of shorts. Had she known she was going on a picnic with Cliff, she would have washed her hair that afternoon and tried to do something different with it. That would have pleased Joan. Suddenly her thoughts came to an abrupt halt. She was traipsing on dangerously thin ice with this playboy.

"I've been meaning to ask you what kind of car this is?" she asked as he closed the trunk.

"A Lamborghini."

"Oh." She didn't know a lot about sports cars, but this one had a name that sounded expensive.

The girls were waiting at the table for them when Diana and Cliff arrived. Joan had unfolded the blanket and spread it out beneath a tall fir tree.

"Can we go looking for seashells?" Joan asked.

"I want to eat first," Katie complained. "I'm hungry."

"I bought plenty of food." Cliff said, opening the sack and setting out four individual boxes. Each one contained a complete meal.

"What's for dessert?" Already Katie had ripped open the top of her box, and a chicken leg was poised in front of her mouth.

"Ice cream cones, but only if you're good," Cliff answered.

"What he means by 'good,'" Joan explained in a hushed voice, "is giving him plenty of time alone with Mom. They need to talk."

Diana's eyes flared with indignation. "Did you tell her that?" she demanded in a low whisper.

Cliff looked astonished enough for her to believe in his innocence. "Not me."

From the corner of her eye, Diana saw him give Joan a conspiratorial wink, and was all the more upset. Rather than argue with him in front of the children, Diana decided to wait. However, maintaining her anger with Cliff was impossible. He shared the picnic table bench with Katie and sat across from Diana. He was so charming that he had all three females under his spell within minutes. Diana found it only a little short of amazing the way he talked to the girls. He didn't talk down to Joan and Katie, but treated them as miniature adults, and they adored him for it. From Diana's point of view, this man could do with fewer worshiping females.

The girls finished their meal in record time and were off to explore. While Diana tossed their garbage into the proper receptacle, she shouted out instructions.

"Don't you dare come back here wet!" she cried, and doubted that they'd heard her.

"Wet?" Cliff asked.

"Leave it to them to decide to go swimming."

"Once they find out how cold the water is, they'll change their minds," he said confidently.

Cliff had moved from the picnic table to the blanket and sat with his back propped against the tree, watching Diana as she made busywork at the picnic table.

"I'm sure the birds will appreciate your dumping those crumbs on the ground," he said, and patted the area beside him. "Come and sit down."

Unwillingly Diana did as he asked, but sat on the edge of the blanket. It was too dangerous to get close to Cliff; such raw masculinity unnerved her. She'd been three years without a man, and this one made her feel things she would have preferred to forget.

"I wish you hadn't done this," she said in a small, quiet voice.

"What?"

"Don't play dumb with me, Cliff Howard. You know exactly what I'm talking about."

"Why are you sitting so far away from me?"

"Because it's safe here."

"I don't bite." His mouth curved up in a sensual smile that did uncanny things to Diana's equilibrium.

"Maybe not, but you kiss," she told him irritably.

His eyes held hers. "It was good, wasn't it?"

She nodded. "Too good."

His smile was lazy. "Nothing can be *too* good."

Diana couldn't find it within herself to disagree, although she knew she should. "What's this about your suggesting to Joan that they give us time together alone?"

His mouth broadened into a deeper grin. "Actually, that was her idea."

Diana rolled her eyes heavenward. That sounded exactly like something Joan would suggest.

"I like your girls, Diana," he said gently. "You've done a good job raising them."

"They're not raised yet—besides, you're seeing their good side. Just wait until they start fighting. There are days when I think they're going to seriously injure each other."

"My brother and I were like that. We're close now, although he's living in California." Cliff paused and told her a couple of stories from his youth that produced a smile and caused her to relax. "Rich and I talk at least once a week now. Joan and Katie will probably do the same once they leave home."

Bringing her legs up, Diana rested her chin on top of her knees. One hand lazily picked up a long blade of grass. It felt right to be with Cliff. Right and wrong.

"Why haven't you married?" The question was abrupt and tactless, slipping out before she could temper the words.

Cliff shrugged, and then his answer was as direct as her question. "I haven't found the right woman. Besides, I'm having too much fun to settle down."

"Usually, when a man's over thirty there's a reason . . . I mean . . . some men can't make a commitment, you know." Oh, heavens, she was making this worse every minute.

"To be honest, I've never considered marriage." There hadn't been any reason to. That wasn't to say he hadn't been in love any number of times, but generally the emotion was fleeting and within a few weeks another woman would capture his attention. Once he'd had a girl move in with him, but those had been the most miserable months of his life, and the experience had taught him valuable lessons. Expensive ones. He would never again accept that kind of arrangement.

"Shirley mentioned a Becky somebody."

Bless Shirley's black heart, Cliff mused. "She lived with me for three months."

"You didn't want to marry her?"

"Good grief, no. I was never so glad to get rid of anyone in my life."

Diana frowned. The knowledge that Cliff had lived with a woman proved that he was a swinging single, as she'd suspected. That he'd want to spend time with her was only a little short of amazing. Perplexed, she wrapped her arms around her legs and briefly pressed her forehead to her knees.

"You don't approve of a man and woman living together?" The troubled look that clouded her eyes made her opinion all the more evident.

Diana lifted her head and her eyes held his. "It isn't for me to approve or disapprove. What other people do is their own business as long as it doesn't affect me or my children."

"But it's something you'd never do?"

Her hesitation was only slight. "I couldn't. I have Joan and Katie to consider. But as I said, it's not up to me to judge what someone else does."

Her answer pleased him. Diana was too intelligent to get caught in a dead-end relationship that would only end up ripping apart her heart.

Unfortunately Cliff had been forced to learn his lessons the hard way.

"You were on my mind every day, all day, all week," he said softly, enticingly. "I thought about you getting up and taking the girls to school. Later, I remembered you telling me you wanted to plant marigolds. That's what you did today, isn't it?"

Diana nodded and closed her eyes. "I had a crummy week." She didn't want Cliff to court her. Her attraction to him was powerful enough without his telling her he hadn't been able to get her off his mind.

"The fact is, I couldn't stop thinking about you," he added.

"I filled out an application for a job with the school district this morning," she told him brightly. She was desperate for him to stop leading her on. She didn't need for him to say the things a woman wants to hear. They weren't necessary; she had been fascinated from the moment he'd walked into her house. "There's a good chance they'll be able to hire for September."

"When I wasn't thinking about you," he continued, undaunted, "I was remembering our kisses and wondering how long it would be before I could kiss you again."

Her fingers coiled into hard fists. "I'll probably be working as a teacher's aide," she said, doing her utmost to ignore him.

"Don't make me wait too long to kiss you again, Diana."

Her hands were so tightly bunched that her fingers ached. She forced herself to ignore him, to pretend she hadn't heard what he was saying. Closing her eyes helped to blot out his image, but when she opened them again, he had moved and was sitting beside her.

"How long are you going to make me wait?" he asked again, in a voice that would melt concrete.

His eyes rested on her mouth. Diana tried to look away, but he wouldn't let her. Even when he raised his hand and turned her face back to him, his gaze didn't stray from her lips. He pressed his index finger over her mouth and slid it from one corner of her lips to the other. Diana couldn't have moved to save her life.

"You don't need to tell me anything. I know what you're thinking and that you weren't able to get me off your mind, either. I know you want this."

One of his hands cupped the side of her face, and her eyes fluttered closed. His other hand slipped around her waist as he brought her into his arms. In that moment Diana couldn't have resisted him to save the world. He knew her, knew that he'd been on her mind all week, knew how much she regretted that things couldn't be different for them.

Cliff lowered his head and pressed his lips over hers. The kiss was gentle and so good, that Diana felt her heart would burst. Emotionally rocked, she trembled as though trapped in the aftermath of an earthquake.

Slowly his mouth worked its way over hers, and she opened her lips to him in silent invitation, the way a flower does to the noonday sun, seeking its warmth, blossoming. Diana groaned, and her arms curled around his torso until her hands met at his spine. Before she was aware of how it had happened, Cliff placed his hands on her shoulders and pressed her backward, anchoring her to the blanket. He raised his head, and his eyes delved into hers.

Diana sank her fingers into the dark hair at his temples and smiled tentatively. It was the sweetest, most tender expression Cliff had ever seen, filled with such gentle goodness that he felt his heart throb with naked desire. He longed to press her body under his.

"Do you feel it, too?" he asked, needing to hear her say the words.

Diana nodded. "I wish I didn't."

"No, you don't," he returned with supreme confidence. A surge of undiluted power gripped him.

"I think he kissed her."

A girlish giggle followed the announcement.

"Katie?" Cliff asked Diana.

She nodded.

Cliff levered himself off Diana and helped her into a sitting position. Self-conscious in front of her children, Diana ran her fingers through her hair, lifting it away from her face.

"We found a starfish," Joan said, delivering it to her mother and sitting on the blanket.

Diana didn't notice the proud find as much as the fact that her daughter's shoes were missing and the bottoms of her jeans were sopping wet. Chastising Joan in front of Cliff would embarrass the eleven-year-old, and Diana resisted the urge.

"Isn't he gorgeous?" Katie demanded.

"Who?" Diana blinked, thinking her daughter could be talking about Cliff.

"The starfish!" Both girls gave her a funny look.

"Yes, he's perfectly wonderful. Now take him back to the water or he'll die."

"Ah, Mom . . ."

"You heard me." She brooked no argument.

Joan picked up the echinoderm and rushed back to the beach. Katie lingered behind, her head cocked at an angle as she studied Cliff.

"Do you like to kiss my mother?" she asked curiously.

Cliff nodded. "Yes. Does that bother you?"

Katie paused to give some consideration to the question. "No, not really, as long as she likes it, too."

"She likes it, and so do I."

Katie's pert nose wrinkled. "Does she taste good?"

"Real good."

"Gary Hidenlighter offered me a baseball card if I'd let him kiss me. I told him no." She wrapped her hands around her neck, then, graphically pretending to strangle herself. "Yuck."

"It matters who you're kissing, sweetheart," Diana explained. A fetching pink highlighted her cheekbones at her daughter and Cliff talking about something so personal.

Having satisfied her curiosity, Katie ran toward the pathway that led to the beach and to her elder sister.

"I have the feeling that if Gary Hidenlighter had offered her Kentucky Fried Chicken, she would have gone for it."

Cliff chuckled, his eyes warm. "What do I need to trade to gain your heart, Diana Collins?"

Ignoring the question, Diana picked up the blanket and took care to fold it with crisp corners. She held the quilt to her stomach as a protective barrier when she finished.

"I asked you something."

"I have no intention of answering such a leading question." In nervous agitation she flipped a stray strand of hair around her ear.

"Can I see you again tomorrow?" he asked. "Dinner, a show, anything you want."

Diana's heart constricted with dread. Now that she was faced with the decision of whether to see him again, the answer was all too clear.

"Listen," she murmured, wrapping her arms around the blanket to ward off a chill, "we need to talk about this first."

"I asked you to go to a movie with me."

"That's what I want to talk about."

"Is it that difficult to decide?"

"Yes," she whispered.

Cliff stood and leaned against the tree, bracing one foot against the trunk. "All right, when?"

Diana was uncertain. "Anytime the girls aren't around."

"Later tonight?"

She'd never felt more unsure about a man in her life. The sooner they talked, the better. "Tonight will be fine."

"Don't look so bleak. It can't be that bad."

It was worse than bad. Shirley's warnings echoed in her ears, reminding her that she'd be a fool to date a prominent woman-izer who was said to have little conscience and few scruples.

Diana's insides were shaking and her nerves were shot. She was a mature woman! She should be capable of handling this situation with far more finesse than she was exhibiting.

"I—I wish you hadn't come back." Her emotions were so close to the surface that she tossed the blanket on the picnic table and stalked away, upset with both Cliff and herself.

For half a minute, Cliff was too stunned to react. This woman never ceased to astonish him. She'd wept in his arms when he'd kissed her, and when he'd told her how attracted he was to her and asked her out again, she'd stormed away as though he'd insulted her.

Driven by instinct, Cliff raced after her, his quick stride catching up with her a few feet later.

"Maybe we should talk now," he suggested softly, gesturing toward a park bench. "We can see the girls from here. If there's a problem, I don't want it hanging over our heads. Now tell me what's got you so upset."

She gaped at him. He honestly didn't know what was wrong. He was driving her crazy, and he seemed completely oblivious to the fact. Gathering her composure, Diana nodded in silent agreement and sat down.

Cliff joined her. "Okay, what's on your mind?"

You! she wanted to scream, but he wouldn't understand her anger any more than she did. "First of all, let me tell you that I am very flattered at the attention you've given me. Considering the women you usually date, it's done worlds of good for my ego."

A frown marred his brow. "I don't know what you're talking about."

"Oh, come on, Cliff," she said in an effort to be flippant. "Surely you realize that you're 'hot stuff.'"

"So they tell me."

She expelled her breath slowly, impatiently. "A date with you would quicken any female's heart."

"I'm flattered you think so."

"Cliff, don't be cute, please—this is difficult enough."

He paused, leaned forward and clasped his hands. "I don't understand what any of this has to do with a picnic supper. I like you. So what? I think your daughters are wonderful. Where does that create a problem?"

"It just does." She felt like shouting at him.

"How?" he pressed. Women generally went out of their way to attract his attention. He found it an ironic twist that the one woman who had dominated his thoughts for an entire week would be so eager to be rid of him. Her defiance pricked his ego. "All right, let's hear it," he said, his voice low and serious.

Still, he wouldn't look at her, which was just as well for Diana, since this was difficult enough.

"I don't want to see you again," she said forcefully, although her voice shook. There—it was out. Considering the way she responded to his kisses, she must be out of her mind. Although she had to admit she didn't feel especially pleased to decline his invitation, it was for the best.

Cliff was silent. The thing was he knew she was right, but he felt he was on the brink of some major discovery about himself. Ego aside, he realized he could have just about any woman he wanted, except Diana Collins.

"I suppose Shirley told you I have the reputation of being some heartless playboy. Diana, it's not true."

Diana paused to take in several deep breaths. She'd hoped that he'd spare her this. "I think you're wonderful . . . ."

"If you honestly felt that way, you wouldn't be so eager to be rid of me."

"Don't, Cliff," she pleaded. She wasn't going to be able to explain a thing with his interrupting every five seconds.

"What I can't understand," he said, shaking his head, "is why you're making it out to be some great tragedy that I find you attractive."

"But I'm not your . . . type," she declared for lack of a better description. "And if we continue to see each other, it will only lead to problems for us both."

"It seems to me that you're jumping to conclusions."

"I'm not," she stated calmly.

Cliff was losing his temper now. "And as for your not being my type, don't you think I should be the one to decide that?"

"No," she argued. Diana could hardly believe she was telling the most devastating man she'd ever known that it would be better for them not to see each other again.

"Why not?" he shot back.

"Because."

"That doesn't make a lot of sense."

Diana clamped her mouth closed. It wasn't going to do any good to try to reason with him. He probably was so accustomed to women falling into his arms that he wasn't sure how to react when one resisted. A few years earlier she would have been like all the others, she noted mentally.

"Diana," he said after a calming minute. "I don't know what's going on in that twisted mind of yours, but I do think you're being completely unreasonable. I like you, you like me . . ."

"The girls . . ."

"Are terrific."

"But, Cliff, you drive a Lamborghini."

The car bothered her! "What's that got to do with anything?"

Diana wasn't sure she could explain. "It makes a statement."

"So does your Ford SUV."

"Exactly! What I can't understand is why a man who drives an expensive sports car is interested in seeing a thirty-year-old widow who plows through traffic in a ten-year-old bomber."

"Bomber?"

Diana's grin was fleeting. "That's what the girls call the Ford."

Cliff's gaze drifted to the two youngsters running along the rolling surf. Their bare feet popped foam bubbles with such mindless glee that he found himself smiling at their antics.

Diana's gaze followed his and her thoughts sobered.

"This doesn't really have anything to do with what cars we drive, does it?"

"No," Diana admitted softly. "Shirley warned me about you."

"I'm not going to lie," Cliff murmured. "Everything she said is probably true. But of all the women I've met, I would have thought you were one to form your own opinions."

"If it were just me, I'd be accepting your offer so fast it would make your head spin," she answered honestly. "But the girls think you're the neatest thing since microwave popcorn and they're at a vulnerable age."

"Somehow I get the feeling that what's bothering you isn't any of these things. Not the car, not the girls, not the other women I date."

He read her thoughts so well it frightened her. She clenched her hands together and nodded. "I can't be the woman you want."

He frowned. "What do you mean?"

"I haven't got the body of a centerfold or the looks of a beauty queen. I've had children."

"Hey, I'm not complaining. I like what I see."

"You might not be so sure if you saw more of me."

"Is that an offer?"

Color bloomed full force in her cheeks. "It most certainly was not."

"More's the pity."

"That's another thing. I'm . . . not easy."

"You're telling me. I've spent the past fifteen minutes trying to talk you into a movie. After all this I certainly hope you don't intend to turn me down."

She laughed then, because refusing him was impossible. He was right; she was the type of person to make up her own mind. Shirley would have her hide, but, then, her neighbor hadn't been the sole subject of his considerable charm.

"You will go with me, won't you?"

"Where?" Katie cried, running up from behind them.

"Cliff wants to take me to a movie."

Katie clapped her hands. "Oh, good. Can Joan and I go, too?"

Four

"I hope you know what you're getting yourself into," Diana's neighbor muttered, her brow puckered. She paused and stared at the bottom of her empty coffee cup. "George told me he's seen Cliff Howard bring lesser women to their knees."

"Listen, Shirley, I'm a big girl. I can take care of myself."

Shirley snickered softly. "The last time you told me that was when you decided to figure your own income tax, and we both know what happened."

Diana cringed at the memory. In an effort to save a few dollars a couple of years back, she'd gone over her financial records and filled out her own tax forms. It hadn't appeared so difficult, and to be truthful, she'd been rather proud of herself. That was until she'd been summoned for an audit by an IRS agent who had all the compassion and understanding of a grizzly bear. It had turned out that she owed the government several hundred dollars and they weren't willing to take Mastercard. They were, however, amicable to confiscating her home and children if she didn't come up with the five-hundred-dollar discrepancy. Scraping the money together on her fixed income had made the weeks following the audit some of the most unpleasant since her husband's death.

"I just don't want to see you get hurt," Shirley added in thoughtful tones. "And I'm afraid Cliff Howard's just the man to do it."

"What I want to know is why I've never seen Cliff before now?" Diana asked in an effort to change the subject. "You know so much about him, like he was a longtime family friend. I didn't even know he existed."

"George plays golf with him a couple of times a month. They meet at the country club. Until the other night, Cliff had only been to our house once." Her mouth tightened. "I should have known something like this would happen."

"Like what?"

"You falling head over heels for him."

Diana laughed outright at that. "Rest assured, I am not in love with Cliff Howard."

"But you will be," Shirley said confidently. "Every woman falls for him eventually. Some of the stories going around the clubhouse about him would shock you."

"Well, you needn't worry. I'm not going to fall for him."

"That's what they all say," Shirley told her knowingly.

Diana avoided her friend's gaze. Her neighbor wasn't saying anything she hadn't already suspected. She liked Cliff, was strongly attracted to him, but she wasn't going to fall for him. She was too intelligent to allow herself to be taken in by a notorious playboy. But, no matter what her feelings, Diana couldn't completely discredit Shirley's advice. Her neighbor could very well be right, and Diana could be headed down the slick path to heartache and moral decay.

She paused and cupped her hands around her coffee mug. "He's been wonderful with the girls," she said, hoping that alone was excuse enough to date Cliff.

"I know," Shirley answered softly, shaking her head. "That confuses me, too. I never thought Cliff Howard would like children."

"Mikey thinks he's great."

"Yeah, but Cliff won him over early by bringing him an autographed baseball."

Shirley had a point there. Besides, Mikey was the friendly sort and not easily offended. "Joan and Katie are crazy about him."

Shirley's eyes narrowed. "Just don't make the mistake of thinking you're different from all the other women who have wandered in and out of his life."

Diana pondered her friend's words. Shirley had gone to great lengths to describe Cliff's "women." To hear her neighbor tell it, Cliff Howard hadn't so much as looked at a woman over thirty, much less shown an interest in dating one. It went without saying that he usually avoided women with children. Cliff had told her himself that she was the first widow he'd taken out. Diana didn't know what was different about her, wasn't sure she wanted to know. He seemed to honestly enjoy being with her and the girls, and for now that was enough.

"What makes you think you'll be different?" Shirley pressed.

"But I am different. You said so yourself," Diana answered after a lengthy pause, holding her neighbor's concerned gaze.

"I don't mean it like that." An exasperated sigh followed. "Just keep reminding yourself that Cliff could well be another Casanova."

Diana laughed outright. "Unfortunately he's got his good looks."

"You're about as likely to have a lasting relationship with Cliff as you are with Casanova, so keep that in mind."

"Yes, Mother," Diana teased softly. She found Shirley's concern more touching than irritating.

"Just don't make me say 'I told you so,'" her neighbor returned, and the doubt rang clear in her voice.

Diana mused over their conversation for most of the day. Shirley wasn't telling her anything she hadn't already considered herself. She'd been playing with fire from the minute she'd agreed to that first dinner date with Cliff, and she knew it, but the flickering flames had never been more attractive. She was thirty, and it was time to let her hair down and kick up her heels a little.

For his part, Cliff wasn't stupid, Diana realized. He knew what kind of physical response he drew from her, knew she had been teetering with indecision when he had suggested they see each other again. So when Katie had piped in and asked to go to the movies with them, Cliff had jumped on the idea. By including the girls, he'd known she wouldn't refuse. How could she, with Joan and Katie doing flips over the idea? The man was a successful attorney and he'd read her ambivalence with the ease of a first grade primer. Although she'd been determined to put an end to this silliness, her well-constructed defenses had tumbled with astonishing unconcern and she was as eager for the drive-in as the girls. It was one of the last left in the country and in South King Country, in the countryside.

"Mom," Katie cried as she rushed into the kitchen the minute the school bus dropped her off. "Can Mikey go to the drive-in movie with us?"

Diana hedged. "I don't know, honey. Cliff has to agree."

"He won't care. I know he won't, and besides, he knows Mikey and Mikey's parents know Cliff." She slapped her hands against her side as though that fact alone were enough for anyone to come to the same decision, then grinned beguilingly.

Arguing with such logic seemed fruitless. "Let's wait and talk to Cliff once he arrives."

"Okay."

Diana watched in amazement as Katie grabbed an apple from the fruit basket and dashed out the front door to join her friends. Usually Diana was subjected to a long series of arguments whenever the girls were after something, and Katie's easy acceptance pulled her up short.

"Well, all right," she muttered after her daughter, still bemused.

By the time Cliff arrived, Diana was convinced that half the neighborhood was waiting. He parked his sports car in the driveway, and was instantly besieged by a breathless, excited Joan and two or three of Joan's friends. Katie and Mikey followed a second later. Both Diana's girls grabbed for Cliff's hand, one trying to outdo the other. With a patience that pleased and surprised Diana, Cliff stopped their excited chatter. He directed his first question to Joan.

Watching the humorous scene from the front porch, Diana saw her elder daughter issue an urgent plea for Cliff to allow her to invite their very best friends in all the world to the drive-in with them.

Katie started in next. Cliff's gaze went from the girls to a series of neighborhood kids who stood in the background, awaiting his reply.

From her position, Diana could clearly see Cliff's confusion. He'd asked for this, she mused, having trouble holding in her laughter.

"Hi," she greeted him, coming down the steps.

"Hi." His bewildered gaze sought hers as he motioned toward Joan and Katie and the accumulated friends. "What do you think?"

"It's up to you."

"Please, Cliff," Katie cried, her hands folded as if praying.

Cliff glanced down on Diana's daughter and released a long, frustrated sigh. He'd thought about this evening all day, and planned—or at least hoped—the drive-in movie would quickly put the girls to sleep so he could kiss Diana. Once again he'd discovered she'd dominated his thoughts most of the afternoon. His plans certainly hadn't included dragging half the neighborhood to the drive-in with him.

"I thought of a way it could work," Diana told him. "Come inside, and we'll talk about it."

Her compromise wasn't half bad, Cliff mused an hour later as he parked his sports car beside the SUV full of kids at the drive-in. They'd agreed earlier to take Diana's vehicle simply because his car wouldn't hold everyone. Diana had suggested they drive both cars and park next to each other. That way the adults could maintain their privacy and still manage to keep an eye on the kids, who were feeling very mature to have their own car. Now that he thought about it, Diana's idea had been just short of brilliant.

"How does everyone feel about popcorn?" Cliff asked once they'd situated the cars halfway between the screen and the snack bar.

"I already popped some," Diana informed him, climbing out of the driver's seat. Joan eagerly replaced her, draping her wrist over the steering wheel and looking as though she were Jeff Gordon ready for the Indy 500.

Diana sorted through something in the rear of the SUV and returned with her arms full. She handed each child his own bag of popcorn and a can of soda. "Don't eat any until the movie starts," she instructed, and was greeted by a series of harmonizing moans. "That goes for you, too," she told Cliff, her eyes twinkling.

He grumbled for show and shared a conspiratorial wink with Joan, who, he could see, had already managed to sample her goodies. He held his car door open for Diana before walking around the front and joining her in the close confines of his Lamborghini.

Diana scooted down low enough in the seat to rest her head against the back of the thick leather cushion. The contrast between them had never been more striking. She wore Levi's and a pink sweatshirt, while Cliff was fashionably dressed in slacks and a thick crewneck sweater. Diana sincerely doubted that any of his other dates had ever dressed so casually. Nor did she believe other women had six kids tagging along. Knowing Cliff's game, Diana considered the neighborhood tribe poetic justice.

"This is turning into a great idea," he said, wondering how much longer it would take before it got dark.

Before Diana could answer, a Road Runner cartoon appeared on the huge white screen. The kids in the car next to them cheered with excitement, and even from her position in Cliff's sports car, she could hear them rip into their bags of popcorn.

"You're a good sport," Diana said, feeling self-conscious all of a sudden. "I mean about the kids and everything."

"Hey, no problem."

"How'd work go?" She felt obligated to make small talk, certain he wouldn't possibly be interested in the cartoon.

"Good. How about your day?"

"Fine." She clenched her hands together so hard her fingers ached. "Joan went to the orthodontist." Now that made for brilliant conversation! She'd bore him to death before the end of the previews.

"So she's going into braces?"

Diana nodded and reached for her bag of popcorn so she'd have something to do with her hands. "I told her she's enough of a live wire as it is."

Cliff chuckled. "I'm glad to hear she's going straight."

Now it was Diana's turn to laugh. What had seemed the perfect solution an hour before now had the feel of a disaster in the making. Alone with Cliff, she'd seldom been more uncertain about anything. Joan and Katie had been her shield, protecting her from the wealth of emotion Cliff was capable of raising within her. She sat beside him, quivering inside, never having felt more vulnerable. He could make cornmeal mush of her life if he chose to, and like a fool, she'd all but issued the invitation for him to do so. Shirley's warnings sounded in her ears like sonic booms, and for an instant, Diana had the sinking feeling that one of Custer's men must have experienced the same sensation as he rode into battle, wondering what he was doing there. Diana wondered, too. Oh, man, did she wonder.

The credits for the Lucas film rolled onto the huge screen, but Diana's thoughts weren't on the highly rated movie. The open bag of popcorn rested on her lap, but she dared not eat any, sure the popcorn would stick halfway down her desert-dry throat.

"Diana?"

She jumped halfway out of her seat. "Yes?"

Cliff's smile was lazy and gentle and understanding. "Relax, will you? I'm not going to leap on you."

If there'd been a hole to crawl into, Diana would have gladly jumped inside. "I know that."

"Then what's the problem?"

There didn't seem to be enough words to explain. She was a mature, capable woman, but when she was around him, all her hard-earned independence evaporated into thin air like an ice chip on an Arizona sidewalk. He brought back feelings she preferred to keep buried, churning emotions that reminded her she was still a young, healthy woman. When she was with Cliff, she was a red-blooded woman, and her body felt obliged to remind her of the needs she didn't want to remember. With Cliff so close beside her, the last thing on her mind was motherhood and apple pie. His proximity caused her to quiver from the inside out. She wanted him to kiss her, longed for his touch. And it scared her to death.

"Diana?"

Slowly she turned to look at him. Her face felt hot against the crisp evening air, and Cliff's look brushed lightly over her features. He was kissing her with his eyes, and she was burning up with fever. Suddenly the interior of the car made her feel claustrophobic. She set the popcorn aside and reached for the door handle.

His hand stopped her. "You're beautiful."

He whispered the words with such intensity that Diana felt them melt in the air like cotton candy against her tongue. She wanted to shout at him not to say such things to her, that it wasn't necessary. She didn't need to hear them, didn't want him to say them. But the protest died a speedy death as he reached for her shoulders. His gaze held her prisoner for what seemed an eternity as he slowly slid his hand from the curve of her shoulder upward, until he found her warm nape. He didn't move, hardly breathed, anticipating her reaction. When he could wait no longer for an invitation, he wove his fingers into her hair and directed her mouth toward his.

Cliff's lips claimed hers in a fury of desire. His mouth slanted against hers in a full, lush kiss that spoke of fervor and timeless longing. The shaking inside Diana increased and she raised her hands to grip his shoulders just to maintain her equilibrium. Her skin was hot and cold at the same time.

Suddenly it all seemed too much. Using her arms as leverage, Diana abruptly broke away. Head bowed, she drew in ragged breaths. "Cliff, I . . ."

He wouldn't allow her to speak and gently directed her mouth back to his. All the resolve she could muster, which wasn't much, had gone into breaking off the kiss. When he reached for her again, unwilling to listen to any argument, there was nothing left with which to refuse him. His mouth opened wider, deepening the kiss, and Diana let him. Folding her arms around his neck, she leaned into his strength. He brought her against him possessively until her ribs ached and the heat of his torso burned its way down the length of her own. Cliff felt her body's natural response to him and he groaned. At this moment he'd give anything to be anyplace besides a drive-in. He wanted to lift the sweatshirt over her head and toss it aside. The pain of denial was strong and sharp as he buried his face in the sloped curve of her neck. With even, steady breaths, he tried to force his pulse to a slow, rhythmical beat as he struggled within himself. It had been a long time since he'd experienced such an intensity of need.

The battle that waged inside Diana was fierce. She wanted to push herself away from him and scream that she wasn't like his other women. There'd been only one lover in her life, and she wasn't going to become his next conquest simply because her hormones behaved like jumping beans whenever he touched her. But the words that crossed her mind didn't make it to her lips.

"Diana . . ." Cliff spoke first, his voice filled with gruff emotion. "Listen, I know what you're thinking."

"Don't, Cliff, please don't." She twisted her face away from him, unable to form words to explain all that she was thinking and feeling. She felt both tormented and compelled by what was happening to them.

Cliff tensed, and his fingers dug into her shoulders.

"What's wrong?" She lifted her head and bravely raised her gaze to meet his own.

"Don't look now, but we've got an audience."

"Joan?"

"And . . . others."

"How many others?"

"Five."

"All six of the kids are staring at us?" The hot flush that had stained her neck raced toward her cheeks and into the roots of her hair. She'd assured all the neighborhood parents that the drive-in movie was rated PG, and here she was giving them an R-rated sideshow.

"Six noses are pressed against the window, and six pairs of eyes are glued on us," Cliff interjected with little humor.

"Oh, no," Diana groaned, hanging her head in abject misery.

"Joan's giving me the thumbs-up sign, Katie looks shocked and Mikey's obviously thoroughly disgusted. He's decided to cover his eyes."

"What should we do?" Diana asked next, horribly embarrassed.

"Good grief, why ask me? I don't know a thing about kids."

His hold was tight enough to cause her shoulders to ache, but Diana didn't complain. She was as much at a loss about what to do as Cliff was. "I think we should smile and wave, and then casually go back to watching the movie."

"This isn't the time to be cute."

"I wasn't trying to be funny. That was my idea."

"If that's the best you can come up with, then I suggest you turn in your Mother of the Year Award."

"What?" Diana cried.

"We could be warping young minds here, and all you're doing is coming up with jokes."

"Oh, for heaven's sake, I think it's safe to assume they've seen people kiss before now," Diana said, growing more amused by the moment.

"Hey, Mom."

Joan's shout interrupted their discussion. Forcing herself to appear calm and collected, Diana twisted around, painted a silly smile on her face and rolled down the window. "Yes, sweetheart?" she answered in a perfectly controlled voice. She was actually proud of herself for maintaining her cool. She prayed her expression gave away none of the naked desire she'd been feeling only moments before.

"Why are you arguing with Cliff?"

"What makes you ask that?"

"You weren't fighting a minute ago."

"You were kissing him real hard," Katie popped in. She was leaning from the back seat into the front and sticking her head out the side window next to her sister. "Judy Gilmore's boyfriend kissed her like that the time she baby-sat for us. Remember?"

"Say, aren't you kids supposed to be watching the movie?" Cliff asked, having trouble disguising his chagrin.

"It's more fun looking at you," Joan answered for the group.

"Mom, I've got to go to the bathroom."

"Me, too." Three other voices chimed in from behind Katie.

"I'll take you." Diana couldn't get out of the car fast enough. Rarely had she been more grateful for the call of nature.

By the time Diana returned, Cliff's mood had improved considerably. He was munching on popcorn and staring at the screen. When she eased into the seat beside him, he glanced in her direction and grinned. "The movie's actually pretty good."

Diana suspected it wasn't half as amusing as they'd been. She had to give Cliff credit—he really was a good sport.

By the time the second feature had started, Joan, Katie and their friends were sound asleep.

"I should have waited until now to kiss you," Cliff joked, staring across at the car filled with snoozing youngsters. "Problem was, I was too eager."

That had been Diana's trouble, as well. From the minute she'd sat beside him and they'd been alone, she'd known what was bound to happen. She'd wanted it too much.

Cliff looped his arm around her shoulder and brought her head down to his hard chest. "Now that we haven't got a crowd cheering us on, do you want to try it again?" He gave her a self-effacing, enticing half smile.

Diana laughed, and although the console prevented her

from cuddling up close to his side, she adjusted herself as best she could. "When I was a teenager, we used to call the drive-in the 'passion pit.'"

"Hey, I'm game. I don't know if you recognize it or not, but there's chemistry between us." He brushed the hair from her brow and pressed his lips there.

"I noticed it all right." His kiss just then was like adding water to hot grease. "It's more potent than I care to dwell on."

"I'll say."

He did kiss her again during the second movie, but more for experimentation than anything. His fingers, tucked under her chin, turned her mouth to his as his warm lips touched, stroked and brushed hers. Temporarily satisfied, Cliff settled back and watched the movie for a few minutes more. He reached for her again later and nibbled along her neck. He refused to hold her tight, as aware of the danger as she of these explosive fireworks between them. A drive-in movie with a carload of kids parked in the next space was not the place to get overly romantic.

The second movie over, Cliff met her back at the house after Diana had dropped off Joan and Katie's friends. Both girls were more interested in sleeping than climbing out of the car. Finally Cliff lifted the sleeping Katie into his arms and carried her inside and up the stairs. A dreamy-eyed Joan followed behind, yawning as she went.

Diana tucked the blankets around her elder daughter. Joan planted her hands beneath her pillow and rolled onto her side. "Mom?"

"Yes, honey."

"Thank Cliff for me, okay?"

"Will do."

Joan forced one eye open. "Are you going to see him again?"

"I . . . don't know, honey. He hasn't asked me out."

"You should invite him to dinner. You make great spaghetti."

"Honey, I don't think that's a good idea."

"I happen to love good spaghetti," Cliff answered.

Diana turned and found him standing in the doorway of Joan's bedroom. "Why don't you make up a batch and bring it sailing?"

"Sailing?"

"You and the girls." Having heard Diana's hesitation, he re-signed himself to including her daughters in every outing until she learned to trust him. "We'll make a day of it."

"When?"

Cliff thought about waiting another week to see Diana again, and knew that was much too long. His schedule for the next week was hectic and he'd be lucky to find the time to spend more than an hour or two with her. He had two cases going to trial and a backlog of work awaiting his attention. "Tomorrow," he suggested.

Joan bolted upright. "Hey, that sounds great. Count me in."

Irritated, Diana glared down at her daughter. "Cliff, I don't know. I'd think you'd have had your fill of me and the girls for one weekend."

"Let me be the judge of that."

"I've never been sailing before," Joan reminded Diana, her two round eyes gazing up at her pleadingly. "And you know how Katie loves anything that has to do with the water."

"We'll talk about it later," Diana told her firmly, and walked out of the bedroom. Cliff followed her down the stairs.

"Well, what do you say about tomorrow?" he asked, stand-ing in front of the door.

"I'm . . . not sure." She remained on the bottom step, so that when he walked over to her, their eyes were level.

He smiled at her then and slipped one arm around her waist to pull her against him. In an effort to escape, Diana pried his arm loose and climbed one stair up so she rose a head above him.

If she thought he was going to let her go so easily, Cliff mused, then Diana Collins had a great deal to learn about him.

He brought her into his arms and kissed her until everything went still as hot, tingling shivers raced through Diana. She closed her eyes and stopped breathing.

"Tomorrow," she said in a tight, strained whisper. "What time?"

"Noon," Cliff mumbled, and dropped his hands.

Diana gripped the banister until her nails threatened to bend. "Thank you for tonight."

It was all Cliff could do to nod. He backed away from her as though she held a torch that was blazing out of control. Already he was singed, and all he could think about was coming back for more.

Five

"How long will it take before I catch a fish?" Katie asked impatiently. Her fishing pole was poised over the side of the sailboat as the forty-foot sloop lazily sliced through the dark green waters of Puget Sound.

"Longer than five minutes," Diana informed her younger daughter. She tossed an apologetic glance in Cliff's direction. He'd been the one so keen on this outing. She wasn't nearly convinced all this time together with the girls would work. Cooping the four of them up in the close confines of a sailboat for an afternoon wouldn't serve anyone's best interests as far as she could see. But Cliff had assured her otherwise, and the girls continued to swoon under the force of his charm. With such resounding enthusiasm from both parties, Diana certainly wasn't going to argue.

"The secret is to convince the fish he's hungry," Joan said haughtily with the superior knowledge of a girl three years Katie's senior.

"How do you do that?"

Diana was curious herself.

"Move your line a little so the bait wiggles," Joan answered primly, and gyrated her hips a couple of times as an example. "That makes the fish want to check out what's happening. In case you weren't aware of it, fish are by nature shy. All they need is a little encouragement."

"All fish are shy?" Diana muttered under her breath for Cliff's benefit.

"Especially sharks," he returned out of the corner of his mouth.

"I've met a few of those in my time." Chuckling, Diana watched as he finished baiting Joan's hook and handed her the pole. Cliff could well be a shark, but if so, he was a clever one.

When he'd completed the task, he paused and grinned at her.

"What about you?" Diana asked as he settled down by the helm. "Aren't you going to fish?"

"Naw." He slouched down and draped his elbow over the side of the sloop. Squinting, he smiled into the sun and expertly steered the sailboat into the wind.

For a full minute, Diana couldn't look away. Shirley had painted Cliff in such grim tones—a man without conscience who freely used women. When he was finished, Shirley had said, he hurled them aside for fresh conquests. Looking at him now, Diana refused to believe it. Cliff was patient with the girls, and exquisitely gentle with her. Just being with him was more fun than she could remember having had in months. He appeared completely at ease with her and Joan and Katie. But, then, she reminded herself, women were said to be his forte. If Cliff were indeed the scoundrel her neighbor so ardently claimed him to be, then he'd done an excellent job bamboozling her.

"Mom, come and look," Katie called, and Diana moved closer to her daughter.

Cliff smiled. He was enjoying this outing with Diana and her family. Getting the girls occupied fishing had helped. He had them using his outdated equipment, so nothing expensive could be ruined. Actually, he was rather proud of himself for being so organized. He'd set the fishing gear the girls could use on one side of the boat and his own on the other. That way, there would be no confusion.

Now, with the girls interested in catching "shy" fish, he could soak up the sun and take time to study Diana. She was nothing like the women he was accustomed to dating. The attraction he felt for her was as much a shock to him as it apparently had been to her.

She'd finished with Katie and sat next to him. They were so close that Cliff could feel the warmth radiating from her. He longed to put his arm around her and bring her closer to his side. Okay, he'd admit it! He wanted to kiss her. Her butterscotch kisses were quickly becoming habit forming. All he'd need to do was lean forward. Their torsos would touch first, and his mouth would quickly find hers. No matter where he looked—the sky, the green water, the billowing sails, anyplace—he couldn't dispel every delicate, womanly nuance of Diana. Frustrated, he deliberately turned his thoughts to other matters.

"How's it going, girls?" he called, seeking a diversion.

"Great," Joan shouted back.

Cliff was impressed with her enthusiasm.

"All right, I guess," Katie said, peering over the side. "Here, fishy, fishy, fishy."

"That isn't going to help," Joan snapped, and as if to prove her point, she swung her fishing pole back and forth a couple of times, looking superior and confident.

Contented, Cliff grinned, and his gaze drifted back to Diana. She was a widow, no less. He'd always pictured widows as old ladies with lots of grandchildren, which was illogical, he realized. Diana was his own age. It wasn't that he'd avoided dating women thirty and over, he simply hadn't been attracted to any.

But he was attracted to Diana. Oh yes, was he attracted! He wasn't so naive not to realize his playboy reputation had put her off. He'd give his eyeteeth to know what she'd heard—it would do wonders for his ego. Smiling, he relaxed and loosened his grip on the helm. He didn't know what George Holiday had told his wife, but apparently Shirley had repeated it in graphic detail. Luckily Diana had a decent head on her shoulders and was smart enough to recognize a bunch of exaggerations when she heard them.

Diana had never been on a sailboat before and she loved it, loved the feeling of relaxed simplicity, loved the wind as it whipped against her face and hair, loved the power of the sloop as it plowed through the water, slicing it as effectively as a hot butcher's knife through butter. Earlier, Cliff had let her man the helm while he'd moved forward to raise the sails, and she had been on a natural high ever since.

"You're looking thoughtful," Cliff said to Diana a moment later.

Her returning smile was slow and lazy. She closed her eyes and let the wind whip through her hair, not caring what havoc the breeze wreaked. "I could get used to this," she murmured, savoring the feel of the noonday sun on her upturned face.

"Yes," Cliff admitted. He could get used to having her with him just as easily. When he stopped to analyze his feelings, he realized that she was the down-home type of woman he didn't feel the need to impress. He could be himself, relax. He was getting too old and lazy for the mating rituals he'd been participating in the past few years.

"Cliff!" Joan screamed into the wind, her shrill voice filled with panic. "I've . . . got something." The fishing pole was nearly bent in two. "It's big."

"Joan caught a whale," Katie called out excitedly.

"Hold on." Cliff jumped up and gave the helm to Diana.

"Here, you take it," Joan cried. "It's too big for me."

"You're doing fine."

"I'm not, either!"

"Joan, just do what Cliff says," Diana barked, as nervous as her daughter.

"But he hasn't said anything yet."

"How come Joan can catch a fish and I can't?" Katie whined. "I wiggled my hips and everything."

"Honey, now isn't the time to discuss it."

"It's never the time when I want to ask you something."

"Reel it in," Cliff shouted. The urge to jerk the pole out of the eleven-year-old's hands and do it himself was strong. The once confident Joan looked as if she would have willingly forgotten the whole thing.

Cliff watched as the fifth grader's hand yanked against the line. "Don't do that—you'll lose him!"

"I don't care. You do it—I didn't really want to kill a fish, anyway."

"Don't be a quitter," Cliff said, more gruffly than he'd intended. "You're doing fine."

"I am not!"

Exasperated, Cliff moved behind Joan and helped her grip the pole. With his hand over hers, he reeled for all he was worth, tugging the line closer and closer to the boat.

"I can see him," Katie shouted, jumping up and down.

"It's a salmon," Cliff called out as they got the large fish close to the boat. "A nice size sockeye from the look of him." He left Joan long enough to retrieve the net, then leaned over the side of the boat to pull the struggling salmon out of the water.

"Gross," Joan muttered, and closed her eyes. "No one told me there was going to be blood."

"Only a little," Diana assured her.

"I want to catch a fish," Katie cried a second time. "It's not fair that Joan caught one and I didn't."

"Don't worry about it," Joan said with a jubilant sigh. "I'll help you."

"I don't want your help. I want Cliff to show me."

"Cliff has to steer the sailboat," Diana explained to her younger daughter. She knew this peaceful afternoon was too good to be true. The girls would erupt into one of their famous fights and shock poor Cliff. He wasn't used to being around children— he wouldn't understand that they bickered almost constantly.

"I'm hungry," Katie decided next.

In order to appease her younger daughter, Diana climbed below deck to the galley, where Cliff had stored the picnic basket, and got Katie a sandwich and a can of her favorite soda.

Within a half hour, both girls were back to fishing, and serenity reigned once again.

"How much longer will it take?" Katie demanded within a few minutes. The irritating question was repeated at regular intervals.

Cliff's smile was getting stiffer by the minute. He wished he hadn't invited the girls along. He wanted Diana to himself, but he realized she would have refused the invitation if Joan and Katie hadn't been included. For the past thirty minutes, he'd been sitting watching Diana and wanting to kiss her. He couldn't do half the things he longed to do with Joan and Katie scrutinizing his every move. They were good kids, but it wasn't the same as being alone with Diana. And with Katie whining every few minutes, Cliff sorely felt the need for a little peace and quiet. His musings were interrupted by Katie's excited shout.

"Mommy, I got a fish, I got a fish!"

"I'll show you how to bring him in!" Joan yelled, and quickly moved to her sister's side, dragging her fishing pole with her.

"Hey! Watch your lines." Cliff's warning came too late, and

before anyone could do anything to prevent it, the two fishing lines were hopelessly entangled.

"What do we do now?" Joan asked, tossing Cliff a look over her shoulder.

Once Cliff had assessed the situation, he shrugged and sadly shook his head. "There's nothing to do. I'll have to cut both lines."

"But my fish . . ."

"Honey, you can't reel him in now," Diana hastened to explain, praying Katie wouldn't be too terribly disappointed.

Cliff hated to cut the fishing lines, too, and was angry for not having warned the girls about what would happen if they didn't mind their poles. In addition to losing the fish, he was throwing away good lures and weights. Thankfully, there was nothing of real value like his—It was then that he saw his open tackle box on the other side of the boat. Cliff went stark still. He'd given both girls specific instructions to stay out of his gear. His swift anger could not be contained.

"Who got into my stuff?" he demanded, and knelt down to examine his box. His worst fears were quickly realized. "My lucky lure is missing. Who took my lucky lure?"

"Joan, Katie, did either of you get into Cliff's box?" Already Diana feared the answer. Cliff looked as though he'd like to strangle both girls for so much as touching his equipment.

"Where is my lucky lure?" Cliff repeated, his face hard and cold.

"You . . . you just cut it off." Katie's head dropped so low Diana could see her crown.

For a minute it looked as though Cliff would jump overboard in an effort to retrieve his silver lure from the murky green waters.

"That was my lucky lure," Cliff repeated, as if in a daze. "I caught a forty-pound rock cod with that silver baby."

"Katie," Diana coaxed, "why did you get into Cliff's equipment when he asked you not to?"

Cliff slammed the lid to his tackle box closed, and the sound reverberated around the inside of the sailboat like a cannon shot. He stood and turned his back to the three women. Diana and her girls couldn't appreciate something like a special lure. To them it was just a five-dollar piece of silver. To him it was his "sure bet." The success of an entire fishing expedition depended on whether he had that silver lure. He might as well hang up his fishing pole for good without it. A woman couldn't be expected to appreciate how much it meant. Burying his hands inside his pants pockets, Cliff muttered something vile under his breath and decided there wasn't anything he could do about it now. The lure was gone.

"Mom, I just heard Cliff swear," Joan whispered.

"Cliff, I'm sorry." Diana felt obliged to say something, although she realized it wasn't nearly enough. She felt terrible. With one look at the way the hot color had circled his ears, she knew how truly angry he was.

"It's my fault," Katie blubbered, hiding her face against her mother's stomach. "Joan caught a fish and I wanted one, too, and I thought Cliff's pretty lure would help."

"You'll replace the lure out of your allowance money," Diana said sternly.

Tears welled up in the small, dark eyes as she nodded, eager to do anything to appease Cliff.

With slow, deliberate action, Cliff returned to the helm and sat down heavily. His brooding gaze avoided Diana and the girls. "Don't worry about it," he said as calmly as possible.

"I'm sorry, Cliff," Katie whispered in a small, broken voice.

He forced his gaze to the youngster. "Don't give it a second thought," he said almost flippantly.

"I'll buy you a new silver lure just as pretty."

"I said, don't worry about it."

If possible, Katie's brown eyes grew more round. Tears rolled down her pale cheeks.

"How about something to eat?" Diana interjected, rubbing her palms together, hoping to generate interest in the packed lunch.

"We're not hungry," Joan answered for both her and her sister.

"Cliff?"

"No, thanks."

"I guess I'm the only one." She got out a sandwich and even managed to choke down a couple of bites.

Cliff's gaze drifted to Diana, who was valiantly pretending nothing was wrong. If she didn't watch it, she was likely to gag on that sandwich. Joan and Katie were huddled together, staring at him like orphans through a rich family's living room window on Christmas Eve. Joan had her arm draped over her sister's shoulders, while Katie looked thoroughly miserable. Finally Cliff couldn't stand it anymore.

"How come she loses my lure and I'm the one feeling guilty?" If there'd been a place to stalk off to, he would have done it. As it was, he was stuck on the boat with all three of them, and he wasn't in the mood for company or conversation.

"I think it's time to head back to the marina," Diana murmured, and sat beside her daughters.

Cliff couldn't have agreed with her more. He mumbled some reply and quickly tacked across the wind, heading in the direction of Des Moines Marina. Every now and then, his gaze reverted to Diana and her daughters. The three sat in the same dejected pose, shoulders hunched forward, eyes lowered to the deck, hands planted primly on their knees. The sight of them only made Cliff feel worse. All right, he'd lost his temper, but only a little. His conscience ate at him. So he shouldn't have yelled, and Joan was right, he had sworn. He'd overreacted. Talk about the wrath of Khan! But for crying out loud, Katie had gotten into his equipment, when he'd given specific instructions for her to stay out.

Diana longed to say or do something to alleviate this terrible tension. Cliff had every reason to be upset. She was angry with Katie, too, but the eight-year-old was truly sorry, and other than replacing the lure, which Katie had already promised, there was nothing more the little girl could do.

"Cliff . . ."

"Diana . . ."

They spoke simultaneously.

"You first," Cliff said, and gestured toward her, unable to tolerate the silence any longer.

"I want you to know how sorry I am." When Cliff opened his mouth, she knew before he spoke what he planned to say, and it irritated her more than an angry argument. Squaring her shoulders, she gritted her teeth and waved her index finger at him. "Please don't tell me not to worry about it."

"Let's forget it, okay?" His smile was only a little stiff. He didn't want this unfortunate incident to ruin a promising relationship. When it came to dealing with women, he did fine— more than fine. It was Joan and Katie who had placed him out of his element.

"It's obvious you're not going to forget it."

"It's just that it was a special lure," Cliff said, although that certainly didn't excuse his anger.

Katie placed her hands over her face and burst into sobs.

If Cliff had been feeling guilty before, it was nothing compared to the regret that shot through him at Katie's teary tirade. He'd lost his favorite lure; *he* felt guilty, and she was crying. He didn't understand any of this, but the one thing he did know was that he couldn't bear to see the youngster so miserable. Without forethought, he left the helm and went over to Katie.

He picked her up and hugged her against his chest before turning to steer the sloop with Katie cradled in his lap. "It's all right, sweetheart," he whispered, wrapping his arms around her.

"But . . . I . . . lost . . . your . . . lucky lure," she bellowed.

"It was just an ordinary lure. You can buy me another one just like it, and then that one will be my luckiest lure ever."

"I'm . . . so-o-o sorry." She kept her face hidden in his shoulder.

"I know."

"I'll never ever get into your fishing box again. I promise."

She raised her head, and Cliff wiped a tear from the corner of her eye. The surge of tenderness that overtook him came as a surprise. He'd been angry, but he was over that. There were more important things in life than a silly lure, and he'd just learned that an eight-year-old's smile was one of them.

"We've both learned a valuable lesson, haven't we?"

Katie responded with a quick nod. "Can I still be your friend?"

"You bet."

Her returning grin was wide.

"You want to learn how to steer the sailboat?"

She couldn't agree fast enough. "Can I?"

"Sure."

Diana felt the burden of guilt lift from her shoulders. She enjoyed Cliff's company and liked the way he'd included the girls in their dates. He'd gone out of his way to be good to her, and she would have hated to see everything ruined over a lost lure. He had a right to be upset—she was mad herself—but anger and regret weren't going to replace his "silver baby."

Diana watched as Cliff patiently showed Katie the importance of heading the sailboat into the wind. The eight-year-old listened patiently while Cliff explained the various maneuvers. He looked up once, and their eyes happened to meet. Cliff smiled, and Diana thought she'd never seen anything more dazzling.

From now on she wasn't listening to anything Shirley Holiday had to say. She knew everything she needed to know about Cliff Howard.

Remembering how good Cliff had been with Katie after she'd lost his lure made the days that followed the sailing trip pass quickly as she anticipated seeing him again. They'd left the marina, had dined on Kentucky Fried Chicken, Katie's favorite, and had headed back to Diana's house. Cliff had discreetly kissed her goodbye, invited her to dinner and promised to phone.

Joan sauntered into the kitchen, paused and glanced at the two chicken TV dinners sitting on top of the kitchen counter. "Is Cliff taking you to dinner?"

"Good guess."

Joan wrinkled up her nose. "I hate to tell you this, but Katie's not going to eat chicken unless it's from the Colonel."

Diana opened the microwave and placed the frozen meals inside. "She'll live."

"A starving woman wouldn't eat that, either."

Diana sighed. "You'll enjoy the chicken, so quit worrying about it."

"Okay."

The phone rang, and Joan leaped to answer it as if there were some concern that Diana would fight her for it.

"Hello."

Diana rolled her eyes as her daughter's voice dipped to a low, seductive note, as though she expected Justin Bieber to phone and ask for her.

"Oh, hi, Cliff. Yeah, Mom's right here." She placed the receiver to her stomach. "Mom, it's Cliff."

Diana wiped her hands dry on a kitchen towel and reached for the phone. "Hello."

"Hi."

The sound of his voice did wondrous things to her pulse. She wouldn't need an aerobics class if she talked to Cliff Howard regularly. "The kids' dinner is in the microwave, and the girls are going over to Shirley's afterward, so I should be ready within the hour."

"That makes what I have to tell you all the more difficult." He'd been looking forward to this dinner date all week and was frustrated.

"You can't make it?" Diana guessed. She should have known something like this would happen. Everything had gone too smoothly. The girls were going to Shirley's, she'd found a lovely pink silk dress on sale and her hair looked great, for once. Naturally Cliff would have to cancel!

"I'm sorry," he stated simply, and explained without a lot of detail what had happened. A court date had been changed and he had to prepare an important brief by morning. He wouldn't be able to get away for hours. He hated it, would have done anything to get out of it, but couldn't. Then he waited for the backlash that normally followed when he was forced into breaking a dinner engagement.

"I know you wouldn't cancel if it wasn't something important," Diana said, hiding her disappointment.

"You're not angry?"

His question took Diana aback. "Should I be?"

"I . . . no."

"I'm not saying I won't miss seeing you." She marveled that she was so willing to admit that. When it came to Cliff, she continued to feel as though she were standing on shifting sand. She was afraid of letting her emotions get out of control, and she didn't want to rely on him for more than an occasional date. And yet every time he asked to see her again, she was as giddy as Joan over the rock group U2.

"I'll make it up to you," Cliff promised.

"There's no reason to do that."

"How about dinner Thursday?"

Diana checked the calendar beside the phone. "The PTA is electing its officers for next year, and since I'm a candidate for secretary, I should at least make a showing."

"How about—"

"Honestly, Cliff, you don't need to make anything up to me. If you're so—"

"Diana," he cut in, "I haven't seen you or the girls in three days. I'm starting to get withdrawal symptoms. I actually found myself looking forward to watching the Disney Channel this week."

Diana laughed.

"If you can't go out with me Thursday, then how about Friday?" Now that he'd gained her trust, he felt more comfortable about having her accept an invitation without having to include her daughters.

"Cliff, listen, I'm already going to be gone three nights this week."

"Three?"

"Yes, I went to a Girl Scout planning meeting on Monday. I had a quick Sunday school staff meeting Tuesday and now the PTA thing on Thursday. I don't mind leaving the girls every now and then, but four nights in one week is too much. If you want the truth, it's probably a good thing you have to cancel tonight. I don't like being gone this much."

Cliff leaned back in his desk chair and chewed on the end of his pencil. After the fishing fiasco, he'd hoped to avoid including the girls in any more of their dates for a while. "Okay," he said reluctantly, "let's do something with the girls on Friday."

"Cliff, no."

"No?"

"Really. Both Joan and Katie have been up late every night this week. Katie's got a cold, and I really don't want to take her out again. Friday night, I planned on ordering pizza and getting them both down early." She wasn't making excuses not to see him, and prayed he understood that. Everything she'd said was the complete truth.

"Saturday night, then?" He wasn't giving up on her, not this easily.

Her breath was released on a nervous sigh. "All right."

Six

The house was still, and Diana paused for a moment to cherish the quiet. After loud protests and an argument with Joan, who seemed to think a fifth grader should be allowed to stay up and watch MTV, both girls were in bed. Whether they were asleep or not was an entirely different question. Peace reigned, and that was all that mattered to Diana.

She brewed herself a cup of tea and sat with her feet up, reading. In another two weeks school would be out, and then Joan and Katie would find even more excuses to put off going to bed. If it were up to those two ruffians, Diana knew they'd loiter around until midnight. Only Diana wouldn't let them. In some ways she was eager to spend the summer with the girls, and in other ways she dreaded three long months of total togetherness. Her parents had insisted on having them fly to Wichita and had even paid for their airline tickets. Diana was looking forward to those two weeks as a welcome reprieve. She missed seeing her family and in the past had briefly toyed with the idea of moving back to her hometown. That had been her original intention after Stan had died. Her parents had planned to come and help her with the move, but Diana had hedged, uncertain. Now she was convinced she'd made the right decision to stay in the Seattle area. With the loss of their father, the girls had already experienced enough upheaval in their young lives. A move so soon afterward wouldn't have been good for any of them. Although Diana dearly loved her family, she did better when they weren't hovering close by.

Her wandering thoughts were interrupted by the doorbell. She paused and checked the time. It was only a few minutes past nine, but she rarely received company this late.

Setting aside her book and her tea, she answered the door. "Cliff."

"Hi." His ready smile was filled with charm. "Did you win the election?"

Diana was more than a little surprised to see him. After their telephone conversation a couple of days before, she hadn't known what to think. She stepped aside so he could come in. "Win the election?" she repeated, not following his line of thought.

"Yes, you told me you were up for PTA secretary."

"Oh, yes. I was running unopposed, so there wasn't much chance I'd lose."

"Is that Cliff?" Katie, dressed in her pink flannel nightgown, appeared at the top of the stairs.

"Hi, Katie." Cliff raised his hand to greet the youngster, his smile only a little forced. He preferred to spend time with Diana alone tonight.

"Katie, you're supposed to be asleep."

"Can I give Cliff his lure?"

"Okay." Diana knew it would do little good to argue. While shopping in a local store the day before, Katie had found a similar fishing lure, and they'd bought it as a replacement for Cliff's. At the time, Diana had wondered if there would be an opportunity to see Cliff again. He had asked to see her on

Saturday, but she half expected him to cancel. She wasn't sure where their relationship was headed. He seemed determined to see her again, but she hadn't heard a word from him since their abrupt telephone conversation a few days earlier.

Katie flew down the stairs and raced into the kitchen. "Mom, where'd you put it?"

"In the junk drawer."

As if by magic an exasperated Katie reappeared, hands on her hips. "Mom," she said with a meaningful sigh, "all the drawers are filled with junk."

Rather than answer, Diana stepped into the kitchen and retrieved the fishing lure for her daughter.

Katie eagerly ripped it from Diana's fingers and hurried back to Cliff, who was sitting in the living room. "Here's another lucky lure," she said, her eyes as round as grapefruits. "I'm real sorry I lost yours."

Cliff's gaze sought Diana's as he accepted the lure. "I told you not to fret over it."

"But you got real angry, and I felt bad because I wasn't supposed to get into your fishing gear and I did. Mom's making me pay for it out of my allowance."

"I'd rather you didn't." Cliff directed the comment to Diana.

Before Diana could respond, Katie broke in. "But I have to!" she declared earnestly. "Otherwise I won't learn a lesson—at least that's what Mom said."

"Moms know what's best," Cliff managed to murmur, looking uncomfortable.

Katie brightened. "Besides, I thought that if I bought you another lucky lure, then you'd take Joan and me out in your sailboat again. Next time I promise I won't get into your fishing box." As though to emphasize her point, she spit on the tips of her fingers and dutifully crossed her heart.

Before Cliff realized Katie's intention, the little girl hurled her arms around his neck and gave him a wet kiss on the cheek.

Diana smiled at his shocked look. "Tell Cliff good-night, honey."

Without argument, Katie paused long enough to give her mother another hug and kiss, then dutifully traipsed back upstairs.

"It seems women have a way of throwing themselves into your arms," Diana teased once Katie had left the room. She hoped to lighten the mood. She didn't know why Cliff had come, especially when he looked as though he'd rather be any-place else in the world than with her.

"I sincerely hope the trait runs in this family," Cliff teased back. He held out his arms to her, then complained with a low groan when Diana chose to ignore his offer.

Cliff wasn't exactly sure what was going on with him. After their last adventure on the sailboat, he'd decided that although he enjoyed Joan and Katie, he preferred to keep the kids out of the dating picture. It was Diana who interested him. In fact, he couldn't stop thinking about her.

She wasn't as beautiful as other women he'd seen. Her hips were a tad too wide, but where physical attributes had seemed important in the past, they didn't seem to matter with her.

When it came to women, Cliff wasn't being conceited when he admitted he could pick and choose. Yet the one woman who filled his thoughts was a young widow with two preteens. He'd been so astonished at the desire he felt for Diana that he'd phoned his brother in California and told him about her.

Rich had listened, chuckled knowingly and laughed out-right when Cliff mentioned that Diana was a widow with two daughters. Then he'd made some derogatory comment about it being time for Cliff to find a real woman. Cliff had been vaguely disappointed in the conversation. Subconsciously he'd wanted his brother to tell him to wise up and stay away from a woman with children. Cliff had almost *wanted* Rich to tell him to avoid Diana and insist that a relationship with her would be nothing but trouble. Maybe that was what Cliff wanted to hear, but it wasn't what he felt.

Even if Rich had advised him to break things off with her, he doubted that he would have been able to. She was in his blood now, increasing the potency of his attraction each time they were together. That evening as he'd sat in his office, he hadn't been able to get his mind off Diana. Twice he'd picked up the phone to call her. Twice he'd decided against it. He didn't like what was happening to him. No one else seemed to notice that he was sinking fast. And there wasn't a life preserver in sight.

Sitting in the overstuffed chair beside Cliff, Diana took a sip of her tea and attempted to put some order to her thoughts. She was happy to see Cliff. More than happy. But a little apprehensive, too.

"How was your day?" she asked finally when he didn't seem inclined to wade into easy conversation.

"Busy. How about yours?"

"I went in for a job interview with the school district this morning." Cliff couldn't possibly understand what courage that had taken. She hadn't worked outside the home since Joan had been born, and had no real credentials. "I'm hoping they'll hire me as a teacher's aide. That way I'll have the same hours as the girls."

"Do you think you'll get the job?"

Diana answered with a soft shrug. "I don't know. The principal from Joan and Katie's school gave me a recommendation, since I've done a substantial amount of volunteer work there. The last school levy passed and the district's been given the go-ahead to hire ten teacher's aides. I have no idea how many applications they took or how many they interviewed."

"If that doesn't pan out, I'm sure I could find a part-time position for you in my law firm." The minute Cliff made the offer, he regretted it. Having Diana in his office two or three times a week could end up being a source of personal conflict.

"Thank you, Cliff, but, no."

"No?" This woman continued to astonish him. He'd expected her to jump at the offer. "Why not?"

"It's downtown, and I'd prefer to be as close to the girls as I can in case they get sick and need to come home . . . ." That was the first plausible excuse to surface. Although it was the truth, Diana didn't have a great deal of choice when it came to finding employment. She'd turned down his offer because she preferred not to work in the same place as Cliff.

"I can understand that," he said, relieved and irritated at the same time. Diana had him so twisted up in knots he couldn't judge his own emotions anymore. He shouldn't have come tonight, he knew that, but staying away had been impossible.

"I'm pleased you stopped by," Diana said next.

He was happy she was pleased, because he was more confused than ever. He had thought that if he stopped off and they talked, then maybe he'd know what was happening to him. Wrong. One look at Diana and all he wanted to do was make love to her.

"I want you to know I feel bad about our conversation the other day." Diana felt as though she were sailing into uncharted waters, her destination unknown. Their telephone conversation had gone poorly, and she wasn't sure whose fault it was. Cliff had kept insisting on seeing her again, and she had kept refusing, finally giving in. More than that, it seemed that Cliff had been expecting her to be angry because he'd had to cancel their dinner date. She hadn't been. Then Cliff had sounded as though he'd wanted to start an argument and was confused when she wouldn't be drawn into a verbal battle.

"You feel bad because I canceled dinner?" Cliff asked.

"No, because I had to turn down your offer for another date."

Cliff felt more than a little chagrined. He'd admit it—her refusal had irked him. For all his suave sophistication, he wasn't accustomed to having a woman turn him down. It had taken a fair amount of soul-searching to decide he wanted to see Diana again—without Joan and Katie. Her rejection, no matter how good her reasons, had been a blow to his considerable pride.

"You turned me down for dinner *and* Friday night," he reminded her.

"I thought I explained . . ."

"I know."

Diana lowered her gaze to her mug of tea, which she was gripping tightly with both hands. "You don't know how hard that was."

"Then why did you?"

"For the very reasons I told you."

His brow puckered into a deep frown.

"I like you, Cliff. Probably more than I should." She didn't know what weapon she was handing him by admitting her feelings, but she was too old for silly games, too wise to get tangled up in a web of emotion and too intelligent not to look at him with her eyes wide open. They weren't right for each other, but that hadn't seemed to matter. They'd weathered their relationship much better than she had ever imagined they would. If they were going to continue to see each other, then she preferred that they be honest about their feelings. Honest and up-front.

"I like you, too, Diana," he admitted softly, his eyes holding her all too effectively. "I'm not sure I'm ready for what's developing between us, but I want it. I want you."

The muscles in her stomach constricted with his words. She'd asked for his honesty, and now she was forced to deal with her own reactions to it. Cliff frightened her because he made her feel again; he'd reawakened the deep womanly part of her that craved touch. Intuitively she'd known the first time he'd kissed her how potent his caress would be. In the years since Stan had died, she'd effectively cast the hunger for love and desire from her life.

Until Cliff.

Knowing this made each minute they spent together all the more exciting. It made each date all the more dangerous.

Diana tore her gaze from his. "What are we going to do about it?"

"I don't know."

"I . . . don't, either."

Cliff drew in a hard breath and held out his arms to her. "Come here, Diana."

Of its own volition, her hand set the tea mug aside. She stood and walked over to Cliff and offered no resistance when he pulled her down and cradled her in his lap. Her hands rested against his shoulders as his eyes gently caressed her face. It was almost as if he were asking her to object.

She couldn't. She wouldn't. A long, uninterrupted moment passed before Cliff lifted her hair from her shoulder and tenderly kissed the side of her neck. His lips felt cool against her skin, and she turned her head to grant him the freedom to kiss her where he willed.

At the sound of her soft gasp, his tongue made moist forays below her ear. Cliff loved the scent of her. Other women relied on expensive perfumes, and yet they couldn't compare to the fresh sunshine smell that was Diana's alone.

An all-too-warm, tingling sensation raced through Diana. Against her will, she closed her eyes. Her fingers gripped his shirt collar as his lips slowly grazed a trail across the underside of her chin.

"Cliff . . ." she moaned. "Please . . ."

"Please what?"

Her throat constricted, and she felt as if she were going to cry again. When she spoke, the words came out sounding like someone trying to speak while trapped underwater. "I want you to kiss . . . me."

His hands covered each side of her face and directed her mouth to his. Their lips slid across each other's with sweet familiarity. Diana was eager, so eager, but the urgency was gone, leaving in its wake a pure electric, soul-stirring sensation.

She clung to him even as the tears burned their way down her face. When he paused, as though unsure, she kissed him back, her mouth parted and pliant over his. She'd come this far and she refused to let him back away from her now.

Diana's kiss was all the encouragement Cliff needed. His arms tightened around her, and he gently rocked her, unable to get close enough. He felt the moisture on her face and tasted the salt of her tears. The reason for their being there humbled him. She was opening up to him as she never had before, trusting him, granting him custody of her wounded heart.

Diana moaned as his hands roamed over her back, bringing her as close as it was humanly possible.

At her soft cry tenderness engulfed him like a tidal wave. He wanted Diana in that moment more than he'd ever craved anything in his life. The passion she aroused in him was almost more than he could bear. He tried to tell her what she did to him by kissing her again and again, but it wasn't enough. Nothing seemed to satisfy the building fire within him. "Diana," he moaned, "I'm afraid if we continue like this we're going to end up making love in this chair."

The words made no sense to Diana. Cliff had transported

her from limbo into heaven in a matter of moments. She had no desire to leave her newly discovered paradise. Her only response was a strangled, nonsensical plea for him not to stop.

"Upstairs," he said a minute later. "I want to make love to you in a bed."

Somehow the words made it through the thick haze of desire that had clouded her brain. He wanted to make love to her in a bed! Upstairs. Joan and Katie—her daughters—were upstairs.

"No," she managed.

"No?" Cliff echoed, shocked.

"The . . . girls."

"So? Aren't they asleep?"

"I . . . don't know. It doesn't matter."

"It matters to me," he argued. "I need you, Diana."

She didn't need to guess how much he wanted her—she was feeling the same urgency. It had been slowly building in her for three long years.

"I want you," he reiterated forcefully. Pressing his hands over her ears, he kissed her long and hard so she'd know he wasn't just muttering the words.

Diana drove her fingers into his hair and slanted her mouth over his in eager response. "I need you, too," she whispered against his lips. "Right now, I could almost die I want you so much."

"Good."

"But, Cliff, I can't. I . . ."

"Come on, honey, don't argue with me. We're mature adults—we both know what we want—so what's stopping you?"

"Cliff, you don't understand."

He closed his eyes and groaned. "Somehow I knew that you were going to say that."

"Joan and Katie are up there."

"They're asleep, for heaven's sake." He could argue with her if she were being reasonable, but he was defenseless against such logic. "They won't even know."

"I'll know."

His hold on her torso tightened as he buried his face in the smooth silk of her skin. He drew in a ragged breath as the battle between his conscience and his raw need raged within him. Without too much trouble, he knew he could change her mind. She wanted him nearly as much as he craved her, and all it would take to convince her of that was a few more uninterrupted minutes. He released an anguished sigh when his conscience won. There would be another chance, another place, and the next time it would be right.

"Are you angry?" Diana asked.

He thought about it a moment, then shook his head. "No."

"I feel like I've been a terrible tease."

"Then tease me anytime you want," he managed on the tail-end of a sigh. "Now," he said, easing her off his lap, "walk me to the door and kiss me good-night while I still have the power to leave you."

She rose unsteadily. The carpet under her feet seemed to buckle and sway beneath her.

Cliff held out his hand to steady her. "Are you okay?"

"I don't know," she admitted with a half smile. She didn't know if she'd ever be the same again. Every part of her was throbbing with need, and yet all she could taste was frustration and regret.

He wrapped his arm around her and let her walk him to the front door. Their kiss was ardent, but brief. His arms continued to hold her. "Saturday night," he reminded her. "I'll pick you up at six-thirty."

It was all Diana could do to nod.

She remained leaning against the door frame long after Cliff had left. A strange chill rattled her as she realized how close she had come to walking up the stairs and making love with Cliff. It was then that she realized there was no real commitment between them, not even whispered words of love, only the pure physical response of a lonely widow to an exceptionally handsome man. Diana gripped her stomach as a wave of nausea passed over her. She felt ill and frightened.

Somehow she made it up the stairs and into bed, but that didn't guarantee sleep. Over and over again she thought about what had nearly happened with Cliff. No doubt women regularly fell into bed with him. Diana couldn't blame them; he would be a wonderful lover. Gentle and considerate. Even now, hours after he'd left, her body tingled from the memory of his touch.

She wanted him, but the situation was impossible. Her life was filled with responsibilities now. She wasn't carefree and single—she was a mother.

After twenty more minutes of tossing and turning, Diana glanced at the clock. Life wasn't simple for her anymore. Not with two daughters who watched her every move. When she'd been dating Stan, there'd been no real thought to the future. It had all been so easy. They were in love, so they got married. Diana was burdened with obligations now on all sides. Ones she willingly accepted.

For two days, she agonized over what she was going to say to Cliff. She wanted to set the record straight, explain that what had nearly happened wasn't right for her. She couldn't deny that she desired him; he'd see through that fast enough.

When Cliff arrived promptly at six-thirty to pick her up on Saturday night, she kissed the girls goodbye and stiffly followed Cliff to his car. Although he'd told her they were going to dinner, he hadn't said where.

"You look as jumpy as a pogo stick," he said once they were seated inside his Lamborghini. He was dying to kiss her. Already he ached with the need to hold her in his arms and taste her kisses.

"I . . . we need to talk."

Cliff placed the key in the ignition, then leaned over to gently brush his mouth over hers. "Can't it wait until dinner?"

Diana shook her head. "I don't think so. It's about what nearly happened the other night."

"Somehow I thought you'd bring that up." His hands tightened around the steering wheel. He'd gone too fast for her, but she'd amazed him with how ready and eager she was. It hadn't been right for them Thursday, but it would be tonight—he'd make certain of that.

"I'm not ready for . . . it." Her face flushed with embarrassment. She'd never talked to a man this way, not even with Stan.

"Lovemaking." If she wouldn't say the word, he would. He didn't know what her problem was. The fact that she would deny what was happening between them surprised him, especially after all her talk about honesty. Their making love was inevitable. He'd known it almost from the first.

He wanted her desperately. Every time he closed his eyes, he pictured her in his bed, satin sheets wrapped around her, with her arms stretched toward him, inviting him to join her. She wouldn't need to ask him twice. These past two days without her had been hell. He wanted her so much that he felt naked and vulnerable without her, and now he was determined to have her. It hadn't felt right to walk away from her the other night. The memory of her kisses had returned to haunt him.

"All right, lovemaking," Diana echoed, her voice firm but low. "After the other night, I'm afraid I've given you the wrong impression."

Cliff reached over and squeezed her fingers. "Don't worry, honey, we're not going to do anything you don't want."

Diana should have felt better with his reassurance, but she

didn't. She'd dreaded this evening from the moment he'd left her, and yet the hours hadn't gone by fast enough until she'd seen him again. She thought she knew what she wanted, but one look at Cliff and she was unsure of everything.

"You didn't say where we were going for dinner," she said, making conversation.

He smiled, and his face lit up with boyish charm. "It's a surprise."

He drove toward Des Moines and Diana was certain he was taking her to the fancy seafood restaurant the marina was famous for, but he drove past it and instead headed up the back roads to the cliff above the water.

"I didn't know there was a restaurant up this way," she confessed.

"There isn't," he told her with a wide grin. "We're going to my condo. I've been cooking all day."

"Your place," Diana echoed, and the words seemed to bounce around the car like a ricocheting bullet. Her heart slammed against her breast with dread.

"I'm a fabulous chef . . . wait and see."

Her responding smile was weak and filled with doubt.

Cliff parked his car in the garage and came around to help her out. He tucked his arm protectively around her waist as she climbed out of his car, then paused to gently kiss the side of her neck. His tender touch went a long way toward chasing away Diana's fears, and she smiled up at him.

Cliff was eager to show her his home and proudly led her into his condominium. The first thing Diana noticed was the flickering flames of the fireplace. The table was set for two, with candles ready to be lighted. The room was dark, and music played softly from the expensive speakers.

As she surveyed the room, a chill shimmied up her spine. "You haven't heard a word I've said, have you?"

Seven

"Of course I've been listening," Cliff insisted. He didn't know what was bothering Diana, but she'd been acting jumpy from the minute he'd picked her up.

"I told you, I'm not ready."

"For dinner?" He couldn't understand why she was so riled up all of a sudden. He'd been looking forward to this evening for days. The crab was cracked for their appetizers, hollandaise sauce simmered on top of the stove, ready to be poured over fresh broccoli. The thick T-bone steaks were in the refrigerator, just waiting to be charcoal grilled. He wanted everything perfect for tonight, for Diana. The wine was chilled—he'd seen to it all.

"In case you weren't aware of it," Diana cried, pointing a finger at her chest, "I live in this body!"

"What in the world are you talking about?"

"This." She gestured wildly with her arm toward the open space of his living room. "Tell me, Cliff, exactly what have you planned for tonight?" She flopped down on his white leather couch, crossed her legs and glared at him with wide, accusing eyes.

"A leisurely candlelight dinner. Is that a crime, or did I miss something in law school?"

Diana ignored his sarcasm. "And that's all? What about after dinner?"

He scooted the ottoman in front of the couch, sat down and leaned forward so his eyes were level with hers. "I thought we'd share a couple of glasses of wine in front of the fireplace."

"And sample a few stolen kisses, as well?" she coaxed.

Cliff grinned, relaxing. "Yes."

The lilting strains of the music from a hundred violins drifted through the room. She noticed the way the lights in the hallway that led to the master bedroom had been dimmed invitingly. The door to his room was cracked open, a ribbon of muted light beckoning to her. The romance in the condominium was so thick, Diana could hardly see the romancer.

"But you're planning on something else happening, aren't you?" she asked, her eyes effectively holding his.

Cliff opened his mouth to deny it, then quickly decided against trying to bluff his way out of the obvious. He didn't have any choice but to be honest with Diana. Before he could say anything, she cut him off.

"Don't lie to me, Cliff Howard," she declared, folding her arms defiantly around her torso. "Do you think I'm stupid? Do you honestly believe I'm so naive to not know that you've planned the big seduction scene?"

"All right. All right." He eased her arms loose and reached for her stiff fingers, holding them between his hands. "Maybe I'm going off the deep end here, but after the other night, I thought maybe . . ."

"Exactly what did you think?"

"That you and I had something special going for us. Something very special."

"You want to make love to me?"

"You're right I do," he murmured, and raised her fingertips to his lips. His gaze didn't leave hers, as though seeking confirmation. "And you want me, too, so don't try to deny it."

"I have no intention of doing so. You're right on target . . . things could easily have gotten out of hand the other night."

Cliff was beginning to feel more confident now. He realized that some women required more assurances. "Then you can understand—in light of Thursday night—why I'm thinking what I'm thinking." He raised his eyebrows suggestively, seeking a way to alter the sober tone of this conversation. Diana was becoming far too defensive over something that was inevitable. Wanting her in his bed shouldn't be considered a felony. Surely she realized that.

Diana felt incredibly guilty. She couldn't be angry with Cliff when she'd given him every reason to believe she was willing to sleep with him. Not until he'd left and her head had cleared did she realized how wrong a physical relationship with Cliff was for her. Unfortunately Cliff had no way of knowing about her sudden change of heart. The anger rushed out of her as quickly as it had come. She freed one hand from his grip and gently traced the underside of his well-defined jaw. She wasn't sure what she'd gotten herself into, but she wanted to make it right for them both.

Cliff captured her hand and held it against his cheek, needing her more and more by the minute. If she didn't stop looking at him with those incredibly lovely brown eyes, he couldn't offer any guarantee he'd be able to serve the meal he'd spent so much time preparing.

"Cliff, I feel bad about all this, but I'm simply not ready."

He stared at her for a full moment, weighing his options. She was frightened, he could see that, and he didn't blame her for acting like a nervous virgin. It had been a long time since a man had properly loved her. Thursday night she'd been as hot as a firecracker. It had hurt Cliff to leave her, both physically and mentally. She had to know him well enough to realize that he wasn't going to rush her into something she didn't want. First he had to make sure everything was right for her.

"Honey," he whispered, and leaned forward to sample her sweet lips. Their mouths clung, and when he sat back down, he closed his eyes at the bolt of passion that surged through him. "Trust me, you're ready."

Diana blinked back the dismay. Nothing she'd said had sunk into Cliff's thick skull. She tugged her hands free and clenched them together. "Answer me this, Cliff. Do you love me?"

Groaning inwardly, Cliff forced a smile. Over the years he'd come to almost hate that word. Women hurled it at him continually, as if it were a required license for something they wanted as much as he did. "I believe there's magic between us."

Diana's returning grin was infinitely sad. "Oh, Cliff, it sounds as if you've used that phrase a hundred times. I expected you to be more original than that."

She shamed him, because he *had* used that line before—not as often as she said, but enough to warrant a guilty conscience. Her look told him how much she disapproved of glib, well-worn words. To hear her tell it, he was another Hugh Hefner. Well, he had news for her—she wasn't exactly Mother Teresa. He didn't know how she could deny the very real and strong sexual tension between them. Diana was warm and loving, and confused. All he wanted to do was show her how good things could be between them, and Diana was making it sound as though he should be arrested for even thinking about taking her to bed.

She dropped her gaze and sighed. "It would be best if I went home."

Her words were as unexpected as they were unwelcome. "No!"

"No?"

"Diana, we've got something magical here. Let's not ruin it." Cliff was grasping at straws and knew it, but he didn't want her to leave.

"What we've got is a bunch of hormones calling out to one another. There's no commitment, no love!"

"You don't believe that."

"Am I wrong?" she asked with eyes that ripped into his soul. "Are you ready to offer your life to me and the girls?" She knew the answer, even if he didn't. Love preceded marriage, and although he cared for her, he didn't love her.

Commitment was another word Cliff had come to abhor. He jerked his fingers through his hair, almost afraid to speak for fear of what he'd say. "I can't believe we're having this conversation."

Already she was on her feet, her purse clenched under her arm. "Goodbye, Cliff."

He stood and crossed the room. "Why are we arguing like this, when all I want to do is make love to you?"

Dejected, Diana paused, her hand on the doorknob. "In case you haven't figured it out, that's exactly our problem."

Cliff was growing more impatient by the minute. Impatient and overwhelmingly frustrated. Okay, so she'd read his intentions; he hadn't exactly tried to cover up what he'd planned for the evening. She could be a good sport and play along, at least until after dinner. He wasn't going to force her into anything if she honestly objected. "Is wanting you such a sin?" he asked.

"No," she answered smoothly, "but I need something more than magic." She couldn't explain it any better. If Cliff didn't understand love and commitment, then it was unlikely he'd be able to follow her reasoning. And she had no intention of trying to justify it anyway.

"Come on, Diana, wake up and smell the coffee. Times have changed. Men and women make love every night."

"I know." She had no more arguments. There was nothing more to say. She twisted the knob and pulled.

Cliff's fist hit the door, closing it with a sharp thud. "I don't know what happened between Thursday night and now, but I think you're being entirely unreasonable."

"I don't expect you to understand."

His anger and disappointment were almost more than he could bear. "Please don't leave."

"I can't see any other option."

He gritted his teeth, trying to come up with some way to make her understand. "Diana, listen to me. I'm a sexual person. I haven't been with a woman in a long time. I've got to have you for the pure physical release, I . . ."

Her stunned look caused him to swallow the rest of what he was saying.

"Goodbye, Cliff," she said, and then jerked open the door and walked out.

Cliff stared at the closed front door for a full minute. He couldn't believe he'd said that to her, as though she and she alone were responsible for easing his sexual appetite. He couldn't have made a bigger mess of this evening had he tried.

Diana didn't know she could walk so fast. Instead of going along the sidewalk, she cut between parked cars and crossed the street. Within a few minutes she was close to the marina. A Metro bus pulled to a stop at the curb, and its heavy doors parted with a whoosh. Without knowing its destination, Diana climbed on board. She had already taken her seat, when she saw Cliff's sports car race past the bus and chase after a taxi. Her eyes followed Cliff and the taxi until they were out of sight.

Diana was able to get a transfer from one bus to another, and an hour later she walked inside her house, exhausted and furious.

"Mom, where were you? What happened?" Joan cried, running to the door to greet her. "Cliff's been calling every ten minutes."

She ignored the question and headed for the refrigerator. For the past half hour, she'd been walking. She was dying of thirst, and her feet hurt like crazy—a lethal combination. Both Joan and Katie seemed to recognize her mood and went out of their way to avoid her.

Diana had been home fifteen minutes, when the phone rang again. Joan sprinted into the kitchen to answer it.

"If it's Cliff, I don't want to talk to him," Diana yelled after her daughter.

Joan reappeared a couple of minutes later. "He just wanted to know that you got home okay."

"What did you tell him?"

"That you were mad as hops."

Diana groaned, sagged against the back of the overstuffed chair and hugged a pillow to her stomach. That wasn't the half of it. The next time she went racing out of a man's condominium, she'd make sure she carried enough cash to take a cab home. She'd ridden on the bus with two winos and a guy who looked like a candidate for the Hell's Angels.

"Are you mad at Cliff, Mom?" Katie wanted to know, plopping down at her mother's feet.

"Yes."

"But I like Cliff."

"Don't worry, kid, I got all the bases covered." Joan sank onto the carpet beside her sister. "Cliff just phoned. I advised him to wait a couple of days, then send roses. By that time, everything will be forgotten and forgiven."

The pressure Diana applied to the pillow bunched it in half. "Wanna bet?" she challenged.

★ ★ ★

Shirley poured herself a cup of coffee and sat at the kitchen table beside Diana. "It's been a week."

"I told you I didn't want to hear from him." Diana continued copying the recipe for yet another hamburger casserole that disguised vegetables. She had only a few minutes before the girls would be home from school, then the house would become an open battlefield. Both Joan and Katie had been impossible all week. Without understanding any of what had happened between Cliff and her, her daughters had taken it upon themselves to champion his case. Diana refused to talk about him and, as a last resort, had forbidden either girl to mention his name again.

For the first few days after their argument, Diana had held out hope that things could be settled between her and Cliff, It didn't take long for her to accept that it was better to leave matters as they were. They were in a no-win situation. The bottom line was that they'd only end up hurting each other. Despite everything, Diana was pleased to have known Cliff Howard. She'd been living her life in a cooler; she'd grieved for Stan long enough. It was time to join the land of the living and soak up the sunshine of a healthy relationship again. Dating Cliff had shown her the way out of the chill, and she would always be grateful to him for that. In the past three years, she'd dated only occasionally. Cliff had helped her to see that she was ready to meet someone, pick up the pieces of her shattered life and move on.

"But I feel bad," Shirley continued, holding the coffee mug with both hands. "George told me I had the wrong impression of Cliff—he isn't exactly the playboy I led you to believe."

"Honestly, Shirley, I'd think you'd be happy. I've finally agreed to a dinner date with Owen Freeman." For two years her neighbor had been after Diana to at least meet this distant relation of hers. Diana had used every excuse in the book to get out of it. She simply hadn't been interested in being introduced to Shirley's third cousin, no matter how successful he was. Cliff had changed that, and Diana would have thought her neighbor would appreciate this shift in attitude.

"I know I should be thrilled you're willing to meet Owen, but I'm not." Shirley ran the tip of her index finger around the rim of her mug. She hesitated, as though she'd noticed the flower vase in the center of the table for the first time. It came from a florist. "Who sent the flowers?"

"Cliff."

"Cliff Howard?"

Diana nodded, intent on copying the recipe. He'd taken Joan's advice and sent the bouquet of red roses with a quick note of apology scribbled across the card. In other words, the next move was up to her. It had taken Diana several days of soul-searching to decide not to contact him. The decision hadn't been an easy one, but it was the right one.

"But if he sent you flowers, then he must be willing to patch things up."

"Maybe." Diana dropped the subject there.

Her neighbor paused. "The least you could do is tell me what he did that was so terrible. If you can't talk to me, then who can you talk to?"

Diana's fingers tightened around the pencil. Shirley wasn't asking her anything Joan and Katie hadn't drilled her about a dozen times. Both girls had been out of joint from the minute Diana informed them she wouldn't be seeing Cliff again. Katie had argued the loudest, claiming she wanted to go on his sailboat one more time. Joan had ardently insisted she liked Cliff better than anyone, and had gone into a three-day pout when Diana wouldn't change her mind. As patiently as she could, Diana explained to both girls that there would be other men they would like just as well as Cliff.

"What I want to know," Diana said, reaching for her own coffee as she studied her friend, "is why you've changed your tune all of a sudden. When I first started going out with Cliff, you were full of dire warnings. And now that I've decided not to see him again, you're keen for me to patch things up with him."

"You're miserable."

"I'm not," Diana shot back, then realized what Shirley said was true. She missed Cliff, missed the expectancy that he'd brought back into her life, the eagerness to greet each day as a new experience. She missed the little things—the way his hand reached for hers, lacing her fingers with his. She missed the way his eyes sought her out when the girls were jumping up and down at his feet, wanting something from him. She hadn't realized how lonely she was until Cliff had come into her life, and now the emptiness felt like a huge, empty vacuum that needed to be filled.

"It's best this way," Diana said after a thoughtful moment.

Shirley's hand patted hers. "Okay," she said reluctantly, "if you say so."

"I do."

Neither spoke for a long time. Finally Shirley ventured into conversation. "When are you having dinner with Owen?"

"Tomorrow," Diana answered. Now all she had to do was pump some enthusiasm into meeting Shirley's third cousin, who taught English literature at the local community college.

The following evening, Diana tried to convince herself what a good time she was going to have. She showered and dressed, while Joan followed her around the bedroom, choosing her outfit for her.

"How come you're wearing your pearl earrings?" Joan demanded. "You didn't wear them for . . ." She started to say Cliff's name, then hurriedly corrected herself since he was a forbidden subject. "You know who—and now you're putting them on for some guy you haven't even met."

Diana's answering smile was weak at best. She needed the boost in confidence, but explaining that to her daughter would be difficult.

When her mother didn't answer, Joan positioned herself in front of Diana's bedroom window that looked down onto the street below. "A car just pulled into the driveway."

"That will be Mr. Freeman. Joan, please, be on your best behavior."

"Oh, no."

"What's wrong?"

"He just got out of the car—he's wearing plaid pants."

Diana reached for her perfume, giving her neck and wrists a liberal spray, and rolled her eyes toward the ceiling. "It's not right to judge someone by the clothes he wears."

"Mom, he's a nerd to the tenth power." Joan sagged onto the end of the mattress and buried her face in her hands. "If you end up marrying this guy, I'll never forgive you."

"Joan, honestly!"

"Mom, Mr. Freeman is here," Katie screamed from the foot of the stairs after peeking out the living room window. She raced up to meet her mother, who was coming out of the bedroom. "Mom," she whispered breathlessly. "He's a geek. A major geek!"

Feigning a smile, Diana placed her hand on the banister and slowly walked down the stairs to answer the doorbell.

As far as looks went, the blonde won over Diana, hands down, Cliff decided. He smiled at the sleek beauty who clung to his arm, and tried to look as though he were enjoying himself. He wasn't. In fact, he'd been miserable from the minute Diana had walked out of his condominium. At first he'd been furious with her. For a solid hour he'd driven around, searching for her, desperate to locate her. Only heaven knew where she'd run off to—it was as though aliens had absconded with her.

Twice he'd broken down and phoned her house, nearly frantic with worry. Joan had assured him, on the third call, that her mother was home and safe. It was then that Cliff had decided that whatever was between Diana and him was over. She was a crazy woman. One minute she was melting in his arms, and the next she was as stiff as cement, hissing accusations at him.

Two days later, after he'd had a chance to cool down, Cliff changed his mind. He'd behaved like a Neanderthal. The remark he'd made about being a sexual person returned to haunt him. It was no wonder she was angry, but she'd played a part in their little misunderstanding, leading him on, letting him think there was a green light in her eyes where it was actually a flashing red one. He didn't possess ESP—how was he supposed to read her mind? Okay, he'd make the first move toward a reconciliation, he decided, and then leave the rest up to her. On his instructions, his secretary ordered the roses with an appropriate message. Cliff had sat back and waited.

When he hadn't heard from Diana by the end of the week, he was stunned. Then shocked. Then angry. All right, he'd play her game—he was a patient man. In time she'd come around, and when she did, he'd play it cool. If anyone was sitting home nights, alone and frustrated, it wouldn't be him. He'd make sure of that.

Hence Marianne—the blonde.

"Who are you going out with tonight?" Joan asked her mother as she sat at the kitchen table and glued on a false thumbnail.

"Not Mr. Freeman again," Katie groaned, and reached for an apple.

"He's a nice man."

"Mom, if you wanted nice, I could set you up with Mr. Rogers or Captain Kangaroo."

Diana hated to admit how right Joan was. Owen Freeman excited her as much as dirty laundry. He'd brought her candy, escorted her to a classical music concert and treated her with kindness and respect. He'd even supplied her with letters from his colleagues attesting to his character, just in case she was worried about being alone with him. Maybe Cliff wasn't so out of line to have mentioned magic. She felt it with him, but she certainly didn't with Owen Freeman. There were so many frogs out there and so few princes.

"Have you read through his references yet?" Joan asked.

"Honey, that was a very nice gesture on Mr. Freeman's part."

"He's a geek."

"Katie, I want you to stop calling him that."

Her younger daughter shrugged.

Joan spread contact cement across the top of the nail on her little finger. A pile of fake fingernails rested in front of her. "It's your life, Mom. You know how Katie and I feel about Mrs. Holiday's cousin, but you do what you want."

"Well, don't worry about it—you're not having dinner with him. I am."

Joan rolled her eyes toward the ceiling. "Lucky you."

Owen arrived a half hour later. He brought Joan and Katie a small stuffed animal each and a small bouquet of flowers for Diana. He really was an exceptionally nice man, but, as Joan had said, so were Mr. Rogers and Captain Kangaroo.

When Owen headed toward Des Moines and the restaurant at the marina, Diana tensed. Of all the places in the south end to eat, he had to choose this one.

"I understand the food here is excellent," Owen said once they were seated.

"I've heard that, as well," Diana said, looking over the top of her menu. Her heart was pumping double its normal rate. She was being silly. There was absolutely no reason to believe she would run into Cliff Howard simply because this restaurant was close to his condominium. No sane reason at all.

Owen ordered a bottle of wine, and Diana nearly did a swan dive into the first glass. Alcohol would help soothe her jittery nerves, she reasoned. After tonight, Diana decided, she would tell Owen that it simply wasn't going to work. He was such a nice person, and she didn't want to lead him on when there was no reason to believe anything would ever develop between them. Her mind worked up a variety of ways to tell him, then she decided to take the coward's way out and leave a voice mail message after he dropped her off following dinner.

"You're quiet this evening," Owen said softly.

"I'm sorry."

"Are you tired?"

She nodded. "It's been a long week." Diana turned her head and looked out over the rows and rows of watercraft moored in the marina. Without much trouble, she located Cliff's forty-foot sloop.

"Do you sail?" she asked Owen, without taking her eyes from Cliff's boat.

"No, I can't say that I do."

"Fish?"

"No, it never appealed to me."

Diana pulled her gaze away. Owen was forty, balding and incredibly boring. Nice, but boring.

"I did go swimming once in Puget Sound," he said, his voice rising with enthusiasm.

Diana's smile was genuine. No doubt, Owen saw himself as a real daredevil. "I did, too—once, by accident."

"Really?"

She nodded, and the silence returned. Finally she said, "I enjoy picnics."

Owen's forehead puckered into a brooding frown. "I don't get much time for outdoor pursuits."

"I can imagine . . . with school and everything."

"Bridge is my game."

"Bridge," Diana repeated, amused. Owen Freeman was really quite predictable. "I imagine you're good enough to play in tournaments."

The literature professor positively gleamed. "As a matter of fact, I am. Have you ever played?"

"No," she admitted reluctantly.

The hostess escorted another couple to the table across from their own. Diana didn't pay much attention, but the blonde was stunning.

"I would thoroughly enjoy teaching you," Owen continued. "Why, we could play couples."

"I'm afraid I don't have much of a head for cards." Except when it came to her VISA or Mastercard. Then she knew all the tricks.

"Don't be so hard on yourself. You've just lacked a good teacher, that's all. I promise to be patient."

Diana felt someone's stare. She paused and looked around and didn't recognize anyone she knew. Taking another sip of her wine, she relaxed. "Is it warm in here? Or is it just me?" she asked Owen.

"It doesn't seem to be overly warm," Owen responded, and turned around as though to ask the opinion of those sitting at the table closest to their own.

Feeling feverish, Diana frantically fanned her face. It was then that she saw Cliff. The voluptuous blonde she'd noticed a few minutes before sat beside him, her torso practically draped over his arm. Diana's hand froze in midair as her breath caught in her lungs. Her worst nightmare had just come true. Cliff was dating Miss World, and she was with Captain Kangaroo.

Eight

"Katie, will you kindly come down from that tree!" Diana yelled as she jerked open the sliding glass door that led to the backyard. It seemed she was going to have to cut down the apple tree in order to keep her younger daughter from climbing between its gnarled limbs. The girl seemed to think she was half monkey. Two days into summer vacation, and already Diana was beginning to sound like a banshee.

"Mom . . ."

"Katie, just do it. I'm in no mood for an argument." She slammed the door, furious with herself for being so short-tempered and angry with Katie for disobeying her. A rush of air escaped her lungs as she slouched against the kitchen wall and hung her head in an effort to get a firm grip on her emotions.

"Mom?"

Diana lifted her eyes to find Joan standing on the other side of the room, studying her with an odd look. She frowned. "What?"

In answer to her mother's question, Joan pulled out a chair

and patted the seat. "I think it's time for us to have another of our daughter-mother talks."

If her preteen hadn't looked so serious, Diana would have laughed. Not again! Diana had only just recovered from the first such conversation. Joan had spoken to her about the importance of not doing anything foolish—such as marrying Owen on the rebound from Cliff.

"Again, Joan?" she asked, her eyes silently pleading for solitude.

"You heard me."

Diana rolled her eyes toward the ceiling and seated herself. While Diana waited, Joan walked around the counter and brewed a cup of coffee. Once she'd delivered it to her mother, she took the chair across from Diana and plopped her elbows onto the tabletop, her hands cupping her face as she stared at her mother.

"Well?"

"Don't rush me. I'm trying to think of a diplomatic way of saying this."

"I've been a grouch. I know, and I apologize." Diana could do nothing less. She'd been snapping at the girls all week. School was out, and it took time to adjust. At least, that was what she told herself.

"That's not it."

"Is it Owen? You needn't worry. I won't be seeing him again."

In a spontaneous outburst of glee, Joan tossed her hands above her head. "There is a God!"

"Joan, honestly!"

"So you're not going to date Owen anymore. What about . . ." She paused abruptly. "You know . . . the one whose name I've been forbidden to mention."

"Cliff."

Joan pointed at her mother's chest. "He's the one."

"What about him?" Diana asked, ignoring her daughter's attempt at humor.

The amusement drained from the eleven-year-old's dark eyes. "You still miss him, don't you?"

Diana lowered her gaze and shrugged. She preferred not to think about Cliff. Ever since the night she'd seen him with that bimbo clinging to him like a bloodsucker, Diana had done her best to avoid anything vaguely connected with Cliff Howard. It was little wonder they hadn't been able to get along. Obviously, Cliff's preference in women swayed toward the exotic. Their breakup had been inevitable. He might have been satisfied with apple pandowdy for a time, but his interest couldn't have lasted. Not when he could sample cheesecake anytime he wished. Diana had been intelligent enough to recognize that from the first, but she'd been so flattered—all right, attracted to Cliff—that she'd chosen to ignore good old-fashioned common sense. Joan was right, though. She did miss him. But more important, she'd gotten out of the relationship with her heart intact. No one had been hurt; she'd been lucky.

"Anyway, Katie and I have been thinking," Joan continued.

"Now that's dangerous." Diana took a sip of her coffee and nearly choked as the hot brew slid down the back of her throat. Joan had made it strong enough to cause a nuclear meltdown.

"Mom, Katie and I want you to know something."

"Yes?"

"Whatever Cliff did, *we* forgive him. We think that you should be big enough to do the same."

Marianne batted her thick, mascara-coated lashes in Cliff's direction, issuing an invitation that was all too obvious. He pulled her into his arms and kissed her hard. Harder than necessary, grinding his mouth over hers, angry with her for being so transparent and even angrier with himself for not wanting her.

The woman in his arms moaned, and Cliff obliged by kissing her again. He didn't need to be an Einstein to realize he was seeking something. Every time he kissed Marianne, it was a futile effort to taste Diana.

The blond wound her arms around his neck and seductively rubbed her breasts over his torso. Cliff couldn't force any desire for her, and the realization only served to infuriate him.

His hands gripped Marianne's shoulders as he extracted himself from her grasp.

She looked up at him, dazed and confused. "Cliff?"

"I've got a busy day tomorrow." He offered the lame excuse, stood and reached for his jacket. "I'll give you a call later." He hurried out the door, hardly able to escape fast enough. Once inside his car, he gripped the steering wheel with both hands and clenched his jaw. What was happening to him? Whatever it was, he didn't like it. Not one bit.

Diana stood at the sliding glass door and checked the sleeping foursome on the patio. In an effort to make up for her cranky mood, and in a moment of weakness, she'd agreed to let the girls each invite a friend over for a slumber party. Now all four were sacked out in lawn chairs, with enough pillows, blankets, radios and stuffed animals to supply a small army. They'd talked, laughed, carted out half the contents of the kitchen and had finally worn themselves out. Peace and goodwill toward men reigned for the moment.

Diana had just poured herself a cup of decaffeinated coffee, when the doorbell chimed. Surprised, she checked her watch and noticed it was after ten. She certainly wasn't expecting anyone this late.

Setting aside her coffee, she moved into the entryway and

pressed her eye to the peephole in the front door. Her gaze met the solid wall of a man's chest—one she'd recognize anywhere. Cliff Howard's.

There wasn't time to react, or time to think. Her heart hammered wildly as she unbolted the lock and gradually opened the door.

"Hi," he said awkwardly. "I was in the neighborhood and thought I'd stop in. I hope you don't mind."

He was dressed in a dinner jacket, his tie was loosened and the top two buttons of his shirt were unfastened. Cliff didn't need anyone to tell him he looked bad. That was what he felt like, too. So the dragon lady wasn't going to come to him. Fine, he'd go to her, and they'd get this matter settled once and for all. Hard as it was to admit, he missed her. He even missed Joan and Katie. It hadn't been easy swallowing his pride this way, and he sincerely hoped Diana recognized that and responded appropriately.

"No, I don't mind." Actually, she was pleased to see him now that she'd gotten over the initial shock. They hadn't exactly parted on the best of terms, and she wanted to clear the air and say goodbye without a lot of emotion dictating her words. "I'd just poured myself a cup of coffee. Would you care for some?"

"Please." He followed her into the kitchen, sat down, noticed the open drape and pointed toward the patio. "What's going on out there?"

"School's out, and the girls are celebrating with a slumber party."

He grinned and nodded toward the large pile of blankets. Only one hand and the top of a head were visible. "I take it the one with the six-inch bright red fingernails is Joan."

Grinning, Diana delivered his cup to the table and nodded. "And the one clenching sixteen Pooh bears is Katie." As she moved past Cliff, she caught a whiff of expensive perfume and the faint odor of whiskey.

"It's good to see you, Diana." The fact was, he couldn't stop looking at her.

"There wasn't any need to tear yourself away from a hot date to visit, Cliff. I'm here most anytime." Her words were more teasing than angry, and she smiled at him.

He smiled back. "The least you could do is pretend you're happy to see me."

"But I am."

She really did have the most beautiful eyes. Dark and deep, wide and round. They were capable of tearing apart a man's heart and gentle enough to comfort an injured animal. He remembered how their color had clouded with passion when he'd kissed her, and wondered how long it would be before he could do it again. He longed for Diana's kisses as much as he missed her quick wit.

Diana settled herself in the chair across from him, not wanting to get too close. Cliff had that look in his eyes, and she was beginning to recognize what it meant. If she gave him the least amount of encouragement, he would reach for her and cover her mouth with his own. Then everything she'd discovered about herself these past days without him would be lost in the passion of the moment.

"Why did you come? Did your dinner companion turn you down?"

She didn't know the half of it, he thought to himself.

Diana grinned into her coffee cup. "Was she the same girl as the other night?"

"Yes," Cliff admitted sheepishly. "Unfortunately all her brains are situated below her neck."

"Now, Cliff, that was unkind." So her own estimation of Miss World had been right on; the blonde was a bimbo. It was tacky to feel so good being right about the other woman. Tacky, but human.

"Well, your date certainly resembled William F. Buckley."

Diana was unable to hold back her laugh. "He brought me references."

"What?"

"He's Shirley's third cousin, and apparently he thought I needed to know something more about him. Honestly, Cliff, I thought I'd die. He'd had someone from Highline Community College write up a letter telling me what a forthright man he is, and there was another letter from his dentist and a third from his apartment manager."

They laughed together, and it felt incredibly good. Diana wiped a tear from the corner of her eye and sighed audibly. "Joan and Kate were scared to death I'd marry him."

"How have the girls been?"

"They're great." Actually, Diana was grateful both her daughters were asleep; otherwise they might have launched themselves into Cliff's arms and told him how miserable their mother had been without him.

"And you?"

"Good. How about yourself?"

"Fair." Cliff didn't know the words to describe all that had been happening to him. Nothing had changed, and yet everything was different. He'd dated one of the most sought-after women in Seattle, and she'd left him feeling cold. His little black book was filled with names and phone numbers, and he hadn't the inclination to make one phone call.

"Actually, I'm glad you stopped by," Diana said, wading into the topic they'd both managed to avoid thus far. "I owe you an apology for running off on you that way."

"Diana, honestly, I still don't know what I did that was so terrible."

"I realize that."

"I thought we had something really good going. I didn't

mean to rush you—I assumed—falsely, it seems—that you were as ready for the physical part of our relationship as I was."

Diana lowered her gaze, and her hands tightened around the mug. "I wish I could be different for you, but I can't."

"You wanted me. I knew that almost from the first."

She still did, but that didn't alter her feelings. "Unfortunately I need something more than magic."

"What?" If he could give it to her, he would.

Her eyes were infinitely sad, dark and soulful. "You know the answer to that without my having to spell it out for you."

At least she had the common sense not to say it: love and commitment. He wasn't pleased at the thought of either one.

"Listen," she said, slowly lifting her eyes to capture his. "I'm glad you're here, because we do need to talk. A lot of things have been going through my mind the past couple of weeks."

"Mine, too."

"I like you, Cliff. I really do. It would be so easy to fall in love with you. But I'm afraid that if I did, we'd only end up hurting each other."

Feeling confused, he frowned darkly at her. "How do you mean?"

"When we first started going out, you automatically included the girls—mainly because I had them gathered around me like a fortress, and you recognized that you had to deal with them in order to get to me."

He grinned because she was right on target; that had been his plan exactly.

"Later, after the fishing fiasco, you realized that having the girls around wasn't the best thing for a promising relationship. I can't say that I blame you. There's no reason for you to be interested in children—a ready-made family isn't for you, and children do have a tendency to mess things up."

Cliff opened his mouth to contradict her, then realized that basically she was right. After the sailing trip, he had more or less decided the time had come to wean Diana away from her girls. To be honest, he'd wanted her all to himself. Oh, he'd planned to include Joan and Katie occasionally, but he was mainly interested in Diana. Her daughters were cute kids, but he could easily have done without them, and as much as possible, he'd hoped to keep them in the background of anything that developed between him and Diana.

"You make me sound pretty mercenary." Actually, when he thought about what he'd been doing, he realized that his actions could be construed as selfish. All right, so he'd been selfish!

"I don't mean to place you in a bad light."

"But it's true." It hadn't been easy for him to admit that, and he felt ashamed.

"Herein we have the basic problem. I can't be separated from the girls. You may be able to ignore them, but I can't. We're one, and placing me in the middle and asking me to choose between you and my daughters would only make everyone miserable."

Cliff's smile was wry. "You know, you would have made a great attorney."

"Thanks."

"The way I deal with Joan and Katie could change, Diana." His gaze continued to hold hers. She was right; he'd been thinking only of himself, and he'd been wrong. But now that the air had been cleared, he was more than willing to strike up a compromise.

"Perhaps it could change." She granted him an A for effort, and was pleased that he cared enough to want to try. "But there's more."

"There is?"

"Cliff, for some reason you have a difficult time making a

commitment to one woman. I suspect it has a lot to do with the girl who lived with you. Shirley told me about her."

"Becky." He didn't even like to think about her or the whole unfortunate experience. It had happened a long time ago, and as far as he was concerned, the whole affair was best forgotten.

"You might not be thrilled with this, but I think you cared a great deal for Becky. I honestly believe you loved her."

Unable to remain seated, Cliff stood and refilled his coffee cup, even though he'd taken only a few sips. "She was a selfish bitch," he said bitterly, his jaw tight.

"That makes admitting you loved her all the more difficult, doesn't it?"

"Who do you think you are? Sigmund Freud?"

"No," she admitted softly. "Believe me, I know what you went through when she moved out. Although the circumstances were different, I was unbelievably angry with Stan after he died. I'd take out the garbage and curse him for not being there to do it for me. I'd never been madder at anyone in my life. As crazy as it sounds, it took me months to forgive him for dying."

"Stan's death was absolutely nothing in common with what happened between me and some airhead. Becky wandered in and out of my life several years ago and has nothing to do with the here and now."

"Perhaps you're right."

"I know I am," he reiterated forcefully.

"But ever since then, you've flitted in and out of relationships, gained yourself a playboy reputation and you positively freeze at the mention of the word love. I'd hate to think what would happen if marriage turned up in casual conversation."

"That's not true." He felt like shouting now. Diana hadn't even known Becky. He was lucky to have gotten away from the two-timing schemer. Diana had it all wrong—he was planning on falling in love and getting married someday. It wasn't as if he'd been soured on the entire experience.

"I understand how you feel, believe me. Loving someone makes us vulnerable. If we care about anyone or anything, we leave ourselves wide open to pain. Over the years, the two of us have both shielded our hearts, learned to keep them intact. I'm as guilty as you are. I've wrapped my heart around hobbies. You use luxuries. The only difference between the two of us is that I have Joan and Katie. If it hadn't been for the girls, they might as well have buried me in the casket with Stan. It would have been safe there—airless and dark. Certainly there wouldn't have been any danger of my heart getting broken a second time. You see, after a while the heart becomes impenetrable and all our fears are gone."

Standing across from her, Cliff braced his hands on the back of the chair. He said nothing.

"I guess what I'm trying to say is that I finally understand the reason I couldn't sleep with you. Yes, you were right on target when you said I was physically ready, but emotionally and spiritually I'm miles away. You were right, too, when you claimed there was magic between us. After dating Owen, I recognized that isn't anything to sneeze at, either." She paused, and they shared a gentle smile. "But more than that, I realized that without love, without risking our hearts, the magic would fade. A close physical relationship would leave me vulnerable again and open to pain." She dropped her gaze to the tabletop. "It hurts too much, Cliff. I don't want to risk battering my heart just because something feels good."

When she'd finished, the silence wrapped itself around them.

Diana was the first one to speak. "But more than anything, I want you to know how grateful I am to you."

"Me? Why?"

"You woke me up. You made me feel again."

"Glad to oblige, Sleeping Beauty." Cliff hadn't liked what she'd said—maybe because it hit too close to the truth. She was right; he had changed after Becky, more than he'd ever realized. He wasn't particularly impressed with the picture Diana had painted of him, but the colors showed through all too clearly. She was right, too, about surrounding himself with luxuries. The sailboat, the fancy sports car, even the ski condo—they were extravagances. They made him feel good, made him look good.

After a long moment, Cliff moved away and emptied his coffee cup into the sink. "You've given me a lot to think about," he said with his back to her.

She'd given them both a lot to think about. Diana walked him to the front door and opened it for him. "Goodbye, Cliff."

He paused for a moment, then reached for her, folding her in his arms, pressing his jaw against the side of her head. He didn't kiss her, didn't dare, because he wasn't sure he would still be able to walk away from her if he did.

Diana slowly closed her eyes to the secure warmth she experienced in his arms. She wanted to savor these last moments together. After a while, she gently eased herself free.

"Goodbye, Diana," he whispered, and turned and walked away without looking back.

"Hey, Cliff, how about a cold beer?"

"Great." He stretched out his hand without disturbing his fishing pole and grabbed for the Bud Light. Holding the chilled aluminum can between his thighs, he dexterously opened it with one hand and guzzled down a long, cold drink.

"This is the life," Charlie, Cliff's longtime fishing buddy, called out. His cap was lowered over his eyes to block out the sun as he leaned back and stretched out his legs in front of him. The boat rocked lazily upon the still, green waters of Puget Sound.

"It doesn't get much better than this," Cliff said, reaching for a sandwich. The sun was out, the beer was cold and the fish were sure to start biting any minute.

The weather forecast had been for a hot afternoon sun. It was only noon, and already it was beginning to heat up. Charlie and Cliff had left the marina before dawn, determined to do some serious fishing. Thus far neither man had had so much as a nibble.

"I'm going to change my bait," Charlie said after a while. "I don't know what's the matter with these fish today. Too lazy, I guess. It looks like I'm going to have to give them reason to come my way."

"I think I'll change tactics, too." Already Cliff was reeling in his line. It was on days like this, when the fish weren't eager and the sun was hot, that he understood what it meant to be a fisherman. Once he had his pole inside the boat, he reached for his tackle box and sorted through the large assortment of hand-tied flies and fancy lures. A flash of silver stopped his search. His replacement lucky lure. His fingers closed around the cold piece of silver as his thoughts drifted to Katie. She was rambunctious and clever, and whenever she walked, the eight-year-old's pigtails would bounce. Grinning, he remembered how she'd leaned over the side of his sailboat and called out to the fish, trying to lure them to her hook before her sister's. His grin eased into a full smile as he recalled the girls' antics that Saturday afternoon.

"You know what I've been thinking?" Charlie mumbled as he tossed his line over the side of the boat.

Cliff was too caught up in his thoughts to care. He'd done a lot of thinking about what Diana had said the other night. In fact, he hadn't stopped thinking about their conversation. He hadn't liked it, but more and more he was beginning to recognize the truth in what she'd had to say.

"Cliff?"

Sure, he'd missed Diana, regretted his assumptions about their casually drifting into a physical relationship. But he missed Joan and Katie, too, more than he'd ever thought he would. The instant flare of regret that constricted his heart at the sight of the lure shocked him. He was beginning to care for those two little girls as much as he did for their mother.

"Cliff, good buddy? Are you going to fish, or are you going to kneel and stare into that tackle box all day?"

There was a reason Diana hated Monday mornings, she decided as she lifted the corner of Joan's double bed and tucked the clean sheet between the mattress and the box spring. She hated changing sheets, and once a week she was reminded of the summer job in her junior year of high school. She'd been a hotel maid and had come to hate anything vaguely connected with housekeeping.

When she finished with the girls' sheets, she was going to wash her hair, pack a picnic lunch and treat Joan and Katie to an afternoon at Seahurst beach in Burien, another South Seattle community. She might even put on a swimsuit and sunbathe. Of course, there was always the risk that someone from Greenpeace might mistake her for a beached whale and try to get her into the water, but she was willing to chance it.

Chuckling at her own wit, Diana straightened and reached for a fresh pillowcase. It was then that she heard a faint but sharp cry coming from outside, and recognized it immediately as something serious. It sounded like Katie. She tossed the pillow aside and started out of Joan's bedroom. The last time she'd looked, both girls were in the backyard playing. Mikey Holiday had been over, as well as a couple of other neighborhood kids.

"Mom!" Joan shrieked, panic in the lone word. "Mom! Mom!"

It was the type of desperate cry that chills a mother's blood. Diana raced down the stairs and nearly collided with her elder daughter. Joan groped for her mother's arms, her young face as pale as the sheet Diana had just changed.

"It's Katie . . . she fell out of the apple tree. Mom, she's hurt . . . real bad."

Nine

Diana walked briskly down the wide hospital corridor. Katie was at her side, being pushed in a wheelchair by the nurse who'd met her at the emergency entrance. The eight-year-old sobbed pitifully, and every cry ripped straight through Diana's soul. She hadn't needed a medical degree to recognize that Katie had broken her arm. What did astonish Diana was how calmly and confidently she'd responded to the emergency. Quickly she had protected Katie's oddly twisted arm in a pillow. Then she'd sent Joan and Mikey over to his house with instructions for Shirley to contact Valley General Hospital and tell them she was on her way with Katie.

"You'll need to fill out some paperwork," the nurse explained when they reached the front desk.

Diana hesitated as the receptionist rose to hand her the necessary forms.

Katie sobbed again and twisted around in her chair. "Mom . . . don't leave me."

"Honey, I'll be there as fast as I can." It wasn't until Katie had been wheeled out of sight and into the cubical that Diana began to shake. She gripped the pen between her fingers and started to complete the top sheet, quickly writing in Katie's name, her own and their address.

"Could . . . I sit down?" Now that her hands had stopped trembling, her knees were giving her problems. The entire room started to sway, and she grabbed the edge of the counter. She was starting to fall apart, but couldn't. At least not yet, Katie needed her.

"Oh, sure, take a seat," the woman in the crisp white uniform answered. "There are several chairs over there." She pointed to a small waiting area. A middle-aged couple was sitting there watching the *Noon News.* Somehow Diana made it to a molded plastic chair. She drew in several deep breaths and forced her attention to the questionnaire in front of her. The last time she'd been in Valley General was when Stan had been brought in.

Her stomach heaved as unexpected tears filled her eyes, blurring her vision as she relived the horror of that day. Three years had done little to erase the effects of that nightmare. Her throat constricted under the threat of overwhelming sobs, and again Diana forced her attention to the blank sheet she needed to complete.

But again the memories overwhelmed her. She'd been contacted at home and told that Stan had been in an accident. Naturally she'd been concerned, but no one had told her he was in any grave danger. She'd left the girls with Shirley and rushed to the hospital. Once she'd arrived, she'd been directed to the emergency room, given a multitude of forms to complete and told to wait. There'd been another man who'd just brought his wife in with gall bladder problems, and Diana had even joked with him in an effort to hide her nervousness. It seemed they kept her sitting there waiting for hours, and every time she inquired, the receptionist told her the doctor would be out in a few minutes. She asked if she could see Stan and was again told she'd have to wait. Finally the physician appeared, so stiff and somber. His eyes were filled with reluctance and regret as he spoke. And yet his message was only a few, simple words. He told Diana he was sorry. At first, she didn't understand what he meant. Naturally, he was sorry that Stan had been hurt. So was she. It wasn't until she asked how long it would be before her husband could come home and seen the pity in the doctor's eyes that she understood. Stan would never leave the hospital, and no one had even given her the chance to say goodbye to him. Diana had been calm then, too. So calm. So serene. It wasn't until later, much later, that the floodgates of overwhelming grief had broken, and she'd nearly drowned in her pain.

Katie's piercing cry cut sharply into Diana's thoughts. Her reaction was instinctive, and she leaped to her feet. The hospital staff hadn't let her go to Stan, either.

She stepped to the receptionist's desk. "I want to be with my daughter."

The woman took the clipboard from Diana's numb fingers and glanced over the incomplete form. "I'm sorry, but you'll need to finish these before the doctor can treat your daughter."

"Please." Her voice cracked. "I need to be with Katie."

"I'm sorry, Mrs. Collins, but I really must—"

"Then give her something for the pain!" The sound of someone running came from behind her, but Diana's senses were too dulled to register anything more than the noise.

"Diana." Cliff joined her at the counter, his eyes wide and concerned. "What happened?"

"Katie . . . they won't let me be with Katie."

Tears streamed down her face, and Cliff couldn't ever remember seeing anyone more deathly pale. It was then that he realized that he'd never imagined that Diana could be so unnerved. One look at her told him why he'd found it so urgent to rush here. Somehow he'd known that Diana would need him.

Until a half hour ago, his day had been going rather smoothly. He'd been eating a sandwich at his desk, thinking about a case he was about to review, when his secretary had stuck her head in the door and announced that someone named Joan was crying on the phone and asking to speak to him. By the time Cliff had lifted the receiver, the eleven-year-old was almost hysterical. In between sobs, Joan had told him that Diana had taken Katie to the hospital. She'd also claimed that her mother couldn't afford to pay the bill. Cliff had hardly been able to understand what had happened until Shirley Holiday had gotten on the line and explained that Katie had broken her arm. Cliff had thanked her for letting him know, then had sat quietly at his desk a few minutes until he'd decided what he should do. After a moment he'd dumped the rest of his lunch in the wastepaper basket, stood and reached for his suit jacket. He'd tossed a few words of explanation to his secretary and crisply walked out the door.

A broken arm, although painful, was nothing to be worried about, he'd assured himself. Kids broke their arms every day. It wasn't that big a deal. Only this wasn't just any little kid, this was Katie. Sweet Katie, who had tossed her arms around his neck and given him a wet kiss. Katie who would sell her soul for a bucket of Kentucky Fried Chicken. Diana's Katie—his Katie.

He hadn't understood why he felt the urgent need to get to the hospital, but he did. Heaven or hell wouldn't have kept him away. It was a miracle that the state patrol wasn't after him, Cliff realized when he pulled into the hospital parking lot. He'd driven like a crazy man.

"Mrs. Collins has to complete these forms before she can be with her daughter," the receptionist patiently explained for the third time.

Diana's hand grasped Cliff's forearms, and her watery eyes implored him. "Stan . . . never came home."

Cliff frowned, not understanding her meaning. He reached for the clipboard and flipped the pages until he found what he wanted. "Diana, all you need to do is sign your name here." He gave her the pen.

"I'm sorry, but I will have to ask Mrs. Collins to fill out all the necessary—"

Cliff silenced the receptionist with one determined look. "I can complete anything else."

Diana scribbled her name where Cliff had indicated and gave the clipboard back to him.

"Take Mrs. Collins to her daughter," he stated next in the same crisp, dictatorial tone.

The woman nodded and stood to walk around the desk and escort Diana to where they'd wheeled Katie.

Cliff watched Diana leave, reached for the clipboard and took a seat. It wasn't until he read through the first few lines she'd completed that he understood what Diana had been trying to tell him about Stan. The last time she'd been in the hospital was when her husband had been brought in after the airplane accident. From the information George Holiday had given him, Cliff understood that Stan had been badly burned. On the advice of Stan's physician, Diana had never seen her husband's devastated body. One peaceful Saturday morning, Diana kissed her husband goodbye and went shopping with her daughters, while he took off in a private plane with a good friend. And she never saw her high-school sweetheart again.

Less than an hour later, Diana appeared and took a seat beside Cliff. She'd composed herself by this time, embarrassed to have given way to crying as she had.

"They're putting a cast on Katie's arm," she said when Cliff looked to her. "She's asking to see you."

"Me?"

"Yes, Cliff, you."

They stood together. Diana paused, feeling a bit chagrined, but needing to thank him. "I don't know who told you about the accident or why you came, but I want you to know how much I appreciate your . . . help. Something came over me when we arrived at the hospital, and all of a sudden I couldn't help remembering the last time I was here. I got so afraid." Her voice wobbled, and she bit into her bottom lip. "Thank you, Cliff."

"No problem." He was having a hard time not taking her in his arms and offering what comfort he could. His whole body ached with the need to hold her and tell her he understood. But after their last discussion, he didn't know how she'd feel about him touching her. He buried his hands in his pants pockets, bunching them into impotent fists. "I'm here because I want to be here—there's nothing noble about it."

Although he made light of it, Diana knew he'd left his law office in the middle of the day to rush to the hospital. His caring meant more than she could ever tell him. She wanted to try, but the words that were in her heart didn't make it to her tongue.

"Cliff!" Katie brightened the minute he stepped into the casting room.

"Hi, buttercup." Her face was streaked with tears, her pigtails mussed with leaves and grass and a bruise was forming on the side of her jaw, but Cliff couldn't remember seeing a more beautiful little girl. "How did you manage that?" He nodded toward her arm.

"I fell out of the apple tree," she told him, and wrinkled up her nose. "I wasn't supposed to climb it, either."

"I hope you won't again," Diana interjected.

Katie's young brow crinkled into a tight frown. "I don't think I will. This hurt real bad, but I tried to be brave for Mom and Joan."

"I broke my leg once," Cliff told her. The thought of Katie having to endure the same pain he'd suffered produced a curious ache in the region of his heart. He watched as the PA worked, wrapping her arm in a protective layer of cotton. Then he dipped thick plaster strips in water and began to mold them over Katie's forearm and elbow.

"I've missed you a whole lot," the little girl said next.

"I've missed you, too." Cliff discovered that wasn't a lie. He'd tried not to think about Diana and her daughters since the night of their talk. The past couple of days, he'd been almost amused at the way everything around him had reminded him of them. He'd finally reached the conclusion that he wasn't going to be able to forget these three females. Somehow, without his knowing how, they'd made an indelible mark on his heart. What Diana had said about Becky and him had been the truth. Funny, he'd once told Diana to wake up and smell the coffee, and yet he had been the one with his head buried in the sand.

"Mom missed you, too—a whole bunch."

"Katie!"

"It's true. Don't you remember you were cranky with me and Joan, and then you told us you were sorry and said you were still missing Cliff and that was the reason you were in such a bad mood."

A hot flush seeped into Diana's face and circled her ears. With some effort, she smiled weakly in Cliff's direction, hoping he'd be kind enough to forget what Katie had told him.

"Don't you remember, Mom? Joan thought it was Aunt Flo again and you said—"

"I remember, Katie," she said pointedly.

"Who's Aunt Flo?" Cliff wanted to know.

"Never mind," Diana murmured under her breath.

"Will you sign my cast?" Katie asked Cliff next. "The only boys who can sign it are you and Mikey."

"I'd be honored."

"And maybe Gary Hidenlighter."

"Who's he?" The name sounded vaguely familiar to Cliff, and he wondered where he'd heard it.

"The boy who offered her a baseball card if she'd let him kiss her."

"Ah, yes," Cliff answered with a lopsided grin. "I seem to recall hearing about the dastardly proposition now."

"Kissing doesn't seem to be so bad," Katie added thoughtfully after a moment. "Mom and you sure do it a lot."

Cliff lightly slipped his arm around Diana's shoulders and smiled down on her. "I can't speak for your mother, but I know what I like."

"I do, too," she responded, looking up at Cliff, comforted by his feathery touch.

Getting Katie out of the hospital wasn't nearly as much a problem as getting her in had been since Cliff was there to smooth the way. While Diana filled in the spaces Cliff had left blank on the permission forms, he wheeled Katie up to the hospital pharmacy and had the prescription for the pain medication filled. By the time they returned, Diana had finished her task. As the two came toward her, the sight of them together filled her with an odd sensation of rightness.

"Can I ride in Cliff's car?" Katie asked once they were in the parking lot.

"Katie, Cliff has to get back to his office."

"No, I don't," he countered quickly, looking almost boyish in his eagerness. "While we were waiting, I phoned my secretary and told her I was taking the rest of the day off."

"Oh, goodie." Katie's happy eyes flew from her mother to Cliff and then back to Diana again. "Since Cliff isn't real busy, can I go in his car?"

Diana's gaze went to Cliff, who acquiesced with a short nod.

All the way into Kent, Katie chatted a mile a minute. The physician had claimed that the pain medication would make the little girl drowsy, but thus far it had had just the opposite effect. Katie was a wonder.

"I used my new lucky lure the other day," Cliff said when he was able to get a word in edgewise.

"Oh, good. Did it work?"

"Like a dream." His change in luck had astonished him and had amazed Charlie, who'd wanted to know where Cliff had bought that silver lure. Cliff had sailed back into the marina that afternoon with a good-size salmon and a large flounder, while Charlie hadn't gotten so much as a curious nibble.

Katie let out a long sigh of relief. "I was real afraid the new one wouldn't have the same magic."

"Then rest assured, Katie Collins, because this new lure seems to be even better than the old one. In fact, you might have done me a favor by losing the original."

"Really? Are we ever going to go fishing on your sailboat again? I promise never to get into your gear unless you tell me I can."

"I think another fishing expedition could be arranged, but let's leave that up to your mother, okay?" He wasn't sure Diana would agree to seeing him again, and didn't want to disappoint Katie.

"That sounds okay," Katie assented.

When Cliff pulled into the driveway behind Diana's gray bomber, it seemed that half the kids in the neighborhood rushed out to greet Katie.

They followed her into the house, and she sat them down, organized their questions and patiently answered each one, explaining in graphic detail what had happened to her. As he looked on from the kitchen, it seemed to Cliff that she was holding her own press conference.

While Katie was hailed as a heroine, Diana brewed coffee and brought a cup to Cliff. "Do you mind if I take a look around your garage?" he asked her unexpectedly after taking a sip.

"Sure, go ahead." She wondered what he was up to and was mildly surprised when he reappeared a couple of minutes later with a handsaw.

"Here," he said, handing her his suit jacket, and marched outside.

Katie noticed he was gone right away. "What's Cliff doing?"

Diana was just as curious as her daughter and followed him out the sliding glass door. She paused, watching him from the patio as he methodically started trimming off the lower branches of the backyard's lone tree.

By the time he'd finished, Cliff had loosened his tie, unfastened the top buttons of his starched shirt and paused more than once to wipe the sweat from his brow.

Grateful for his thoughtfulness, Diana started issuing instructions. Soon the neighborhood kids had gathered around him and stacked the fallen limbs into a neat pile. Diana was so busy watching Cliff and telling the kids to keep out of his way that he was nearly finished before she noticed that Joan was missing.

Diana wandered through the house, looking for her daughter. When she didn't find her on the lower level, she wandered up the stairs.

"Joan?"

She heard a muffled sob and peeked inside the first bedroom, looking past all the Justin Timberlake posters to her daughter, who had flung herself across the top of her half-made bed.

"Joan?" she asked softly. "Don't you want to come and see Katie?"

"No."

"Why not? She wants you to sign her cast."

"I'm not going to. Not ever."

Diana moved to her daughter's side and sat on the edge of

the mattress. Puzzled by Joan's odd behavior, she brushed the soft wisps of hair from the eleven-year-old's furrowed brow.

Huge tears filled the preteen's dark brown eyes. She muttered something about Cliff that Diana couldn't understand.

"You phoned him at his office?"

Joan nodded. "I . . . I don't know why. I just did."

"Do you think I'm angry with you because of that?"

Joan shrugged in open defiance. "I don't care if you are mad. I wanted to talk to Cliff and I did . . . Katie was hurt and I thought he had the right to know."

The realization that both girls had turned to Cliff in the emergency was only a little short of shocking to Diana. Katie had asked about him even before Diana had had a chance to tell the youngster he was in the hospital waiting room, filling out the forms. And Joan had contacted him at his office, knowing she would probably be punished for doing so. No other man Diana had ever dated had had this profound effect on her daughters. Without trying, without even wanting to, Cliff Howard had woven himself into their tender hearts. Although it hurt, Diana understood now that she'd made the right decision to break off her relationship with him. Cliff possessed the awesome power to hurt her children, and it was her duty, as their mother, to protect them.

"Mom," Joan sobbed, straightening up enough to hurl herself into her mother's arms, "I was so afraid."

"I know, sweetheart." Fresh tears filled Diana's eyes at the memory of those first minutes at the hospital. "I was, too."

"I . . . thought Katie would never come home again."

Diana's own fears had been similar. In all the confusion, she hadn't considered what had been going on in Joan's mind. As the eldest, Joan could remember the day her father had died. She had only been eight at the time, and although she might not have understood everything, she could vividly remember the horror, just as Diana had earlier in the day.

"You can have my allowance if you need it . . . ."

"I don't need your allowance, honey."

Embarrassed now by the display of emotion, Joan wiped the moisture from her cheek and gave her mother a determined, angry look. "That Katie can be really stupid. You know that, don't you?"

"Cliff cut off the lower limbs so Katie won't be able to climb into the apple tree again."

Joan nodded approvingly. "It's a good thing, because that Katie can be so stupid. Knowing her, she wouldn't learn a single lesson from this. If something hadn't been done, she'd probably break her other arm next week."

Diana hid her smile, and the two hugged each other. "Come downstairs now, and you can talk to your sister."

Joan nodded. "All right, but don't get mad at me if I tell Katie she's got the brains of a rotting tomato."

"Mom, is there room in your suitcase for my iPad?"

Diana groaned, glanced toward the ceiling and prayed for patience. "Unfortunately I need some space for my clothes," she said, and attempted to shut the suitcase one last time. It wouldn't latch. "Your iPad has low priority at the moment."

"Mom!" Katie hurried into the bedroom. "Did you tell Cliff we were going to Wichita to visit Grandma and Grandpa?"

Diana hedged, trying to recall if she had or not. She had, she thought. "Yes."

"How come he hasn't come over since he brought me home from the hospital?"

The tight, uncomfortable feeling returned to Diana's chest. "I . . . don't know."

"But I thought he would."

So had Diana. She'd laid her cards out on the table, and the next move was his. He'd been wonderful with Katie that day she'd broken her arm, more than wonderful. While Katie had slept during the afternoon from the effects of the medication, he'd taken Joan out shopping. Together they'd purchased Katie a huge stuffed Pooh bear. At dinnertime he'd insisted on providing Kentucky Fried Chicken, much to her younger daughter's delight. But after they'd eaten, he'd said a few words of farewell, and that had been the last Diana or the girls had heard from him.

Actually, Diana was grateful for this vacation. These next two weeks with her parents would help all three of them take their minds off one Cliff Howard.

"He didn't even sign my cast."

"I think he forgot," Diana said, sitting on her suitcase in an effort to latch it.

"I think we should call him," Joan chimed in.

"No."

"But, Mom . . ."

One derisive look from Diana squelched that idea.

"What is it with that man, anyway?" Joan asked next. "I don't understand him at all."

Joan wasn't the only one baffled by Cliff.

"I thought he was hot for you."

"Joan, please."

"No, really, Mom. The day he brought Katie home, he could hardly take his eyes off you."

Diana had done her share of looking, too. She'd wanted to talk to him, let him know how much she appreciated what he'd done for her and the girls, but he had left before the opportunity arose, and they hadn't heard from him in four days. Now that she'd had some time to give the matter thought, she'd decided not to protect the girls from the danger of Cliff denting their tender hearts. She'd seen how wonderful he'd been with Katie and how thoughtful with Joan. He'd never intentionally hurt them.

"Cliff told me he'd take me fishing again," Katie said. Her cast was covered with a multitude of messages and names in a variety of colors, but she'd managed to save a white space for Cliff under her elbow. "But he said if we went again, it would be up to you. We can go, can't we, Mom?"

Before Diana could answer Katie, the phone rang. Joan pounced on the receiver next to Diana's bed like a cat on a cornered mouse.

"Hello," she said demurely, sat down and grinned girlishly. She crossed her legs and thoughtfully examined the ends of her fingernails. "It's good to hear from you again."

It was obviously a boy, and Joan was in seventh heaven.

"Yes, she's recovered nicely. Katie always was the brave one. Personally, at the sight of blood, I get the vapors. It's a good thing my mother kept her wits about her."

Diana bounced hard on the suitcase and sighed when the latch snapped into place. Success at last.

"Yes, she's sitting right here. She's packing. You do remember we're leaving for Wichita tonight, don't you? You didn't? Well, that's strange . . . Mom claims she did tell you. Yes, of course, just a minute." Grinning ear to ear, Joan held out the phone to her mother. "It's for you, Mom. It's Cliff."

Diana's heart fell to her knees and rebounded sharply before finally settling back into place. Joan had to be joking. "Cliff Howard?"

"Honestly, Mother, just how many Cliffs are you dating?"

"At the moment, none."

As diplomatically as possible, Joan steered her younger sister out of the bedroom and started to close the door.

"But," Katie protested, "I want to talk to Cliff, too."

"Another time," Joan said, and winked coyly at her mother.

Clearing her throat, Diana lifted the telephone receiver to her ear. "Hello."

"Diana? What's this about you leaving for Wichita?"

"Yes, well, I thought I mentioned it."

A short silence followed. "How long are you going to be gone?"

"Two weeks."

Her answer was followed by his partially muffled swearing. "Listen, would it be all right if I came over right away?"

Ten

Cliff pulled his sports car into Diana's driveway and turned off the engine. For a long moment he kept his hands on the steering wheel, his thoughts heavy. Maybe Diana had told him about this trip to Wichita, but if she had, he sure didn't remember it. He'd reached a decision about himself and his relationship with Diana and her girls. The process had been painful, but now that he knew his mind, he wasn't going to let a planned two-week vacation stand in his way.

Determined, he climbed out of his car, slammed the door and headed for the house.

Diana met him on the front porch, and once again Cliff was struck by her simple beauty. Her dark eyes with their long, thick lashes searched his face. Her lips were slightly parted, and a familiar ache tightened Cliff's midsection. If everything blew up in his face today, if worse came to worse and he never saw Diana Collins again, he'd always remember her and her kisses. They'd haunt him.

"Hello, Cliff." Diana was amazed how cool and unemotional she sounded. She wasn't feeling the least bit controlled. From the minute they'd finished their telephone conversation, she'd been pacing the upstairs, wandering from room to room in a mindless search for serenity. She'd never heard Cliff sound quite so serious. Now that he'd arrived, she noted that his piercing blue eyes revealed an unfamiliar intensity.

"Hello, Diana."

She opened the screen door for him.

"Where are the girls?" he asked once he was inside the house. He kept his hands in his pockets for fear he'd do something crazy, like reach for her and kiss her senseless. He'd been thinking about exactly that for four long days. Being with her only increased his need to taste her again.

"Joan and Katie are saying goodbye to all their friends in the neighborhood. You'd think we were going to be gone two years instead of two weeks." Actually, this time alone with Cliff had been Joan's doing. Her elder daughter hadn't been the least bit subtle about suggesting to Katie that perhaps they should take this opportunity to bid their friends a fond au revoir. Katie, however, had been far more interested in seeing Cliff. Diana estimated they'd have fifteen minutes at the most, before Katie blasted into the house.

Cliff jerked a hand out of his pocket and splayed his fingers through his hair. Now that he was here, he found he was tongue-tied. He'd practiced everything he wanted to say and now he didn't know where to start.

"Would you like some coffee?"

"No, thanks, I came to talk." That sounded good.

"Okay." Diana moved into the living room. Whatever was on Cliff's mind was important. He hadn't so much as cracked a smile. She imagined his behavior was similar when he stood in the courtroom before the jury box. Each move would be calculated, every word planned for the maximum effect.

Diana lowered herself into the overstuffed chair, and Cliff

took a seat directly across from her on the sofa. He sat on the edge of the cushion, his elbows resting on his thighs, and clenched his hands into tight fists.

"How's Katie?"

Diana's smile came from her heart. "She's doing great. After the first day she didn't even need the pain medication."

"And you?"

Without his having to explain, Diana understood. "Much better, I . . . I'm not exactly sure I know what happened that day in the hospital, but emotionally I crumbled into a thousand pieces. I was about as close to being a basket case as I can remember. I'll always be grateful you were there for Katie and me."

"Her accident taught us both several valuable lessons."

"It did?" Diana swallowed around the uncomfortable tightness in her throat. She hardly recognized the Cliff who sat across from her; he was so grim-faced and unreadable.

Cliff seemed unable to take his eyes off her. There was so much he longed to tell her, and he'd never felt more uncertain about how to express himself. Knowing she would be leaving for her parents' had thrown him an unexpected curveball. He wished he could have taken her to an expensive restaurant and explained everything on neutral ground. Now he felt pressured to clear the air between them before she left for Wichita.

"Until Katie broke her arm," he went on to say, "I'd more or less decided, after our late-night conversation, that you were right and it was best for us not to see each other again." He sat stiffly, feeling ill at ease. "It didn't take you long to see through me—I'm definitely not the marrying kind, and you knew it. You appealed to my baser instincts and I appealed to yours, but anything more than that between us was doomed. Am I right?"

Out of nervous agitation, Diana reached for the pillow with the cross-stitch pattern and fluffed it up in her lap. "Yes . . . I suppose so."

"Not seeing me again was what you wanted, wasn't it?" Cliff challenged.

Regretfully Diana nodded. It was and it wasn't. A relationship with Cliff showed such marvelous promise, and at the same time contained the coarse threads of tragedy. If the only threat had been *her* heart and *her* emotions, Diana might have risked it.

At least those had been her thoughts before the accident, when she'd seen how good Cliff had been with her girls. Joan and Katie were already involved.

"I see."

Diana wasn't sure he did. If he understood all this, then there wasn't any reason for this urgent visit now. Suddenly she understood what he was getting at. Her cheeks flushed, and she stood, holding the decorator pillow to her stomach. "Cliff, I apologize."

"You do?" He was the one who wanted to ask her forgiveness.

"Yes. I had no idea Joan would contact you when Katie was hurt. I'll make sure it doesn't happen again. I don't know why she did it . . . but I've talked with her since and explained that she should never have made that call, and she promised she . . ."

Cliff stormed to his feet. "I'm not talking about that!"

"You're not?"

"No." He lowered his voice, paused and ran his hand along the back of his neck a couple of times. "Listen, I'm doing a poor job of this."

She stared at him in wide-eyed wonder, not knowing what to think.

"Sit down, would you?"

Diana lowered herself back into the chair.

Cliff paced the space in front of her as though she were a stubborn member of the jury and he were about to make the closing argument in an important trial. He couldn't believe he was making such a mess of something this basic. Talking to Diana should have been a simple matter of explaining his change of heart, but once he arrived, he felt as nervous as a first-year member of a debate team.

Diana pressed her hands between her closed knees and studied Cliff as he moved back and forth in the small area in front of her chair. It was on the tip of her tongue to tell him that if he didn't hurry, the girls would be back and then their peace would be shattered. With Katie doing cartwheels at the sight of him, there wouldn't be a chance for a decent discussion.

Perhaps, Cliff decided, it would be best to start at the beginning. "Do you remember the night I came over after work and we sat and talked?"

Diana grinned and nodded. "As I recall, we did more kissing than talking."

Cliff relaxed enough to share a smile with her, and when he spoke his eyes softened with the memory of how good the gentle lovemaking between them had been then. "It didn't feel right to walk away from you that night."

Diana's gaze dropped to the carpet. It hadn't felt right to her, either, but there was so much more at stake than her feelings or his.

"After I left you, I decided a romantic evening alone together in my condo would be just the thing to seal our fates. Do you remember?"

She wasn't likely to forget. "Listen, Cliff, I don't know what your point is, but . . ."

Cliff wasn't entirely sure anymore, either. "I guess what I'm having such a difficult time telling you is that I don't bed every woman I date." Diana was special, more than special. She had never been, and never would be, a number to him—someone he'd use to boost his ego. He wanted to explain that, and it just wasn't coming out the way he'd planned.

"It's none of my business how many women you've slept with." If he was going to make some grand confession, she wasn't interested in hearing it.

"But this does involve you."

She stood again, because it was impossible to remain seated. "Listen, Cliff, if you're going to tell me you slept with that . . . that bimbo blonde then . . . don't."

"Bimbo blonde? Oh, you mean Marianne. You think I made love to her? Diana, you've got to be joking."

"No, I'm not." The unexpected pain that tightened her chest made it almost impossible to talk evenly. The power Cliff Howard wielded to injure her heart was lethal. Diana had recognized that early in their relationship and had taken steps to protect herself. Yet here he was, stirring up unwelcome trauma.

"I didn't sleep with her! Diana, I swear to you by all that I hold dear, I didn't go to bed with Marianne." His words were little more than a hoarse whisper.

She walked across the room and looked out the window. Where were the girls when she could really use them? "That's hardly my business."

"I'm trying to make a point here."

"If so, just do it," she said, and whirled around to face him, shoulders stiff. She was on the defensive now and growing more impatient by the minute.

"I want to apologize for . . ."

"That's exactly what I thought," she flared, resisting the urge to place her hands over her ears to blot out his words. "And I don't want to hear it . . . so you can save your breath."

"For the night at my condominium," Cliff continued, undaunted. "I set up that seduction scene because we both felt the magic, and I wanted you." He lowered his voice to an enticing whisper of remembered desire. "Heaven knows I wanted you." And nothing had changed.

Now it was Diana's turn to pace, and she did so with all the energy of a raw recruit eager to please his sergeant. She stopped when she realized how ridiculous she must look and slapped her hands against the sides of her thighs. "Just what is your point?"

For a minute Cliff had forgotten. "When you walked out on me that night, I can't remember ever being angrier with anyone in my life. I figured if you were into denial, then fine, but I was noble enough to be honest about my feelings."

"I wonder if there's a Pulitzer Prize for that," she murmured sarcastically, and wrapped her arms around her waist.

Cliff ignored her derision. "Later I had a change of heart and decided I could be forgiving, considering the circumstances. I gave you ample time to come to me, and when you didn't, I was forced to swallow my pride and bridge the uneasiness between us. You may be impressed to know that I don't do that sort of thing often."

A snicker slipped from Diana's clogged throat. She tightened her grip on her waist. The longer he spoke, the more uncertain she was as to how to take Cliff. He was being sarcastic, but it seemed to be at his expense and not hers.

"That night you lowered the boom and told me a few truths," Cliff continued. "Basically, let it be known that you weren't interested in falling into bed with me because of some mystical, magical feeling between us. You also took it upon yourself to point out a couple of minor flaws in my personality. As I recall, shortly afterward I was left to lick my wounds."

A smile cracked the tight line of Diana's mouth. "Was I really so merciless?"

"Wanna see the scars?"

"I didn't mean to be so ruthless," she said tenderly, filled with regret for having injured his pride, although she'd known the nature of their talk would be painful for him.

"The truth hurts—isn't that how the saying goes?"

Diana nodded.

"I've done a lot of thinking since that night." Only a few feet separated them, and he raised his hands as though to reach for her and bring her close to him. Reluctantly he dropped his fists to his side and took a step in the opposite direction.

"And?" Diana pressed.

"And I think we may have something, Diana. Something far more valuable than magic. Something I'm not likely ever to find again. I don't want to lose you. I realize I may have ruined everything by trying to rush you into bed with me, and I apologize for that. I'd like a second chance with you, although I probably don't deserve one."

His eyes softened and caressed her with such tenderness that Diana stopped breathing until her lungs ached. When she spoke, the words rushed out on the tail end of a raspy sigh. "I think . . . that could be arranged."

"Whatever it is between us is potent—you'll have to agree to that."

Diana couldn't deny the obvious.

"I know you have your doubts and I honestly can't blame you. But if you agree to letting me see you again, I promise to do things differently. I'm not going to pressure you into lovemaking—you have my word on that."

"I've made my share of mistakes, too, and I think it would only be fair if I came up with a few promises of my own."

He looked at her as though he hadn't had a clue as to what she was talking about.

"I have no intention of rushing you into making a commitment. And the word *love* will be stricken from my vocabulary." Feeling almost giddy with relief, she smiled warmly.

Cliff smiled in return. "I wonder if we could seal this bargain with a kiss."

"I think that would be more than appropriate."

Cliff had reached for her even before she'd finished speaking. He needed to hold her again and savor her softness pressing against him. She was halfway into his arms, when the front door burst open.

"Cliff!" Katie leaped into the living room with all the energy of a hydroelectric dam. Her pigtails were swinging, her eyes aglow. "I didn't think you'd ever get here. You forgot to sign my cast, and I saved you a space, but it's getting dirty."

Joan followed shortly after Katie. "Hi, Cliff," she said nonchalantly. She tossed her mother an apologetic look.

Cliff pulled a pen from inside his suit pocket and knelt in front of Katie.

"What took you so long?" Katie demanded as Cliff started penning his message on her cast.

"I don't know, buttercup," he answered, looking up to Diana and smiling.

"I can't get over how much the girls have grown," Joyce Shaffer, Diana's mother, said with an expressive sigh, alternately glancing between Joan and Katie.

"It's been a year, Mom." The long flight from Seattle to Wichita had left the girls and Diana exhausted. Joan and Katie had fallen asleep ten minutes after they arrived at Diana's family home. Diana longed to join her daughters, but her parents were understandably excited and wanted to chat. Diana and her mother gathered around the kitchen table, nibbling on chocolate chip cookies, drinking tall glasses of milk and talking.

"Poor Katie," her mother went on to say sympathetically. "Is her arm still hurting?"

"It itches more than anything."

Burt Shaffer pulled up a chair and joined the two women. "Who's this Cliff fellow the girls were telling me about?"

Diana hesitated, not exactly sure how to explain her relationship with Cliff. She didn't want to lead her family into thinking she was about to remarry, nor did she wish to explain that she and Cliff had reached a still untested understanding.

"Cliff and I have dated a few times." That was the best explanation she could come up with on such short notice. She should have been prepared for this. The minute the girls had stepped off the plane, Katie had shown her grandparents where Cliff had signed her cast and told the detailed story of how he'd let her ride in his car on the way home from the hospital. First Katie, then Joan, had spoken nonstop for a full five minutes, extolling his myriad virtues, until Diana had thought she'd scream at them both to cut it out.

"So you've only dated him a few times." Her father nodded once, giving away none of his feelings. "The girls certainly seem to have taken a liking to him. What about you, rosebud? Do you think as highly of this Cliff fellow as Joan and Katie seem to?"

"Now really, Burt," her mother cut in. "Don't go quizzing poor Diana about the men in her life the minute she walks in the door. Diana, dear, did I tell you Danny Helleberg recently moved back to town?"

Diana and Danny had gone to high school together a million years ago. Although they'd been in the same class, Diana had barely known him. "No . . ."

"I talked to his mother the other day in the grocery store and I told her you were flying out for a visit. She says Danny would love to see you again."

"That would be nice." Not really, but Diana didn't want to disappoint her mother.

"I'm glad you think so, honey, because he phoned and I told him to call again in the morning."

"That'd be great." Her smile was weak at best. She had hardly

said more than a handful of words to Danny Helleberg the entire time they were in school together. Recounting the memory of their high-school days should take all of five minutes. It
was the only thing they had in common.

"His wife left him for another man. I did tell you that, didn't
I? The poor boy was beside himself."

"Yes, Mom, I think you did mention Danny's marital problems." She tried unsuccessfully to swallow a yawn, gave up the
effort and planted her hand over her mouth, hoping her parents
got the hint.

They didn't.

"Danny and his wife are divorced now."

Diana did her best to try to look interested. It was the same
way every visit—her parents seemed to think it was their duty to
supply her with another husband. Every summer a variety of men
were paraded before her while Diana struggled to appear grateful.

"Tell us about Cliff," her dad prompted.

Diana's fingers tightened around her milk glass. "There really isn't much to tell. We've only gone out a few times."

"What's his family like?" her mother wanted to know, looking as though she already disapproved. If Diana was going to
remarry, it was her mother's opinion that the man should be
from Wichita. Then Diana wouldn't have any more excuses to
remain in Seattle.

"Really, Mom, I don't have any idea—I haven't met his
parents."

"I see." Her mother exchanged a look with her father that
Diana recognized all too well.

"Cliff's an attorney," she added hurriedly, hoping that would
impress her parents.

"That's nice, dear." But her mother didn't seem overly swayed
by the information. "We just hope you aren't serious about this
young man."

"Why?" Diana asked, surprised.

Her mother looked more amazed than Diana. "Why, because Danny Helleberg is back in town. You know how well his mother and I get along."

Diana felt like grinding her teeth. "Right, Mom."

Cliff leaned back on his leather couch and stretched out his legs in front of him, crossing his ankles. Diana's first email had arrived. Already adrenaline was pumping through him. Four days. She'd been gone only four days, and he missed her more than he thought it was possible to miss another human being. He thought about their last minutes together while he'd driven her and the girls to the airport. Diana had lingered as long as she could, seeking to delay their parting. So much had remained unsaid between them. She'd wrapped her arms around his neck and kissed him soundly. The memory of that single, ardent kiss still had the power to triple his pulse rate. It was the type of kiss men remember as they go into battle. A kiss meant to forge time and distance. She'd looked as dazed as he felt. Without saying anything more, she'd turned and left him, rushing into the airport with Joan and Katie at her side. Cliff had remained at the airport drop-off point far longer than necessary, wishing she were back in his arms. Two weeks, he'd thought. That shouldn't be so long, but the way the time was dragging, each minute seemed longer than the one before. Two weeks was an eternity.

He grinned as he read over the first few lines that told him about Joan and Katie and how Katie had told her parents about him before Diana had had the opportunity to mention his name. The smile faded when he read how her parents were pressuring her to move to Wichita so they could look after her properly. He sighed audibly as he scrolled down to the second page. Diana assured him this was an old argument and that she had no intention of leaving Seattle. She loved her parents, but being close to them would slowly, surely, drive her crazy. Cliff agreed with that. He loved his family, but they had the same effect upon him.

Cliff continued reading. Diana told him she regretted the impulsive kiss at the airport. Now all she could think about was getting back to Seattle and seeing him again. Nothing had ever been that good—not even their first kiss at the marina under the starlight.

Cliff agreed.

If she experienced half the emotion he had over that kiss, she'd call her family vacation short and hurry back to him. All he could think about was Diana coming home and his holding her again.

He left the computer and went into the kitchen to fix himself something for dinner. Five minutes later he returned, pausing over the last few words she'd written about the kiss.

On impulse he reached for the phone. If he didn't hear her voice, he'd be the one to slowly, surely, go crazy. Getting her parents' number wasn't a problem, and he quickly punched it out, checking his watch and figuring out the time difference.

"Hello."

Cliff would have staked his life savings that Joan would answer. He was right.

"Hi, Joan."

"Cliff! How are you?"

"Fine." Okay, so that was a minor exaggeration; he would be once he talked to Joan's mother.

"We went to Sedgwick County Zoo today. It was great. I saw a green snake and a black-necked swan."

She paused, and Cliff heard muffled arguing.

"Joan," Cliff called after a long pause, "are you there?"

"Yes, Cliff," she said a bit breathlessly. "It seems my darling younger sister wants to talk to you."

"Okay." Briefly Cliff wondered if he'd end up speaking to

everyone in the entire household before he was able to talk to Diana.

"Hi, Cliff," Katie shouted. "I told Grandma and Grandpa all about you, and Grandpa says he's going to take me fishing here in Wichita."

"That sounds like fun. Where's your mother?"

"There was a bad storm the other night and there was lightning and thunder, and I woke up scared and Mom came in and told me there was music in the storm. Did you know that? And guess what? She was right. I went back to sleep, and in the morning I could still remember the funny kind of drums that played."

Cliff was impressed at Diana's genius. "I'm glad you're not afraid of thunder anymore."

Once again Cliff heard muffled words and then silence. "Katie? Is someone on the phone?"

"Hello, Cliff."

Joan again. "Listen, sweetheart, could I speak to your mother?"

"I'm afraid that poses something of a problem," Joan whispered huskily into the receiver, as though she'd cupped her hand over it.

"It does?"

"Yes. You see, she isn't here at the moment."

"What time do you expect her back?"

"Late. Real late."

"How late?"

"She didn't get in until after midnight last night."

Cliff grinned. "I suppose she's seeing a lot of her old high-school friends."

"Especially one old friend. A *boyfriend*," Joan said heavily.

"Oh?"

"Yes, his name is Danny Helleberg. He's not nearly as good-looking as you, but Grandma told me that looks aren't everything. Grandma insists that Danny will make an excellent stepdad. Katie and I aren't sure. Out of all the men Mother's been dating—including the man with references—we vote for you."

Eleven

A week! It hadn't even taken Diana a week to forget about him. The minute she was out of Cliff's sight, she'd started dating another man behind his back. Outrage poured over him like burning oil, scalding his thoughts. He should have learned from Becky that women weren't to be trusted. He'd been a fool to allow another woman, someone he'd thought he could trust, to do this to him a second time.

Pacing seemed to help, and Cliff did an abrupt about-face and marched to his living-room window with a step General Mac Arthur would have praised. All along, Diana had probably planned and plotted this assault on his pride. Look at how cleverly she'd manipulated him thus far! Why, she'd had him eating out of the palm of her hand! With his fists clenched tightly at his sides, Cliff turned away from the unseen panorama before him and stepped into his kitchen, opening the refrigerator. He stared blankly at its contents, shook his head, wondered what he was doing there and closed the door. Diana was ingenious, he'd grant her that much. She had him right where she wanted him—lonely, miserable and wanting her. From the minute he'd met her, he hadn't been himself. It was as though he were out of sync with his inner self while he mulled over what this young widow and her daughters were doing in his life. He'd listened to her while she tore him apart, searched deep within himself and recognized the truth of what she'd said. And all the while she'd waited patiently for him to return to her. And he had. Diana had been so confident that she hadn't so much as tried to contact him. Not once.

Then this sweet, innocent widow had duped him into believing this two-week jaunt to Wichita was a vacation to visit her family. She was visiting all right, but it wasn't her family she'd been so eager to get home to see. Oh, no, it was some old-time boyfriend she could hardly wait to date again. While she'd been looking at Cliff with those wide, deceiving eyes of hers, she'd been scheming to hook up with this Danny whatever-his-name-was.

And another thing—some mother she turned out to be, leaving Joan and Katie this way. Both girls had bubbled over with excitement, they'd been so happy to hear from him. The poor kids were lonely. And what children wouldn't be, left in a strange house with people they hardly knew, while their mother was gallivanting around Wichita with another man?

Cliff knew one thing. If Diana was painting the town, he wasn't going to idly sit at home, pining away for her. He was through keeping the *TV Guide* company, through missing Diana or even thinking about her. In fact, he was finished with her entirely, he decided suddenly. He didn't need her, and it was all too obvious that she didn't need him, either. Fine. She could have it her way. In fact, she could have her old high-school boyfriend. Being the noble man he was, Cliff determined that he would quietly bow out of the picture. He'd even wish the two childhood sweethearts every happiness.

Now that he'd made a decision, Cliff took out his little black book and flipped through the pages. The names and phone numbers of the women listed here would give Diana paranoia. Grinning, he ran his finger down the first section and stopped at Missy's phone number. One look at Missy, and Diana would know she was out of the running. Already he felt better. The thought of Diana comparing herself to another one of his dates and falling short was comforting to his injured ego. As he'd told himself a minute before, Cliff Howard didn't need Diana Collins.

He reached for the phone and hit the first three digits of Missy's number, then abruptly disconnected. He wasn't in the mood for Missy. Not tonight.

Determined, he turned the page and smiled again when he saw Ingrid's name. The pretty blond Swede was another one Diana would turn green over. This time, however, it wasn't the voluptuous body that would pull the widow up short, although heaven knew Ingrid was stacked in all the right places. No, Ingrid was a well-educated corporate attorney, in addition to being independently wealthy. Cliff knew how much Diana would have loved to get her college degree. Soothed by the thought, Cliff reached for the phone and punched out a long series of numbers, but he hung up before the first ring.

Diana wasn't such a terrible mother. Look at how she'd calmed Katie down in the middle of a thunderstorm. The unexpected, unwanted thought caused him to frown.

Okay, so she hadn't exactly left her daughters in the hands of strangers, but Joan and Katie hardly knew their grandparents. It seemed to Cliff that Diana would want to spend her time with her mother and father. He sagged against the back of the couch and let out his breath in a heated rush.

He didn't want to be with Missy tonight, not Ingrid, either. Diana was the only woman who interested him, and had been the only one for weeks. He had an understanding with Diana, unspoken, but not undefined. They had something wonderful going—they wanted to test these feelings, explore this multifaceted attraction. If she felt the need to date other men, then that was up to her. For his part, he'd been living in the singles world for a long time; he didn't need another woman in his arms to tell him what he already knew. His gaze fell to the black book in his hands. He riffled through the pages, stopping now and again at a name that brought back fond memories. Yet there wasn't anyone listed whom he'd like to wrap in his arms, no one he longed to kiss and love. Given a magic wand and a bucketful of wishes, Cliff would have conjured up Diana Collins and only Diana Collins. Widow. Mother. And, he added painfully, heartbreaker.

Cliff must have dozed off watching television, because the next thing he was aware of was the phone. Its piercing rings jolted him awake. He straightened, rubbed his hand over his eyes, then reached for his cell.

"Hello."

"Cliff, it's Diana."

The sound of her voice was enough to send the blood rushing through his veins. When he spoke, he attempted to hide the sarcasm behind banter. "So how was your hot date with Danny Heartthrob?"

"That's what I called about. Listen, Cliff, I don't know what the girls told you . . ."

"Quite a bit, if you must know." Again he made it sound as though the entire evening had been a joke to him.

"Are you mad?"

She sounded worried and uptight, but Cliff thought it was poetic justice. "Should I be?"

"No!"

"Then why all the concern?"

Diana hesitated, not liking the condescending note in his

voice. "I thought, you know, that you might have gotten upset because . . . well, because I'd gone out to dinner with Danny."

"Two nights in a row, according to Joan."

"I swear I don't even like him. He's a dead bore, but my mother's got this thing about my remarrying before I shrivel up and become an old woman. To hear her tell it, that's likely to happen in the next six weeks. Time is running out."

"Listen, if you want to see this Danny every night of your vacation, it's fine with me."

"It is?" came Diana's stunned response. "I . . . thought we had an understanding."

Cliff felt shut out and hurt, but he wasn't about to let her know that. Yes, they did have an agreement, but apparently it didn't mean a whole lot to Diana. Obviously she considered herself free to date other men, when he still hadn't recovered from the shock of not finding a single name in his black book that interested him. The only woman he wanted was Diana Collins, but unfortunately she was with another man.

"If you think I'm going to fly into a jealous rage, then you've got me figured all wrong. I'm just not the type," Cliff said, wondering exactly what this bozo Danny looked like. "The way I see it, you're on vacation and you're a big girl. You can do what you want."

Diana pondered his tone more than his words. She'd been sick when Joan and Katie had told her Cliff had phoned. He wouldn't understand that she'd gone out with Dan to appease her mother. These two dates had been part of a peacekeeping mission.

"You mean you're honestly not angry?"

"Naw."

"If the circumstances were reversed, I'm not sure I'd be as generous." She made an impatient, breathy sound, then burst out, "I know this is none of my business, but maybe you're being understanding about this because you've been seeing someone . . . since I've been in Wichita?"

Cliff would have loved to let her think exactly that, but he wasn't willing to lie outright. Misleading her, however, was an entirely different story.

"I'm sure there's been ample opportunity," Diana added, feeling more miserable by the minute.

"Well, as a matter of fact . . ."

"Forget I asked that," she insisted. "If you're going out with Bunnie or Bubbles or any of the other girls listed in your bachelor directory, I'd rather not know about it."

"Do you doubt me?" he asked, trying to sound casual. She had a lot of nerve. He was the one sitting home nights staring at the boob tube while she was flirting with everything in pants on the other side of the Rocky Mountains.

"It isn't a matter of trust," Diana answered after a long moment.

"Then what is it?"

"I'm not sure." The frustration was enough to make her want to cry. "We had so little time together before I had to leave. I'd been looking forward to this trip for weeks and then I didn't even want to go. There was so much I wanted to tell you, so much I wanted to say."

A pulsating silence stretched between them.

"It's ten-thirty here," Cliff said at last, checking his watch and figuring the time difference. It was past midnight there. "Did you just get in?"

"About twenty minutes ago."

"Did you have a good time?"

"No."

Naturally she'd tell him that, and just as naturally he believed her, because it hurt too much for him to think otherwise.

"I will admit that I was a little bit jealous when I first talked to Joan." He didn't like telling her that much; it went against his pride. But letting her know his feelings would help.

Diana relaxed and closed her eyes.

"But it wasn't anything I couldn't work out myself," he added magnanimously. "I didn't like it one bit, if you're looking for the truth, but beyond anything else, I trust you."

The line went quiet for a moment. "Oh, Cliff, I've been so worried."

"Worried," he repeated, realizing Diana was close to tears. "Whatever for?"

"After what happened with you and . . . Becky, I had this terrible feeling that you'd think I was . . . I don't know, cheating on you."

"You haven't even cheated *with* me yet."

Her soft laugh was like a refreshing sea mist on a hot, humid afternoon. Cliff savored the sweet musical cadence of her voice.

It struck him then, struck him hard.

He was in love with Diana. No wonder he'd reacted like a lunatic when Joan had told him her mother was out with an old high-school flame. He'd been a blind fool not to acknowledge his feelings before now. He'd been attracted to her physically almost from the first, and the pull had been so strong that sharing a bed with her had been the only thing on his mind. Her reaction to that idea had left him reeling for days. She wanted more, demanded more. At the time he hadn't learned that the physical response she evoked in him only skimmed the surface of his feelings for her.

"I can't tell you how boring tonight was," Diana went on. "Dan doesn't like women who wear Levi's. Can you believe that, in this day and age? I spent the entire evening listening to his likes and dislikes, and I'm telling you—"

"Diana," Cliff interrupted her.

"Yes?"

The need to say it burned on his tongue, but he held back. A man didn't tell a woman he loved her over the phone. "Nothing."

The line went completely silent for a moment. "I'm not seeing him again. I made that perfectly clear to Dan tonight." She could deal with her mother's disappointment more readily than she could handle another date with a fuddy-duddy thirty-year-old.

"Don't let me stand in your way," Cliff returned almost flippantly. He was still shaking with the realization that he loved Diana. When a man cared this deeply for a woman, he shouldn't need those kinds of reassurances.

Suddenly angry, Diana frowned at the receiver. "That's a rotten thing to say."

"What is?"

"Oh, don't play stupid with me, Cliff Howard. I hadn't planned on seeing Dan again, but since you have no objection, then fine."

He could feel the heat of her anger a thousand miles away. Her words were hurled at him with the vehemence of a hand grenade. "What's made you so mad?"

"You. Do I honestly mean so little to you?"

"What on earth are you talking about?"

"That . . . that last statement of yours about my dating Dan, as though you couldn't care less and . . ."

"I couldn't care less," he echoed, and feigned a yawn.

"Fine, then."

Cliff couldn't so much as hear her breathe. It was as though they'd been caught up in a vacuum, both struggling to find an escape, but discovering they were trapped.

She'd do it, too. Diana would go out with this clown again

just to spite him. Women! He'd made a major concession on her behalf, and she didn't have the good sense to appreciate it. "Okay, you want me to say don't go out with Dan . . . then I'm saying it."

It was exactly what Diana had needed to hear five minutes before. Unfortunately his admission had come too late. "You've got no claim on me. I can see anyone I please, and you . . ."

"The hell I don't have a claim on you."

"The hell you do!"

"I love you," he shouted. "That must give me some rights."

"You don't need to shout it at me!"

"How else am I supposed to get you to listen?"

"I . . . I don't know." If she had felt like crying before, it was nothing compared to what she was experiencing now. "You honestly love me?" Her voice was little more than a whisper.

"What's wrong now?" True, he hadn't planned on telling her like this, but he expected some kind of reaction from her. What he'd honestly hoped she'd do was to burst into tears and tell him she'd been crazy about him from that first night when he'd repaired her sink.

"Why did you tell me something like this when I'm a thousand miles away?"

"Because I couldn't hold it inside any longer. Are you going to keep me in suspense here? Don't you think you should let me know what you feel toward me?"

"You already know."

"Maybe, but I'd still like to hear you say it."

"I love you, too." The words were low and seductive, rusty and warm.

"How much longer are you going to be gone?" he asked, having difficulty finding his voice.

"Too long."

Cliff couldn't have agreed with her more.

★ ★ ★

"Will Cliff be at the airport?" Joan wanted to know, returning the flight magazine to the pocket in the seat in front of her.

"Yeah, Mom, will he?" Katie asked, tugging on Diana's sleeve.

Diana nodded. "He said he would."

The Boeing 737 was circling Sea-Tac airport before making its final approach for landing.

Joan and Katie had been far less impressed with flying on the return trip from Wichita, and Diana felt mentally and physically drained after coming up with twenty different ways to keep the pair entertained.

Cliff had promised he'd be waiting in the airport when they landed. Although Diana was dying for a glimpse of him, she almost wished she had time to take a shower and properly touch up her makeup before their reunion. She felt haggard, and it wasn't entirely due to the long flight.

Diana had made the mistake of admitting to her parents that she was in love with Cliff. She'd been honest in the hope that her mother would understand why she didn't want to date anyone else while she was in Wichita. Instead the announcement had been followed by a grueling question-and-answer session. Her mother and father had demanded to know everything they could about Cliff and his intentions toward her and the girls. Diana couldn't reassure them since she didn't know herself. Instead of being pleased for Diana, her parents seemed all the more concerned. Consequently, her last week in Wichita had been strained and uneasy for everyone except the girls.

"You talked to him lots."

"Who?" Diana blinked, trying to listen to Katie.

Her younger daughter gave her a look that told Diana she was losing it. "Cliff, of course. Every time I turned around, you two were on the phone."

"We spoke a grand total of six times."

"But for hours."

"Yeah," Joan piped in. "The first week we were there, you hardly mentioned his name. In fact, you got mad at Katie for telling Grandma and Grandpa about him and then the second week you hogged the phone, talking to him every minute of the day."

"I did not hog the phone!"

"Someone could have been trying to get through to me, you know," Joan said defensively.

"Who?"

"I . . . don't know, but someone, maybe a boy."

"Is Cliff going to marry you?" Katie asked. "I think I'd like it if he did."

Oh, no, not the girls, too. First her parents wanted to know his intentions, and now Joan and Katie. It was too much. "I have no idea what's going to happen between Cliff and me," Diana answered forcefully. It was little wonder that Cliff hated the word *commitment*—she was beginning to have the same reaction herself.

"I, for one, think it would be fabulous to have a father who looks like Cliff," Joan said, tilting her head in a thoughtful pose.

"Speaking of rock stars," Diana said pointedly, her gaze narrowing on her elder daughter, "did you really tell the boy who carried out Grandma's groceries that we're a distant relation to Phil Collins?"

Joan's bemused gaze slid to the other side of the plane. "Well, I'm sure we must be related one way or another. Just how many Collinses could there be? It is a small world, Mother, in case you hadn't noticed."

The plane landed on the runway with hardly more than a timid bounce, then the taxi to the receiving gate took an additional ten minutes. By the time the 737 had pulled to a stop and passengers were starting to disembark, Diana's nerves were frayed. The girls were right; she had talked to Cliff nearly every night. But now that they were home, she was skittish and self-conscious. She wished she'd done something glamorous with her hair before they'd left Wichita, but at the time, she'd been so eager to get on the plane and back to Seattle that she hadn't planned ahead.

Joan and Katie tugged at her arms, urging her to hurry as they briskly walked down the narrow jetway. It seemed as if everyone was hurried toward baggage claim, and although Diana didn't readily see Cliff, she knew he was there.

"Diana."

She'd just made it past the first large group crowding around the carousel.

"Over here."

Before Diana could think, Joan and Katie had left her side and hurled themselves at Cliff as though they'd just spent the past ten years in boarding school.

He crouched to receive their bear hugs and nearly toppled when he looked up and smiled at Diana.

"Welcome home," he said, straightening. Lightly he wrapped his arm around her shoulder and brushed his lips over hers. He paused to inhale the fragrance of spring that was hers alone and briefly closed his eyes in gratitude for her and the girls' safe return.

"Do you want to see my suntan?" Joan asked.

"Sure." Cliff was so glad to have them back that he would have agreed to anything.

"I got another Pooh bear from Grandma."

Cliff grinned down on Katie, and would have willingly given her a whole warehouse full of her favorite bear. Oh yes, it was good to have them back.

"What about you?" Cliff asked, slipping his arm around Diana's waist. "Is there anything you want to show me?"

"Maybe."

"Later?"

"Later," she agreed with a soft smile.

They weren't back in the house five minutes before Joan and Katie were out the door, eager to let their friends know everything about Wichita.

Cliff had just finished delivering the last suitcase to Katie's bedroom. He paused at the top of the stairs and waited for Diana to meet him.

"If I don't get to properly kiss you soon, I'm going to go crazy." He held his arms out to her. "Come here, woman."

Without hesitation, Diana walked into his arms as though she'd always belonged there. It didn't matter to her that the front door was wide open, or that the girls were likely to burst in at any minute. All that concerned her was Cliff.

His hands knotted at the base of her spine as his gaze drifted hungrily over hers. "Did you see any more of Danny-boy?"

"You know I didn't."

"Good, because I was insanely jealous." His mouth found hers in an expression of fiery need, and he poured everything he'd learned about himself into the kiss. Everything he'd learned about what was right for them. Nothing had gone according to schedule while Diana was away. Every second, every minute of their separation had only heightened his need to have her back. Again and again he kissed her, needing her and showing her how much. His lips branded her and cherished her, and his tongue dipped into the secret warmth of her mouth.

Fire streaked through Diana's veins, and a delicious throbbing ache spread through every part of her body. The Boeing aircraft had landed in Seattle, she had even carried her suitcases into the house, but she hadn't been home until exactly this minute. The realization of how much Cliff had come to mean to her in such a short time was both powerful and frightening. She slid her arms around him, needing the reassurance of his closeness. Her hands traced his back, slowly playing over his ribs and the taper of his spine. She savored the feel of this man who held her and loved her and needed her as much as she needed him.

Diana's breathing became raspy when Cliff's mouth moved from her lips to the side of her neck. She trembled and snuggled closer in his embrace.

"Welcome home, Diana." His own breathing was shaky.

"If I go to the grocery store, to the dentist, to the bank, any-where, promise you'll greet me this way when I return."

"I promise." His grip on her shoulders relaxed, but he didn't release her. Not yet.

"Oh, I nearly forgot." She broke away and hurried into her bedroom. "I brought you something."

Cliff followed her inside. "You did?"

Already Diana had tossed her suitcase on top of the mattress and was sorting through a stack of neatly folded clothes for the T-shirt.

"Diana?"

"It's right here. Just hold on a minute."

"Listen, I know this is soon and everything . . ."

"It's blue—the same color as your eyes." When she'd first seen the T-shirt, her heart had almost broken, she'd missed him so much.

Cliff buried his hands in his pockets. This wasn't exactly how he planned to do this, but he'd done a lot of thinking while Diana had been away and seeing her again proved every-thing he thought to question. "Diana . . ."

"It's here. I know it is." She paused and twisted around. "I may have tucked it in Joan's suitcase." Determined to find it, she hurried into her daughter's bedroom, paused and whirled around. "I'm sorry, Cliff, what were you saying?"

"Nothing." He felt like a fool.

"Okay." Diana went back and started rooting through the

suitcase. The shirt was perfect for Cliff, and she was eager to give it to him.

"Actually, I had some time to mull over our relationship while you were away, and I was thinking that maybe we should get married."

At last Diana found the shirt, lifted it out and turned to face him, her eyes wide with triumph. The excitement drained from her as quickly as water through a sieve.

"What was it you just said?"

Twelve

"Mom, what do you think?" Joan paraded in front of her mother as though the eleven-year-old were part of a Las Vegas floor show. She wiggled her girlish hips and demurely tucked her chin over her shoulder while placing her hands on bended knee. "Well?"

Diana successfully squelched a smile. "You look at least fifteen, if not older."

Joan positively glowed with the praise.

"How come we have to wear a dress?" Katie grumbled, following her sister into the living room. Diana's younger daughter wasn't the least bit thrilled at the prospect of a dinner date with Cliff if she had to wear her Sunday clothes. "How come Cliff can't just bring over KFC? I like that best."

"Hey, dog breath, I want to eat in the Space Needle," Joan blasted her.

In a huff, Katie crossed her arms and glared defiantly at her sister. "I think it's silly."

The dinner date with the girls to announce their engagement had been Cliff's suggestion. He'd wanted to take Joan and Katie someplace fancy and fun and had chosen the famous Seattle landmark from the 1962 World's Fair.

"Come on, girls," Diana pleaded, "this night is special, so be on your absolute best behavior."

"Okay," the two agreed simultaneously.

Cliff arrived ten minutes later, dressed in a crisp pin-striped three-piece suit and looking devilishly handsome. The minute he walked in the house, the girls burst into excited chatter, gathering around him like children before a clown. Although he was listening to Joan and Katie, his eyes sought out Diana's and were filled with warmth and gentle promise. One look confirmed that his wild imagination hadn't conjured everything up out of desperation and loneliness. She did love him, and heaven knew he loved her.

Seeing Cliff again made Diana feel nervous, impatient and exhilarated. She'd only arrived back in Seattle the day before, and her whole world had been drastically changed within a matter of a few hours. The memory of Cliff standing on the other side of Joan's bedroom from her, looking boyish and uncertain as he suggested they get married, would remain with Diana all her life. Anyone who knew this man would never have believed the confident, sophisticated Cliff Howard could be so unsure of himself. In that moment, Diana knew she would never again doubt his love. She didn't recall how she'd answered him. A simple yes or a nod—perhaps both. What she did remember was the joy of Cliff crushing her in his arms and kissing her until they'd been forced to part when Joan and Katie returned.

"Can I order KFC at the Space Needle?" Katie asked a second time, breaking into Diana's musings.

"Every restaurant serves chicken, dummy," Joan inserted. "Personally, I'm going to order shrimp."

If dishes were wishes, Cliff would order two weeks alone in a hotel room with Diana. He dreamed about making love to her, about lying in bed and experiencing the feel of her skin brushing against him. He thought about waking up with her in the morning and falling asleep with her at night. Night after night, day after day. The mere suggestion excited him, filled him with anticipation for the good life that lay before them. The physical desire he felt for her was deep, honest and powerful. On the twenty-minute drive into Seattle, both Joan and Katie were excited and anxious and kept the conversation going, bantering back and forth, then squabbling, then joking.

The elevator ride up the 605-foot Space Needle left Joan and Katie speechless with awe. Diana treasured the brief silence. She didn't know what had gotten into her girls lately, but they seemed either to be constantly chattering or else endlessly bickering.

The hostess seated them by a window overlooking Puget Sound and the Olympic mountain range. The two girls sat together, and Cliff sat beside Diana. Once they were comfortable, they were handed huge menus. Diana's eyes skimmed over her own, and when she'd made her decision, she glanced in the girls' direction.

"Katie," she whispered, both embarrassed and amused, "honey, the napkin's not a party hat. Take it off your head."

"Oh." Katie's dark eyes were filled with chagrin.

Joan smothered a laugh, which only proved to embarrass Katie more.

"How was I supposed to know these things?" Katie demanded.

Joan opened her mouth to explain it all to her younger sibling, but Diana interceded with a scalding look that instantly silenced her oldest daughter.

Cliff set his menu aside when the waitress appeared, and after everyone had made their selection, he ordered champagne cocktails for the adults and Shirley Temples for the girls. While waiting for their drinks to arrive, Cliff placed his arm around Diana, cupping her shoulder. She raised her hand and linked her fingers with his. His touch was light, almost impersonal, but Diana wasn't fooled. Cliff was as nervous about this evening as she was. So much rested on how Joan and Katie reacted to their news.

"Cliff and I have something we'd like to tell you," Diana said softly after the waitress had placed a drink in front of each one of them. She knew how much the girls liked Cliff, but she wasn't sure how they'd feel about him becoming a major part of their lives. It had been just the three of them for a long time.

Joan took a long sip of her Shirley Temple. Her eyes were raised, but her head was lowered. She looked like a crocodile peering at them from just above the waterline. For her part, Katie was busy spreading out the linen napkin across her lap.

Diana resisted the urge to shout at them both that this was important and they should pay attention.

"Cliff and I are trying to tell you something," Diana said forcefully, gritting her teeth with impatience.

"What?"

The fact that they'd decided to get married wasn't something to be blurted out without preamble. Diana had hoped to start off by explaining to her daughters how she'd come to love Cliff and how her love would affect Joan's and Katie's life.

"Cliff and I have discovered that we love each other very much." Diana's fingers tightened around his. Just being able to say the words and not having to hide them in her heart produced a special kind of joy.

"So?" Katie murmured, lifting the tiny, plastic sword from her drink and shoving both maraschino cherries into her mouth at once.

"I already knew that," Joan said knowingly.

"So," Diana said slowly, and expelled her breath, "Cliff and I were thinking about getting married."

"And we wanted to know your feelings on the matter," he inserted, studying both Joan and Katie. He was as uptight about this evening as Diana. But the girls seemed more concerned about sucking ice cubes than listening to what their mother had to say.

Joan shrugged. "Sure, if you want to get married, I don't care."

"Me, either," Katie agreed, and juice from the two cherries slid down the side of her chin.

"Oh, gross," Joan cried, and pointedly looked in the opposite direction.

Diana's patience was quickly wearing thin. "Girls, please, we're not talking about what we're going to have for breakfast tomorrow morning. If Cliff and I do get married, it's going to be a major change in all our lives." She was about to relay that the marriage would mean they'd be moving and the girls would be changing schools, but Joan interrupted her.

"Will I get a bigger allowance?"

"Can I have a new bike?" Katie asked on the tail end of her sister's question.

"Can I tell people we're going to be rich?" Joan asked without guile.

"If we're going to be rich, then I should be able to get a new bike, shouldn't I?"

"We are not going to be wealthy because I'm marrying Cliff," Diana cried, raising her voice and doing a poor job of hiding her disappointment in her daughters. She wasn't sure what she'd expected from Joan and Katie but it certainly hadn't been indifference and greed.

"Gee, Mom, why are you so mad?" Joan asked, studying her mother with a quizzical frown. "Katie and I already knew you were in love with Cliff. We couldn't help but know from the way you've been acting all summer."

Both girls seemed to want an answer.

"I see," Diana answered softly, briefly regaining a grip on her emotions.

"Then neither of you has any objection to our getting married?" Cliff asked.

Diana was as tense as a newly strung guitar. What upset her most was the way the girls were behaving; the entire dinner was about to be ruined.

Joan and Katie shared a look and answered his question with a short shake of their heads.

"I think it'd be great if you married Mom," Joan answered. "But if it's possible, I'd like to be able to get my ears pierced before the wedding." Briefly she fondled her thin earlobe. "What do you think, Cliff?"

As an attorney, Cliff was far too wise to get drawn into those mother-daughter power games. "I think that's up to your mother."

"And you already know my feelings on the matter, Joan!"

"Okay. Okay. Sorry I asked."

Any further argument was delayed by the waitress, who delivered their order, and for a brief time, all dissension was forgotten. Katie dug into her crispy fried chicken, while Joan daintily dipped her jumbo shrimp in the small container of cocktail sauce.

"Mom, will Cliff be my father?" Joan asked a minute later, cocking her head in a thoughtful pose.

"Your stepfather."

Joan nodded and dropped her gaze, looking disappointed. "But would a stepfather be considered a real enough father for the banquet?"

It took Diana only a moment to understand Joan's question. The Girl Scout troop Joan had been involved with throughout the school year was sponsoring a father-daughter dinner at the end of the month. Diana had read the notice and not given the matter much thought. Unless someone from church volunteered to escort them, the girls generally didn't attend functions that involved fathers and daughters.

"I'm sure a stepfather will be acceptable," Cliff answered. "Would you like me to take you to the banquet?"

"Would you really?"

"I'd be more than happy to."

It seemed such a minor gesture, but a feeling of such intense gratitude filled Diana's heart that moisture pooled in her eyes. She turned to Cliff and offered him a watery smile. "Thank you," she whispered. She wanted to say more, but speaking was quickly becoming impossible.

His eyes held hers in the most tender of exchanges, and it took all the strength and good manners Cliff could muster not to kiss Diana right there in the Space Needle restaurant. His insides felt like overcooked mush. He was ready for a wife, more than ready, and he was willing to learn what it meant to be a father.

It wasn't his intention to take the memory of Stan away from Joan and Katie, nor would he be the same kind of father they'd known. He was sure to make mistakes; he wasn't perfect and this father business was new to him, but he loved Joan and Katie and he planned to care for them as long as he lived. Somewhere along the way to discovering his feelings for Diana, her daughters had neatly woven strings around his heart.

"It's because of me, isn't it?" Katie asked, waving a chicken leg in front of Diana's and Cliff's nose as though it were a weapon.

"What is?" Diana asked.

"That you and Cliff are going to get married."

"How come?" Joan asked sharply, reaching for her napkin. "I think it's because of me."

"No way!" Katie cried. "I was the one who broke my arm and Cliff came back to Mom because of that!"

"Yeah, but I was the one who called and told him you were in the hospital—so it's all my doing. If it hadn't been for me, we could have ended up with Owen, or worse yet, Dan from Wichita, as our new dad."

"Will you girls kindly stop arguing?" Diana hissed. Embarrassment coated her cheeks a shade of hot pink. People were turning around to stare at them. Diana was certain she could feel disapproving looks coming their way from the restaurant staff.

"Who did it, then?" Katie demanded.

"Yeah, who's responsible?"

Both girls stopped glaring at each other long enough to turn to look at their mother.

"In a way you're both responsible," Diana conceded, praying the two would accept the compromise.

"Ask Cliff." Once again the chicken leg was waved under their noses.

"Yeah, Cliff, what do you think?"

"I think . . ."

"Drop it, girls," Diana insisted in a raised voice the girls readily recognized as serious. "Immediately!"

The remainder of the dinner was a nightmare for Diana. Whereas Joan and Katie had chattered all the way into Seattle, they sat sullen and uncommunicative on the drive home to Kent. A couple of times Cliff attempted to start up a conversation, but no one seemed interested. Diana knew she wasn't.

Back at the house, Joan and Katie went upstairs to their rooms without a word.

Diana stood at the bottom of the stairs until they were out of sight and then moved into the kitchen to make coffee. Cliff followed her and placed his hands on her shoulders as she stood before the sink.

Miserable and ashamed of her children's behavior, Diana hung her head. "I am so sorry," she whispered when she could speak.

"Diana, what are you talking about?"

"The girls—"

"Were exhausted from a two-week vacation with their grandparents. You haven't been back twenty-four hours, and here we are hitting them with this." Gently his hands stroked her bare arms. He felt bad only because Diana did. "I love you, and I love the girls. Tonight was the exception, not the norm. They're good kids."

She nodded because tears were so close to the surface and arguing would have been impossible. Cliff must really love her to have put up with the way Joan and Katie had behaved. Diana couldn't remember a time when her daughters had been worse. After all these years as a single mother, Diana had prided herself on being a good parent and in one evening she'd learned the truth about her parenting skills.

"Diana," Cliff whispered, "put that mug down. I don't want any coffee. I want to hold you."

The mug felt as if it weighed a thousand pounds when Diana set it on the counter. Slowly she turned, keeping her eyes on the kitchen floor, unable to meet his gaze.

His arms folded around her, bringing her against him. He didn't make any demands on her, content for the moment to offer comfort. His chin slowly brushed against the top of her head, while his hands roved in circles across her back. The action had meant to be consoling, but Cliff had learned long before that he couldn't hold Diana without wanting her. Diana looped her arms around his neck and directed his mouth to hers. The kiss was possessive, filled with frustration and undisguised need. Diana shuddered at the wild, consuming kiss.

Cliff was pacing outside the gates of heaven. He loved this woman, needed her physically, mentally, emotionally—every way there was to need another human being. But she was driving him crazy. The drugged kiss went on unbroken, and so did the way she moved against him. "Diana," He pulled his mouth from hers and buried his face in her shoulder while he came to grips with himself.

They remained clenched in each other's arms until their strained, uneven breathing calmed. Gathering her courage, Diana tilted back her head until she found his eyes.

Cliff smiled at her, bathing her in his love. His thumb brushed the corners of her mouth, needing to touch her.

Little could have gone worse tonight, and Diana felt terrible. "You don't have to go through with it, you know."

He frowned, not understanding.

"With the wedding . . . After tonight, I wouldn't blame you if you backed out. I think if the situation were reversed, I'd consider it."

Cliff's frown deepened. She had to be nuts! He'd just found her and he had no intention of doing as she suggested. He saw the doubt in her eyes that told him of her uncertainty. He met her gaze steadily, his own serious. "No way, Diana," he whispered, and cupped her face, tilting her head upward to meet his descending mouth. The kiss was deep and long, warm and moist. When he broke away, his shoulders were heaving and his breathing was fast and harsh. He didn't move a muscle for the longest moment. Then, slowly, regretfully, he dropped his arms.

"I'd better go," he said with heavy reluctance. It was either go now or break his promise to her.

Diana wanted him to stay, needed him with her, but she couldn't ask it of him. Not tonight, when everything else had gone so wrong. Wordlessly she followed him to the front door.

He paused and lifted his hand to caress her sweet face. Diana placed her own over his and closed her eyes.

"I'll call you tomorrow."

She nodded.

* * *

"Mom, when will Cliff be here?"

Diana finished removing Joan's hair from the hot curler before glancing at her wristwatch. "He's due in another hour."

"Do you think he'll like my dress?"

"I'm sure he'll love it. You always did look so pretty in pink."

"Really?"

Diana couldn't remember Joan ever being more anxious for anything. The Girl Scout banquet was a special night for her daughter and for Cliff. The wedding was set for the second week of August; they'd found a house near Des Moines that everyone was thrilled with, and they planned to make the big move before the first day of school. Diana had already started some of the packing.

Her parents were flying out for the ceremony, as were Cliff's. His brother, Rich, and his wife and family were driving up from California. But for Joan, the wedding and all the planned activities that went along with it ran a close second to the father-daughter banquet. Cliff had told her he was ordering an orchid for Joan, and out of her allowance money Joan had proudly purchased a white rose boutonniere for Cliff.

The phone pealed in the distance, and a minute later Katie stuck her head in the bathroom door. "It's for you, Mom. It's Cliff." Katie paused and glanced at her elder sister. "Wow, you look almost grown up."

"You really think so, Katie?"

Smiling, Diana hurried into the upstairs hallway and picked up the telephone receiver. "Hi, there. Oh, Cliff, you wouldn't believe how pretty Joan looks. I've never seen her—"

"Diana, listen . . ."

"She's more excited than on Christmas morning—"

"Diana." This time his voice was sharp, sharper than he'd intended. He was in one heck of a position, torn between his job and his desire to be with Joan for her special night. He didn't mean to blurt it out, but there didn't seem to be any other way to say it. "I can't make it tonight."

Diana was so stunned she sagged against the wall and closed her eyes. "What do you mean you can't make it?" she asked after a tortuous moment when the terrible truth had begun to sink in. Surely she'd misunderstood him. She hoped there was some kind of mix-up and she hadn't heard him right.

"The senior vice president has asked me to take over a case that's going to the state supreme court. I just found out about it. The first briefing is tonight."

"But surely you can get out of one meeting."

"It's the most important one. I tried, Diana."

"But what about Joan?" This couldn't be happening—it just couldn't. The new dress, Joan's first pair of panty hose, her hair freshly permed and set in hot rollers. "What about the father-daughter banquet?"

Cliff couldn't feel any worse than he already did. "I phoned George Holiday, and he's agreed to take her. There will be other banquets."

"But Joan wants to go with you."

"Believe me, if I could, I'd take her. But I can't." He was growing impatient now, more angry at the circumstances than with Diana, who couldn't seem to believe or accept what he was telling her.

"But surely they'd have let you know about something this important before now."

"Diana, I'll explain it to Joan later. I've got to get back to the meeting. I'm late now. Honey, believe me, I'm as upset about this as you are."

"Cliff," she cried, "please, you can't do this to her." But it was too late, the line had already been disconnected. When she turned around, Diana discovered Joan watching her with wide brown eyes filled with horror and distress.

"Cliff's not going, is he?" she asked in a pained whisper.

"No . . . he's got an important meeting."

Without a word, Joan turned and walked into her bedroom and closed the door.

The minute it was feasibly possible, Cliff prepared to leave the meeting. He shoved the papers into his briefcase and left with no more than the minimal pleasantries. He felt like a heel. His conscience had been punishing him all night. Okay, okay, it wasn't his fault, but he hadn't wanted to disappoint Joan. His only comfort was that he'd be able to take her to the father-daughter banquet the following year and the year after that. Surely she'd understand this once and be willing to look past her disappointment.

The porch light was on at Diana's, and he hurriedly parked the car. To his surprise, Diana met him at the front door. She looked calm, but she didn't fool him; he knew her too well. Anger simmered just below the surface. He'd hoped she would be more understanding, but he'd deal with her later. First he had to talk to her daughter.

"Where's Joan?"

"In her room. She cried herself to sleep."

"Oh, no." Cliff groaned. He moved past Diana and up the stairs into the eleven-year-old's bedroom. The room was dark, and he left the light off and sat on the corner of her mattress. His heart felt heavy and constricted with regret as he brushed the curls off her forehead.

"We need to talk," Diana whispered from outside the doorway. Her arms were crossed over her chest and her feet were braced apart, as though to fend off an attack.

"How did the banquet go?" he asked as he followed her down the stairs.

Diana shrugged. "Fine, I guess. Joan hardly said a word when she got home."

"Honey, I'm sorry, I really am. This kind of thing doesn't come up that often, but when it does, there's nothing I can do."

"You broke her heart."

Cliff didn't need Diana piling on any more guilt than what he already had. It wasn't as though he'd deliberately gone out of his way to disappoint Joan. He certainly would rather have spent the night with Diana's daughter than cooped up in a stuffy, smoke-filled office.

"I know a banquet with an eleven-year-old girl isn't high on your priority list . . ."

"Diana, that's not true—"

"No . . . you listen to me. You want to break a date with me, then fine. I'm mature enough to accept it. But I can't allow you to hurt one of my children. I absolutely refuse to allow it."

Cliff ran his fingers through his hair and angrily expelled his breath. "You're making it sound like I deliberately planned this meeting just so I could get out of the banquet."

"All I know," Diana said, holding in the anger as best she could, "is that if it had been Stan, he would have been here!"

Stan's name hit Cliff with all the force of a brick hurled against the back of his head. He reeled with the impact and the shock of the pain. "Are you going to throw his name at me every time something goes wrong?"

"I don't know," she murmured. "All I know is that I don't want you to hurt Joan and Katie."

"You're making it sound like I'm looking for the opportunity."

"I've had all night to think about what I want to say," Diana confessed, dropping her gaze, unable to meet the cutting, narrowed look he was giving her. "All of a sudden I'm not so sure marriage would be the best thing for me and the girls."

Cliff knotted his hands into tight, impotent fists. "Okay, you want to call off the wedding, then fine."

His willingness shocked her. "I don't know what I want."

"Well, you'd better hurry up and decide."

A horrible silence stretched between them like a rolling, twisting fog, blinding them from the truth and obliterating the love that had once seemed so strong and invincible.

"I'll give you a week," Cliff announced. "You can let me know then what you want to do." With that, he turned and walked out the front door.

Thirteen

"Are you making poached eggs again?" Joan whined when she came down the stairs for breakfast.

"Yes," Diana said. "How'd you know?"

"Oh, Mom, honestly." The preteen plopped down at the kitchen table and shook her head knowingly. "You always make poached eggs when you're upset. It's a form of self-punishment—at least, that's what I think. Katie says it's because you still haven't made up with Cliff." She paused to study her mother. "Katie's right, too. You know that, don't you?"

Mumbling something unintelligible under her breath, Diana cracked two raw eggs over the boiling water. A frown gently creased her forehead. "Just how many times this week have I served poached eggs?"

"Three," Joan came back quickly. "Which is exactly as many days since you and Cliff had your big fight."

"We didn't have a big fight," Diana answered in a calm, reasonable voice.

Joan shrugged and took a long drink of her orange juice before answering. "I heard you. You and Cliff were shouting at each other—well, maybe not shouting, but your voices were raised, and I could hear you all the way upstairs." She paused as though considering whether to add a commentary. "Mom, I think you were wrong to talk to Cliff that way."

Diana groaned and scraped the butter across the top of the hot toast. "This isn't a subject I want to discuss with you, Joan."

"But I saw Cliff when he came into my bedroom, and he felt terrible about missing the banquet."

"I thought you were asleep!"

"I wasn't really . . . I had my eyes closed and everything, but I was peeking up at him through my lashes. He felt really bad. Even I could see that."

Diana wielded the butter knife like a sword, waving it at her daughter. "You should have said something then."

Looking guilty, Joan reached for her orange juice a second time. "I was going to, but you started talking and saying all those mean things to Cliff, and I was glad because I was still angry with him." She paused and sighed. "Now I wish I'd let him know I was awake. Then maybe I wouldn't be eating poached eggs every morning."

Diana served her daughters breakfast, but she didn't bother to eat any herself. She didn't need a week to decide if she wanted to marry Cliff. Within twenty-four hours after their argument, she recognized that she'd behaved badly. Joan and Katie were far more than willing to confirm her suspicions about the way she'd acted. Diana was forced into admitting she'd been unreasonable. More than anything, she deeply regretted throwing Stan's name at Cliff. Beyond whatever else she'd said, that had been completely unfair. She owed Cliff an apology, but making one had never come easy to her—the words seemed to stick in her throat. But if she didn't do it soon, she'd have a mutiny on her hands. Already Katie had hinted that she was going to move in with Mrs. Holiday if she had to eat poached eggs one more morning.

The girls went swimming that afternoon, and while they were at the pool, Diana paced the kitchen floor, gathering up the courage to contact Cliff. With a stiff finger, she punched out the number to his office as she rehearsed again and again what she planned to say.

"Hello," she said in a light, cheerful voice. "This is Diana Collins for Cliff Howard."

"I'll connect you with one of his staff," the tinny receptionist's voice returned.

Diana was forced to ask for him a second time.

"Mr. Howard's in a meeting," his secretary explained in a crisp professional tone. "Would you like to leave a message?"

"Please have him return my call," Diana murmured, defeated. She was convinced Cliff had given his secretary specific instructions to inform her that he was out of the office. The suspicion was confirmed when, hours later, she still hadn't heard from him. He'd said a week, and he seemed determined to make her wait that long, Diana mused darkly after Joan and Katie were in bed asleep. He wanted her to sweat it out. Either that, or he'd decided to cut his losses and completely wash his hands of her.

Depressed and discouraged, Diana sat in front of the television, flipping channels, until she stumbled upon an old World War II movie. For an hour she immersed her woes in the classic battle scenes and felt tears course down her cheeks when the hero died a valiant death. The tears were a welcome release. Once she started, she couldn't seem to stop. Soon there was a growing pile of damp tissue on the end table beside her chair.

The doorbell caught her by surprise. There was only one person it could be. Cliff. Loudly she blew her nose, then quickly rubbed her open hands down her cheeks to wipe away the extra moisture. With her head tilted at a regal angle, she moved into the entryway, her heart pounding at a staccato beat.

"Hello."

Cliff took one look at her and blinked. "Are you okay?"

She nodded and pointed to the television behind her. "John Wayne just bit the dust, but he took the entire German army with him."

Cliff stepped inside the house. "I see."

He looked good, Diana thought unkindly. The very least he could do was show a little regret—a few worry lines around the mouth. Even a couple of newly formed crow's-feet at his eyes would have satisfied her. At the very least, he could say something to let her know he'd been just as miserable as she. Instead he was the picture of a man who had recently returned from a two-week vacation in the Caribbean. He was tan, relaxed, lean and so handsome he stole her breath.

"I understand you called the office," he said stiffly.

Diana nodded, but couldn't manage to get the practiced apology past the clog in her throat.

"You wanted something?"

Again she nodded. His expression was tightening—she was losing him fast. Either she had to blurt out how sorry she was, or she was going to let the most fantastic man she'd ever met silently slip out of her life.

"Is it so difficult to tell me?"

Confused, she nodded, then abruptly shook her head.

Cliff released a giant sigh of frustration and impatience, then reached for her, gripping her shoulders. His fingers dug deep into the soft flesh of her upper arms. "I'm not letting you go this easily."

"What?" She blinked at the shock of his harsh treatment.

"I know what you're going to say and I refuse to accept it."

She slapped her hand over her heart, her eyes as round and as wide as full moons. "You know what I'm going to say?"

In response, he nodded, released her shoulders and instead captured her face. If she'd wished to witness his pain and regret, she saw it now. It filled his face, twisting his mouth and hardening his jaw. "I love you, Diana." With that, he lowered his mouth to hers in a punishing kiss that robbed her of her breath and her wits.

Cliff groaned, and Diana slipped her arms around his neck, melting her body intimately against his. "Cliff." Reluctantly she broke away, lifting her soft brown eyes to capture his. Her hands bracketed his face as a slow, sweet smile turned up the corners of her mouth. "I love you so much. I'm so sorry for what happened—I was unreasonable. Forgive me. Please."

Shock and disbelief flickered briefly across his taut features.

"You can't honestly believe I'm going to cancel the wedding," she whispered, humbled by this man and his love for her. "The reason I called you today was to tell you how much I love you." The moisture that brightened her eyes now had nothing to do with the emotion brought on by the sentimental movie. These tears came all the way from her heart.

Cliff looked for a moment as though he didn't believe her. He kissed her again because he couldn't remain with his arms wrapped around her and not sample her familiar sweet taste. He felt weak with relief and, at the same moment, filled with an incredible, invincible strength.

Cliff's kiss filled Diana with desire, left every muscle in her body quivering. Her passion matched his. Cliff pressed his lips over hers in mounting fervor, and Diana rose onto her toes to align herself more intimately with his body.

"Diana." He groaned and tore his mouth from hers. "We . . . we have things to settle here."

"Shh." She kissed him hungrily, slanting her mouth over his as she wove her fingers through his thick hair, savoring the feel and taste of him.

Cliff could refuse her nothing. The golden glow of a crescent moon outlined her beautiful face. Cliff released a deep sigh of awe at the priceless gift she was granting him—herself, without restraint, without restriction.

"Let's go upstairs," she whispered.

Cliff blinked and raised his hands to capture her face, holding her steady so he could look into her passion-drugged eyes. When he spoke, his voice was husky and deep. "Aren't the girls up there?"

"Yes, but . . . ?"

Their breaths warmed each other's mouths. "I can't believe I'm doing this," he groaned, and closed his eyes to a silent agony.

"Doing what?"

"Refusing you."

"Cliff, no." Diana couldn't believe it, either. After all the times he'd tried to seduce her, now he was turning her down. "Why?" she choked. "I want you."

"Believe me, honey, I want you, too—so much it hurts." He spoke through clenched teeth, his hands gripping her upper arms. Diana went still in his arms, and he relaxed as though a great tension had eased from him.

"Not the first time we make love," he murmured into her hair, his voice low and raw. "Not like this. We'll be married in ten days. I can wait."

"I don't know that I can," she complained.

"Yes, you can. The loving is going to be very good between us."

If it was going to be like it had been tonight, Diana didn't know if she'd survive the honeymoon.

It took Cliff almost an hour to find the headstone. He'd wandered around the graveyard in the early morning sunlight, intent on his task. Today was to be his wedding day. Friends and relatives crowded around him at every turn. His sane, sensible mother had become a clucking hen. His father kept slapping him across the back, smiling and looking proud. Even his brother seemed to follow him around like a pesky shadow, just the way he'd done in their youth. There were a thousand things left to be done on this day, but none so important as this.

Now that he'd located the place, Cliff wasn't sure what had driven him here. He squatted and read the words engraved with such perfection into the white marble: STANLEY DAVID COLLINS, HUSBAND, FATHER. The date of his birth and death were listed. No epitaph, no scripture verse, just the blunt facts of one man's life.

Slowly Cliff stood and placed his hands in his pockets as he gazed down at the headstone. His heart swelled with strong emotion, and in that space of time, he knew what had driven him to this cemetery on this day. He hadn't come to seek solitude from all the hustle and bustle, nor had he sought escape from the people who had suddenly filled his home. He didn't need a graveyard to be alone. He'd come to talk to Stan Collins. He'd come because he had to.

"I wish I'd known you," he said, feeling awkward, the words low and gruff. "I think we would have been friends." From what he'd learned from George Holiday and the information he'd gleaned from Diana and the girls, Stan had been a good man, the type Cliff would gladly have counted as a friend.

Only silence greeted him. Cliff wasn't sure what he'd expected, certainly no voice booming from heaven, no sounds from the grave. But something—he just didn't know what.

"You must have hated leaving her," he said next. He didn't know much about Stan's death, only bits and pieces he'd picked up from Diana the day he'd gone to the hospital when Katie had broken her arm. Between Diana's nonsensical statements and her panic, he'd learned that she hadn't been able to see Stan when they'd brought him into the emergency room. There'd been no time for goodbyes. The realization twisted a tight knot in Cliff's stomach. "I know what thoughts must have been in your mind." He bowed his head at the grim realization of death. "I would have been filled with regrets, too."

A strange peace settled over Cliff, a peace beyond words. He relaxed, and a grin curved his mouth. "You'd be amazed at Joan and Katie. They're quite the young ladies now." Diana was letting both girls stand up with her today as maid of honor and bridesmaid. She'd sewn them each a beautiful long pink dress with lace overlays. Joan had claimed she looked at least fourteen. Heels, panty hose, the whole nine yards. Katie was excited about getting her hair done in a beauty shop. Cliff laughed out loud at the memory of the eight-year-old insisting they serve Kentucky Fried Chicken at the wedding reception. Joan had been thrilled with the prospect of having an extra set of grandparents at Christmastime. Within minutes both girls had had his parents eating out of their hands. They'd been enthralled with Diana's two daughters from the minute they'd been introduced.

"You'd have reason to be proud of your girls," he said thoughtfully. "They're fantastic kids."

The humor drained from his eyes as his gaze fell once more to the engraved words on the headstone. The word *father* seemed to leap out at him. "I guess what I want to say is that I don't plan on trying to steal you away from Joan and Katie." Stan would always be their father; he had loved his children more than Cliff would ever know until he and Diana had their own. Now Cliff would be the one to raise Joan and Katie and love and nurture them into adulthood, guiding them with a gentle hand. "I know what you're thinking," he said aloud. "I can't say I blame you. I'm new to this fatherhood business. I can't do anything more than promise I'll do my best."

Now that he'd gotten past the girls, Cliff was faced with the real reason he had come. "I love Diana," he said plainly. "I didn't expect to, and I imagine you'd be more than willing to punch me out for some of the things I've tried with her. I apologize for that." His hands knotted into tight fists inside his pants pockets. "I honestly love her," he repeated, and sucked in a huge breath. "And I know you did, too."

The sun had risen above the hills now, bathing the morning mist with its warm, golden light so that the grass glistened. After a long reverent moment, Cliff turned and traced his steps back to the parking lot.

He took a leisurely drive back to his condominium and found his brother parked outside waiting for him.

"Where have you been?" Rich demanded. "I've been all over looking for you. In case you've forgotten, this is your wedding day."

Undisturbed, Cliff climbed out of his car and dropped the keys into his pants pocket.

Still Rich wasn't appeased. "I didn't know what to think when I couldn't find you." He checked his watch. "We were supposed to meet Mom and Dad ten minutes ago."

"Did you think I'd run away?" Cliff joked.

"Yes. No. I didn't know what to think. Where the blazes did you go that was so all-fired important?"

Cliff smiled into the sun. "To talk to a friend."

"Mom, I've got a run in my panty hose," Joan cried, her young voice filled with distress. "What am I supposed to do now?"

"I don't like the feel of hair spray," Katie commented for the tenth time, bouncing her hand off the top of her head several times just to see what would happen to the carefully styled but stiff curls.

"I've got an extra pair of nylons in the drawer," Diana answered Joan first. "Katie, keep your hands out of your hair!" Her mother was due any minute, and Diana didn't know when she'd been more glad to see either parent. Surprisingly, she wasn't nervous. She was more confident about marrying Cliff than any decision she'd made in the past three years. He loved her, and together they would build a good life together.

"You're not wearing your pearl earrings," Joan said with astonishment, and loudly slapped her sides. "Good grief, is any date more important than this one?"

Diana wrinkled her brow. "What do you mean?"

"Don't you remember? Honestly, Mom! I wanted you to wear the pearls the first night you went to dinner with Cliff, and you told me you wanted to wait for something festive to impress him."

Diana smiled at the memory. "I think you're right," she said, and traded the small gold pair for the pearls. "Nothing's more important than today." Her knees felt weak, not with doubts, but with excitement, and she sat on the corner of the mattress. "How do you girls feel?" she asked, watching her two daughters carefully.

"We're doing the right thing," Joan said with all the confidence of a five-star general. "Cliff's about the best we're going to do."

"What?" Diana asked with a small, hysterical laugh.

"Really, Mom," Katie came back. "For a while, I thought we'd get stuck with that Danny fellow from Wichita."

"Or Owen," Joan added. Both girls looked at each other and made silly faces and cried, "Oou!"

"Who's Owen?" Diana's mother asked as she stepped into the bedroom.

"He's the major geek I was telling you about who brought the references," Joan explained before Diana had the chance. He really was a dear man and someday he'd find the right woman. Fortunately, according to Joan and Katie, it wasn't her.

"Ah, yes," Joyce said, sharing a secret smile with her daughter. "You look lovely, sweetheart."

"Thanks," Joan answered automatically, then looked and gave her grandmother a chagrined smile. "Oh, you mean my mom."

"All three of you look beautiful."

Joan and Katie beamed at the praise.

"Watch, Grandma," Katie said. Tucking her arms close to her side, Katie whirled around a couple of times so the hemline of her dress flared out.

"Stop behaving like an eight-year-old," Joan cried. "You're supposed to be mature today."

"But I am eight!"

Joan opened her mouth to object, then realized she'd already lost one of her press-on fingernails. For a wild minute, there was a desperate search for the thumbnail. Peace ruled once they located it.

"Mother, would you check Katie's hair?" Diana asked. "She can't seem to keep her fingers out of it."

"Sure. Katie," Joyce called to her granddaughter, "let's go into the ladies' room."

Three hours later, Diana stood in front of the pastor who had seen her through life and death in the church where she sat each Sunday morning. Her parents, Cliff's family and a small assortment of close friends were gathered behind them. Joan and Katie stood proudly at her side.

The man of God warmed them all with a rare, tranquil smile. Diana turned, and her gaze happened to catch Cliff's. He did love her, more than she'd ever dared to dream, more than she'd ever thought possible. He stood tall and proud and eagerly held her eyes, his love shining through for her to read without doubt, without question. He was prepared to pledge his life to her and Joan and Katie. The commitment she sought he was about to willingly vow.

Witnessing all the love in Cliff's eyes had a chastising effect upon Diana. The man she'd once considered an unscrupulous womanizer had chosen her to share his life. He was prepared to love her no matter what the future held for them, prepared to raise her daughters and guide their young lives. Out of all the beautiful women he'd known, Cliff had chosen her. Diana didn't know what she'd done to deserve such a good man, but she would always be grateful. Always.

The minister opened his Bible, and Diana focused her attention on the man of the cloth. Her heart was full. Happiness had come to her a second time when she'd least expected it.

When the moment came, Cliff repeated his vows in a firm, assured voice, then silently slipped the solitary diamond on her finger. Diana prepared to do the same.

Her pastor's words echoed through the church. When he asked her if she would take Cliff as her lawfully wedded husband, she opened her mouth to say in an even, controlled voice that she would. However, she wasn't given the chance.

Joan spoke first. "She does."

Katie chimed in. "We all do."

Fourteen

So much for the small, intimate wedding party, Cliff thought good-naturedly several hours later. Everywhere he looked, there were family and friends pressed around him and Diana, shaking his hand, kissing Diana's cheek and offering words of congratulations. Each wished to share in their day and their happiness, and Cliff was pleased to let them. If it wasn't their guests pressing in around them, then it was Joan and Katie. The two popped up all over the hall, jostling gaily around the room like court jesters. Every now and again Cliff captured Diana's gaze, and the aching gentleness he saw in her eyes tore at his soul. Beyond a doubt, he knew that she was just as eager to escape as he was.

Other than their meeting in the church, Diana hadn't had more than a moment to talk to this man who was now her husband. They stood beside each other in the long reception line and were so busy greeting those they loved that there wasn't an opportunity to speak to each other.

When there was a small break in the line of relations and friends, Cliff leaned close and whispered in her ear, but she scarcely recognized his voice. His aching whisper was filled with raw emotion. "I adore you, Mrs. Howard."

Her eyes flew to his as the shattering tenderness of his words enveloped her. So many things were stored in her heart, so much love she longed to share. Because she couldn't say everything she wanted to, Diana moved closer to Cliff's side. Very lightly she pressed her hip against his. Cliff slipped his hand around her waist, drawing her nearer and tighter to him. For the moment at least, they were both content.

Hours later they arrived at the hotel room, exhausted but excited. A bottle of the finest French champagne, a gift from Cliff's brother, awaited them, resting in a bed of crushed ice.

Cliff gave the champagne no more than a fleeting glance. He wasn't interested in drinking—the only thing he wanted was his wife. He wrapped his arms around Diana and kissed her hungrily, the way he'd been fantasizing about doing all afternoon. He was starving for her, famished, ravished by his need.

Diana eagerly met his warm lips, twining her arms around his neck and tangling her fingers in the thick softness of his dark hair. She luxuriated in the secure feel of his arms, holding her so close she could barely breathe. She smiled up at him dreamily and sighed.

"I didn't think we were ever going to be alone," she whispered, her voice shaky with desire. Pausing, she pressed her face against the side of his strong neck.

"Me, either." His voice wasn't any more controlled than hers. His gaze fell on the bed, and the desire to make love with Diana wrapped itself around him like a fisherman's net, trapping him. He didn't want to rush Diana—he'd hoped their lovemaking would happen naturally. It was only late afternoon. They should have a drink and a leisurely dinner first, but Cliff doubted that he could make it through the first course. "Shall we have a drink?" he asked, easing her from his arms. Over and over again, he silently told himself to be patient, to go slow. There was no reason to rush into this when they had all the time in the world.

"I don't want any champagne," Diana answered in a husky whisper.

"You don't?"

Smiling, she shook her head. "I want *you*. Now. Don't make me wait any longer."

Cliff's knees went weak with relief, and he turned to face her. His heart pounded like a giant jackhammer in his chest.

"Oh, Cliff," she murmured, holding out her arms in silent invitation. "I don't think I can wait a minute more. I love you so much."

His eyes glowed with the fire of his passion as he reached for her. He kissed her once, twice, hardly giving her a chance to breathe. Their bodies strained against each other, needing and giving more.

Wildly Diana returned his kisses, on fire for her husband, desiring him in a way that went beyond physical passion.

In response to Diana, Cliff wrapped his arms around her, bringing her close to him so she would know beyond a doubt how much he longed to make her his. Somehow, while still kissing, they started to undress each other. Deftly Diana loosened his necktie, rid him of his suit jacket and unfastened the buttons of his shirt. When she splayed her hands over his bare chest, she sighed and reveled in the firm, hard feel of him.

With some difficulty, Cliff located the zipper in the back of Diana's dress and fumbled with it. Diana sighed into his mouth and reluctantly tore her lips from his. She whirled around, sweeping up the hair at the base of her neck to assist him and resisted the urge to stamp her foot and demand that he please hurry.

Their clothes were carelessly tossed around the room one piece at a time. By the time they'd finished, Diana was breathless and weak with anticipation. She'd thought to hide her imperfect body from Cliff, eager to climb between the sheets and hide, but he wouldn't allow it.

Cliff broke away long enough to study Diana. His sharp features, hardened now with excitement, softened with indescribable tenderness. Just looking at her made the breath catch in his throat and the blood surge through his veins in a violent rush. His senses were filled with the sight of her as his eyes swept her body in one long, passionate caress. His breath was labored when he spoke. "You're so beautiful."

"Oh, Cliff." Tears pooled in her eyes. Her body carried the marks of childbirth, but her husband saw none of her flaws. He viewed her with such a gentle love that he was blinded to her imperfections. Her heart constricted with emotion, and Diana was certain she couldn't have loved Cliff Howard more than she did at that precise moment.

His self-control was cracking, Cliff realized as he pulled back the sheets from the king-size bed and tossed the pillows aside. He wanted Diana so much his breath came quickly, no matter how hard he tried to slow it, and his heart beat high in his throat. He kissed Diana again and pressed her back against the mattress. After the lovemaking their arms and legs remained tangled as they lay on their sides facing one another. Cliff was trapped in the web of overpowering sensation. He saw her tears and felt his chest tighten with such a tender love that he could have died at the moment and not suffered a regret. Everything in his life until this one moment seemed shallow and worthless. The love he shared with Diana was the only important thing there would ever be for him. He'd found more than a wife; he'd found his life's purpose, his home.

Murmuring her love, Diana slipped her arms around his neck and pulled his head to hers. Her kiss was full, holding back nothing. Again and again Cliff kissed her. They were soft, nibbling kisses; the urgency of their lovemaking had been re-moved. They both slept and woke late in the evening. While Diana soaked in a hot bathtub, Cliff ordered their dinner from room service. Her stomach growled as the smell of their meal wafted into the large pink bathroom. She was preparing to climb out of the water, when Cliff came to her, holding a fat, succulent shrimp.

"Hungry?" he asked.

Diana nodded eagerly. It'd been hours since she'd last eaten—morning, to be exact—and at the time she'd been too excited to down anything more than a glass of orange juice.

"Good." He plopped the shrimp in his mouth and greedily licked the sauce from the ends of his fingers. Darting a glance in her direction, he laughed aloud at her look of righteous in-dignation.

He left the room and returned a couple of moments later with an extra shrimp, taking delight in feeding it to her. Diana hurriedly dried off and dressed in a whispery soft peignoir of sheer blue. The lacy gown had been a gift from Shirley Holiday, with instructions for her to wear it on her wedding night.

When she reappeared, Cliff had poured them each a glass of champagne. He turned to hand her hers and stopped abruptly when he viewed her in the sheer nightgown, his eyes rounding with undisguised appreciation.

"Do you like it?" she asked, and did one slow, sultry turn for effect.

Cliff only nodded; to speak was nearly impossible.

Diana took a sip of the champagne and pulled out a chair. One by one, she started lifting domed lids to discover what he'd ordered. "Oh, Cliff, I'm starved."

He dragged his gaze from the dark shadow of her nipples back to their meal. His gaze fell to the table. Food. Their dinner.

"Filet mignon," Diana said, and sighed her appreciation. "I

can't believe how famished I am." She looked up to discover her husband's eyes burning a trail over her.

Cliff moistened his lips. Diana's gown teased him with a soft cloud of thin material that fell open to reveal her thigh and the top of her hip. He found he couldn't tear his eyes off her. Wistfully he cast a glance at the bed. He dared not suggest it—not so soon after the last time. Diana would think he was some kind of animal.

"Cliff?" Diana whispered.

He squared his shoulders and forced a smile.

"Cliff Howard." Although he made a gallant effort to disguise what he wanted Diana knew. This man was a marvel. "Now?"

He looked almost boyish. "Do you mind?"

She glanced longingly at her dinner, grabbed a second shrimp and smiled. Standing, she reached for his hand and led him toward the bed.

"Married life seems to agree with you," Shirley Holiday commented three weeks later, after Cliff and Diana had returned from their honeymoon.

There'd been some adjustments, Diana mused. They'd recently moved into their two-story house, situated between Des Moines, and Salt Water State Park and were still unpacking. The girls had settled into their new school and were learning to adjust to sharing their mother, which was something they hadn't realized would happen once she and Cliff had married.

"It has its moments," Diana agreed. Like the first night they were in their new house! Cliff had just started to make love to her, when Katie burst into the bedroom, crying because of a bad dream. Cliff murmured something about having a nightmare of his own, while Diana scrambled for some clothes. The first thing the following morning, Cliff had put a lock on the bedroom door. Then, later in the same week, Diana and Shirley had planned on hitting a sale at Nordstrom's, when Cliff had shown up at the house unexpectedly. She'd thought, at first, that he'd come to take her to lunch, but he'd had other plans. Giggling, Diana had phoned her friend and said she'd be a few minutes late.

"I can't remember the last time I saw you this happy," Shirley said with an expressive sigh. "You know, I feel responsible for all this."

"For what?" Diana asked, joining her friend at the kitchen table.

"For the two of you getting together."

It took a supreme effort on Diana's part not to remind her former neighbor that she had done everything within her power to discourage Diana's relationship with the known playboy and womanizer, Cliff Howard.

"So when do you start your college classes?" Shirley asked while Diana poured them each a second cup of coffee.

The bride glanced in the direction of the kitchen calendar that hung beside the phone. "In a couple of weeks." After the wedding, Cliff had insisted Diana give up her job with the school district. As far as her future was concerned, Cliff had other plans.

"I think it's wonderful the way Cliff's encouraging you to go back to school. How long will it take you to get your nursing degree?"

Grinning, Diana propped her elbows on top of the oak table. "About ten years, the way we plan it."

Shirley's eyes widened with surprise. "That long—but whatever for?"

"I plan to take a couple of long breaks in between semesters."

"But, Diana, that doesn't make sense. This is a golden opportunity for you. I'd think . . ."

"Shirley!" Diana stopped her. "We're planning on me having a baby as soon as possible." And another the following year, if everything went according to their schedule. From the way Cliff had been working at the project, Diana believed she was bound to be pregnant by the end of the month. Not that she was complaining. The lovemaking between them was exquisite, just as she'd always known it would be. Each time her husband reached for her, she marveled at how virile he was. And how gentle.

The conversation between the two women was interrupted by Cliff, George and the girls, who came through the front door, returning from a golfing match.

"We're back," Cliff said, leaning over the chair and kissing Diana's cheek.

"Cliff let me drive his golf cart," Joan announced proudly as she entered the kitchen. "It's only a few more years, you realize, till I'll be old enough for my driver's permit."

"All Cliff let me do was steer," Katie complained, plopping herself down in the seat beside her mother.

"Next year you can drive the cart," Cliff told her.

Katie responded by folding her arms and pinching her lips together in a pretty pout. "It's not fair. Joan gets to do everything."

"The older one always does," Joan answered with a superior air.

"Are you going to let her talk to me that way?" Katie demanded. "Just what kind of a mother are you?"

"Girls, girls," Cliff said, without raising his voice. Joan and Katie stopped arguing, but when they didn't think he could see, Katie stuck her tongue out at Joan, and Joan eagerly reciprocated.

Cliff did his best to disguise a smile. He was smiling a lot lately. Marrying Diana and taking on the responsibility for Joan and Katie had changed him. There'd been so many wasted years when he'd drifted from one meaningless relationship to another, seeking an elusive happiness, finding himself chasing after the pot of gold at the end of the rainbow. But now he'd found real love, experienced it firsthand, and it had altered the course of his life.

That night, Diana fell asleep in her husband's arms. A loud clap of thunder woke her around midnight. She rolled onto her back and rubbed the sleep from her face.

"I wondered if the storm would wake you," Cliff whispered, raising himself up on one elbow in order to kiss her.

Diana kissed him back and looped an arm around his neck. "Have you been awake long?"

"About five minutes." Once more, his mouth tenderly grazed hers. "Have I told you lately how much I love you?"

"You *showed* me a couple of hours ago!"

He nuzzled her neck and the familiar hot sensation raced through Diana, and she sighed her pleasure.

Cliff kissed her in earnest then, wrapping her in his arms. "What have you done to me?" He growled the question in her ear. "I can't seem to get enough of you."

"Do you hear me complaining?" Completely at ease now with his body, she touched and kissed him in places she knew would evoke a strong reaction.

"You little devil," Cliff whispered raggedly.

"Want me to stop?"

"No," he answered on a low growl. "I'm crazy about you, woman."

Diana stiffened and turned her head toward the bedroom door.

Cliff was instantly aware of the change in her mood. "What is it?"

"Katie."

"I didn't hear her."

"She's frightened of storms." Already Diana was freeing herself from his arms.

Mumbling under his breath, Cliff rolled onto his back and swallowed down the momentary frustration. "I'm beginning to relive a nightmare of my own. When are you going to be back?"

"In a minute." Diana climbed out of the bed and reached for her robe.

"Give me a kiss before you go," Cliff insisted, then yawned loudly. "Wake me if I go back to sleep."

Diana willingly obliged. "I shouldn't be long."

"Hurry," he coaxed, and yawned a second time.

Diana was gone only a matter of minutes, but by the time she returned and slipped between the sheets, Cliff was snoozing.

"Sweetheart," she whispered, gently shaking him awake.

He rolled over and automatically reached for her.

"Honey," Diana murmured.

"Just a minute," he whispered sleepily. "I need to wake up." He nibbled softly on her earlobe.

"It's Katie," Diana told him.

"What about her?"

"She's frightened by the storm."

"I'm frightened, too, but I understand—go ahead and go back to comfort Katie."

Diana pushed the hair from his face and gently kissed the side of his jaw. "She doesn't want me—she requested you."

"Me?"

"You."

A slow, easy smile broke out across Cliff's handsome features. Comforting his daughter in a storm. It was exactly the kind of thing a father would do.

★ ★ ★ ★ ★